St Martin's Summer

Rose was conscious only of the beat of Simon's heart and the caress of his lips and hands. A new self-esteem, her lost miserable youth restored in joy, kisses such as she had never known before – Simon showered all these gifts upon her as he held her in his arms.

It was then, when past and future seemed divided inexorably by the sword of the present holocaust, that the telephone uttered its shrill summons.

At first Simon ignored it. The tide of desire was running strongly in him, and the prize was almost his. Hers was the beauty of spirit, the simplicity and sincerity of mind that he had longed for but never found. She was at once both mother and lover, in a miraculous fusion which overwhelmed him.

The telephone continued to sing its harsh song. Under that sustained cacophony something vital died out of their love-making. With a groan, Simon picked up the receiver.

"Hallo." He stopped, listening. "Okay. We'll be over as soon as we can."

He looked down at Rose, passion fading in the face of crisis. "Clive wants you to go home. Robert is missing."

St Martin's Summer

Jane Anstey

A Wings ePress, Inc.
Mystery Romance Novel

Wings ePress, Inc.

Edited by: Jeanne Smith
Copy Edited by: Christie Kraemer
Executive Editor: Jeanne Smith
Cover Artist: Trisha FitzGerald-Jung

All rights reserved

Names, characters and incidents depicted in this book are products of the author's imagination or are used fictitiously. Any resemblance to actual events, locales, organizations, or persons, living or dead, is entirely coincidental and beyond the intent of the author or the publisher.

No part of this book may be reproduced or transmitted in any form or by any means, electronic or mechanical, including photocopying, recording, or by any information storage and retrieval system, without permission in writing from the publisher.

Wings ePress Books
www.wingsepress.com

Copyright © 2018 by Jane Anstey
ISBN 978-1-61309-658-1

Published In the United States Of America

Wings ePress Inc.
3000 N. Rock Road
Newton, KS 67114

Dedication

To my daughters.

No man is an island entire of itself; every man is a piece of the continent, a part of the main; if a clod be washed away by the sea, Europe is the less, as well as if a promontory were, as well as any manner of thy friends or of thine own were; any man's death diminishes me, because I am involved in mankind.
And therefore never send to know for whom the bell tolls; it tolls for thee.

—John Donne

One

Rose was waiting in the playground when Robert finished school, waiting for the burst of shining happiness that always filled her when she caught sight of his small, slight form ambling out of the building. Today, as usual, his fair hair was awry, and his coat undone, his schoolbag bumping along on the ground behind him. But today, the happiness quickly faded as she recalled how soon these enchanted evenings with her son might become only a nostalgic memory. Her husband Clive had just decreed, with typical autocratic decision, that eight-year-old Robert should go away to prep school, as soon as possible. How on earth would he cope without her, away from home and its security? And how would *she* cope without *him*?

She put the thought aside, and they walked home slowly hand-in-hand in the early evening twilight, chatting cheerfully about nothing in particular. They waved to old Ben Cartwright, the sexton, who was putting away his shears in the shed at the back of the church. They exchanged a smile with George Warrendon, one of the local farmers, as he paused, shotgun over his shoulder, at the entrance to Church End Farm. They greeted the rector, a tall, ascetic figure reminiscent of a medieval monk in his plain black cassock and clerical cloak, on his way home from parish visiting. Then they stopped as usual to pat the grassy top of the broken-down wall at the far end of the churchyard, the wall that a younger Robert had pretended was an old pony grazing.

Around them, night was falling gently on St Martin-on-the-Hill. The last lingering sunlight lay across the village green, casting long shadows on the school playground, and the two ancient oaks that stood sentinel by its gate. The shadows broke and shifted as the tree branches moved in the light wind, and a few dry leaves fluttered down. Lights showed at uncurtained windows, and the darkness of the lane was punctuated by luminous pools from porch lamps switched on against the autumn dusk. It was all familiar and homely, the place where they belonged, where nothing exciting or terrifying ever happened, and their lives seemed safely wrapped within a close community.

And then they were home. They walked slowly up the path between the flowerbeds, where elderly bedding plants were growing straggly and sparse, to the front door of the big, square 1930's house. Rose unlocked the door and switched on the lights. She hung up their coats in the cupboard and made her way to the kitchen at the back of the house to make sandwiches for Robert's tea. On Tuesdays, they came home from school later than usual because of French Club, and he was always ravenous.

"Wash your hands, Robert," she called, as she took the sliced loaf out of the breadbin. "Tea in five minutes." She waited, listening for an answering call. Sometimes, he drifted off into the playroom and failed to register practical reminders about such things as washing.

A distant answer reached her, which might, with the ear of faith, have come from the bathroom. She poured milk into his mug and set a knife beside the plate. Then she reached down *The Hobbit* from the shelf, where it sat beside Rose's own well-thumbed editions of the nineteenth-century classics.

While she read to him, Robert munched his sandwiches silently, his big eyes behind their plastic-rimmed glasses staring intently at her, careful not to miss a word. He was a good reader, and could have finished the book himself ages ago, had he wished, but weekday supper-time reading was Mummy's special treat, and he would not dream of depriving her of it.

"'They had escaped the dungeons of the king and were through the wood, but whether alive or dead still remains to be seen,'" read Rose, and marked the place with an old envelope. "I think that's enough for tonight, darling. It's the end of a chapter."

Robert nodded and drank the remaining milk in his glass. To Rose's secret regret, he never asked for another chapter. It was always her own sense of the rightness of things which determined the place to stop each evening. Often, she was tempted to read on just a little further, to prolong their special hour. Today the temptation was especially strong, with the knowledge that supper-time reading might soon be a thing of the past. But she resisted it and closed the book firmly.

She cleared away his sandwich plate and mug and loaded them haphazardly into the dishwasher. Straightening up, she looked around the room with contentment. No designer had planned its colour scheme or its utilitarian fitments. The red velour curtains at the windows were faded and the brown hardwearing cord carpet had seen better days. The big scrubbed wooden table in the middle of the room was covered by an undistinguished green checked cloth with a waterproof backing, and the old dog basket in the corner had one corner chewed. But the room was warm from the presence of the Aga, and from the absence of her strong-minded organizing husband. Clive disliked the cosy shabbiness of it, and its persistent untidiness, but to Rose, the kitchen's imperfections were a comfort. It was the only room in the house where she did not feel the weight of Clive's contempt. Here, although sometimes her cakes sank when they should have risen, or her pastry turned out heavy, the room never reproached her.

"Mummy, I want to finish what I was doing yesterday with my railway," said Robert, breaking in upon her thoughts. "I've finished my tea, and it isn't even six o'clock yet."

Rose smiled at him. "Did you have any homework from school?"

"Not today."

"I'll run your bath at seven," promised Rose. "Perhaps Daddy will be home in time tonight to play with the electric railway."

Robert's face grew a little tight at this prospect, but he nodded bravely and turned to go.

~ * ~

Clive had been immersed in a succession of high-level meetings until mid-afternoon, leaving his personal assistant in charge of his office. When he got back, she was waiting for him, calm and poised, as always, in her black business suit, faultless make-up and well-cut blonde hair.

Clive dumped his briefcase on the desk. "Okay, what have we got?"

Olivia pointed to the open Excel file on her PC. "The report on the Leicester building," she said. "It's over-budget and behind schedule."

"We'd better see the project managers, then, and quickly," he responded, running a hand through his thinning hair. "Can you arrange a meeting for tonight? Tomorrow night latest."

Olivia nodded. "They can make tonight at six," she said. "I've booked the conference room."

"We need to check the penalty clauses."

"Done. I've printed them off."

"Good," he said. She was the best personal assistant he'd ever had. As with most things, you got what you paid for, and she was worth every penny, in all departments. He summoned up a full-wattage smile for her and picked up the folder of documents she'd left ready for him for his first meeting.

He sat at his desk, oblivious to the breath-taking view across the City in the late afternoon light and thought briefly about his wife's reaction to the idea of sending Robert away to school. It was a pity she couldn't see it his way. But Robert had to grow up. He had passed some smart blazer-clad schoolboys on the station on his way to work this morning, and the contrast with his own son, last seen at the breakfast table wearing rather childish teddy-bear pyjamas, had been painful.

Olivia watched him, keen to get on with the task in hand, but aware that when he was at his desk he didn't like to be disturbed. She had worked hard to make herself indispensable to Clive and trusted to helm the office ship when he was busy elsewhere. She arrived every morning well before eight to check on the day's schedule, sort the mail, and prepare printouts of the papers he would need for the various meetings. Once he walked through the door, their working day usually whirled into action at once. She enjoyed the hectic lifestyle, the business trips abroad, the cut and thrust of working closely with someone in a position of power in a big company. She was his equal in ability, and they both knew it, but she had chosen a PA career deliberately, seeing in it opportunities that a managerial career in her own right might not have given her. Feminism did not appeal to her. The glass ceiling still existed, but when a woman was a trusted, essential right-hand to a man in a powerful position, he took her up with him. Co-operation, not competition, with men was what had worked for her, spiced whenever possible with a sexual liaison on the side. Praise was a bonus, something Clive didn't hand out often. No one who needed their ego stroked all the time would last long with him, and she had worked for him for seven years. She wasn't in the least moved, either, by the charm he turned on occasionally to keep her sweet. It didn't mean a thing. In fact, she wasn't convinced that Clive really *liked* women in general, though he certainly tried to dominate them if he could. He terrorised his wife and most of the female members of the office staff. Some of them even seemed to enjoy it. Olivia herself had never allowed him to get the upper hand of her, nor had she made the mistake of bringing feminine wiles into the office. She had other means of getting her own way.

Clive roused himself from his reverie and leaned across her to look at the figures on her screen. His aftershave and the clean smell of his suit fabric filled her nostrils.

"You'd better ring Rose," he said to her. "Tell her I'll be late tonight."

Olivia made a note on her jotter and turned back to the computer screen. *Ring Mrs Althorpe,* she had written. *As late as possible*, her mental note added. Competition with women, especially wives, was a different matter altogether. *Keep her waiting. Keep her guessing.* Not that Clive's wife had ever seemed worthy of her notice, let alone offered her any competition. A poor submissive washed-out woman, Olivia thought her, from whom twenty-odd years of marriage to Clive had long removed any assertiveness. If she had wanted to annex Clive emotionally there would be no effective resistance from his wife. Still, wives must know their place. She would phone just before they went to the meeting. That would be time enough.

~ * ~

Rose could hear Robert singing gently to himself above the hum and rattle of the electric railway as she ran his bath. She laid out his favourite teddy-bear pyjamas on the heated towel rail and patted them fondly, thinking warm maternal thoughts of their owner, and trying not to feel a frisson of fear that Clive would have his way, and remove Robert from her orbit for half the year.

The telephone rang, and she turned off the bath taps in order to answer it.

"Mrs Althorpe?" She recognised the voice at once. She and Olivia Landry had never used first names, and the formality maintained the distance between them…which suited them both for different reasons.

"Oh, yes, Miss Landry." So, Clive was going to be late again after all. That was a relief.

"Mr Althorpe," the secretary informed her, in cold, efficient tones, "has been delayed in an important meeting." Miss Landry clearly felt that even informing his wife that Clive would be late showed more consideration than the occasion merited. Apologies were certainly not required. Rose sighed and hoped that Miss Landry had not heard her.

"Oh. I see. Well, thank you for letting me know."

She put the receiver back in its cradle and returned to the bathroom in the discouraged frame of mind that usually followed any contact she had with Olivia Landry. Perhaps it was because she entertained certain suspicions about the nature of the relationship between Clive and his PA; or perhaps Miss Landry's crisp voice reminded her of the contrast between them. Whenever they met—which was infrequently, at office social events—she was invariably dressed in designer clothes and beautifully groomed; and according to Clive, she was an excellent ballroom dancer as well as being a byword for efficiency in the office. Competing with such a paragon, Rose felt, would be useless, even if years of struggling against the devastating contempt of her husband had not sapped in her any desire to make the effort.

It was fortunate, she reflected as she went back to the kitchen, that she had not prepared Clive a special meal, to sit spoiling in the oven. The plain and uninspired casserole she had prepared could wait safely with the heat turned down low.

"Robert," she called, as she passed the playroom door on the way to the kitchen, "Your bath's ready."

An indistinguishable murmur came from behind the door. She looked in and watched him playing for a moment, trains and track spread around the room, his imagination clearly thoroughly engaged in their operation. "Robert?"

He looked up vaguely.

"Bath time."

"Okay. I'll just fix this bridge in here, Mummy. Then I'll come."

~ * ~

When Clive finally arrived home, there was little time left for further argument about Clive's plans for Robert, but Rose made the most of the hour when they sat opposite each other in the dining room at the big mahogany table, with its heavy candlesticks and the enormous cut-glass vase Clive's mother had given them as a wedding present. However adamant Clive was, she was equally determined to put her point of view.

"Robert's quite happy where he is, here at the village school," she told him. *And he's all that makes my life here bearable*, she added silently.

"The local primary is all very well in its way," Clive replied, his blue eyes cold and unyielding. "But he won't meet any very suitable friends there. Look at the two boys he brought home last weekend! And the academic standards won't get him into anywhere decent when he's older, either. No, he'd better go away to prep school, next term, if possible."

He handed her the brochures Olivia had downloaded for him that morning, the pages already marked with pale yellow post-it notes. Rose put them on the table in front of her without looking at them. She was struggling to think of something, anything, to say, afraid that silence would be taken for consent.

"Surely eight's too young to go to boarding school? Sarah didn't go till she was eleven." The comparison wouldn't help much, she knew, for their daughter Sarah, now 22, was a different kind of person altogether and had thrived on boarding school. But Robert's happiness was too important for her to surrender without a struggle. "And I don't really believe he's the kind of child to do well away from home, anyway," she went on, trying to build on her earlier argument. "He's not like Sarah."

Clive snorted. "I'm well aware of *that*. Sarah could hold her own against anyone even as a small child. The trouble is, you just don't want him to grow up."

"That's not true," she blurted out, stung by the way Clive was turning the discussion into an attack on *her*. "That's not fair. It's your ambition that's the trouble! No one associated with you must fail, must they? It was all right for Sarah. She wanted to be a success. She enjoyed all the academic pressure, the sport, the exams, the good results. But Robert's different. He likes the simple things..." Her voice died away.

"Like you?" he suggested dryly, but in a deceptively gentle tone which did not in the least hide his contempt.

Rose choked. The weight of Clive's low opinion of her, and his determination that his son should not resemble her, stifled her protests. All she knew was that she didn't want Robert to change or go away. She wanted him to stay at home with her, and remain that sweet, rather disorganised, dreamy individual whom she adored.

"He's not that immature," she pleaded, aware that she was fighting a rear-guard action in a hopeless position, where her only chance of success, however slim, had been in attack. "Some children develop more slowly than others. Honestly, Clive, I think he'd be terribly unhappy away from home at the moment."

"Don't baby him, Rose."

She sighed. Clive knew only too well that to ride roughshod over her opinions was the most effective way of demolishing any feeble arguments she might come up with. She tried desperately to think of some new defence.

"If Robert is at school during term time, you'll be able to do more entertaining for me," went on Clive, pressing home his advantage. "You could even come away with me on business trips," he suggested, in a silky tone.

Rose's heart sank. She was uncomfortable with the fast-paced lifestyle he led on those trips, and she had always used the children—first Sarah and now Robert—as an excuse for staying at home. Calling his bluff and agreeing to accompany him might bring about an end to his business trips with his secretary as sole companion, possibly even to the extra-curricular activities she felt sure they indulged in on those occasions. But the cost to her own peace of mind was too high.

As she hesitated, Clive took her silence for capitulation. "Good, that's settled." He pointed at the small stack of coloured pamphlets. "We can look at these over coffee. I marked the school I thought was the best one. I'll make us an appointment to visit it next week."

Two

After she had cleared the dinner dishes, Rose found she couldn't face drinking coffee and looking at school brochures with Clive. Instead she went upstairs to check on Robert. She stood for a while watching him while he slept, trying not to think of the possibility that he might soon be sleeping somewhere else, far from her loving watchfulness. Beside the bed, the nightlight he still insisted upon gave off a soft gleam, highlighting the shadows on his small face. As if aware of her scrutiny and resenting it, Robert turned in his sleep to face the wall. His mother smoothed the quilt over him, tucking it round him more snugly.

She picked her way carefully back across the bedroom floor, rescuing an errant dirty sock on her way. An old neglected teddy bear that had once belonged to Sarah sat in dignified retirement on the chest of drawers beside the door, his worn face expressing peaceful resignation. Sarah had thrown the teddy out when she left home, but Rose had rescued him from the dustbin sack where he lay amid assorted outgrown toys, posters and books, and placed him in Robert's room.

She herself possessed no mementoes of childhood. Her mother had let her take nothing with her at the age of twelve when they fled from the house they shared with her violent stepfather. In the years that followed, she had not cared to buy anything new to be lost or broken in the succession of state-funded bed-and-breakfast hostels they had inhabited until her mother died when Rose was sixteen.

For Rose, Sarah's teddy represented the security and warmth of her children's upbringing in contrast with her own. She smiled at him as she left and closed the door softly behind her.

As she washed up the casserole dish, Rose resolved not to involve Robert in her disagreement with Clive over his schooling. It would be so easy to enlist him, to ask carefully couched questions which would elicit the response that yes, he did want to stay at the village school, and no, he didn't want to board. But to do so would be close to manipulation, and however genuinely the answers she elicited might reflect his true feelings, she would not stoop to it. Robert should not feel that his parents were at odds about his education. It might worry him, and she could not bear to have him worried.

Clive, she soon discovered, had no such scruples. He was already at home when they arrived from school the following evening, and immediately took Robert off to the playroom to build a new railway layout. Over his supper, instead of listening to the next instalment of Tolkien's masterpiece, Robert spoke to Rose excitedly of the new school he was to go to next year, and all the new friends he would make among the boys there. Daddy had said he was too big for the village school now, and he would find the new school much more interesting. There would be a big sports field and a proper science laboratory and...

"But Robert," cried Rose, interrupting this eulogy. "Do you *want* to go away from home? I thought you'd be so unhappy about the idea."

Robert reached out and took her hand in his comfortingly. "Mummy, I know you'll miss me terribly, and of course I'll miss you too, but it will be really fun to sleep in a dormitory with the other boys. We'll have midnight feasts and pillow fights and things," he added with happy anticipation.

Rose sighed at this naivety. Clive had prepared his ground well. In the rosy fictional picture he had painted of boarding-school life, there was no place for the loneliness, the homesickness, and the sense of being uprooted which many of those who have experienced it remember with pain.

She felt she could not let Clive's strategy succeed. She said good night to Robert and marched into the drawing room, determined to put up a fight. But Clive at once reminded her that it was Wednesday, and that Wednesday was bell-ringing practice.

"You missed last week's practice. We had Honor and Jeffrey over, remember. So, you'd better go tonight, hadn't you? Can't let Geoff down."

For a brave moment she thought of resisting him, of telling him that discussing Robert's future was more vital than her commitment to the bellringing band. But as she opened her mouth to speak, he picked up the phone and started to make a call. He would only ignore her if she spoke, or look at her with such irritation she would turn, like a chastised dog with her tail between her legs and do what he suggested in the first place. In a state of impotent rebellion, she followed the sound of the bells to church.

Sundials was less than a hundred yards from the church, so that by setting off down the lane as soon as she heard the bells begin to sound, Rose was able to slip into the ringing chamber at the back of the church while they were still being raised. She leant against the stone wall, feeling the slight swaying of the tower as the bells swung on their mountings, and watching her fellow ringers with admiration... particularly the vice-captain, Simon Hellyer.

Simon was ringing the sixth bell, the tenor, the heaviest in the tower, which set the pace for the others. She watched him pulling the rope smoothly and economically, the strong muscles in his forearms tightening with each pull. A wiry man in his late thirties, of middle height, his dark striking good looks and quiet charisma had, she suspected, some effect on all the women who came within his orbit. Yet, in spite of his undoubted sexual magnetism, he made a point of rejecting female advances when they occurred and prevented them from being made if he could. She had herself made none and would have expected no welcome from him if she had.

She was ashamed of her instinctive reaction to him and would have much preferred to be indifferent. But the fact remained that he stirred something deep and primitive in her and had done so from the first moment he had come to join the ringing band eighteen months before. She was only grateful (she told herself) that he lived three miles away in the parish of Two Marks, and that their paths therefore crossed only on bell-ringing occasions.

"Stand!" commanded Geoff, the tower captain, a big broad-shouldered countryman with a slow smile and much quicker wits. With a last pull, the ringers brought their bells to a halt. Knots were tied in the rope ends, and the silence of human voices was broken.

"Hallo there, Rose," called Janice from across the tower. A dumpy garrulous woman in her late fifties, she chatted interminably about her numerous family and their various concerns unless firmly quelled, as well as possessing a voracious curiosity about others. Rose lacked the ruthlessness required to snub her effectively, and consequently dreaded talking to her.

"Fine, thanks," she responded automatically, trying not to give Janice any encouragement.

Geoff and his son Ken, at the other side of the tower, were discussing with the visiting ringer the intricacies of one of the more complicated change-ringing methods and had no attention to spare for Rose. But Simon was regarding her thoughtfully. She had the uncomfortable feeling that he knew very well that her cheerful demeanour was deceptive. Somehow, she must forestall any personal questions.

"The bells went up in peal well tonight," she said to him, overcoming her shyness with an effort and trying not to blush. "I listened to you all the way up the lane. Nice and even."

He nodded. "It wasn't bad. But you should learn to raise in peal yourself, Rose."

"You need more practice raising a bell on your own first," put in Geoff, overhearing from across the ringing chamber. "Come five minutes early one practice night, and we'll give it a bit of work."

Rose's heart sank. Her attempt at a casual, carefree remark had backfired badly. Raising the bells scared her. She had visions of losing control of the bell rope, whereupon Geoff would have to come charging across the tower to rescue her. It had happened once or twice while she was learning to ring, and she shrank from repeating the experience.

"Maybe after the St Martin's Weekend," she prevaricated. "I'm a bit busy with things for the fête at the moment." The annual fête, held as part of the church's patronal festival in November, and the highlight of the village's year, was less than a week away, and the excuse sounded plausible.

"Come to think of it, we should practise St Martin's Doubles tonight," said Geoff. "We'll be ringing a quarter-peal after the service on Sunday evening, as usual. And I want you to ring the treble this year, Rose."

Rose's expression made Simon laugh. "You look as though we've condemned you to be boiled alive in oil, or something equally medieval and terrifying," he said, smiling at her. "You've rung the treble for St Martin's Doubles before."

"Ye-es," said Rose, struggling to explain her horror at the proposal. "But a quarter-peal... that's forty minutes' ringing without a break! I'm sure I couldn't concentrate that long. I'll let you all down."

"No, you won't," Geoff assured her bracingly. "And if you did," he added, seeing that she was about to protest further, "I'd soon set you right again."

"Yes," she said in a small voice. It was impossible to explain the fears which beset her. Geoff would sort out her mistakes to the best of his considerable ability; but she would still know it was her fault if the quarter-peal failed.

"Catch hold for a touch of St Martin's Doubles," said Geoff to the rest of the band. "Simon, you stand with Rose and help her if she goes wrong. Fill in, everyone. Don't forget, places in front and dodging in the middle."

Ropes were taken up and ringing began again. With a great effort of concentration, Rose managed to ring her simple part in the method correctly for the first few minutes, counting her places carefully. Then, acutely conscious of Simon so close beside her, her mind wandered for a moment and the music faltered, the bells suddenly chiming in chaotic cacophony instead of ordered melody.

"You're just coming down to lead, Rose," said Simon quickly from beside her. "Lead now. The three takes you off."

With difficulty, Rose found her place again in the intricate pattern, but she finished the exercise hardly more confident than she had started it, and certainly not at all convinced of her ability to ring a quarter-peal in less than a week's time.

After the practice, the ringers walked across the road to the local pub, appropriately named The Bell, as they often did on a Wednesday night. Rose rarely joined them, since her conscience usually drove her home to attend to the needs, imagined or otherwise, of her family. But tonight, still smarting from her failure to stand up to Clive, she allowed herself to be persuaded.

Inside, the pub was warm and the public bar rather crowded.

"Let's go through into the lounge," said Simon, leading the way through a big dark oak door into the quieter room on the other side of the bar area. The two men went off to the bar and came back with a tray of glasses.

Simon raised his glass to Rose. "Cheers," he said, his eyes meeting hers with a twinkle. She found herself colouring and looked away. It was ridiculous that Simon could make one feel so *befriended* with so little apparent effort.

She looked around her at the warm lounge with its dark oak tables, some set for eating. Red soft furnishings and a deep red carpet, rows of horse brasses and racing prints on the walls, with their cream paint and dark panelling, all contributed to the sense of cosiness and comfort. She relaxed into the cushions on the bench seat where the men had decreed she should sit, while they perched on wooden chairs and leant their elbows on the table. *I should do this more often. It wouldn't matter if I were a little later getting home on a Wednesday.*

Half an hour later, Rose emerged from the pub doorway just ahead of the others to find torrential rain falling like a bead curtain from the gutters above. She recoiled involuntarily and bumped into Simon, who was following her out.

"Steady! What's happened?"

Rose put out a hand and balanced herself against the porch wall. "Sorry. It's absolutely pouring."

He peered out. "Yes. In fact, I think that could be said to be an understatement. Can I give you a lift home?"

Rose demurred. "I'll be all right. It's probably only a heavy shower. I wouldn't dream…"

"Don't be daft," he told her. "You'd be half-drowned before you got out of the car park. You can't wait for a shower this size to go over…it might take an hour. I pass your door anyway on my way home. Hang on there, and I'll go and open the car door."

Without waiting for her reply, he sprinted away down the path to the little car park next to the road. After a few moments, Rose pulled her coat more closely round her, turned up her collar, and followed him. The car was waiting for her at the bottom of the path, and the passenger door swung open as she reached it. She scrambled in and the car turned slowly out into Church Lane, the windscreen wipers swishing busily across the glass in front of her.

"Thanks, Simon," she said, brushing the raindrops off her hair. "It's certainly foul. It had better not be like this on Saturday!"

He glanced at her. "You hold the fête inside, don't you?"

"Yes, but lots of people don't come if it rains. And the ball really will be a wash-out if we all have to wear wellington boots to get to it!"

He laughed. "I've never been to this ball of yours. In fact, I have to admit, I didn't even come to the St Martin's fête last year. Extraordinary how parochial we all are, each in our own little patch, out in these villages."

"We *call* it a ball," she said. "But it's really more of an informal hop. There's a band, but they play a variety of stuff…a bit of ballroom dancing, and some old-fashioned jiving. And we usually finish off with barn dancing, with a caller. Ben Cartwright sometimes plays the accordion for the barn dance part, although I wonder whether he will this year. His bronchitis and his rheumatism both seem to be troublesome."

Simon changed down for the sharp corner. "You'll have to tell me which house is yours."

"The one with the white gate…just there, on the right."

He pulled up in front of the gate. "Wait a minute, Rose. Let the rain ease up a bit or you'll be soaked again before you get to the front door. I like the sound of this ball of yours. Can you sell me a ticket? What do we wear? DJs and cummerbunds or jeans and a sweatshirt?"

She laughed. "I don't suppose anyone will care either way. Clive and I don't usually bother dressing up, but some people do. You could always take the DJ off for the jiving and the barn dancing! I'll have to go inside and get you a ticket. I haven't any with me."

"I'll give you the money now," he said, reaching into the inside pocket of his sports jacket for his wallet. "I don't want you to have to come out again in this weather. Give me the ticket on Saturday at the Fête … you're a stallholder, aren't you?"

"I'm helping on the Bring & Buy," she confirmed.

"That's all right, then. How much do you want for this ticket?"

"Fourteen pounds," said Rose, feeling slightly apologetic.

"H'm. What do I get for that?"

"The dancing and the band, of course, and a light supper… it's usually quite good. And there are the fireworks at the end, because of Guy Fawkes."

He handed her a £10 note and fished a couple of two-pound coins out of his pocket. "I'll look forward to it."

She tucked the money away, thanking him, and for the first time she forgot to be shy of him, and consequently awkward, and raised her eyes to his. She found them smiling at her with amusement. There was nothing in his gaze to disturb or embarrass her, and for a moment, she smiled back, acutely conscious of his nearness. *Goodness. What am I thinking of?* She groped for the car door hurriedly.

"Thank you very much for the lift, Simon," she said, and her tone was formal and stilted again.

If he noticed the change, Simon gave no sign of it. "See you on Saturday," he said. "Run now."

She ran. The rain was still falling in sheets, whipping into her face with the gusts of wind blowing round the side of the house. Gasping, she made for the side door and almost fell into the kitchen, water running off her coat in little rivulets. Dolly arose from her basket and came to greet her, stooping to lick the water from the floor.

She bent to pat the spaniel and froze. From the direction of the sitting room came Clive's voice, raised in anger.

"You stupid bitch, don't rant at me. I can't possibly come this weekend. I've got family commitments here." There was a pause. Clearly the person at the other end of the telephone had something to say about this. "You shouldn't have been such a fool," Clive went on ruthlessly. "I've told before you not to book things without consulting with me first. Okay, I know you're a bloody fine PA and more besides, but you don't own me, and you never will."

Rose straightened up. Clive clearly had no idea that she had come in, though she was later than usual. He must be talking to Olivia Landry. Upbringing and principle suggested to Rose that she should indicate her presence to Clive. Instinct told her to keep quiet and listen hard. At least she would know the truth, not simply harbour suspicions, corrosive to her peace but without firm foundation, easily laughed off by her plausible, contemptuous husband. Instinct won hands down. With rising dismay, she listened, and between the pauses, the truth emerged loud and clear.

"I'm going to the fête and the dance here in the village, if you must know.... No, of course it isn't that important, Olivia. But be reasonable. I've said I'll be there, and I've bought tickets for the dance. Rose will be disappointed if I don't take her... That's stupid, you know she isn't... Look, don't compete, you don't have to. She'll never measure up to you in anything that matters... What do you care about that? Would you really want to be a dull, dowdy middle-aged housewife with no conversation and no looks? No, that's what I thought. When's my next trip to the States? Book yourself on that, and we'll take an extra day or two, go down to Florida and get an autumn tan... God, Olivia, you don't give up, do you? All right. I've promised Robert I'll be here for the fête on Saturday, and I'm not going back on that. But I'll get out of the rest of the high-jinks. You go up on Saturday morning, and I'll fly up and join you. That do?... I can hear Rose at the door. I've got to go. See you tomorrow."

Rose had not moved at all. Clive could not possibly have heard her in the kitchen. But clearly, mention of her return was a well-prepared excuse to ring off. She was rocked by a sudden wave of anger. She had always suspected that her husband was having an affair with his secretary, but Clive had never provided any proof; and all the time he was stringing them both along, having his cake and eating it, lying to her, putting Olivia Landry off when he chose. She clenched her fists. How dare he treat her with such contempt? As for clever "Miss Landry," Rose had no sympathy for her. Clive had met his match there; she was as self-seeking, as manipulative and ruthless, as Clive himself.

She took one step in the direction of the sitting room, fully intending to throw the telephone conversation in her husband's face. Then she stopped. If she did that, it would be the end. Clive would walk out, and Olivia would undoubtedly be waiting for him.

I won't give in that easily, she declared to herself, haunted by all the years of giving in gracefully. *I should have fought for him years ago.* "Dull, dowdy and middle-aged," *am I? Well, I'll show him!*

Three

It was impossible to hide her anger from Clive, impossible even to dissemble the reason for it. When she walked into the sitting room, her eyes blazed as they met his, and it was clear he guessed that she had heard at least part of his telephone conversation.

"Rose," he began, his tone almost an apology. "Don't…"

She did not wait for him to finish. Even if he were shaken enough to offer excuses instead of plausible explanations for once, she was too angry to listen. She had made up her mind, in those cataclysmic few minutes in the kitchen, that she would not speak to him about what she had heard. If she stopped and listened to anything he had to say, the anger would pour out of her in vocal torrents. She would shout and scream and cry, and any dignity with which she might shame him would be irrevocably lost. So, she turned away from him and marched up the stairs.

As drama, it was lost on Clive. As she reached the landing, her resolution was shaken by hearing him laugh. She almost turned and vented her rage upon him there and then. But she controlled herself and continued along the landing to the bedroom they shared. She took her nightclothes and her cosmetics and went into the spare bedroom. Sarah slept there when she visited them for a night occasionally, and the bed was always made up. Clive was justified in thinking her reaction bad theatre, though the memory of his laughter galled her. Yet she found, uncomfortably, that in the real dramas of life, emotions can be as unsubtle and violent as in any tawdry soap opera. She shook all over with reaction.

Although it was early, she had a bath and went to bed, trying to relax. She read for hours in an attempt to calm herself enough to sleep, but even so she spent a disturbed night. Her anger woke her at intervals, and her mind churned over her wrongs interminably. "I'll show him!" she said to herself again.

Quite what she was so determined to show him, Rose did not stop to analyse carefully, either then or later. Her fury carried over to the following day, fuelling her actions with an energy which she would never normally possess. She remained in her room until Clive had left for the office and resolved not to speak to him when he came home. Even Robert became aware of her anger and asked somewhat plaintively whether he had done something wrong, which stopped her in her tracks.

~ * ~

The commuter platform was crowded, and Clive had to push his way through the mass of Suits and their briefcases in order to position himself for the Quiet Coach. On the opposite platform, he saw again the group of schoolboys in their red-and-blue blazers and neatly pressed trousers, waiting for a train going south. They reminded him that he had not yet made the promised appointment for himself and Rose to visit the boarding school he had chosen for Robert. The spat with Rose, and later his own anger with Olivia, had driven it out of his mind.

His train came in, and he shrugged off personal concerns and wedged himself and his laptop into the slim space remaining beside an enormously fat woman clutching a bulging holdall. He skimmed the headlines in the *Financial Times*, his mind juggling the experts' predictions of long-term trends in financial markets as a consequence of the Brexit vote, and the short-term cash-flow problems of the company he worked for. The inhabitants of the Quiet Coach as usual took a relaxed view of the concept of silence, in spite of the notices pasted so prominently by the train company.

Assorted mobile phones rang and were answered, and opposite him two women in casual clothes appeared to be discussing the more lurid details of their weekend clubbing experiences. He opened his laptop quickly and started to re-read the text of a report he had taken home with him the evening before.

The train disgorged its passengers at Waterloo an hour later, to fight their way through the ticket barriers and on to the Underground; a human torrent flowing down the escalators deep into the bowels of London. Clive felt the rustling breath of warm air stirred up by the Tube trains as they clanked and hummed along the Drain, gathering up office workers and depositing them unceremoniously at Bank for the start of the working day. Up the steep escalators they rode, to emerge into the cool damp air of the City of London and join the crowds of other hurrying, worrying commuters on their way to work: solicitors, barristers, bankers and financial gurus, senior and middle managers, and the multifarious support personnel they required to keep the City punching above its weight in the world. The experience of being part of that buzz of activity and purpose normally energised him. Today, it felt alien and impersonal, and he was glad to arrive at the sanctuary of his own desk.

Olivia wasn't in the office when he arrived. Her absence was irritating, especially as he suspected it was a deliberate attempt at provocation, and ironically it made him keener than he would otherwise have been to think of ways of placating his wife.

He had tried using a gentle supplicatory approach to Rose that morning, one which would normally have mollified her and persuaded her to forgive him for any wrongdoing, real or imagined. But this time, it seemed she had gone beyond such simple remedies. Each time he spoke, she glared at him and left the room. Clive was not only baffled by her attitude but annoyed. He made generous financial provision for Rose and the children, he reminded himself self-righteously, and, in general, felt that he had always fulfilled his family duties more than adequately. It was true that he had not intended to let Rose find out about his liaison with Olivia, but then he had never considered his casual double-life as in any way problematic, either practically or morally.

He was disconcerted, too, by Olivia's attitude. She belonged in his business world as the cool, unemotional assistant who hid a surprising (not to mention exhilarating) ability to throw off her professional mask and become an inspired mistress, spicing their clandestine assignations with wildcat sexuality before retiring again into her smooth, enigmatic poise. But on the phone on Wednesday night, it had been clear that for the first time she had determined to cross the line into his personal life. It unsettled him more than he was willing to admit. Something would have to be done to restore the equilibrium, or Olivia would have to go. But he didn't want that to happen. She was too valuable to him in too many ways. He would have to look at all the options and see whether the situation could be retrieved.

~ * ~

On Friday morning, equipped with a long mackintosh and an umbrella, and reflecting that the fête organisers were wise to have opted for an inside venue, Rose braved the rain and caught the thrice-weekly bus to Winchester. Clothes shopping normally meant buying skirts, slacks and sweaters in pastel colours and shades of tweedy brown or green; sensible country clothes. But today, she needed to be extravagant. She spent an hour window shopping before she chose a boutique. Then she went inside and put herself into the hands of the experienced and skilful saleswoman.

She came home with a complete outfit for the ball, a smart trouser suit for the church service and the quarter-peal on Sunday evening, and a hair appointment booked for Saturday morning. She had spent more on her wardrobe in one day than she normally spent in six months, but she grudged the expenditure not at all. If Clive could be made to look twice at her, to realize that she was anything but "dull, dowdy and middle-aged"—how those words had stung her, not least because she had been foolish enough to let them be true—the money would have been well spent.

She walked back to Sundials from the bus stop with a spring in her step. Buying new outfits had lifted her spirits. She had seen herself in the mirror in the dress shop in the dance dress which suited her so well, and the sight had made her feel more confident. No longer could she be described, even by a scornful husband, as dowdy. She realised that she had allowed her relationship with Clive, not to mention her whole life, drift for far too long. From now on, things would be different.

That afternoon she and Robert went to the rectory after school. Robert usually preferred to go straight home rather than mixing with his peers, and Rose did not usually cut across his natural inclinations. But on this occasion, she was firm. She had her own reasons for wanting to visit the rectory.

"We've been invited so often, Robert," she had said when she met him in the playground. "And this time we're going to go. It's ages since I had a proper chat with Liz."

They walked along the narrow lane quietly side by side for the short distance between the school and the rectory. Children ran hither and thither energetically on their way home, followed, more or less, patiently and diligently by mothers, child-minders and a sprinkling of fathers.

St Martin's Rectory was a big Victorian house set back off the road, flanked by trees and approached by a winding drive punctuated by overgrown shrub borders and rough grass. It sprawled splendidly across its half-an-acre of garden in a slightly shabby, down-at-heel way. Quite why it had not been sold off long ago to some London magnate with money, like so many other Victorian rectories, leaving Jeremy Swanson and his family to be re-housed in a modern brick-built box, Rose had never thought to ask. *It must be very expensive to heat,* she thought to herself, as she rang the bell.

The heavy oak door was opened by the rector himself, clad in casual trousers and a heavy round-necked sweater, above which emerged a clerical collar. "Hallo, Rose. Liz is expecting you," he said, as he ushered them in. "I think Chris is in the playroom, Robert," he added, smiling down at the boy kindly. "Why don't you go and find him?"

Robert let go of his mother's hand, which he had been absent-mindedly holding as they came up the drive and went off down the passage-way to find Chris. Jeremy gave Rose a friendly smile and disappeared through the door into his study. Rose stood for a moment irresolutely in the centre of the threadbare hall carpet, while the soft tramp of Robert's feet faded away, leaving a heavy, dust-laden silence. So conscious was she at that moment of the rectory's prosperous ecclesiastical past, she almost expected to see maids in starched linen arrive from the nether regions of the house to collect her coat and hat and usher her into the presence of the rector's wife.

Instead, a familiar voice hailed her from a room across the hall that would once have been the rectory drawing-room. "Rose, I'm in here. Come and have some tea."

Rose pushed open the door and found her hostess, a tall, willowy woman in her late thirties with fair hair tied up in a French plait, plumping cushions and rearranging chairs. Five afternoons a week, from one o'clock to three-thirty, the rectory hosted the village preschool group.

"It's amazing," said Rose, "the way you can get it tidy again, after having all those three- and four-year-olds running about in here."

"Part of my bargain with Remy," Liz replied. "I'm allowed to use the sitting room so long as it's all tidy by five o'clock in case he wants it for a church meeting. Sometimes," she admitted, pushing back a few tendrils of loose hair absent-mindedly, "it's quite a struggle to meet the deadline. But it's really the only space we have that's big enough for the activities they need."

She straightened the last cushion, picked up a tray containing mugs and a large bone china teapot which had been resting on top of the upright piano, and placed it on a low table beside the sofa.

"Now," she said, fixing her eyes on Rose. "Tell me what's new. Apart from that nice sweater, that is. I haven't seen that before."

"It's been in my wardrobe for ages," said Rose, pleased to see that Liz appreciated her efforts to furbish herself up. She didn't think Clive had noticed.

"Well, I'm glad to see you wearing it, then. Now, I've been trying to get you to come and have tea with me for weeks, and you haven't managed it until today. So, I deduce something very particular brought you along. Give."

"Oh, Liz, I really haven't been able to come before," Rose began to explain awkwardly. "Robert likes to go straight home after school most days, you see… and then Clive hates it if the meal's late… and…"

"Rose, you don't need to explain," said Liz cheerfully. "I'm just glad that whatever it is actually over-rode all these other considerations and put you down on the doorstep. So – what's new?"

Rose sighed. "You're right, of course. I wanted to pick your brains."

Liz poured tea into small, rather pretty mugs and passed one to Rose. "Pick away," she invited. "There are biscuits in that tin if you want one."

Rose took the cup and sipped the warm liquid absent-mindedly. How much did she feel justified in sharing with Liz? They were friends, but she didn't want to tell her about Clive and Miss Landry. It was too raw, and the last thing she wanted to do was burst into tears.

"I thought I might look for a job," she said at last. "And I'm not sure how to go about it. I haven't got many qualifications, for a start. I mean, two A-levels aren't going to get me far, are they? And I can't even use a word-processing program on the computer."

"That really is a new idea, Rose," said Liz.

Rose squirmed slightly, though she knew Liz was only teasing her. An inadequate housewife was all she was, after all. It was no wonder that Liz thought the idea of her getting a job a revolutionary one.

"Not that I don't think it's an excellent notion for you to get a job," Liz added quickly, seeing Rose's reaction but misunderstanding the reason for it. "Those menfolk of yours might appreciate you more if you made them fend for themselves a little."

The very thought of asking Clive to fend for himself brought her out in a cold sweat. But was it not a desire to be more independent that had sent her to ask Liz's advice? She hesitated again over how much to divulge to Liz. "Clive wants to send Robert away to school," she explained at length. That was a safe enough topic. "If Robert isn't here, it will feel a bit lonely at home. But, of course, I'd have to have the holidays free."

"Mm." Liz looked shrewdly at her friend. "And what do *you* think about Robert going away to school? How long has this been mooted, anyway?"

"Last Monday," Rose admitted.

"And you'd rather keep him at home."

"Well, of course I would, Liz! He's so young, and... vulnerable. I'm afraid he'd be bullied. Chris is awfully sweet to Robert, but some of the other boys aren't very kind." She sighed. "That's why Clive says Robert must go. He thinks it would toughen him up... make him mature a bit. But Liz, I don't want Robert to go away." She could hear the desperation in her own voice, try as she might to suppress it.

"Then why not *tell* Clive that? Surely you have a say in this too, Rose?" Was there a hint of exasperation in Liz's tone, Rose wondered? Liz often exhorted her to be more assertive, but Rose had never been able to work out how to start. Perhaps if Clive saw her new look and realised that she wasn't going to let him get away with the affair with Olivia too easily, things might change. But already she could feel her newfound resolution ebbing away.

"Well," said Liz, after waiting in vain for a response. "You could volunteer to help at the school. Fran already knows you, after all, so I'm sure she'd find you something useful to do. I think they have volunteers listening to the children read, for example. Or you could train properly as a teaching assistant, which would make you employable in other schools too, and then you'd get paid. Either of those would make it easy for you to have holidays with Robert, although sometimes private school terms are different, of course. Or perhaps you could work from home as a proof reader. I don't think you'd need a degree for that, and you might be able to do a course by correspondence."

"Oh, but Liz, that would mean running my own business, wouldn't it? I'd never manage to do that." She began to wish that she hadn't mentioned the idea to Liz, who would be sure to follow up her enquiry by asking her periodically how she was getting on with her search. Perhaps voluntary work at the school would be the easiest thing. Already the idea of getting a job was losing its attraction.

"You can do more than you think, Rose. What you need is a bit of positive thinking. You've got a lot to offer, you know. Believe in yourself."

Rose heard the words but couldn't connect with the thought behind them. What she had to offer was, in reality, so little, it seemed to her. "Thanks," she said at last. "Thanks for giving me all those ideas, too. Now, I'd better take Robert home and let you get on with cooking for Remy and the family."

"Oh, I shan't cook tonight," said Liz airily. "It's Remy's turn. I've got a class tonight."

Admiration warred with envy in Rose's breast. As well as running the preschool group, Liz taught an evening class in Northchurch every Friday. How did she manage it all? She certainly couldn't imagine Clive cooking a meal to enable *her* to go out to work.

"It's really good of you to have fitted me in," she said sincerely. "I'd forgotten tonight was your evening class."

She picked up her handbag and coat and went down the passage to the rectory playroom. "Robert! It's time to go now."

"Let him stay if he wants, Rose," Liz called from the hall. "He won't be in our way and there's always plenty to eat. I can drop him off on my way out."

But Rose wanted to have Robert at home with her for his supper, and to keep all their comfortable routines intact. It might not be very long before they would all have to be changed, radically.

Four

On her return from her early hair appointment the next morning, Rose set off round the village for some last-minute selling of raffle tickets for the fête, a headscarf protecting her new coiffure from any treacherous gusts of wind. The residents of St Martin-on-the-Hill, the rain having relented, were occupied in washing their cars, and taking the opportunity of a fine autumn morning for some pruning of shrubs. Although she was essentially shy, Rose liked being part of a village community. This week especially, with her domestic affairs in chaos, it was soothing to be out in the village among her friends.

St Martin-on-the-Hill lived up to its name, being built on top of a chalk ridge that formed part of the rolling country to the south of the Berkshire downs. St Martin's church and its attendant farm, once the glebe, perched on the apex facing northwards across open country, with a semi-circle of brick-and-flint cottages and the village green directly adjacent on the southern side of the hill. This section was the oldest part of the village and still the heart of it, although the erection of an estate of fifty modern houses some fifteen years before, on land originally owned by Brian Warrendon, one of the local farmers, had shifted the geographical centre of the village south-eastwards.

She walked slowly up the hill past the churchyard, where old Ben Cartwright was clipping the hedge. His ancient black Labrador bitch lay beside the yew tree, watching her master.

"I'll buy some of them tickets," said Ben in his Hampshire burr, straightening up for a moment. "But you'll 'ave to ask the wife for the money." He turned out the pocket of his ancient corduroy trousers as he spoke, revealing an old bus ticket, half a dog biscuit and a penknife, but no coins.

Rose smiled. Ben had lived in the village for most of his life, latterly acting as sexton, and was a stalwart supporter of church and village activities. He still rang the bells before church on a Sunday whenever he could, pulling the ropes with a slow strength which spoke of fifty years' practice.

"I'll stop at the cottage," she said.

Passing the village school, its doors closed for the weekend, she tried not to remember that Robert's days there might be numbered. *Why is Clive so determined to send him away? What am I doing wrong?*

She stopped at Ben's cottage and was given the raffle ticket money by Ben's redoubtable Cornish wife. A group of Jehovah's Witnesses had parked their cars in the village car park that served both the school and the church and were walking in pairs, carrying sober briefcases, and attired in suits and ties, on their regular Saturday morning efforts to evangelise the villagers. They came often, in spite of the suspicion, resistance or apathy with which their advances were generally met. Jeremy, Rose remembered, smiling to herself, had been heard to say mildly that they probably found it a pleasant way of spending a fine Saturday morning out in the country. Whether the comment was intended to be barbed she had no idea. The rector's observations were often impenetrable.

At Church End Farm, she tramped across the gravel to the back door of the farmhouse, fending off the friendly greetings of two collies who came out to meet her. The back door was open, offering the visitor a view of a long dusty passage furnished only with wellington boots and clumps of dog hair.

"George? Are you there? It's Rose."

After a moment, the farmer emerged, running a hand over his grey hair. He was a tall, rather bony man in his late sixties, clad in old-fashioned grey flannel trousers and an elderly woollen pullover with a hole under one elbow.

"Sorry to disturb you, George. Would you like any raffle tickets?"

For a moment, George appearerd completely bewildered by this question. Then his mind seemed to refocus on her, and he patted his pockets hopefully.

"Come in a minute, Rose. I'll find some cash."

Rose followed him through the passage and into the farm office which led off it. The desk was strewn with paperwork, and a half-empty mug of congealing coffee stood on the window-sill.

"Sorry. I seem to have disturbed something important you were working on, George."

"No, it's all right. I was glad to get away from it for a minute, as a matter of fact. Just business, you know. Accounts. Hateful stuff."

Rose laughed. "Don't let Sarah hear you saying things like that. She'd think it was sacrilege."

George's worn face relaxed. "Takes all sorts, eh, Rose? Same with my brother Brian, you know. He could never understand why I don't like hassle. Of course, it's the hassle that makes the money, I suppose." His voice trailed away rather sadly. Rose wondered whether his wife Lucinda had been expressing dissatisfaction with George as a provider.

Times were poor for farmers countrywide, even those with plenty of land, like the Warrendons, and Lucinda, had aspirations to gentility that George simply couldn't afford.

Alternatively, it might have been the thought of his longstanding quarrel with his brother that prompted the sadness in his voice. The two had not spoken in years, rumour said, though they lived at opposite ends of the same village. Born and brought up in St Martin, the Warrendons continually found grievances against each other on matters as varied as land use, personal behaviour and community involvement. As a young man, Brian had taken the first opportunity to leave the village and study law, while George, after a brief period in the army, had come home to help run the farm. Yet, his father had been inordinately proud of his younger son and had drained family capital to support Brian's legal career and pay the debts he incurred. He had had the justice to divide the land equally between them when he died, but there was no doubt that Brian's share represented the better part of the inheritance, for the Home Farm land was in good heart and the buildings in good repair, while Church End Farm, rented out to tenants, had been neglected during their father's lifetime. Brian Warrendon had certainly made more of a success of farming than his brother, partly because of his willingness to build houses for sale on spare pieces of land whenever the planning department allowed it. As well as helping to perpetuate the bad blood between the brothers, this practice had made him hated and, to a large extent, ostracised by village people, whilst George himself was well liked.

Rose tucked the farmer's five-pound note away in her money bag and picked up the box of raffle tickets. "Thanks, George. I'd better be on my way."

George followed her out of the door. He looked around the yard, taking deep breaths of the mild air. "Splendid, isn't it? I love this place." He gestured at the outlook across the countryside enjoyed by the hilltop farmhouse.

Rose nodded. It was indeed a wonderful view, stretching six or seven miles across both Warrendon farms to the river, some hundred feet below; typical undulating North Hampshire countryside, with mingled arable pasture and copse, and wide fields separated by lanes and hedgerows. She left him standing on his back doorstep, still drinking in his beloved view, and set off home to prepare lunch.

~ * ~

At Sundials, she found that Sarah had arrived a few minutes before to join the family for the village festivities. Her daughter's greeting was brief and cool, as usual. She had taken to calling Rose "Mother" when she went away to boarding school, perhaps aping the manners of her peers, and their relationship had suffered a temperature drop as a result. Clive, however, she treated affectionately and with as much respect as any twenty-two-year-old daughter might be expected to show.

"I like your hair," she said to Rose this morning, to her mother's surprise. "It looks different. Did you have it done specially?"

"Yes," Rose admitted. "I thought I'd have it styled for the dance this evening." The proprietor of the salon, informed of the importance of his efforts, had, she felt, risen to the occasion. The only cloud on the horizon was that, although her daughter had admired the styling, Clive himself did not appear to notice anything. She had secretly hoped he would be impressed. Perhaps when he saw her new dress that evening he would feel differently.

Sarah and her father disappeared into Clive's study to talk over some matter of finance. Sarah liked to play the Stock Exchange and was accustomed to asking her father's advice on the subject of her investments. They would emerge for lunch later, but until then, Rose was free. Robert was playing with a friend, and no more maternal activity would be expected of her until he returned.

She walked down to the church to look at the flowers while the lunch cooked. It would be nice to spend a little time there in the quiet of the old building, and it would be open because of the festive weekend, so she wouldn't have to disturb the Swansons at the rectory for the key. Not that Remy would mind, she knew. He never minded putting himself out for his parishioners. He annoyed some of them by showing a distressing enthusiasm for new forms of worship and no taste for elaborate ritual, and others by having an offbeat sense of humour and too much of a liking for crosswords, crime novels and other apparently unspiritual pastimes; but one could always rely on him to be helpful.

She sat in a pew to admire the flowers. The flower arrangers had done a beautiful job, she thought. The window embrasures were a riot of late autumn colour, and the pulpit was almost obscured by an enormous display of late dahlias. Remy did not encourage elaborate flower arrangements in church except for special festivals, but she thought even he would appreciate his parishioners' efforts on this occasion.

Rose liked being in the church on her own; the quietness created by the atmosphere of age and accumulated prayer was soothing. It was not difficult for her to ask for divine help with her problems; she frequently brought them here. Alone in this place, she ceased to feel ashamed of her failures or her inability to live up to her own expectations, never mind other people's. No doubt God was just as aware of her shortcomings as everyone else, but she never felt that He reproached her for them; and she usually went home feeling stronger for her prayers.

After a few moments, she knelt and bowed her head, looking for the usual feeling of reassurance and peace. Today, however, her prayers seemed to reach no higher than the vaulted roof of the church. The energy given her by her make-over had quickly drained away. Now that her first flush of anger about Clive and Olivia had departed, she felt depressed and inadequate to the task she had set herself of recapturing his interest, and pain stabbed her at the very thought of being separated from Robert. A few tears escaped her closed eyes and trickled down her cheeks. She fumbled in her pocket for a handkerchief and found the pocket empty.

"Damn!" she said, with no thought for the sacredness of her surroundings. "I don't know what happens to my handkerchiefs."

"Mummy, are you talking to yourself?"

She looked round. Robert was standing at the door of the church.

"I went home, but you weren't there. I thought you might be here. The flowers are lovely, aren't they?"

Rose hugged him. "How clever of you to find me," she said, wiping the tears from her cheeks surreptitiously with the back of one hand. "Daddy and Sarah are talking about some business thing or other, so I thought I'd come down here while nobody needed me for anything. Did you have a good time with Darren?"

He nodded. "Yes, I did. I like Darren's family. There's lots of them, and they all play together."

Darren lived on the modern housing estate off Copse Lane. This, in itself, made him unacceptable to Clive as a friend for his son, for Clive had thought the estate a monstrosity when it was built six years before and had never forgiven Brian Warrendon for selling the land to a developer in the first place. Rose herself was determined that Robert should find his own friends rather than having them handpicked by his parents. Accordingly, she had connived at her son's less-than-truthful account of his friend when his father had subjected him to interrogation. Darren had emerged from this eulogy as a model companion, well-behaved and brought up among a charming and good-mannered family of substance, none of which had much foundation in reality.

"Why were you talking to yourself?" Robert demanded, as usual not easily deflected from a subject on which he wanted information. "You *were*, Mummy."

"Yes, I know," she replied. "I had a sniff, and I couldn't find my handkerchief. I never can. They always seem to walk out of my pockets when I'm not looking."

"Like mine," he said helpfully. "Mine walk into very odd places sometimes."

She laughed. "I know they do. I'm the one that finds them, remember!"

"Have you finished looking at the flowers?" he asked. "It's past one o'clock, and I'm hungry."

"Is it that late?" Rose said, feeling slightly flustered. "We'd better get moving, then."

Together they shut the church door and latched it. Robert ran on ahead of Rose down the path through the churchyard and stopped to wait for her at the gate. As she reached it, he shrank back towards her, away from something or somebody on the other side of the hedge. Rose looked over the gate in surprise. "What is it, Robert?" she asked.

He shook his head, white-faced.

From beyond the gate there was a grumbling bellowing noise reminiscent of a charging bull. There was no doubt, however, that it was a human sound. As she stepped out of the churchyard Rose identified it. The human in question was Brian Warrendon, and from the sound of it he was extremely angry. His chest heaved alarmingly, and a steady stream of more or less incomprehensible profanity poured from his lips, underpinned by the angry growling which had so alarmed Robert.

Staring at his flushed, empurpled countenance, Rose stood still. Robert, holding tightly to her hand, ceased to drag backwards against her arm and hid behind her instead. The village knew and respected Brian Warrendon's temper, which was easily aroused and virtually ungovernable. He had twice come close to being sued for assault, but in each case his victims had preferred to accept minor injuries with resignation rather than face his highly paid barrister in cross-examination in court. Although he was usually affable and charming to Rose whenever they met at village functions, she knew better than to draw attention to herself at this moment.

They waited in silence until the raging bull, apparently unaware of their presence, had passed them by. Rose put her arm round her son. "It's all right, Robert. He's gone now." She took his hand again, and as they set off home she murmured half to herself, "But I wonder what on earth made him so angry?"

~ * ~

Brian Warrendon drove home and stood beside his front door looking down over his fields to Copse Lane. His temper had cooled, but unlike his brother, he saw no idyllic rural view, unspoilt by human rapacity, basking in the late autumn sunshine. To him, land was a business venture, owned and worked entirely for profit. The old copses remained uncleared because they were necessary to breed pheasant chicks. They were managed efficiently by the forester and gamekeeper he employed, and the shooting, leased commercially, was a profitable side line during the winter months. The pasture land produced good-quality grass-fed, beef cattle which he bred scientifically himself. And beyond the pasture was the Copse Lane housing estate, still one of his fondest triumphs over the sentiment of the villagers and the bureaucracy of the local planners. But the housing estate was as nothing to what he had in mind for the future. The surveyors were coming down again on Tuesday, and he saw no reason why he should not be able to sell the field by the river for a small—perhaps even a large—fortune. It was merely, he told himself, a question of thinking in grand enough terms. *If it comes off*, he thought to himself, *it'll really show those stuffy villagers...and George, too.* He chuckled, his anger forgotten. Nothing was so much fun as shocking your neighbours rigid.

Five

The whole family set off for the fête together straight after lunch. Rose, carrying two tins of soup and a cashmere sweater which had never suited her, made her way through the throng in the village hall to help on the Bring & Buy Stall, while Clive and Robert, armed with Robert's pocket money, augmented for the afternoon by his father, began their survey of the attractions at the tea marquee attached to one end of the hall. Sarah abandoned the other members of her family and joined up with friends of her own generation who had also returned to the nest for the traditional weekend of festivities.

The village was unusual in having no summer fête, but instead put all its energies into the events of its patronal weekend. The fête on Saturday afternoon, the dance in the evening followed by fireworks, and the special evensong late on Sunday afternoon to mark Remembrance Day, with which it usually coincided, left the villagers exhausted, but the result was usually both financially and communally worthwhile.

The village hall premises were large, and the proceedings were well-known in the surrounding countryside, the event drawing people from all the local villages. This year the hall was packed; the tea tent positively bulged at the seams, and the stalls, competitions, and other attractions did their usual roaring trade.

Laura, the stallholder, and Rose were kept busy on the Bring & Buy stall all afternoon. They had paused from their labours to drink the welcome cup of tea provided for stallholders towards the end of the proceedings, when Rose's attention was drawn by a familiar voice.

"How's trade?" asked Simon, pausing in front of the stall.

She looked up. "Oh, Simon. I've got your ticket for the dance somewhere in my bag. Wait a minute." She rummaged ineffectually in the handbag. "I know I put it in this little zipped pocket...."

"No rush, Rose. I'll have a look on your stall while you're hunting for it. Got anything decent left?"

Laura bustled forward and began showing him the somewhat sorry articles which had been Brought but not yet Bought. Rose could not help admiring, out of the corner of her eye, the courtesy with which he thought up plausible reasons for refusing all of them.

"I've found it!" she exclaimed at last, pleased to be releasing him from his perusal of the unattractive goods. "I'm sorry, it's got a bit bent at the corners..."

Simon took the piece of card from her without examining it and tucked it away in his jacket pocket. "I like that new hairdo of yours, Rose. Is it a wig?"

Flustered and colouring up, Rose began to explain, but he cut her short. "I'm only teasing you," he said, gently. "It's pretty, really. Did you buy a new dress to go with it?"

She stared at him. "How did you know?"

He grinned. "I shall look forward to seeing it tonight. 'Bye."

He turned and strode away without looking back, leaving Rose bewildered and Laura intrigued. Fortunately, his remarks had clearly been made humorously, and both Rose and Simon were such unlikely participants in romantic intrigue that she rejected suspicion out of hand.

~ * ~

Sarah and Rose left the village hall to the sound of the first explosions of the firework display on the village green. Robert had gone to see it with the rectory children, and Liz had promised to see him home afterwards as Clive had disappeared half way through the fete.

"Daddy had a real stand-up row with Brian Warrendon this afternoon," said Sarah. "Did you hear them? What a beastly man that is."

Rose concluded, with some inner irony, that she was referring to Brian and not her father. She remembered her near-encounter with the farmer earlier that day. He had been angry then, too. "What were they arguing about?" she asked rather absent-mindedly.

"I think it was something to do with oil. But I can't think why. Dad was so fed up he went home early."

Poor Robert, thought Rose. *He was so looking forward to going to the fete with Clive.* "Perhaps the oil tanker put mud on the road coming out of the farm," she suggested vaguely.

"And who was that extremely fanciable man talking to you and Laura just before you packed up?" asked Sarah, her eyes alight with mischief.

Rose's attention sharpened, wary of the question. "Which one?"

Sarah laughed. "Were there many? About thirty-five, medium height, dark curly hair, drop-dead gorgeous…very nice going, Mum. Will he be at the dance tonight? I think I may try to get off with him."

To her dismay, Rose found herself resenting this. "I don't know," she snapped. "And he's far too old for you, anyway."

"I like older men," said Sarah provocatively, and disappeared into the twilight to collect her car and return to her flat to dress up for the evening.

~ * ~

Simon had not noticed Sarah particularly at the fete. He had done his share of romancing girls as a young man, but now he would rather be single than flit from one woman to another. He hated fending off both the willing nymphets, young and otherwise, and the disappointed, damaged relicts of others' callousness, with their pathetic yearning for love and commitment. For the moment, at least, he was armoured against them all, and did not expect his citadel to be breached any time in the near future, if ever. Instead, he put his emotional energy into enigmatic, ironic poetry, and was content with his own company.

There were lines of verse bubbling at the edges of his consciousness this evening, arising from his afternoon at the village fete with its host of comic rural characters. He scribbled a couple of ideas down quickly, but there wasn't time to develop them. It was time to change for the dance. He was not, as Rose had earlier divined, much given to party-going, and certainly not to formal dances. But this evening's informal hop, as described to him by Rose, sounded pleasant and innocuous enough.

He pushed aside the curtain covering the wardrobe in his tiny cottage and found a colourful casual shirt and a pair of well-cut trousers. Teamed with a plain dark jacket, they would have to do.

He wondered how Rose would cope with ringing at the quarter-peal the following evening after evensong. He knew she would be nervous and racked h

is brains as to how he could help. He liked Rose, not least because she never flirted or coquetted, never made a play to engage his attention. He found her a restful person, with her focus on her little son and his doings, her desire to please others, and her self-abnegation. He was vaguely aware that she wasn't very happy, and it troubled him a little. Rose was a good woman and deserved better. He hoped she would enjoy herself this evening.

~ * ~

At six o'clock Rose had a bath and began to assemble her finery for the dance. The dress was hanging in the spare-room wardrobe, together with a silk wrap and a pair of evening sandals, hidden from Clive's sight. Like a girl getting ready for her first grown-up party, Rose lifted the outfit lovingly from the hanger and laid it across the bed. She brushed her hair and lowered the dress carefully over her head. Then reverently she admired her reflection in the mirror, from which a new and exciting stranger looked back at her.

Her dark sleek head with its newly cut waves rose triumphantly from the square neck of the red dress, whose colour set off her pale skin and dark brown hair to perfection. The boutique saleswoman had identified the few good features she did have: her smooth dark hair still untouched by grey, her fine high cheekbones, the elegant line from chin to breast. Looking at her reflection now, she believed for the first time that her outward appearance could sway her fortunes. Olivia possessed a hard-edged sophistication which she would never try to emulate. But she realised that her simpler style of good looks was well worth having, and believing in. She forgot her anger and bitterness and looked forward with simple pleasure to the moment when Clive would see her in all her glory.

She spent time over her make-up, including a lipstick chosen to match the dress exactly. It was seven o'clock when she was finally satisfied; half-an-hour before the dance began. She rose carefully from the chair in front of the mirror and glided along the landing to the main bedroom. Sounds of preparation could be heard within.

"Clive...are you ready?"

"No," came muffled tones from within. "I'm not going with you to this dance, Rose. I'm catching a plane in an hour. I've got business in the North...something came up unexpectedly. I'll be back tomorrow night, or perhaps Monday, I'm not sure."

A noose seemed to fasten itself around Rose's neck, tightening painfully until she could hardly breathe. "Clive, you can't..."

"Sorry, Rose," came the heartless voice. "I'm committed now. I'd promised Robert the fête, but I have to..."

"You promised *me* the dance," she interrupted fiercely.

"You've got the tickets, haven't you?" was the careless reply. "Sarah wants to go. She can pick you up. I told her to come round."

"You told her... You've got it all worked out, haven't you?" she said, indignation almost choking her. "You might have thought of telling *me*."

This time Clive did not reply. Rose could hear drawers opening and shutting as he piled clothes into a suitcase.

"I bought a special dress for this," she began, and stopped. A pleading note had crept into her voice, and she was determined not to beg.

"Too bad," was the answer. "Wear it some other time for me. It'll keep."

Wild, desperate thoughts and emotions surged up in Rose. She forced them down. "The dress may keep," she said, in a cold voice. "But I won't. And as for your 'business,' Clive, I know perfectly well what that means. I hope you enjoy her."

She walked with as much dignity as she could back to the spare bedroom. But Clive didn't follow her. He seemed to have ignored— or perhaps not even heard—her parting shot.

Rose sat down again in front of the mirror, but this time her reflection gave her no reassurance. She did not even consider her make-up, applied with such care, as the tears squeezed between her eyelids and coursed down her cheeks. A vice seemed to be crushing her windpipe and her stomach muscles were knotted together. Her heart pounded. She heard Clive's footsteps going down the stairs and the front door slam behind him. The slam, and the absence of any farewell, suggested that her final comment had at least penetrated his indifference. But she hardly cared.

Sarah arrived ten minutes after her father had left, to find her mother sitting in a kind of catalepsy, motionless before the mirror, staring sightlessly at her reflection.

"Mother!"

The unusual concern in her daughter's voice penetrated Rose's trance.

"Your father isn't coming tonight," she said.

"No, he told me. He had to go to Newcastle, or was it Edinburgh? Up north somewhere, anyway. Business, he said."

Rose hesitated. The temptation to enlist her daughter as partisan was hard to resist. But Clive's infidelities should be no concern of Sarah's; she idolised her father.

"I didn't know he was going away until the last minute," she said, trying to control her voice. "I'm not sure I'll bother to go to the dance. I'm not really in the mood."

"Poor Mother. When you had your hair done specially. And this lovely dress. Did you buy it for the dance?"

Rose lifted her tear-stained face to look at her daughter. It might be rather patronising, this sympathy of Sarah's, but it was sympathy of a kind. She tried to smile.

"I did," she said. "That's why I was so disappointed that Dad couldn't go with me. Silly of me. Do you really want me to come anyway?"

"Seems a pity not to, when you're all dressed up. I'll go and check Robert is on his way to bed."

"Maddie next door said she'd come and babysit. She'll be here in a minute."

"Good." Sarah peered at her carefully. "You can't go all streaked like that, though."

Rose smiled rather tearfully. "I'll put some more foundation on."

"It's a blessing you never wear mascara," said Sarah.

~ * ~

The dance was well under way by the time Rose and Sarah arrived. The village hall had undergone a transformation since five o'clock. The stalls had become trestle tables covered with food, the floor had been swept of its fête debris, and turntables and loudspeakers took up the whole of the stage. The band was just starting to play a tango.

Sarah was whisked away by a young man whom Rose recognised vaguely as a boyfriend of her daughter's teenage years.

None of her admirers ever appeared to command her allegiance for more than a few months, even now. Either she grew bored with them and discovered some new and more exciting love interest, or her boundless energy and intellectual drive caused them to retire exhausted from the lists. Sarah seemed not to need emotional security. She was confident, self-assured and competent, and clearly found the challenges of her career more attractive than anything she might discover in a long-term relationship. Perhaps, Rose reflected rather ruefully, thinking of her own less-than-blissful experience of marriage, she was wise.

Rose found herself standing among the other unaccompanied middle-aged women, watching the couples on the dance floor. To her annoyance, she felt her eyes misting. Clive should have been there, admiring her for once, dancing with her, attending to her. This was to have been her evening of triumph, when Olivia Landry was defeated once and for all. Instead, she was alone and unappreciated, and Olivia was no doubt meeting up with Clive at the airport.

The tango ended, and a Beatles number took its place. Sarah and her partner were twisting energetically, legs bent, hips gyrating. Across the room she saw the door open. Simon showed his ticket and moved through the crowd in her direction, though she did not think he had seen her. Instinctively, Rose began to move away. She could not face Simon tonight. As she turned she saw Jeremy Swanson, the rector, beside one of the tables behind her. She would probably not be able to hide her distress from him either. Trapped between the two, undecided, she turned back a little towards Simon, and, at that moment, he caught sight of her.

Their eyes met, and he began to move purposefully in her direction. When he reached her he said nothing, his eyes taking in her face and finery with admiration and, she felt uncomfortably certain, also perceiving all too clearly her inner distress.

"Are you on your own?" he asked.

She nodded, the tears coming to her eyes. She brushed them away angrily.

He reached for her hand and said abruptly, "Come and dance."

The twist had finished, and the DJ was playing a slow ballad. At first, Rose moved stiffly in Simon's arms. Then as he said nothing, holding her closely but still gently, she began to relax. A waltz followed the ballad, and then a quickstep. Simon was a good dancer, light on his feet, guiding her without pressure, and she began to enjoy herself. Clive had always complained that her ballroom dancing was atrocious; she moved awkwardly, and her feet were always in his way. But either it was Clive himself who was the poor dancer, or Simon was a brilliant one. At least, he inspired Rose. She danced foxtrots, waltzes and another slow ballad with him; she even managed to follow his expert lead and spin and swing to the rock and roll numbers. She forgot everything except the enjoyment of the dancing, the movement of her feet and her body, the skill and inspiration of Simon.

At last he led her off the floor. "That's enough for a bit," he observed, smiling.

"Yes," said Rose, breathing hard. "But it was fun. Thank you so much, Simon. Clive couldn't come tonight, and I…"

"I'm glad he couldn't," he said. "But he's a fool to be missing it. You look wonderful, Rose."

She was speechless, looking down at the dress, remembering again the hopes that had been centred on it. "I – I'm glad you like it," she stammered.

"I do like it," he said. "But that's not what I said. *You* look wonderful, Rose."

She looked up again. There was an ardent expression in his eyes which she had never expected to see, and certainly not when they were looking at her. She felt herself blush.

"Come and get some food," he said, and led the way to the tables. But he kept hold of her hand.

Geoff Longman exchanged greetings with them as they filled their plates with cold chicken and salad and reminded them of the quarter-peal scheduled for the following evening. "That is if no one lets me down at the last minute," he added darkly. Since neither Simon nor Rose had intended to let him down (although Rose was still very apprehensive about the ordeal), Lesley was proverbially reliable, and any failure on Ben's part must be due to his rheumatism, this grim foreboding presumably referred to his son. Simon and Rose looked at each other.

"You might ask Janice to stand by in case..." suggested Rose tentatively.

Geoff shook his head. "Not if I can avoid it," he said. "I'm not sure I wouldn't rather call the whole thing off, tradition or no. And while I think of it," he added, "you won't forget the Tower AGM on Wednesday, will you? At your house, Simon, this year, I think we said. You're in the Chair. As you know, I've got to be elsewhere that night, but Ken will come over...probably."

Simon nodded.

"I *had* forgotten all about it," said Rose, feeling guilty, as Geoff strolled away with his plateful of food. "What with the St Martin's weekend and..." her voice tailed away.

"There's not much on the agenda this year," said Simon, considerately ignoring her confusion. "Will Lesley pick you and Ben up on her way as usual?"

"I'm sure she will. I must ask her." She looked round. "I don't think she's here tonight. I'll ask her tomorrow."

Rose had been relieved to find that Geoff did not seem to think it strange to see her with Simon; more extraordinary still, nor did anyone else. Rose felt as though she was in the midst of some outlandish dream, in which people did not behave in the least as one expected them to. Surely, in this setting, to adopt Simon so obviously as her partner for the evening must set all the village tongues wagging? But she could not see any covert glances; no whispers appeared to follow her. It was not until afterwards that she realised that Simon had made it appear so natural and inevitable that in Clive's absence he, one of her fellow bellringers, would squire her, that no one questioned it. There was nothing but friendly proficiency in his dancing, and the ardent look she had seen for a moment in his eyes did not return.

Instead, admiring comments showered upon her from her kinder friends, who seemed genuinely pleased—though unflatteringly surprised—to see her clad in such a dress and so obviously enjoying herself. Past hurts, present problems and future decisions alike were swept away in the enjoyment of the moment. It was an evening of sheer, unalloyed, twenty-four-carat bliss which she would remember forever.

At midnight, the band packed up their equipment while everyone collected their coats and made their several ways home. Sarah had left early in the company of her childhood swain, and with the parting remark that she could see her mother was in good hands, so it was clearly part of the evening's magic that Rose should accept Simon's escort home.

It was a clear starry night, freshly washed by the earlier rain. "Let's walk, shall we?" he said, his hand under her elbow.

She smiled at him and agreed that a walk would be refreshing after the crowded hall.

"And besides, I love to walk when the stars are out," she said, picking her way carefully along the darkened path by the light of Simon's big torch. "They always make me feel that my problems are so small."

He laid his arm lightly along her shoulders. "I'm glad of that," he said, smiling. "When I first set eyes on you this evening, I had the feeling that they seemed pretty enormous."

"Yes," she agreed. How long ago that felt. "I still don't know what to do, but it doesn't seem to matter quite so much now."

There was a silence. She could feel that Simon was waiting for her to confide in him, but somehow she could not. He was no longer the objective, detached individual to whom she had wanted to bring her difficulties over Robert; and to explain her quarrel with Clive now seemed quite impossible. It was better…safer…that he should not have any idea that her marriage was in crisis.

"Has Clive left you?" he asked, after the silence had lasted for two or three minutes.

Rose made a convulsive movement away from him. She did not ask herself how he had divined the nature of her trouble, nor wallow in justifiable annoyance at his attempt to force her confidence. Her whole being was taken up with the effort to maintain a silent, dignified reserve for the few minutes left of the evening. The white gate of Sundials could be seen in the gloom not far ahead.

"Rose, please don't hold out on me," he said as they reached it. For the first time in their long acquaintance, he did not sound as though he felt master of the situation. "I would like to know how things stand."

She found it hard to withstand his sudden vulnerability. "Not now," she faltered. "Not yet. I can't start telling you about it here."

"It might help you to tell me," he said, his voice gentle. "You're holding too much inside you."

They halted by the gate. Simon switched off his torch, and they stood in the gloom for a moment, both of them reluctant to bring the evening to an end.

Rose tried to read Simon's expression by the faint glow thrown by the porch lamp. He had spoken as though he wanted only relief for her, but she was aware that some need of his own had prompted him as well. She had trodden down her own needs for so many years that this longing to confide in him could be stifled along with all the rest. But *his* need she found more difficult to ignore.

Simon took her hand again. "Tell me," he said.

Rose shook her head. "Not today," she said. "I have to see what will happen."

There was a pause, and Rose withdrew her hand awkwardly. "Thank you for a really wonderful evening," she said, not looking at him. "It was so good of you, Simon…so kind."

He made an impatient movement. "I wasn't being kind. Don't thank me, Rose."

It was difficult to move away. She began to explain, disjointedly, why she could not ask him in for coffee, murmuring about the babysitter and the time. He cut her short.

"I'll see you tomorrow," he said, and before she realised what he was about, he bent and kissed her on the lips. For a few seconds, his mouth held hers softly. Then he released her and strode away.

Six

The bells ceased their clamour in the tower of St Martin's church the next morning as Jeremy stood at the rear of the choir procession waiting to announce the first hymn. He watched Rose and Ben sidle quietly out of the ringing chamber and into one of the rear pews. It was always these two ringers who joined the congregation for the service, while the others generally used the outside door of the tower to slip away unnoticed. As for Simon Hellyer, Jeremy had rarely, if ever, seen him in church, even at Christmas.

Jeremy regained control over his thoughts with an effort. Simon was not the first and would certainly not be the last bellringer to ring bells for the love of the pastime rather than for the love of God and His Church. Rose and Ben were already in their places. Liz was looking round from the rectory pew to see what was delaying him. It was time to begin the service for those who had chosen to attend.

"Our first hymn is number two in Ancient and Modern," he declared, wishing yet again that he could persuade the Church Council that *Hymns Ancient and Modern* could no longer even *pretend* to contain much that could be called Modern, whilst most of the Ancient hymns, though still beloved, were completely out of date. "New every morning is the love."

As it was Remembrance Sunday, he had to preach on something relevant, which was often a difficult task. And at

Southover, the service scheduled for eleven o'clock would begin two minutes early with the traditional silence. He had always resisted holding the military-style Act of Remembrance with the Last Post as his predecessor had done, but some of his parishioners still resented it.

He was relieved when the two services were over, when the congregations had been greeted, and the small administrative and parochial details which were always brought to him had been smoothed over or noted for future action. At twelve-thirty he climbed thankfully into his shabby car, waved cheerfully to those of his Southover flock who were still lingering in the churchyard, and drove the two miles home. Family lunch with a glass of wine, and forty winks after it; Sunday afternoon bliss. When there was no service to be taken, he tried to spend at least part of Sunday afternoon quietly, but with the festival evensong at 5 p.m. there was little hope of that today. Sunday was Sunday, the traditional day of rest, and leading services and preaching sermons shouldn't feel like work, he reflected, any more than attending one and listening to the other would count as work for his parishioners in the congregation. The last time he had calculated his parish hours, he had arrived at a horrifyingly large total, especially when he reckoned up how many of his evenings were taken up with visiting, wedding or baptism preparation or other meetings. His own day off, on Monday, rarely if ever lived up to the name. The whole concept of work and leisure for clergy made no sense at all, anyway. To him it was a calling, not a career.

He drove through the village and turned in at the rectory gates. Liz had the lunch ready to serve, as usual. He poured himself his promised glass of wine and took it with him into the dining room, smiling reassurance to her quick frown.

"You do look tired, Remy," she said. "And there's still the St Martin's evensong to come."

"Dad *should* have a rest sometimes," piped up Bethan suddenly.

"Mummy sometimes makes us have a rest after school," agreed Chris. "If we're going out in the evening."

"Dad has his rest after dinner, silly," said Mike, in the superior tone engendered by six years' seniority.

"And he has Monday off," added Lorna.

Jeremy's eyes met Liz's, and they silently agreed that enough had been said in front of the younger members of the family. Liz handed out plates of food, and Jeremy asked Lorna to say grace.

"Can I go out after dinner, Mum?" asked Chris a few minutes later, fork in hand. "Darren has got a new sledge-thingy on wheels and we want to try it out down Copse Lane."

"You know I don't really want you to make a friend of Darren," said Liz. Darren's father's occupation as a somewhat dubious car trader who had once or twice escaped criminal prosecution by the slenderest of margins made him, in Liz's eyes, an unsuitable companion for a clergyman's son. "And Copse Lane is too dangerous to play on," she added, before he could argue.

"But Darren is friends with Robert as well," protested Chris, taking up only the first of her objections. "You *like* me to be friends with Robert." He turned to his father. "I can go, can't I, Dad?"

Jeremy smiled at his son's frustration with parental logic. "Is Robert going with you this afternoon, Chris?" he asked.

There was a moment's silence. Honesty and expediency were obviously at war. Finally, not without a struggle, honesty won. "It was going to be just Darren and me," he said. "Robert tags on…he's younger than we are, and he still wants to join in everything."

"I want to come, too," complained Bethan. "You never let me join in with games when you're out with Darren."

Jeremy sighed. The separation of these fraternal twins into two independent individuals was obviously going to be painful.

"Stay at home and play with Bethan this afternoon," he said to Chris. "I promise you shall go out with Darren another time." He picked up his knife and fork in order to attack his dinner and completely missed the dagger-look directed at him by his wife.

After the meal, Jeremy sat back in his armchair contentedly, a detective novel in one hand. The family was spread out round the drawing room in varying degrees of relaxation. Mike was lying on the floor studying a large Ordnance Survey map of part of the Shetland Islands. For some reason, he was fascinated by maps of all kinds. All his meagre pocket money was spent on them, and his favourite birthday and Christmas presents were always those related to this enthusiasm. Lorna had curled up in one corner of the sofa to read a pop music magazine. A photograph of her latest pop idol, scantily clad and sporting spiky brightly coloured hair, adorned the cover. Liz had given up expostulating about her daughter's taste in magazines or anything else. Lorna was not rebellious or anarchic, nor did her behaviour either at school or at home cause any concern. She had no very dangerous political opinions. She did not experiment with drugs or cultivate unsuitable friends. She simply liked the bizarre, whether in clothes or music or art.

Liz had started knitting, her needles moving briskly and rhythmically across each row. By dedicated and energetic work, she managed to keep most of the family in winter sweaters, but she had turned out Mike's chest of drawers the previous morning and found that not a single one of his sweaters would fit him. Most of them could be passed down to Chris in due course; but the fact remained that not only had Mike's chest measurement expanded yet again, but his limbs were growing longer at an alarming rate. That being so, she would have to knit busily for the next few weeks and face the fact that new items of school uniform would be needed for all the children before long. Jeremy's stipend was adequate, she often told herself, and much better than that earned by some of his colleagues. However, sometimes this truth felt less than self-evident... more a matter of blind faith.

Perhaps she should try to find a full-time job, she thought, instead of teaching one evening class a week at a local college.

Many clergy wives worked full time these days. It was frustrating to know that her qualifications could probably command a higher salary than Remy's. But the ministry was Remy's life. When she married him, she knew she had married his calling, too. How could she rob him of that, or diminish him by suggesting that they would be better off if she were the main breadwinner? And in any case, she had always wanted to give more of her attention to her children than a full-time career would allow. Running the preschool group had seemed ideal, but it didn't bring her in much money to contribute to the family purse; and the weekly evening class paid for her personal needs but not a lot more.

The room was silent, for the twins had been banished to the attic to play. No one knew, and no one cared much, what game they were playing, so long as they were out of earshot. A precious rare peace settled down upon the house. For once, no parishioner felt the need to ring the doorbell or telephone with some real or imagined emergency. The rustle of Lorna's magazine as she turned the pages, the slight crackle of Mike's map, and the click of Liz's knitting needles, combined to soothe Jeremy into slumber. The forty winks became a hundred, but only Liz noticed.

He responded to her hand on his shoulder, more than an hour later, by opening one eye drowsily.

"Don't tell me it's time yet," he said. "I only just closed my eyes for a minute."

"Remy," said his wife severely. "You have been sound asleep for the last hour."

He yawned. "If you say so. It all comes of staying to the end of the dance."

"And drinking three cups of coffee while you argued with Geoff Longman about the history of the St Martin's bells. No wonder you couldn't sleep properly."

Jeremy smiled ruefully. "I should have known I would never convince Geoff by reading up the diocese archives."

He stretched and swung his feet on to the floor. "I hope he won't go to sleep during that quarter-peal of theirs. Though why they have to have it every year..."

"Tradition," said Liz. "They always ring a quarter-peal after the service at the patronal festival. It goes well with Remembrance Day, don't you think? Or with celebrating the Feast of St Martin," she suggested.

"Bellringers like celebrating their own esoteric skill, if you ask me," retorted Jeremy, who was not amused. "You don't find many of them coming to the service beforehand."

"Rose will be there," Liz reminded him quietly. "And Ben."

As Jeremy prepared for the service, he found himself hoping that Liz was right, and Rose would stay for the service as usual. Suddenly, he was visited by an unclerical and most uncharitable desire to wring Clive Althorpe's neck. Why did he not have the sense to appreciate his good fortune? A woman like Rose, positively *created* to be a virtuous, self-denying, considerate wife, deserved a better man as her husband. He had not had a great deal to do with Clive, whose church-going was erratic, but the man's arrogance and his contempt for his wife were evident on the slenderest acquaintance.

Jeremy scolded himself for these condemning thoughts all the way from the rectory to the church gate without making much impression on the unregenerate Adam within. He saw Rose standing beside the lychgate, apparently speaking to someone out of sight beyond. His conscience did not even trouble to suggest that he moved out of earshot; Jeremy had convinced himself many years ago that curiosity was a virtue. He apostrophised it "interest in my parishioners" and considered that justification enough.

"Just tell your husband that he'd better keep his nose out of my affairs, will you?" To Jeremy's ear, the angry voice identified the invisible speaker immediately. Brian Warrendon, in full flow. "It's my business what I do with my land, you tell him."

"I think Clive feels that what happens to the land around the village is everyone's business, whoever the land happens to belong to," Rose replied with surprising temerity… but in defence of the village, not of Clive, Jeremy thought.

"I won't put up with interference from incomers like you and your husband. He'll get what he won't like if he doesn't leave off."

"Even the old villagers feel the same, you know, Brian. The people who've been here even longer than you and George. No one wants any development on the green fields."

"Bit of modern technology would do this village good," stated the farmer flatly. "NIMBY lot!"

"I don't know what modern technology has to do with it," said Rose. "If it's more houses you're thinking of, then you know how people here feel about it." She hesitated, then went on, "Brian, don't you think it's worth considering what the village feels? You have to live here among us, after all. And even your own brother…"

A snort interrupted her. "That milksop George has nothing to say to anything. Him and his beloved countryside… he'd do better to try to satisfy Lucinda. That should keep him busy!"

Rose said no more, and Brian, appearing from behind the gate, nodded brusquely at Jeremy and marched on up the road. One less in the congregation, thought Jeremy. But on the whole the congregation would probably be more comfortable for it.

He raised an eyebrow at Rose and received a slightly rueful smile in return.

"It isn't any use trying to discuss anything with Brian, is it?" she said. "I should know that by now, I suppose. But I can never quite believe he'll be as obstinate as he is. I don't know what on earth he was talking about, anyway, though Sarah did say he'd had a quarrel with Clive yesterday."

"Brian gets in a rage so easily," agreed Jeremy. "I'm always afraid one of these days he'll do something that he'll regret, something that'll get him into real trouble."

The brothers' current estrangement had lasted for the best part of three years. Jeremy had several times asked them to meet with him at the rectory to talk things through, but neither of them had been willing. Yet, surely at some point, they must have been friends? He tried to visualize the two of them growing up together, competing, even fighting perhaps as brothers will, but presumably loving each other. A faint family resemblance suggested their blood relationship still, but this was dwarfed by the contrasts. He saw quite clearly in his mind George's gaunt, pale, rather weary face alongside Brian's broad, red, apoplectic one. A prototype of Cain and Abel before the hatreds led irrevocably to murder. He devoutly hoped it wouldn't come to that.

He became aware that Rose had not responded to his comment. Her face was tight and withdrawn. "It's not always easy to avoid, is it?" she said. "Doing things you'll regret later, I mean. You don't always know what you'll regret, and what you'll think was the best decision you ever made."

Jeremy looked at her sharply. "Come and talk to me, Rose, won't you, before you do anything that serious? Or talk to Liz, if you'd rather. I know she'd want to help. It helps sometimes to air a problem."

"Both of you have helped me a lot in the past," she said. "But I'm not sure anyone can help me now."

They made their way to the door of the church in silence. Rose went inside to take her place near the back of the church, while Jeremy stayed in the porch to greet his parishioners as they came to celebrate the Feast of St Martin.

The church was almost full. Remembrance left behind, a spirit of celebration was easy to conjure up with the congregation feeling cheerful, relieved of the cares of the previous day, recovered from the excesses of the dance, and even mildly elated with the financial success of the weekend. The hymns were the traditional ones for the patronal festival, known by everyone and sung with the gusto associated only with music both known and loved.

Looking around as he mounted the pulpit for the gospel and sermon, Jeremy saw few new faces but missed several old ones. Three deaths the previous winter, the departures of two elderly folk to live with families in distant towns, and of one family whose breadwinner's work had taken them to the Middle East for five years, had thinned the ranks appreciably. Two couples and the local builder had bought the old cottages and renovated them, and two new families had moved in to Copse Lane, but he had seen them only in the course of the pastoral visit he paid to every newcomer to the village. Of recent newcomers, only one, Lesley Trant, had established any connection with the church, and that was merely (and to him regrettably) a campanological one.

The gradual hymn came to an end with a final exultant chord, and the congregation, having listened to the lectionary gospel reading on their feet, as usual, settled themselves in their seats, looking expectantly up at Jeremy. He found himself, unexpectedly, in a dilemma. He had prepared a bland, encouraging, uncontroversial sermon, as usual for this service. People came to be glad, to remember good times past and present, to be hopeful about the future. They did not want to listen to home truths or uncomfortable thoughts from the rector on this occasion... if ever. The few who rattled in the half-empty church like a few sweets in the bottom of a jar on other occasions probably did not listen in any case to his attempts to awaken them from their spiritual torpor. Jeremy stood there silently, more discouraged than he remembered feeling for many years. The thought came to him that he might as well not have lived and worked for ten years in this benefice, for all the change he had effected in the lives of the parishioners. *I'm not suited to a rural parish*, he thought to himself, *even though I love the countryside. They don't want change. They want to keep the clock from ticking, and time from moving on. Why on earth am I wasting my life here?*

The silence grew longer, and a few feet moved restlessly in the pews as the congregation waited. Jeremy's eye fell on the bellringers in the back row. Lesley was there for once, and so, much to his amazement, was Simon, who sat beside Rose nonchalantly, his half-humorous, mocking gaze on Jeremy.

Simon's expression was the last straw. Without further thought, without preamble, Jeremy launched into a quite different sermon, unprepared and a world away from the written notes in front of him; but straight from the heart.

"Have you ever asked yourself why we are here?" he began, looking at the upraised faces before him. "Why do we come, year after year, for the festival, and sit in these pews? We say the words of the service, we sing the hymns, we kneel in the right places.... But why?"

The faces were a little startled. They knew why they came. What was he talking about?

"It's part of the traditional way, you may say," he continued, and there was a rather bitter edge to his voice. "And we are creatures of tradition, aren't we? Whether it's the turkey at Christmas or the lighted candles on the birthday cake. Here in our Hampshire village, we are creatures of tradition.

"Even those of you who have come to the village relatively late in life, because you are prosperous and want to escape from the grim realities of urban life, you want rural customs to stay the same. That's why you came to the country, after all, isn't it?"

The faces were listening now, intent, some of them becoming angry. *I'm glad Clive isn't listening to this,* thought Rose.

"But let me tell you, my friends. It isn't enough to come to church once or twice a year when you're comfortably full of seasonal goodwill or the mellow after-effects of alcohol at the St Martin's ball. It isn't even enough to come every Sunday if it's just part of the traditional way. Not if it doesn't reach down further, into your hearts and minds, and change the way you live your lives. Change for change's sake is sterile. But fear, even fear of change, is worse; it is always destructive."

Jeremy's voice had hardened. He felt all the bitterness of the ten frustrating years he had spent in the benefice spilling over into his words.

"If we are never willing to change," he went on, trying to speak more calmly, "we shall wither and die. Change is the way of nature. We cannot stand still. If the church will not change, it will wither and die too."

He saw George Warrendon wince. Sitting there in the front pew with Lucinda, he seemed to shrink a little, hiding his eyes with his hand. Lucinda showed no emotion of any kind. With sudden compunction for the effect his words were having on George—and perhaps on others—Jeremy continued the sermon more kindly, speaking of St Martin's miracles, changing people's lives for the better.

As Jeremy descended the steps from the pulpit amid a somewhat embarrassed, even hostile silence, he wondered ruefully how much of the sermon he had delivered was directed at himself.

Seven

The three ringers made their way through the door from the back of the church into the tower to find Geoff, Ken and a slightly wheezing Ben already waiting for them.

"Well!" said Simon to Rose as he held the door open for her. "I didn't know the rector had it in him." His voice expressed a slightly grudging admiration which would have surprised Rose if she had had the leisure to consider it. However, nerves were filling her stomach with their butterflies, and her mind was occupied with the fear of what lay ahead, so she let the comment pass.

"You ready, Rose?" Geoff asked her with a slightly forced heartiness. "Ben here isn't too good, so we'll want to get the quarter peal first time." No room for mistakes, was the implication.

"Oh, Ben, what's wrong?" asked Rose, concern for Ben's health instantly banishing her anxieties about the ringing in prospect. She looked at him with more attention, and saw that he looked more stooped than usual, and his face was grey and old.

"Nothing much," was the gruff reply, but she heard the breath wheeze noisily in his chest. "Me re-humatism's not so good today, and I been coughing a bit. Nothing to fuss about."

Rose said no more, but she put her hand on the hunched shoulder for a moment. It would be no use to suggest that they call off the quarter-peal to save Ben the effort and pain of pulling the heavy tenor bell for those thirty-five or forty minutes. Whatever the views of the other ringers, Ben would refuse to allow them to break the St Martin's tradition for his sake.

Her thoughts went back to the sermon Jeremy had given half an hour before, and she was reminded of the power of tradition, especially among country people. The desire to keep a tradition alive had been enough to bring Ben out tonight. Her eyes met Simon's as she moved across the tower to take the treble rope, and he smiled. The warmth in the smile steadied her nerves a little, and she untied the rope more calmly. Simon, she noticed, had taken the rope of the bell next to her, although normally he would have rung one of the heavier bells.

"You just keep that treble hunting up and down," said Geoff, "and we'll do the rest. Simon'll keep an eye out for you."

So, Simon's unusual choice of bell had been prearranged with the ringing captain.

Her mouth felt dry, and she swallowed. "I'll do my best," she promised.

"You'll be fine," Geoff promised her. "We'll have you ringing Surprise Minor in no time at all."

Rose smiled weakly. She knew perfectly well that she would never be able to ring any of the "surprise" methods which only really advanced campanologists could attempt. It was nonsense, but it was meant to cheer her and give her confidence. *Geoff's a dear,* she thought, as she took hold of the woollen sallie.

The quarter-peal could easily have been a disaster. Three times Rose's concentration faltered, and she forgot her place in the pattern of changes. Each time, even before her failure had come to Geoff's attention, Simon's voice spoke quietly beside her, correcting her. After the second incident, she had more confidence, and the third mistake did not trouble her. She found herself turning slightly towards Simon as soon as she was aware that she was in error, sure that the word of assistance would come. Afterwards, she was horrified by the thought of her dependence on him—not only technical but emotional—but at the time it was undoubtedly a source of comfort.

The call of, "That's all. Stand!" which brought the quarter-peal to an end, fell like music upon Rose's ear, and she set the bell to rest on its wooden stay, feeling only relief at having scraped through the ordeal without disgracing her colleagues. The elation of success was far from her thoughts, but her fellow ringers crowded round her, shaking her by the hand and praising her. Simon held back from this, but his smile offered her his congratulations.

"That's a real achievement, Rose. Your first quarter-peal." Geoff pumped her hand energetically, almost crushing it in his strong grasp. "I'll write it up and send the details to the *Ringing World*."

She shook her head inarticulately.

"Don't embarrass her too much, Geoff," advised Lesley, laughing. "Let's ring them down and get home, shall we?"

Geoff picked up the treble bell rope. "Thanks, Rose. And well done. Can you stay for a drink, or must you go?"

"I'd better go, I think. As for the quarter-peal, Simon must take most of the credit. He kept putting me right." She allowed herself to smile at him quickly, across the ringing chamber.

Simon had said nothing to her in words, and was leaning nonchalantly against the wall opposite, but his smile was saying far too much. *Someone will notice something soon if Simon isn't more careful*, thought Rose, and then smothered the thought, aghast at the implication that there was anything for anyone to notice.

As if he knew what she was thinking, Simon picked up the tenor rope, ready to ring down, and spoke casually to Ken beside him. That heart-wrenching smile might never have touched his face. Torn between gratitude and exasperation at his thought-reading, Rose put on her coat. After the strain of the quarter-peal, her knees felt almost too weak to carry her home. Her part in the patronal festival was over. All she had to do now was to go home… and begin to consider her future.

Until this moment she had looked no further than this evening, and the effort she must make not to let the others down. Clive had not yet returned, and she did not expect him until late, if he came at all. What she would say or do when he did return, she had not the least idea. She had put it from her, procrastinating, but she knew she could not continue to do that forever.

~ * ~

Simon had watched Rose leave the tower with thoroughly mixed feelings. Of these, tenderness was uppermost, for he could see that, with the ordeal of the quarter-peal behind her, she was trying painfully to face up to the difficulties that beset her, and he was disconcerted by a sudden and powerful urge to take up her cause and solve all her problems for her. It dismayed him that he could feel so deeply drawn to a woman who possessed neither conventional beauty nor sparkling social skills; a woman older than himself, who moreover had been married to another man for more than twenty years. He knew that the powerful attraction between them was real, and he didn't want to deny it even if he could, but he was still utterly unable to understand what was happening. His long-impregnable citadel had been breached, and powerful emotions were flooding through the gap. But that it should be *Rose* who attracted him so strongly, who was drawing him into a deeper relationship than any he had known in the past, almost defied belief. And why now? He had known her for two years as a fellow ringer, liking her, but feeling for her little more than sympathy towards a woman living gallantly in a situation which clearly brought her little joy. He had not thought his friendship would be of benefit to her, nor even welcome. He had pitied her sincerely, but she had not appealed to him sexually, and in any event her longstanding and apparently stable marriage seemed to put her out of his reach.

Then he had gone to the St Martin's dance, and the dance had been a revelation. Her new dress and hairstyle, and the unexpectedly trim figure they set off, had made him look at her differently, and Clive's absence and her brave defiance in the face of obvious unhappiness and rejection had set up an emotional situation he had neither expected nor sought. As he watched her respond to his admiration, in her unexpected charm and liveliness blooming suddenly into life like the doll under the spell of the Nutcracker, he had seen depths in her that had been hidden before. And as he danced with her, her body close to his, so responsive to him as a partner that they moved as one, that tiny spark of attraction had leaped into flame. He had intended at the start of the dance only to give her his platonic escort and with it the appreciative chivalry her sadness had called forth, but the outcome had not turned out as he had planned. Thinking only of Rose's needs, his own had taken him by surprise.

"Pity Rose had to go," observed Geoff, as they closed the tower door behind them and walked along the path. "I'd have liked to celebrate her first quarter with a drink."

Simon did not reply. Was there a hint of curiosity in Geoff's remarks?

"Nice lady," Geoff went on.

"Yes," said Simon unencouragingly.

Geoff gave it up. "Hope the AGM goes well on Wednesday," he said. "I've made sure everyone knows it's at your place."

Simon nodded. "Thanks."

They paused for a moment outside the church lychgate. Ahead of them the other ringers were strolling down towards the pub in the village.

"Coming for a drink?" asked Geoff. "They're on me tonight."

Simon hesitated. "No, thanks," he said after a moment. "I think I'll be getting back."

"Okay. I'll see you next Sunday, then."

Simon stood watching Geoff's wide solid-looking backview move on down the road; but he made no immediate move towards the car park.

After a while, he turned and began to walk down Church Lane. He stopped at the white gate of Sundials and stood there irresolutely for a moment. The porch lamp was on, but there were no lights in the front rooms of the house. He was just about to open the gate when he heard the sound of a powerful engine coming towards him. He looked round to see the big BMW sweep in at the drive. Clive was home.

Simon's hand dropped from the latch. He turned and walked quickly back to the church and beyond it to the car park. His car moved swiftly past Sundials and on towards Two Marks and home.

~ * ~

Clive's weekend with Olivia had not been an unqualified success. For some reason, the fact that Rose knew where he was, and with whom, seemed to cast a cloud over proceedings. To steal a weekend with another woman while pretending to be on business was an enjoyable adventure, and he had done it quite often. To steal a weekend with a woman who had been both his mistress and his PA for years, leaving behind a wife in whom distress had wrought unprecedented anger, was a different kind of jaunt altogether, especially when he had been more or less forced into the assignation.

Olivia had not been her usual cheerful self, either. She had obviously perceived a potential threat to their relationship from his commitment to his family, though no threat had, in fact, existed. He found it incredible that she should suddenly have waxed jealous, for he had never intended to leave his family for her, nor given her any reason to think he would do. Her unexpected and most welcome possessiveness inevitably caused him to feel very uncomfortable and led to an atmosphere of distrust between them.

Moreover, for the first time, in the face of this jealous possessiveness, some grudging appreciation of Rose had crept unsought into his mind. He almost wished he had stood out against Olivia's cajolery and gone to the St Martin's dance as he had promised. Rose had bought a new dress especially for the evening, and, unless he was much mistaken, especially for *him*. It seemed, on the face of it, unlikely that after twenty-three years of staid housewifery she might be on the verge of spreading some less dowdy wings; but one could never be sure with women, even a woman like Rose.

It was therefore in an unaccustomed mood of interest in his wife that he drove home from the airport. Would she be waiting for him expectantly, dressed stylishly and with a babysitter organised so that they could go out to dinner? Or would she be still nursing her anger and prepared to stand up to him and fight for her rights as a wife? Either, he thought, would be more interesting than the dowdy, spiritless household drudge she normally served up to him. He had married her hoping to mould an 18-year-old waif to his liking, he reflected. He had not meant to crush her. And for the first time, he wondered whether he himself might be partly responsible for the way she had turned out.

As he drove into the village, however, all thought of Rose vanished suddenly and completely as he came close to running down his *bête noir* Brian Warrendon, almost invisible as he walked in black coat and trousers along a dark part of the road just below the Copse Lane turn. Worse, avoiding the pedestrian at the last moment almost caused Clive to wreck the BMW against the old brick and flint wall which leaned outwards into the road on the sharp corner. Cursing under his breath, he wrenched the car away from the dangerous flint projections and pulled up less than a yard from the farmer.

He rolled the window down angrily. "Why can't you use a torch, damn you?" he demanded, relief as well as annoyance making his tone sharp. "Do you *want* to cause an accident?"

"Don't like torches," was the response. "*I* can see perfectly well without them. All the same, you townies, come here complaining about everything—you've no notion about country life."

"Don't start that again," said Clive abruptly. "I've no time for your kind of countryman, making stacks of money out of selling your land for 'development' as you call it, and putting nothing back into the community."

"A bit of progress is what I'm going to put into this community," Brian replied darkly. "Just you wait and see."

He turned his back pointedly and walked away in the direction of his farm. Clive reversed away from the wall, and drove carefully past him in the dark, relieving his feelings with a blast on his horn as he did so. Brian raised his hand in an ungracious, but unmistakable gesture of two-fingered defiance as he passed.

The contretemps did nothing to improve Clive's temper, and as he drove the last half-mile of his journey, his mood deteriorated into a kind of angry self-pity. Olivia's fall from grace had been infuriating; for he had come to rely on her as a stimulating companion as well as PA, good to look at and exciting in bed, yet making no attempt to bind him with the shackles of affection or emotional passion. Her descent into jealousy this weekend, and thus to the level of more ordinary women, had annoyed and disappointed him, although he was still prepared to hope that his wife might achieve a corresponding rise in his estimation. But the problem of Brian Warrendon, he knew, would remain so long as both he and the Althorpes lived in the village.

Clive, whose childhood had been spent in London's suburbia, had initially been eager to enter fully into village life. When he and Rose had bought Sundials some fifteen years earlier, he had immersed himself in its traditional customs with enthusiasm. The isolation of the village, perched on its hilltop two miles from a major road, the narrow, winding lanes into it, and the picturesque cottages round the village green beside the church, had all come to mean a great deal to him. St Martin-on-the-Hill had become his own place, comfortably unchanging in its physical fabric and its social structure, offering a security which met a deep need. Brian

Warrendon, by contrast, born and bred to village life, treated it with contempt and looked only for the opportunity to exploit what he owned for gain.

The discovery that the farmer intended to sell land to developers wherever the local planners would give permission for building had come as a rude shock to Clive. Brian's first successful application for an estate of new houses, ten years ago, represented a rape of the village for which Clive never forgave him. He was not alone in his anger, for many of the longstanding villagers bitterly opposed the scheme and created enough protest to ensure a public enquiry. Clive himself donated large sums to the fund which paid for lawyers and expert witnesses for the village, and he took their eventual defeat personally. The arrival of the new houses, though they were few in number by town standards, seemed to damage irreparably those aspects of village society which had given it its continuity with the past. An essential part of his happiness in the community had been lost, and for this too he blamed Brian Warrendon. He spent less time at home and less effort and money in supporting village activities, but this did not alter his sense of loss.

~ * ~

Rose heard the BMW pull into the drive with a rising panic which clutched at her throat. She had not expected Clive to return until tomorrow, for their parting had hardly been of a kind to inspire in him a longing for reunion. She had counted on another day in which to sort out her chaotic emotions and come to some decision on the future.

Clive's expression as he opened the front door did not encourage her to believe that he was looking forward to their meeting any more than she was. He looked grim and angry, and characteristically she assumed that she was the reason for his black mood. She turned and went back into the kitchen without a word and heard him take his suitcase upstairs and into their bedroom.

He emerged a little later and shared a meal with her. He did not mention the rancour with which they had parted, nor attempt to reassure her about Olivia. Instead, he told her about Brian and his near-miss by Copse Lane.

"That man is a walking disaster area," he said, and Rose realised that his earlier anger had been directed at Brian, not at her. "You'd think he could carry a torch. Honestly, Rose, I very nearly hit him. I almost wish I had," he added bitterly, "The village would be a better place without him."

Rose said nothing. It seemed to her completely wrong to wish someone out of existence, however much they provoked you. Since Clive's anger would very soon turn on her if she voiced this thought, however, she remained silent. She knew she should instead raise the issues that remained unresolved between them, and which hung like a heavy cloud over their relationship… or what remained of it after the events of the weekend. Their mutual silence continued for the next week, and if sometimes Rose thought her husband seemed to be taking a little more interest in her than usual, she put it down to her imagination.

On Wednesday, he left early for his London office and warned Rose that he would be home late.

"I have a Tower meeting at seven-thirty," she reminded him. "Shall I ask Maddie to come round?"

"I'd forgotten you were going out," he said with some irritation. "Yes, you'd better get Maddie. I should be back by then, but if I'm delayed I don't want to have to arrange something at the last minute. I suppose you *have* to go to this meeting? Have you got a lift over there? Is it at Geoff's?"

Rose replied, as casually as she could, "No, it's at Simon's this time. Geoff's away on business, so we'll be a bit short of numbers anyway. Lesley said she'd pick me up."

"Fine. Can't let Geoff down." said Clive, his mind already moving away from home concerns. "I'll see you later."

After he had gone, Rose made a note to herself on the telephone pad to ask her neighbour whether she would be able to babysit for an hour or so. Maddie was usually very helpful. She was a youngish divorcee with no children of her own and rather a boring job at a further education college, and she adored Robert.

Normally her adoration was reciprocated. But on this occasion Robert's reaction to being told that his favourite babysitter was coming to keep him company that evening was rather less enthusiastic than usual. He hung around Rose rather plaintively and seemed restless and nervous. It occurred to her that he might be incubating some illness. However, when she offered to cry off from the meeting and stay at home with him he refused at once and became incommunicative.

At half-past five, Lesley telephoned. "Rose, I'm terribly sorry, but I'm going to be held up tonight. I'm in an emergency publishing meeting on an important project that's run into difficulties, and I can't guarantee it'll be finished in time for me to pick you up. I don't want to keep you waiting. Can you get Clive to run you up to Two Marks? I'll be along later, and I'll give you a lift home."

"Clive may be late home, too," said Rose. "But I'll manage somehow. I'll tell the others you're coming later, shall I?"

"Thanks, Rose. You're sure you'll be all right? Give Simon a ring if there's any problem. He'll come over and get you and Ben, I'm sure."

Rose put the receiver down and stood for a moment rubbing one hand against the other nervously. She could not for the moment think of any other solution to the problem than the one that Lesley had suggested, and she wanted very much to go to the meeting. Apart from the fact that if both she and Lesley cried off, the meeting would hardly be quorate, she wanted to see Simon in his own home. She knew so little about him, because generally he revealed so little. Visiting his house, even for a Tower meeting, would let her come a few steps closer.

Reasoning thus, for the first time, she admitted to herself how important it had become to her to know Simon better, and with that self-revelation a whole host of others presented themselves for her attention. For years, she had pretended to herself that this travesty of a marriage was worth the hurt and humiliation she had suffered for it. Now, suddenly, she saw that she owed Clive neither loyalty nor forbearance, because he had shown her none. And Simon, she had to admit, blushing to herself, was at once the most exciting and the most enigmatic man she had ever met.

Restlessly, she moved towards the window and stood looking out at the garden and beyond it at the valley stretching away to the wood and the river below. The clarity of her thoughts frightened her; the issues could no longer be blurred or put to one side. She must face them, and their implications for her… and for Robert.

Eight

Simon was pouring scotch into a glass when the telephone rang. On the floor beside his armchair stood a half-empty mug of coffee, a plate containing the crumbs of a sandwich, and a pile of exercise books.

He picked up the receiver, tucked it between his shoulder and his ear, and picked up the bottle of scotch again. "Simon Hellyer."

"Hallo." There was a moment's hesitation.

His heart gave a sudden lurch, and then began to beat faster. "Rose?"

"Yes." Her voice sounded strained.

"Is something wrong?"

"No…not really. But Lesley rang to say she'll be late tonight. Clive's out, and I don't think I can get another lift. Lesley was to have brought Ben, too."

"I can come up and get you," he said at once. "I think only Ken is likely to come, apart from you and Ben. Janice doesn't usually make it. I can leave a note on the door…tell Ken to wait, if he gets here first."

"Yes," she said. "Thank you."

The words sounded uncertain, but whether from embarrassment or some other cause, he could not tell.

"What time shall I pick you up? Seven-fifteen all right? That will give us time to come back via Ben."

"All right," she said. "I'll be ready then."

He began to say something to reassure her, but the telephone went dead. Slowly he put the receiver down and looked around the room. He picked up his glass and put it on the draining board then quickly but methodically he began to tidy up.

~ * ~

Maddie arrived to babysit at five past seven, brown hair bobbing, blue eyes sparkling, a bright loquacious woman full of good intentions and entirely without discretion. Rose settled her in front of the television with Robert and went out, shutting the front door behind her, a good five minutes before Simon was due. She much preferred to wait at the gate in the November chill than to be forced to introduce—and explain—Simon to Maddie.

The little red sports car slid to a halt beside her punctually enough to make her glad of the subterfuge. Simon leaned across and opened the passenger door for her, keeping the engine running.

"Well done," he said. "I thought I'd have to come in for you, and we're a bit tight for time." He grinned at her as she pulled the seat belt around her. "I had to tidy up at home, and it took longer than I expected," he explained.

She smiled, and at once felt more relaxed. "I came out a bit early so as not to have to explain you to the babysitter," she admitted in return.

"Clive away on business again?"

Simon's eyes were on the road, but there was something a little too casual about the question. Rose looked at him quickly.

"No, just in London as usual. He'll be home later. My neighbour is always very good about babysitting at short notice. She's very kind..." *Don't explain so much. It's boring.*

Simon swung the car round the corner past the church, and pulled in as close as he could to the front gate of Ben's cottage.

"I'll go in and get him," offered Rose. "He's rather slow these days, Simon. He may need some help."

"I'll turn round while you're gone."

Rose knocked at the cottage door. It was opened by Ben's wife, a little woman with thin grey hair straggling out of an old-fashioned bun. "Come in, Mrs Althorpe," she said, her soft and melodious voice giving a hint of her Cornish origins. "I'm afraid Ben won't be coming tonight. It's his chest."

"Oh, I'm so sorry to hear that. I thought it sounded bad on Sunday night."

"Well, he didn't want to let you all down Sunday, see. But his chest wasn't all it might be then, and I've had the doctor to him twice since. It's these cold damp evenings that does it. Doctor said as he'd better stay indoors after dark in the winter, at least till his chest picks up a bit."

"Yes, I'm sure that's sensible," said Rose, her mind in turmoil. No Ben, and Lesley coming late... Should she cry off herself and go home?

"I hope you have a good meeting, anyway," said Mrs Cartwright comfortably. "Ben didn't know as there was anything special to be discussed?"

"No, I'm not sure either. Simon's 'in the chair' tonight, so I expect Geoff has given him an agenda."

Mrs Cartwright nodded. "Well, I won't keep you now, for you've to get to your meeting. But do come and have a chat with Ben one day, Mrs Althorpe. He's getting right teasy, having to stay indoors so much."

"Yes, I will. I'll come soon." Rose smiled again, rather blindly, and made her escape.

"No Ben?" asked Simon, as he opened the door for her. "His chest, I suppose."

"Yes, that's it. Simon...do you think we should call the meeting off? I mean, we're down to so few. Is it worth having a meeting at all?"

"I'm not calling anything off," said Simon firmly, accelerating past the church, and past Sundials. "Lesley is expecting a meeting, even if she's late. And I don't think Ken will thank me for allowing him to come over from Southover on foot only to send him home again. Besides, I promised Geoff I would host the meeting, and host it I shall."

Rose wondered whether any of the reasons he gave were truthful ones. On the other hand, they were unarguable. She settled back in her seat fatalistically; whatever the evening brought, she would accept.

~ * ~

Clive came home that evening in a very bad temper. Olivia was continuing to sulk and clearly believed that the time had come for him to leave Rose and start what she optimistically called "a new life" with her. All these years she had sold him the story that she didn't care about security, was happy with their relationship as it was, had no desire to settle down, and now suddenly she had changed her tune with a vengeance. He had always thought her the archetypical ambitious career woman, merely enjoying an affair with her boss as a sideline to the job itself, and the discovery that she could be ambitious in a different sense was a major disappointment. *Dishonest bitch, stringing me along like that.*

The thought of finishing with her for good passed through his mind, but he wasn't ready for that yet. She was a good PA, and he would miss her if she left. With hindsight, perhaps he had been unwise to get involved with her sexually... still, he wouldn't have missed even that, taking all in all. He had some very good memories of their times together, although he didn't feel sentimental about them. It had always been a hard-headed relationship on his part, part business, part physical pleasure, with no emotional involvement. Until last weekend, he had thought she felt the same. But there was no accounting for women.

Rose had disappointed him, too. Her anger over his defection from the dance had made him think she was going to put up a fight for his attention, now that she'd found out she had a rival. That had piqued his interest, and he had quite looked forward to developments at home, for once. But she hadn't followed it through. She had been distant with him and acted as though she didn't care. *Wrong move, Rose. A fight I could enjoy. Emotional blackmail and a wounded silence won't get you anywhere.*

He'd forgotten that Rose would be out this evening, until he found Maddie in the house when he got home. She heard his key in the lock and came out into the hall to greet him. She smiled and seemed very pleased that he had arrived. Maybe she wanted to get home early.

"Thanks, Maddie," he said. "You can leave things to me now. Robert in bed?" He looked at his watch. It was well before eight, and at that time, Robert was usually wandering about the house in his pyjamas, resisting the inevitable.

"Yes...he went up soon after Rose went out. I haven't checked on him yet, but I haven't heard him, so I think he must be asleep. Can I get you something to eat, Clive? Or a drink?" She hovered hopefully, brown eyes soft and appealing.

So she wanted to stay. She didn't usually try to socialise with him on the infrequent occasions when she looked after Robert while he and Rose went out together, and he had always thought of her as a mousy little person without much to say for herself, though Rose described her as chatty. But then, Rose wasn't much of a conversationalist at the best of times. Perhaps Maddie felt she had to talk to keep the silences at bay.

He mixed the drink himself but invited her to join him. There was a bottle of white wine in the fridge and he poured her a generous glass. He couldn't remember having talked to her on his own before, and it became rapidly obvious that she fancied him. Her eyes flirted with his, and she giggled under the influence of a second glass of wine. Animated and blushing, she became much prettier, too, and he found himself responding to her artless flattery and flirting with her in his turn. Probably on another occasion he would have soon tired of this and been glad to pack her off home as soon as possible. Tonight, chafing as he was at the shortcomings of both his wife and his mistress, her admiration was a balm.

He looked at his watch and found it was half-past eight. Suddenly, quite coldly and calculatedly, he realised that he wanted to take her to bed. He had felt stressed and over-tired when he came home and frustrated by the unresolved complications of his personal life. A tight band round his forehead had threatened a headache. But already he felt better. Maddie had made him laugh, and the come-on in her eyes was unmistakable. Rose would be out until ten, in all probability, so there was plenty of time.

As she handed him her glass for another refill, he deliberately let their hands touch, and then put the glass down and kissed her, experimentally, but firmly.

Her mouth opened under his. Then she pulled back. "Clive!" The tone was a nice blend of amazement and a kind of guilty excitement. *Fish is hooked*, he thought with a little thrill of exultation. He kissed her again.

"Mm..." she murmured appreciatively, and her arms went round him, hands pressing against his back to bring him closer.

Not much resistance here, he told himself with an inward smile, and put his hand on her breast. *Rose seemed to admire me when she was young, too. But she wouldn't sleep with me until she had a ring on her finger.* Maddie's breast was firm yet soft, and he felt a stir of excitement in his loins. Her type of naive, uncritical admiration was unfamiliar to him, and he was enjoying it. If she kept up that attitude in bed, he could relax and let the tensions evaporate.

He turned her away from him, taking her hand to lead her out of the sitting room. "Come on," he said. "We'll go round to your place."

"What about Robert?" she protested. "I'm supposed to be looking after him."

He had forgotten about Robert. But he didn't want to stop now, and for some reason he didn't feel comfortable taking Maddie to his and Rose's bed.

"Robert is *my* son," he said. "And I'll take responsibility for him. He's safe in bed. He'll be fine for an hour or two until Rose gets back. She said she wouldn't be late. You don't want her walking in on us, do you?"

"But she'll expect one of us to be here..."

"I'll tell her I just got in, and you needed a fuse mending, or something. Come on, Maddie. Do you want it, or not?"

Maddie looked up at him, and he could see her objections falter and fade. She might possibly confess to Rose at some point what they'd done, but who cared? It would teach Rose a lesson, anyway. He'd do what he pleased, and she could get on with it. Didn't he provide for her and Robert, and provide well, too?

He gave Maddie another hard kiss on the mouth, took her by the arm and drew her out of the house, pulling the front door shut behind him. They stumbled along the path and through the side gate to Maddie's front door.

Nine

The village of Two Marks was smaller than St Martin-on-the-Hill, with a population of less than three hundred. It was also considerably older. The earliest surviving cottage at St Martin dated from the seventeenth century, though many of the later ones were thatched in the old style and built of brick and flint. Two or three cottages at Two Marks were thought to have been built before 1500.

"It's a pity it's dark," said Rose, as Simon drove into the village. "I don't think I've been here before."

He glanced at her in surprise. "How long have you lived at St Martin, Rose? I thought you'd been there quite a while."

"I have. Fifteen years. But I don't drive, as you know, and the buses don't come this way. You said yourself we were parochial, didn't you? The nearest I've come to Two Marks would be the woods to the east of the village. I walk that way with Dolly sometimes."

"Well, here we are." He drew up in front of a long hedge. "No drive, I'm afraid. The house is up a bank, and there's no way of making a drive…or a garage, for that matter. But the road's wide enough here. Wait a minute, I'll come and help you out. You're a bit down in the ditch there, but I don't think it's muddy."

He had stopped neatly with the passenger door beside a stile in the hedge, so that there was room for Rose to alight. He came round and put out a hand to steady her as she pulled herself up. She looked up at him as she took his outstretched hand, but it was too dark to see his face.

The cottage was long and low, a single storey under a deep thatched roof. There were five small windows along the white-painted wall, all curtained and lit from within, and a door at the side. The porchway had been built on at a later date, and in a quite different style. Its roof was tiled, and the brick was unpainted. At one end, a small lamp lit the doorway.

Simon took down the untouched note he had left for Ken and unlocked the door. The heavy oak moved back noiselessly. Simon ushered her in ahead of him, and Rose took a step inside and stopped in wonder.

The room was low and beamed, stretching the whole length of the cottage. There were no windows in one long wall, which was lined with bookcases either side of a wide fireplace in which logs were burning steadily. Several armchairs were grouped around the fireplace. At the far end of the room there was a kitchen area, its tiled floor and modern worksurfaces making a striking contrast with the mellow timelessness of the rest of the cottage. Only the solid-fuel stove in the corner of the kitchenette maintained the atmosphere of antiquity.

"Oh, Simon, it's lovely!"

He closed the door, pleased at her exclamation. "I thought it was a real find when I first looked at it. Unusual, though. It wouldn't suit everyone. There's no proper upstairs, for one thing, and it's all one room downstairs. But I like it."

Rose looked around her. "But where do you sleep?" she asked naively.

"I'll show you." He went over to a deep curtained-off alcove opposite the kitchen units, which Rose had imagined must be a storage area.

"It's a bit claustrophobic in summer with the curtains closed," said Simon, drawing the curtains back to show a bed built at waist height into a deep alcove in the wall, with drawers beneath it. "But unusual, as I say."

He closed the curtains again. "Sit down by the fire and get warm, Rose. Will you have some coffee while we're waiting for the others?"

"Thank you." She chose an armchair facing away from the kitchen and gazed up at the bookshelves. There were a few of her favourite authors...Dickens, Austen and Trollope among them, but Simon seemed to favour twentieth-century novels above their earlier counterparts. One set of shelves was filled with poetry from top to bottom: Tennyson, Wordsworth and Keats she recognised. Many other names she did not.

"You read a lot of poems," she said to him as he set a mug of coffee beside her.

"Yes. It's part of my job, for one thing, teaching English. But I love it, anyway." He reached down one of the volumes and thumbed through it. "Do you like poetry?"

Rose coloured a little. "I don't really know much, I'm afraid. I prefer novels. And I don't always feel I understand poetry. I'm not very clever, Simon."

"I don't think cleverness has much to do with it," he said. "Loving poetry isn't only a matter of knowing what the words mean. It's understanding the ideas and feelings the poet is expressing. You should be good at that, Rose."

She coloured rather more deeply. "You don't know me well enough to say that. I'm not... I'm nothing special, Simon, truly."

"Listen to this one," he said, ignoring this disclaimer. "This is something by John Donne, written in the early seventeenth century. It's a meditation, really. More like a sermon than a poem with a metre, but it's very poetic in the way it's expressed. You've probably heard it before, but it's one of my favourites." He smoothed the page and began to read:

"No man is an island, entire of itself, every man is a piece of the continent, a part of the main..."

Rose listened. She listened because the words were beautiful, because the thoughts of John Donne seemed to leap from the words straight into her mind, and she could understand them, and she listened because of the way Simon read them, his warm voice gentle, yet forceful, the vowels and consonants given their perfect weight and beauty.

At last there was silence. Rose lifted her eyes to his and met them steadily as she had never felt able to before.

Simon too was under the spell of John Donne's words. So often he felt as though he *were* an island and not part of the main at all, as though what he thought and did affected no one but himself. He had felt like that ever since he was a child. No one had come close enough to him since then to become attached, to make his island into a peninsula linked to the continent.

"'Never send to know for whom the bell tolls,'" Rose repeated slowly. "'It tolls for thee.' I feel like that when they ring the bell for funerals, Simon. I'm washing up or something and I'll hear the tenor tolling very slowly, the way Ben likes to do it. I always think it's a loss to all of us when someone in the village dies."

"My father read that to me when my mother died," said Simon. "I was ten. I've never forgotten." Even now, the memory had not lost its pain. *Why did I choose to read her that meditation?*

"Oh, how awful for you!" Half-rising, Rose put out her hand to him in sympathy. "How lonely you must have felt."

He took the hand and rubbed it against his cheek. "I did. Sometimes I still do. I need someone to share…the things that matter. But there isn't anyone…"

"Yes," she said. "I know."

Her eyes seem to burn with empathy, and something more. He was acutely aware of the enduring strength under her surface diffidence, and his heart yearned for her suddenly.

"Read some more, Simon," she urged him, her eyes bright and appealing. This was the Rose of the dance again, still young, ardent, holding nothing back.

"More Donne?"

"More anything." She sat down again, chin resting on her hand, her eyes intent.

He reached down some Tennyson from the shelf and read her *The Lady of Shalott*. When he finished, her eyes were full of tears.

"It's so sad, Simon. She loved him, and he couldn't love her in return. And Guinevere wasn't worth it, either. Lancelot was far too good for her."

He laughed, then said seriously, "You may be right. But love isn't like that, is it?"

There was a pause, then she met his eyes. "I don't know much about love, Simon… not that kind of love, anyway. I know now that I don't love Clive. You wanted to know how things stood, remember? I've thought about it, and I know I don't love him. Perhaps I haven't loved him for years. I'm not sure."

He hesitated. "Do you want to tell me about it?"

"No. Yes. N-not now. Ken or Lesley must be coming any time."

Simon looked at his watch. "I think Ken would have arrived by now, don't you? Lesley may not come at all. Tell me."

So she told him. She told him about the contempt Clive had always showed for her, how he had dominated her and bullied her even when they were first married. She told him about the way he had taught Sarah to despise her and how, in the end, even Rose herself had become convinced of her own worthlessness. She told him about Olivia Landry and about Clive's new plans for Robert's education. No longer was he the unapproachable Simon Hellyer whom she had not felt able to consult about Robert all those weeks ago. He was now her friend, to whom it was natural to turn, to confide. And something more than a friend, too. But she didn't want to think about the implications of that just now.

They sat in silence for a little when she had finished. The tears were trickling slowly down Rose's face in spite of her efforts to check them. Simon sat quietly in his chair, his face unreadable.

The telephone's clamour intruded on the silence, and Simon answered it. His half of the conversation consisted mostly of monosyllables to which Rose hardly listened at all. "Hallo? ...Yes...Don't worry...It's fine...I hope so... 'Bye."

He put the receiver back in its cradle slowly. "That was Lesley. She's still in a meeting… they've just taken a break for coffee. She won't be coming. It's just us this evening, Rose."

The last sentence hung in the air, full of a deeper significance.

"I'd better go," Rose said, reaching for her handbag. "Will you give me a lift?"

"Yes, of course I will," he said soothingly. "But stay for a while, won't you? You can't go home looking like that. It's only eight-thirty, anyway. No one's going to expect you just yet." He took out a neatly folded handkerchief. "Come here and let me mop you up."

She allowed him to dry her eyes. The feel of his shirt against her cheek as he put his arms round her brought her comfort, but also a fresh awareness of his body and its hard, muscular strength.

"Why don't you leave him?" he asked her after a while, his arms still holding her close to him, his face against her hair. She felt his heart quicken as he said it.

"But Simon, where would I go? How would I earn a living? I haven't any private income, and I'm not qualified for anything. And there's Robert to think of. I couldn't leave *him,* and Sundials is his home."

There was a moment's pause while Simon assimilated the astonishing fact that her objections were practical ones. She had offered no moral arguments. She had not refused to consider his suggestion. Leaving Clive, it seemed, was not out of the question. He lifted his head from her hair and kissed her. "You know where you can come. You *and* Robert."

She smiled at him through the tears that had welled up again. "Be sensible, Simon. Where would you put us? You said yourself you had no rooms upstairs." Even as she made this reply, the thought occurred to her that this way Robert would not have to be sent to boarding school.

"Robert would love the attic," he said at last. "It has floorboards, and it could easily be made into a real room...there's a space for a window in the eaves above the front door. As for you..." He kissed her again, one hand stroking her hair, feeling the warmth of her body against his. "There's no difficulty about that. Rose... *I want you.*"

The last words carried an emotional charge like a lightning flash, whose electricity seemed to set them both on fire. For Rose, objections of any kind, moral or practical, to the ending of her marriage were swept away by an overwhelming wave of passion. She was conscious only of the beat of Simon's heart, and the caress of his lips and hands. At that moment, nothing else in her life mattered. A new self-esteem, her lost miserable youth restored in joy, kisses such as she had never known before… Simon showered all these gifts upon her as he held her in his arms.

"No! No!" she cried out at last, as he began to unfasten her blouse, and his lips moved across her neck, seeking her breast. "Simon, stop. What are we doing?"

"Darling," he said, his deep voice shaken with laughter as well as passion. "If you don't know by now... Oh, Rose... *Rose...*" He half-led, half-carried her to the bed alcove and pushed the curtains aside.

It was at that moment, when past and future seemed divided inexorably by the sword of this present holocaust, that the telephone uttered its shrill summons once more.

At first Simon ignored it, in the belief that the caller would soon grow tired of waiting for an answer and leave them alone. The tide of desire was running strongly in him, and the prize was almost his. She was beautiful, this woman, with a beauty more than skin deep; more than fine features and soft hair, more than the smooth silk of her olive skin and the shape of her neck and shoulders. Hers was the beauty of spirit, the simplicity and sincerity of mind, that he had longed for but never found. She was at once both mother and lover, in a miraculous fusion which overwhelmed him.

The telephone went on ringing.

"Simon," she said, pushing his face away from her gently. "It might be important."

"Nothing is as important as this," he said huskily, bending his head around her restraining hand and kissing her wrist. "Let me love you, Rose. Don't stop me now."

The telephone continued to sing its harsh song. Under that sustained cacophony something vital died out of their love-making. With a groan, Simon moved away from Rose and picked up the receiver.

"Hallo. Can you ring back later, please? It's…"

He stopped, listening. "Okay. I'll tell her. We'll be over as soon as we can."

Rose sat up, pulling her clothes around her. "What is it, Simon? Something urgent."

He looked down at her, his passion fading in the face of this new crisis. "That was Clive. He wants you to go home. Robert has disappeared."

Ten

There was silence in the car as they drove back to St Martin-on-the-Hill. Rose's mind was filled with all the horror and anxiety of Robert's disappearance, and Simon's thoughts were simply too chaotic to share.

When they arrived, they found Clive waiting for them on the doorstep. He appeared to be completely distracted by what had happened. It had mobilised that having phoned Rose he had taken no further action to find Robert but had simply waited irresolutely for them to return.

"Clive, have you found him?" was Rose's immediate question.

He shook his head. "I don't know where to look."

"When did you find he had gone?"

"Just before I phoned you. I'd…I'd just got in, and I went up to see if he was asleep."

"Have you phoned the police?"

Clive looked at her in bemusement. Simon wondered suddenly whether he might be drunk, though he seemed quite steady on his feet.

"Surely nothing can have happened to him, Rose? He's not in the house, but he can't have gone far, surely?" Clive was clearly trying to persuade himself that there was nothing to be alarmed about. Having phoned Simon with such urgency and demanded Rose's return, he seemed to have completely lost his normal decisiveness.

It was then, to Simon's amazement and admiration, that Rose took the initiative. Within half an hour, she had mobilised Jeremy, Liz and George to search the village. Even Fran, the local headteacher, was consulted, just in case she could throw any light on Robert's movements or intentions. Maddie, who had apparently still been at Sundials when Clive found that Robert was missing, also insisted on joining them, her normal ebullience subdued. But Rose was too busy thinking about Robert's possible whereabouts to notice much about Maddie.

They divided the village into sections in order to search, and set off in three different directions, working in pairs. Clive was left at home to answer the telephone, a strange role for a senior manager with a reputation for business acumen and general competence, but one entirely appropriate for someone in his mental state that evening. Maddie offered, in front of them all, to stay with him, but he rejected the suggestion with apparent horror.

Simon made sure that he was paired off with Rose. He recognised that in this crisis, the search for Robert was of paramount importance, for no one, least of all a schoolteacher, could oppose any course of action necessary for the safety of a child. Yet, at the same time, he felt robbed by the turn events had taken. Rose had so nearly given herself to him, yet he did not feel sure that next time (if there was a next time) the outcome would be the same. The old doubts, submerged or in retreat that evening, might still return to sap her will, or new and more insidious doubts arise. He trusted her to be true—he had never met anyone more transparently honest and loyal. But with his relationship with her still unconsummated, to whom would she feel that fidelity was owed?

In spite of his inner emotional turmoil, Simon searched as diligently as Rose for her missing son. They had chosen the section of the village containing the Copse Lane estate, and they worked their way steadily up the cul-de-sac, knocking on doors and asking if Robert had been seen, checking in back gardens and looking in garages. Simon thought that it would have made their task easier if they had known whether Robert had run away, been kidnapped or simply taken an illicit night-time trip out of bed. But he did not share the thought with Rose. Although she was handling the situation so competently, her powerful maternity bringing out the hidden strength he had known she possessed, he could sense her underlying anxiety and panic. That new closeness which enabled him to be sensitive to her feelings was proving more painful than he had expected. Once or twice, between houses, he put his arm round her comfortingly, but she pulled away. For the moment, she was concentrating totally on Robert's safety. Their relationship meant nothing to her beside that. He swallowed that bitter reflection and rang the next doorbell resolutely.

Rose vaguely recognised the woman who came to the door, her feet in mules a size too big, and her hair streaked in tufts. "It's Tracy Turner, isn't it?" she said. "I'm Robert's mother."

The woman nodded. The tufts bounced up and down as she moved her head. "Darren's in bed a couple of hours ago," she said. "Told me he was tired. Isn't Robert at home, then?" She sounded faintly hostile.

"Robert went to bed about seven-thirty," said Rose calmly. "But my husband went to look at him an hour or so ago and found him missing. We don't know what's happened to him..." Her voice broke, and she swallowed. "We are searching the village," she went on more firmly, "before we call the police."

At this mention of the constabulary, the woman bristled even more. "I don't know nothing about where Robert is," she said. "They none of them care if you're worried, these days. I'm always asking Darren where he's off to, but you know what they are."

"Is Darren actually in his bed at the moment, Mrs Turner?" asked Simon, cutting across this plaint with scant patience.

The direct question caused Darren's mother to register his presence for the first time. "What's it to you?" she asked suspiciously.

"This is Simon Hellyer," explained Rose quickly. "He's a teacher at Northchurch College, and he's helping us to search for Robert."

"I wondered whether it was perhaps possible that the two boys might be out together," said Simon, cloaking his sudden certainty about this with an uncharacteristically diffident and retiring manner which caused Rose to look at him closely.

"Well..." Tracy Turner hesitated, looking behind her vainly in the hope of finding someone to advise her.

"Would you just check for us?" suggested Rose. "It won't take a moment, and it would eliminate one possibility. Please?" She smiled very sweetly at Tracy.

After another moment's hesitation, the woman seemed to make up her mind. "All my kids are in bed," she said, in self-righteous tones. "But I'll look," she added, rather spoiling the effect, and shut the door in their faces.

"Not the most charming woman I ever met," said Simon, wryly. "But at least she's doing what we asked."

"Yes. Thanks for the idea. It's a good one. Do you think Robert and Darren may have gone out on a spree, as it were?"

"I think it's a lot more likely than his going out on his own or being kidnapped from his bedroom while someone baby-sat downstairs, yes."

They waited. After about five minutes the door opened again, and Tracy waved them inside. "Better come in," she said. "The younger ones are in bed, but I can't find hide nor hair of Darren. Bloody lad. His father'll beat the living daylights out of him when he gets home. There's two boys we're looking for, not one."

They sat down in the Turners' living room while Darren's mother explained that she had heard Darren going to bed but had not looked in on him since. "I've been watching the telly in here," she said. "I s'pose he could have crept out the back door easy enough without me hearing him. I locked it up before I come in here, of course, but he could have unlocked it."

"That's easy enough to check," said Simon.

The kitchen was small and poky for the size of the rest of the house and made pokier by having a table in the middle of it. Clutter covered every available surface, including a half loaf of bread, a carton of milk and two stacks of dirty dishes. A large microwave oven dominated one corner, a portable TV another. The outside door was unfastened, with the key still in the lock. "This is the way he went," said Simon.

Rose had followed him. "So the two of them are out together."

"It seems possible, at least. I should think it must have been a stunt they'd agreed to pull. Did Robert seem normal this evening?"

Rose thought back to their supper time, and Maddie's arrival. It seemed aeons ago, a measure of the significance of events between.

"He did seem a bit nervy," she said at last. "I'm afraid I honestly didn't really notice, Simon. I was thinking..." she stopped and met his eyes. "I was thinking about going out myself."

Tracy Turner shuffled into the kitchen, the soles of her mules slapping on the vinyl floor. She looked past Simon at the key in the door. "I keep the key on that hook there when the door's locked. Darren knows that. He must have gone that way. Where have those bloody kids got to?" She sounded quite savage, as though Darren's return would inspire her with as much resentment as relief.

Simon unclipped his phone from his coat pocket. "I think we should check what success the others have had before we decide what to do next. Rose, do you want to ring Clive?" He keyed the number and handed her the phone.

~ * ~

Darren Turner parted from his companions at the bottom of the Copse Lane estate and trudged up the hill towards his own house. It was cold, and rain had started to fall. Behind him on the road he heard the squeal of wheels skidding on the damp surface. He hunched his shoulders inside his anorak and wondered whether the others would get home before they were soaked. Rob Althorpe had been stupid enough to come out in his pyjamas with only a sweater pulled over them. He had probably been so scared of being caught leaving the house that he had chickened out of opening the cupboard and getting out a coat. That would be just like Rob. He and Chris had teased him about it until he was almost in tears. *Silly cry-baby.* But at least they had let him take part in the adventure.

It was a pity they had failed to find the badger. Chris said he had seen it one evening with his dad, and Darren had persuaded him to show him where they'd gone. Still, it had been good fun going out on their own in the dark…at least, he and Chris had enjoyed it. He wasn't so sure about Rob. Rob seemed to feel guilty about going out without telling his mum and dad. All round, it would definitely have been more fun if Rob had not overheard them planning the expedition and begged to come along. They hadn't had any choice then. Rob would probably have told his mum, if they had refused to take him. And Chris seemed to think they should let him come. Perhaps they would be able to fix up to go looking for the badger without him next time.

There seemed to be rather a lot of lights on at his house. He walked quietly up the path to the kitchen door and gently opened it. No one was about. He tiptoed through the kitchen and into the hall, ready to make a quick run for the stairs.

Unfortunately, the hall was not as empty as he had expected. His mother, instead of sitting watching TV in the front room as usual, was standing at the foot of the stairs with Rob's mother and a dark-haired man whom he did not recognize. Rob's mother had a phone in her hand. As he stepped into the hall the man turned sharply and looked at him.

Darren quailed. Often truculent and unruly, he was a match for all but the headteacher at the local school. But there was a menace in the expression in this man's eyes that caused him to experience something very close to fear.

"Just what do you think you're doing?" asked a deep voice quietly. The very quietness of it seemed to pierce Darren's quaking mind.

"I'm...I'm coming in," he murmured lamely.

The man took a step towards him. "From where, may I ask?"

For a moment the whole story trembled on Darren's lips. The truth alone would serve, for he could tell that this man would know at once if he lied. Then, just in time, his mother awoke from the momentary shock caused her by his sudden reappearance and swooped on him.

"You rotten, sly, good-for-nothing," she stormed, shaking him thoroughly. "Where you bin? Up to no good, I'll be bound."

Her familiar physical punishment was an enormous relief to him. No longer did he have to face the interrogation of the man with the steely eyes. His voice rose in its normal whine.

"Mum! I haven't done nothing wrong. Honest, I haven't. I just slipped out to the garage for something. I remembered I hadn't put my bike away. You know how you always say I mustn't leave it outside..."

Tracy was easily satisfied by this explanation. "There!" she said. "And we was looking for you all over... you and Robert."

Darren's eyes opened wider. *They were looking for Rob, too. How did they know? What was going on?*

Rose spoke into the phone. "Clive, Darren has turned up, and he seems only to have been in the garage. So that's a false lead. We'd all better keep looking."

"You'd best get straight back to bed, Darren. Take those trainers off, they're muddy..." Her voice trailed away.

"Where did the mud come from, Darren?" asked Simon, with deceptive mildness.

"I left my bike on the lawn," said Darren. It was worth a try.

"You know, I'm afraid I don't believe you," replied his adversary, in a conversational tone.

"It's true, sir." Where did that 'sir' come from? He never called *anyone* sir.

"Don't you call my Darren a liar," bristled Tracy Turner suddenly.

Simon turned on her, his voice like a whiplash. "I'm trying to discover the whereabouts of a missing eight-year-old boy, Mrs Turner. This is a serious matter. If you think your son never lies, by all means go on thinking so. But personally, I don't believe it. I teach boys who are older and far more adept at lying than your son, and I know the signs very well, believe me. If Robert is missing much longer, it will be a police matter, and Darren will be answering their questions, not mine."

It was the turn of Darren's mother to quail. "Don't speak to me that way," she said, but it was a complaint, not defiance. "You ask Darren what you like, if it'll help find Robert." She looked at Darren. "Answer Mr Hellyer truthfully, like a good boy."

Darren looked back at her doubtfully. He hoped that Mr Hellyer's questions would not range too widely in scope. He had the feeling that his mother would not welcome wholly truthful answers as to the contents of their garage, for example; on the other hand, police involvement was certainly to be avoided.

"So where have you really been, Darren?" asked Simon.

Darren looked at him. "Just up the road," he said. "I went out to get my bike in, like I said," he went on, warming to his story. "And then I remembered I'd promised Chris I'd look for... for a snail."

"A *snail*?"

"Yes," the boy said. This bit was true, anyway, and no one could prove different. "Our teacher asked us to look out for interesting wildlife for a project we're doing at school. Wildlife what comes out at night. And snails come out at night, specially when it's damp..."

"I know when snails come out," said Simon impatiently. "Where did you go, Darren, is what I want to know. And did you see Robert?"

"You should have told me where you were going," said his mother shrilly, relieved to find that Darren could account for his evening expedition so innocently, but keen to deflect him from further revelations. "Don't I always tell you you're not to go out without letting me know?"

"Yes, Mum. Sorry, Mum," said Darren, head down to hide the suspicion of a smirk he could feel forming on his face. With any luck, he and his mother could see off their interlocutor without any recourse to official questioning.

~ * ~

While Simon was grilling Darren Turner, Jeremy and Liz Swanson were making a minute search of the churchyard. If any harm had come to Robert, there were plenty of places here where he might lie hidden. Liz's face was strained in the light of their torches, but Jeremy's looked merely thoughtful. Like Simon, he thought it probable that Robert had undertaken some night-time jaunt and would return in his own good time. Not very much was likely to happen to an eight-year-old boy in this village. Violent crime was almost unheard of here, and even burglary happened infrequently. The only concern he had was the possibility of accident. Falls and sprains were common occurrences on rough ground and an uneven road surface. There was barbed wire, too, in some of the fences, and at the edge of the woods a couple of miles along the road towards Winchester, but the village boys were used to barbed wire... all the farmers used it. In any case, would a young boy go all on his own as far as the woods in search of adventure on a November night?

His thoughts were disturbed by a shout from Liz, exploring the long grass in the older part of the churchyard.

"Remy! I've found him."

Robert was sitting, shivering, beside a large eighteenth-century gravestone upon which the inscription had been all but obliterated by time and weather. His head was hunched between his shoulders. His pyjamas and sweater were soaking, and his shoes scratched. His eyes were open, but they did not seem to see his rescuers.

Liz put her arm round him gently. "Does anything hurt, Robert? Or are you just cold? We'll soon have you home."

Robert said nothing. No sound or movement betrayed that he had heard her, or that he was even aware of her presence. He sat still and shivered.

Jeremy bent down and looked at him. "We'd better get him home as soon as we can," he said. He felt the boy carefully. "I don't think he's hurt, but in any case, he can't stay here and wait for medical attention. He'll contract pneumonia."

Very carefully, he picked Robert up, watching intently for any sign of wincing. Nothing appeared to hurt him, indeed he did not seem to register any change in his circumstances at all. He remained rigidly curled, and Jeremy had to carry him in that position, cradled in his arms. It was awkward, and he was glad the boy was a lightweight, and that it was only a few hundred yards to Sundials.

Liz ran ahead of him to the house and rang the doorbell energetically. "Clive! Clive! We've found him."

Clive came to the door as lethargically as before and peered doubtfully at Liz. The news seemed to take a moment to penetrate his consciousness. Then a relieved smile spread over his face. He looked past Liz to the gate, seeing Jeremy negotiate the opening and start up the path with his precious bundle of humanity.

"Thank God!" he said, and the exclamation sounded like a sincere expression of gratitude. He looked more closely at Jeremy's burden and asked anxiously, "What's wrong with him?"

"I don't know," said Jeremy, as Clive stood aside to let him into the house. "I don't think he's injured, Clive. But something is certainly wrong…seems more psychological than physical. Let's get him warm, and we'll see."

"Where are Rose and Simon?" asked Liz. "We must let them know. And George and Maddie, too."

"George had to go home," said Clive absently, his mind clearly on the curled-up form of his son. "Lucinda rang and asked for him. Simon and Rose phoned just now from somewhere. A house on the Copse Lane estate, I think." Even at this moment of crisis something in Clive's voice expressed distaste at the thought of Rose's presence in one of those shoddy houses on that detested estate. He hesitated. "Shall I get blankets, Remy?"

"Yes, do…and a hot drink."

"I'll get the drink," volunteered Liz. "Does Robert like cocoa?"

Clive looked at her vaguely. "I…I can't remember," he said.

"I expect he does," said Liz practically.

"Can you remember where Rose telephoned from?" asked Jeremy. Clive rubbed his forehead. "I'm not sure. I think she mentioned someone called Darren," he said uncertainly after a moment.

"Darren Turner, Remy," called Liz from the kitchen. "The number's six-o-two."

The boy Liz didn't want to be friends with Chris, Jeremy remembered. "Clive, come and hold Robert. He's still shivering, and I'm not sure whether it's nerves or cold. I'll phone the Turners and tell Rose he's found." he added.

Eleven

Darren, caught uncomfortably between Simon's determination to discover the truth and his own fear of implicating the family in some more or less heinous misdemeanour, had floundered from one lie and half-truth to another, and the smirk on his face had been stillborn. He managed to leave Chris Swanson out of it... he had the feeling that anything he said about Chris might get back to his parents, and they were very strict. Chris would probably be grounded for weeks if they knew he'd gone out without permission. To his surprise, Simon seemed impatient with him more on account of the time spent evading his questions than for the answers he finally gave.

"After a badger, were you? Why on earth didn't you say so earlier? Anyone would think you were burgling the school or vandalising the village hall. Wasting my time like this! *Did you see Robert while you were out?*"

Darren had opened his mouth to answer this question truthfully and without evasion when the telephone in the sitting-room rang. Simon looked up. "Answer it," he said to Tracy sharply.

She glared at him but picked up the receiver. After a moment, she handed it to Rose. "It's the rector," she said briefly.

Trembling, Rose took the receiver and listened to Jeremy's account of events. Then she put out a hand to Simon. "They've found him, Simon. They've found him!" Abruptly she burst into tears.

Simon left Darren and put his arm round her. He took the receiver and said into it, "Thanks, Rector. We'll be back directly." Without another word, he steered Rose out of the front door and down the path, leaving an outraged Tracy Turner on the doorstep behind him.

His arm remained around her, pressing her to his side, as they walked up the street, taking the short cut through the footpath on to Church Lane. "It's over, darling. Don't cry. He's safe."

He walked with her slowly, subduing the thought—unworthy but persistent—that when they arrived at Sundials he must pretend again that they were mere acquaintances, fellow-bellringers with no link other than their shared hobby. This journey in the dark when he could walk with his arm round her, without any prying eyes watching them, seemed suddenly very precious. His determination to move their relationship forward, however, did not falter; another opportunity must be made. Rose must leave Clive as soon as she could; nothing must stand in their way. For he knew in his heart that as yet their relationship was like a frail newborn, vulnerable to the cold winds of chance and needing tender care. Tightening his hold on her as they reached the gate of Sundials, he vowed to himself that nothing should destroy what they had begun.

They found Robert in his bedroom, being examined by the local doctor, a grey-haired, stocky, laconic Scotsman who lived in Southover and had practised in the district for nearly thirty years. He disdained the out-of-hours service run jointly by other practices and preferred to visit his own patients himself, whatever the time.

Liz stood beside him a little anxiously. Robert lay in the foetal position, still shivering in spite of the blankets piled over him, and the hot water bottle Liz had tucked into the bed. His hot chocolate stood untouched on the bedside table. Simon, staying carefully in the background behind Rose as they went up the stairs, noticed that Clive was nowhere to be seen.

"Robert!" breathed Rose, horrified by her first sight of him. "Jim, what's wrong with him?"

The doctor cast a glance over his shoulder at her. "Can't tell yet," he said shortly. "Come in quietly if you're coming, and don't talk to him. I'll have finished examining him in a minute."

Rose moved closer to the bed. At that moment, all her emotions seemed concentrated, via a long-severed but vividly felt umbilical cord, on the rigid, contorted figure on the bed. She was completely unconscious of Simon hovering in the doorway.

The doctor put away his instruments and arose, frowning. "Some kind of psychological trauma," he announced. "Can't tell much till we talk to him. Doesn't seem to be anything physically wrong with him, anyway." He moved back a little from the bed. "Come on, Rose, see what you can get out of him."

She went down on her knees beside Robert and put her arms round him. Perhaps for a moment, it seemed to the watchers, the boy's muscles relaxed a little. Then he rolled away from her and lay on his side with his knees drawn up and his arms hugged protectively round himself.

She put out a tentative hand and touched his shoulder. "Robert! You're quite safe now, darling. You're at home with Mummy... and everything's going to be all right."

There was silence. He neither moved nor made any sound. Rose looked up at Dr Hollins.

"He will be all right, won't he? You said there wasn't anything wrong with him..."

"Nothing physically wrong," amended the doctor. "Don't fret now, woman. Keep him warm and get him to drink something. He's young. He'll recover, given time." He picked up his bag and went to the door. "I'll drop in tomorrow, see how he's doing. Ring me if you're worried about anything."

Rose heard him go away down the stairs; she felt suddenly very alone, and very responsible. Even Dr Hollins did not know what was wrong.

The doctor met Jeremy at the foot of the stairs.

"Have you got a minute before you go, Jim?" the rector asked, detaining him with a hand on his sleeve.

The doctor looked at him in surprise. "Only my bed's waiting for me at home," he said. "What's your problem?"

Jeremy gestured in the direction of the sitting room. "Come in here."

The doctor followed him. On the sofa, head in hands, in an apparent stupor, sat Clive. Apart from the fact that he was sitting rather than lying down, his state closely resembled his son's.

"Drinking?" asked Jim, raising his eyebrows. "Noticed he wasn't in evidence when I went to see the boy. Thought he must be away."

"No, it isn't drink," said Jeremy. "He seemed quite sober when Liz and I brought Robert home. But he hasn't been himself all evening. We had to leave him here to man the phone while we went out looking for Robert. He was obviously going to be no earthly use at all on a search."

Jim Hollins' bushy eyebrows rose another millimetre or two. He sat down beside Clive, felt his pulse and looked under his eyelids. Clive hardly reacted at all, except to flinch slightly at the eye examination.

"Pull yourself together, man," said the doctor bracingly. "Your son's ill, and Rose needs you. Pour him a wee dram, Remy."

Without a word, Jeremy went to the drinks cabinet, poured half a glassful of whisky and held it out to Clive. After a moment Clive took the glass, looked at it vaguely as if from a great distance, and then downed it at a gulp.

"Good," said Dr Hollins briskly. "Go and sit with the boy, now, Clive. He's quite safe. Just needs quiet. Rose's upstairs."

He heaved himself to his feet, patted Clive on the shoulder and ambled out into the hall again. "Let me know if he doesn't cope," he said to Jeremy in an undertone as the latter opened the door for him. "Have to get a shrink to him or something."

Jeremy smiled to himself as he shut the front door. A shrink, indeed! But Hollins himself was as sound as a nut, and no one could fault his commitment to his patients. Suddenly feeling more cheerful, Jeremy went to the bottom of the stairs and called up to Liz. "Any coffee needed up there?"

"Great idea," he heard her reply. "Simon's coming down to help you."

Jeremy went back into the kitchen. Liz, he reflected, was a fine strategist in her way.

~ * ~

On Thursday afternoon, Fran Baker dismissed her class punctually, following them out of the classroom to superintend their departure. Rose had telephoned her late the night before to let her know Robert had been found, and her description of his state of mind had seriously disturbed his teacher. She should go down to Sundials as quickly as possible, she decided, and see what she could do.

A cheerful chaos reigned in the cloakroom, bags and coats slung over the children's shoulders in their haste to escape from the school day prison. Fran stationed herself at the door, persuading pupils that the weather demanded they wear their coats rather than carrying them, that bags and satchels should be fastened neatly, not dragged along untidily, their contents spilling on to the path. It was impossible to smother altogether the natural human instincts of casualness and carelessness characteristic of the mid-primary age group, but she believed a certain curb must be put on them if the children were to emerge at a later stage with any notion of order and grooming. Many of her colleagues considered her old-fashioned, but she was not deterred.

When all her pupils had left, she returned to the classroom, collected up the work to be marked that evening, and loaded it carefully into an enormous shabby handbag. Carrying this on one arm, she made a circuit of the school buildings, and set off along Church Lane. Automatically, she avoided the muddy patches along the edge of the road where a tractor had clipped the bank, and the small piles of excreta left by dogs in spite of her efforts (via both the parish magazine and the school newsletter) to remind dog-owners of the danger thereby posed to children's health.

When she arrived at Sundials, she found the rector on the step.

"I can see Clive in the living room," he said. "But no one's answering the door."

"We'll go round the back," suggested Fran practically.

The kitchen door proved to be unlocked, as she had expected. "I'll look to see if Rose and Robert are upstairs," she said.

Jeremy nodded. "I'll see what I can do with Clive."

This division of labour, however, proved less than fruitful. Rose willingly relinquished her place beside Robert to Fran and went off to make a cup of tea for everyone. But Robert made no response to Fran's voice, though she tried soothing, cajolery and headmistressly firmness. Whatever the trauma that had caused his withdrawal, he was still firmly in its grip.

"Did Robert speak to you?" Rose asked anxiously from the doorway.

Fran shook her head. "No, I didn't have much luck, I'm afraid. Maybe we need to wait until he starts to relax a bit. See what Jim says later." She heaved her bulk out of the low armchair with an effort. "How's Clive? All this seems to have upset him."

"He's in the sitting-room," said Rose. "I've given him a cup of tea, but he hasn't drunk it. Perhaps Jeremy will be able to do something with him."

Fran followed Rose out of the room. "I'll come and see Robert tomorrow," she said. "A bit of continuity—same voices, same questions—that may help."

Rose turned back. "Dr Hollins promised to come in after surgery."

"You're doing a lot for Clive and Robert at the moment, Rose," said Fran. "Is anyone doing anything for you? What about a cup of that tea you made for Clive, for instance?"

Rose smiled suddenly, like a chink of blue sky among thick grey cloud. "That's a sweet thought, Fran. I didn't think to give myself a cup when I made it for Clive and Remy. How silly! Pour one for yourself, too, won't you? I made it in the big teapot."

She watched while Fran made her way slowly down the stairs, before going back into Robert's bedroom. She sat down by the bed, watching him for any sign of movement or awakening, conscious of every breath he took, every flutter of his half-closed eyelids. There was no room in her thoughts while she sat there for anyone or anything other than her son. Clive's withdrawal into himself touched her only peripherally, and then only when he was actually present. Simon Hellyer was completely forgotten.

She heard Fran's heavy tread on the stairs as the headmistress brought her a cup of tea. Fran set it down on Robert's locker beside the bedside lamp and the digital clock.

"Don't forget to drink it," she said firmly. "You can drink tea and watch Robert at the same time. I'll have mine downstairs with Clive and Remy."

Rose nodded absently. "Thanks, Fran."

Fran left her to her maternal vigil. Robert was clearly in shock, and someone must find out what had traumatised him... there might be some danger lurking in the village that could affect other children. Had they alerted the police? She made a mental note to ask the rector. He always knew everything. But in many ways, she was more concerned about Clive's attitude, which she found unnatural and disturbing. Normally competent and worldly, even insensitive, he seemed to have gone completely to pieces. She took a cup from a hook on the dresser and went to pour herself some tea from the pot which sat on a tray beside Clive in the sitting room. His cup, she noticed, was quite untouched.

Jeremy raised his eyebrows enquiringly at her as she sat down. She interpreted the question as relating to Robert and shook her head slightly. They sat in silence, one each side of Clive, watching him intently. But although he sat rather than lying rolled up in a ball, his silence and withdrawal were as profound as his son's. It was eerie, Fran thought; almost enough to make one believe in the supernatural, some ghoul had laid its hold on both of them. What did Remy make of it all? she wondered.

Jeremy was in fact considering the problem with his detective rather than his spiritual hat on. The trauma looked human to him rather than supernatural, although, at present, the process of cause and effect was shrouded in mystery. Sin and folly were at the bottom of it, he felt sure, not the Devil... unless it was in that fallen angel's usual role as orchestrator of evil. There were a number of questions he wanted answered; for a start, why did Robert leave the house? Then there was the matter of who he was with (he felt certain that Robert was not confident enough to go out on his own in the dark), and what had happened to him while he *was* out to cause such an extreme reaction? The most likely explanation seemed to be that Clive and Robert had gone out together when Clive returned home from work. But in that case, how had Clive lost sight of Robert while they were out, so that a search had to be made for the boy? Like Fran, he thought the state Clive was in represented an even greater mystery. What on earth could have happened to traumatise both of them to this degree? But it would clearly be no use asking questions at this stage. Neither of them was in a fit state to respond. However, various possibilities could be considered carefully, with a view to asking the right questions later.

He set his teacup down on the table and got up. "I've got a wedding rehearsal in a few minutes," he said to Fran. "Will you thank Rose for the tea for me? I don't want to disturb her."

Fran nodded. "I must go myself shortly. I promised to go in and speak to the school caretaker tonight. And I must check that she wasn't around last night, too. The churchyard's only just across the road from school. She might have seen something. We must get to the bottom of this, Remy."

"We must," he agreed. He picked up his coat and looked down at Clive. "Goodbye, Clive. I'll come and see you again later. Perhaps it'll help to talk a bit then."

Clive seemed to rouse himself for a moment, but only to shrug his shoulders.

"Well, I'll come anyway," said Jeremy. "You may feel like a chat another time."

Clive said nothing. He wished Fran would go away too and leave him to sort out the turmoil of his thoughts. Talking would do no good at all, he knew that. But at the moment, he couldn't see that action would help either. So he sat quietly, doing nothing, saying nothing, ignoring everyone.

After Fran had gone, the evening wore on interminably. Jim Hollins appeared at about seven o'clock, examined Robert and helped Rose to turn him over carefully so that he lay on his other side. Encouraged in a robust uncompromising manner by the doctor, Clive roused himself sufficiently to make some sandwiches for himself and Rose, and to drink a cup of coffee, but the only change in Robert was that instead of wrapping his arms around himself he clung to Rose's hand. Warmed by the boy's need of her but wrung to the heart by his white face and the tension she could feel in his muscles as his hand gripped hers, she sat by his bedside waiting for any sign of improvement.

Clive went back to the sitting-room, but he didn't have long to spend in thought before the doorbell rang again. It took him a moment to remember who the man on the doorstep was—Simon Hellyer, a bell ringer. He had brought Rose back from the Tower meeting last night and gone out on the search.

Simon was disappointed to see Clive open the door, though he told himself it was only to be expected that Rose would be with Robert. He asked after the boy, and Clive said there was no change, but he did not ask him in. Simon asked after Rose and was told that she was fully occupied with Robert. Any further enquiries he might have made were forestalled. Clive bade him a civil, but curt, goodnight and shut the door.

The sitting-room curtains were open, and as he went away down the path, Simon saw Clive moving about in the room, first towards the cabinet as though to pour himself a drink, then towards the window as though to draw the curtains across, then back to the sofa, to sink down on it as though his legs had given way.

Simon opened the door of his car and stood irresolutely beside it for a moment. He hated to leave Rose alone with a traumatised boy and a man who seemed more in need of support himself than able to give it to her. Yet, the man in question was her husband. He, Simon, he reflected ruefully, had no acknowledged rights at all in the situation. *Rose's friend*, he thought. *That's all I can claim to be… in truth, that's all I am. As far as Clive is concerned, I'm no more than an acquaintance.* She had plenty of those, and Clive would turn them all away tonight.

He swung himself into the driving seat of the car and switched on the ignition. *I wish to God I were her lover*, he thought bitterly.

Twelve

Clive stared blindly out of the window at the departing car. He was sure that something deeper than the casual enquiry of an acquaintance lay behind Simon's visit. Simon had had his arm round Rose when they got back the previous night, though he'd removed it as they came up the path, and he probably didn't know Clive had seen him. It might be that Rose would have wanted him to be let in. Simon might have been able to offer her some support, which was more than he, Clive, was doing, useless jerk that he was.

A further layer of misery added itself to the weight of guilt he was carrying. Yet, he hardly had a right to be jealous. He'd told himself years ago that he was bored with Rose, and it was unreasonable to turn possessive now, given his longstanding relationship with Olivia, not to mention last night's fling with Maddie. If Rose had found someone to care for her, then he shouldn't stand in her way. Yet, he had already done so, almost literally, by turning Simon from the door so unwelcomingly. And he would do the same again, he thought rebelliously, if the situation recurred. She was *his* wife, after all. He still had some rights, and he wasn't going to let them go easily.

It still tortured him to think that if he, Clive, had been in the house when he should have been last night, the boy wouldn't have disappeared. But the come-on from Maddie had been too much for him, what with Olivia sulking, and Rose furious with him. In the end, though, there hadn't been much time to do the thing properly... he'd had to promise they'd spend a night together another time. She had been eager to please and giggly, but their coupling had seemed tame and tawdry, and he came home feeling unsatisfied and irritable. He'd only been with Maddie for an hour or so, and then he'd come back and found Robert gone. He still went hot and cold at the thought of it. Someone must have come and taken him from his bedroom (for surely Robert would never have gone out on his own). What on earth had the boy's abductor done to him to have this effect? Whatever the doctor said about Robert being unharmed, something had terrified the boy, that was clear. And underneath those questions was the terrible knowledge, a knowledge he didn't want to face, that he, the boy's own father, had gone out and left his son vulnerable to attack, kidnap and danger. He hadn't even locked up the house properly when he went next door to shag the baby-sitter. He felt not only panic-stricken but completely overwhelmed by shame. It wasn't an emotion he often experienced, so he didn't know how to deal with it. He had trodden a moral tightrope for years, justifying all kinds of dubious behaviour to himself with observations like "Everyone has affairs; it's part of the lifestyle," and "I'm a good provider, that's what counts," until tonight, when self-gratification had led him to behave in a way even he couldn't justify. For the first time in his life, he despised himself.

Too bad. He flung the thoughts away from him and went back to the drinks cabinet. The whisky bottle stood ready beside the cut-glass tumbler, but he did not touch it. Oblivion via alcohol didn't tempt him. He stood for a few minutes, while more bitter and chaotic thoughts and feelings turned themselves over and over within him like a ball of thorns. Then abruptly he turned away. He needed a much more drastic solution to the problem than anything he could find here. He went out into the hall and selected a warm coat from the cupboard. Without further hesitation, he shrugged himself into it and went out.

~ * ~

Robert's bedroom was warm, and Rose had not slept much the previous night. She heard the front door close downstairs, presumably behind whoever had called, and then there was silence. Robert did not stir. The combination of warmth and quiet and her own tiredness gradually lulled her to sleep, and she dozed peacefully for almost half-an-hour. Then abruptly she realised that Robert was moving. She opened her eyes to find him already half out of bed and putting his feet to the floor.

"Robert, darling!"

With eyes half-closed, and unresponsive to her exclamation, Robert stood up and made his way waveringly to the door. Rose hovered a few inches behind him, hands poised to help him and protect him from harm. He reached the landing and turned left without hesitation. After a few paces, he turned again and opened the bathroom door. Rose followed him, waited while he relieved himself and then walked back behind him, in a silent slow procession, to his bedroom. She wondered whether she should report this development to Dr Hollins. Was it a sign of recovery beginning?

Robert climbed back into bed but did not resume the foetal position. Instead, he sat staring in front of him, with his head resting against the wall. Rose picked up the glass of water beside the bed and offered it to him. After a moment, he took it from her and sat looking at it.

"Drink some, Robert," she encouraged him, remembering Dr Hollins' advice that she should get him to swallow as much liquid as possible.

He lifted the glass, drank half the contents, and allowed her to take it from him.

"Are you feeling better now?" she enquired hopefully, but there was no response.

It came to her that since drink had been acceptable, food might also be welcome.

"I'll go and make you something to eat," she said to Robert. "I'll be very quick."

She ran down the stairs, calling to Clive in the sitting-room as she did so. "Clive, Robert got up to go to the loo. He's had a drink, and I'm going to make a sandwich for him. Will you watch him while I do it, please?"

There was no audible reply from the sitting-room, but she did not wait for one. She sped into the kitchen and began concocting Robert's favourite double-decker peanut-butter-and-banana sandwich.

~ * ~

Jeremy had said Matins in the church and cleared some necessary administrative items from his desk the next morning when the telephone rang.

"Hallo," he answered. "St Martin's Rectory."

"Remy, it's Rose. Could you come down and see me this morning?"

"Of course, I could. Is it Robert?" asked Jeremy at once.

"No. It's not an emergency. He's still much as he was, and Jim Hollins will be down this afternoon to check on him, he said, after surgery. But I need to talk to you."

"On my way," said Jeremy.

He cast an eye quickly over his diary to see which appointments he could cancel. Fortunately, the morning was fairly clear, although he had been planning to do some Bible study in preparation for Sunday's sermons. That would have to wait.

It was a fine morning, but he hardly noticed that as he walked briskly down the lane to Sundials. Rose took some time to answer the door, and he concluded she had been sitting upstairs with Robert. He wondered where Clive was. Perhaps he had gone back to work.

"Has there been any change?" he asked Rose as she took his coat. "I called in last night to see how Robert was, but you can't have heard the bell. I hoped there hadn't been any further crisis."

"When did you call?" asked Rose, surprised.

"Oh, quite late by the time the PCC meeting at Two Marks finished... ten o'clock perhaps."

"I must have been asleep. I put up the camp bed in Robert's room last night, and the doorbell is a bit faint from there. I'm awfully sorry."

"He must be better if you managed to sleep, Rose," said Jeremy, the hint of a teasing tone creeping into his voice.

Rose did not respond to the tone, but answered seriously. "Yes, he is a bit better. He doesn't speak yet, but he moves about, and he's eating and drinking now. Dr Hollins has been this morning, and he says to give it more time. But Remy, the oddest thing..."

"Yes?"

"Clive must have gone out yesterday evening at some point— probably before you came round, if no one answered the door— and..."

"Yes?" said Jeremy again.

"Well...he hasn't come back, that's all."

There was a pause. Jeremy blinked. "He was out all night?"

"Yes. And I haven't a clue where he's gone. I mean, he didn't say anything to me, or leave a note. I'm... I'm a bit worried."

Jeremy quelled his immediate thought, which was that Clive's temporary disappearance removed at least one drain on Rose's emotional resources. "Could he have gone out very early this morning... to work perhaps? Have you tried his office?"

"His bed hasn't been slept in," replied Rose succinctly. "However, that gives me an idea. Thanks, Remy."

"I'll come and see you later, shall I? After lunch, perhaps. I'd like to have a look at Robert myself."

"Yes, all right. I may have found out where Clive is by then."

When Jeremy called in the afternoon, however, Rose was no wiser about Clive's whereabouts.

"I rang his office," she said. "But Miss Landry—that's his secretary—said Clive told her he wouldn't be in until next week.

She rang yesterday afternoon, apparently, because she hadn't heard from him for a couple of days, and there were a number of things waiting for him to deal with." She took a deep breath. "You might as well know, Remy, that Clive and Olivia Landry have been having an affair. I don't know how long it's been going on, but I found out definitely last week, and to be honest, I thought perhaps he was with her last night. I suppose she could be lying about his not being at the office, but it doesn't seem very likely, does it? Clive usually fobs me off with some plausible excuse when he goes off somewhere with Olivia... working weekends and conferences, things like that. This isn't in the pattern at all."

Jeremy sat gazing at her silently for so long that she became restive under his scrutiny. "People in glass houses shouldn't throw stones, is that it, Remy?" she said at last.

"Well, is it?" he asked gently. "I'm not accusing you of anything."

"Not in words," she said indignantly. "You don't have to *say* anything. I always feel you can see straight into me. It's most disconcerting."

"What are you trying to tell me, Rose?"

"I'm not trying to tell you anything. I'm trying *not* to tell you. Besides, there isn't really anything to tell."

He smiled reassuringly. "I'm sorry. Don't tell me. Not unless it will help you."

She sighed. "I expect it will, one day. But not now. I just want to get Robert back to normal, find Clive, and then... then we can try to work something out."

~ * ~

By Sunday morning, Rose was near the end of her emotional tether. Robert was improving slowly, but he was still immersed in an impenetrable silence which made communication with him impossible. And Clive had not contacted her at all, so she had no idea where he was or when, or if, he was coming home. She felt as though the whole weight of responsibility for the family had fallen on her. And in this state of emotional weakness she suddenly and belatedly remembered Sarah.

Oh God, she thought. *I haven't told Sarah that Clive's missing. Or about Robert.*

For a moment she hesitated, torn between conflicting anxieties. Sarah wouldn't necessarily be all that interested in Robert's problems. She was usually quite sweet with Robert and obviously fond of him, but the age gap, and the fact that Sarah had left home, prevented them from being more than distant acquaintances. But she adored her father. Should she let Sarah know Clive was missing, or would that just worry her unnecessarily? The police had seemed certain that Clive would return in his own good time and had refused to set up a hue and cry for the moment. Should she wait for a few days more? On the other hand, Sarah was her daughter and might, just conceivably, be a source of support, support for which she would at this moment be immeasurably grateful.

Rose had deliberately refrained from turning to the other person whose help she knew would be forthcoming. Simon must remain at arm's length. His support, however freely offered in intention, would come at a cost, and she didn't yet know whether she could meet it.

~ * ~

Sarah was contemplating a late breakfast when her mother rang. Saturday evenings were usually clubbing nights, and she had arrived home, well lubricated though not intoxicated, with an escort, at about two o'clock. The remainder of the night, though satisfying in a number of respects, had not been particularly restful, and she had not surfaced from the ensuing slumber until after nine. Her escort had departed with somewhat unseemly haste, refusing her offer of breakfast, so she was sitting in an armchair wrapped in a bathrobe, her hair still tousled from the shower, a cup of tea beside her, when the phone rang.

"Oh, it's you, Mother... Are you all right?... Disappeared? I'm glad you found him again quickly... Oh, poor little boy, but I expect he'll come out of it soon... *What?* Dad's disappeared? Mother, he *can't* have. He must have told you where he was going, but you weren't listening. I mean," she added, trying to make allowances. "You were worried about Robert..."

"Sarah," came the reply with unexpected asperity, "the car is still on the drive and your father hasn't taken even his pyjamas with him as far as I can see."

Her mother sounded brisk and matter-of-fact, confident of her facts, and in the face of this, Sarah found it difficult to persist in disbelief. Robert's traumatic experience, whatever it was, was a little disturbing, and going out in the evening without telling his parents was certainly out of character, but in her view Robert was an over-sensitive, wimpish little boy whom anything out of the ordinary might upset—he could be terrified of his own shadow. But it was unbelievable that *Dad*—whose hard-headed competence and merciless pursuit of whatever he desired at any particular moment had always compelled her admiration—should put on his overcoat, and simply walk out of his house and not return, whatever the provocation. St Martin-on-the-Hill was not the kind of place someone would get kidnapped or mugged in the street. If he had disappeared, then presumably he had meant to do it. But why on earth should he have wanted to?

"You've told the police, Mother?"

"Oh, Sarah! Of course, I have."

"And they said?" Sarah's initial bewilderment was edging over into anger.

"What would you expect? Husbands apparently disappear for a short time quite often, and they won't search for him until he's been gone without word for two weeks."

"Great. And just what are we supposed to do in the meantime?"

"Nothing," said her mother. "Just wait and see, they say. Sarah, I'm worried, too, but I've got Robert to look after and really I can do without chasing after your father as well."

Sarah opened her mouth to object, and then closed it again. Reluctantly, her innate sense of justice had to admit that this was fair enough. "How is the little silly? What on earth was he doing, out on his own like that, anyway?"

"I don't know, Sarah. No one can work out whether someone took him from his room, or whether he went out by himself. Neither seems very likely, really, so we're all mystified. He's better, I think, but he's awfully *silent*. Something frightened him badly, but he won't tell us what it was."

Sarah wondered who "us" was. In the absence of her father, who was supporting her mother? She could imagine just how demanding Robert would be, even in silence.

She wriggled inwardly a little. No doubt many would think it should be Sarah's job to go and help her mother, but she was disinclined to get involved. Robert and she were poles apart in age, character and interests and there was really no reason to suppose she would be able to help much. And her mother sounded quite calm... surprisingly so in the circumstances. But just recently her mother had seemed to be growing out of her quite awful dependence on Dad and becoming rather more of a person in her own right. Not before time, either, and Sarah had no intention of reversing the process by becoming Main Prop in her turn. Of course, it was possible her mother had simply found a substitute crutch in the form of some new friend or other in the village (perhaps that very sexy bellringer who had seemed specially attentive at the ball? Unlikely, she concluded with regret... the sort of support Mother would want would more probably come from the rector and his wife).

"Let me know if you hear anything about Dad, won't you?" she said, signing off before any request for help could be voiced. "I hope Robert perks up soon."

She picked up her tracksuit from the drying rack by the radiator and started to put it on. A trip to the gym would be more beneficial than breakfast. She could have something to eat when she came back.

~ * ~

Balked of support from Sarah and feeling unreasonably constrained by her enforced incarceration in the house, she was relieved and delighted beyond measure when Liz arrived unexpectedly on the way home from church. She opened the door wide, dragged her visitor hastily into the kitchen and plied her with coffee and biscuits, expressing her gratitude all the while.

"It must be awful for you," responded Liz, sympathetically. "I can't think what Clive is thinking about, leaving you like this."

"He seemed terribly upset about Robert," said Rose. "Almost as though he blamed himself. But he wasn't even here when Robert went out. And we can hardly blame poor Maddie, if she was in the sitting room, and Robert deliberately left the house without telling her. It's such a strange thing to have done. I can't believe anyone came and took him from his room... it just seems impossible. On the other hand, something seems to have frightened him badly."

She poured the coffee and handed Liz a cup. "You don't have sugar, do you? Would you like one of these biscuits?"

Liz shook her head. "I won't, thanks, Rose. But do have one yourself... carbohydrates are natural tranquillizers, did you know that?"

Rose did not respond to this nutritional gambit, but she bit into a chocolate biscuit somewhat absent-mindedly. "You don't think anything could have... *happened* to Clive, do you, Liz?"

"Happened in what sense?" asked Liz, cautiously.

Rose hesitated to put the fear into words. "The police didn't seem to take it at all seriously, his disappearing like that, but suppose there's been an accident. I mean, he can't just have... vanished, can he?"

"No," agreed Liz slowly. "But the police would have known if there'd been an accident. He'll be on a list of missing persons somewhere, I expect, even if they aren't prepared to follow it up at the moment. There must be a reason... it's just we don't know what it is." She paused for a moment and then added, "Oh dear, that doesn't sound very helpful. I'm sorry, Rose."

"It's very sweet of you to come when you must have so much to do," responded Rose warmly. "I've been amazed at how good everyone's been to me. But it's embarrassing as well as worrying. I mean, what can I say when people ask why he's gone, or when he's coming back?"

Liz patted her shoulder. "Why don't you go out for a walk with Dolly? I'll sit with Robert. He knows me well enough, wouldn't you think?"

"Oh, I'm sure he wouldn't be upset if you were there instead of me when he wakes. But Sunday's the day you spend with the family. You shouldn't waste it."

"That will not be a waste," said Liz firmly. "Tell you what… I'll go and give them some lunch and come back about two o'clock. Remy always has a nap after lunch on a Sunday and the others are left to their own devices, anyway. You ought to get away from the house for a bit, Rose. You don't know how long all this is going to go on."

"Well, if you're sure…" Rose's voice sounded small and uncertain. "Dolly could do with a walk, it's true."

"Yes, I am. Quite sure. Have you got something to eat for lunch? I don't suppose you've been able to do much shopping the last few days."

"Lesley did some for me on Friday when she went to the supermarket. I couldn't even think straight to give her a list, so she just bought what she thought I'd need. Aren't people kind, Liz? I can't think what I've done to deserve it. I mean, I simply haven't done anything."

"You've just been yourself," said Liz briskly. "Something not everyone manages to do. And they all love you, Rose."

Rose went pink. "Me?"

"You. Now, get yourself something to eat while I feed my ravening hordes. I'll be back later."

Rose watched her from Robert's window as she went down the path and turned left along the lane towards the village. She wondered suddenly whether Liz saw her as a friend, or merely as parish business. How hard it must be to disentangle the two when you were married to a clergyman. But she was very glad of Liz's support in this crisis, friend or not.

Thirteen

When Liz returned, Rose set out with Dolly across the fields above Copse Lane. The first part of the walk crossed Brian Warrendon's land, on a public right of way that doubled as the unmade bridle path leading to his farmhouse. Two large meadows and a stile brought her through a small belt of trees, all that remained of the mixed forest that had once covered the whole area. Beyond that, the land climbed north-eastwards and she crossed the boundary over another stile on to George's property. The path led round the edge of a ploughed field, and eventually, if she followed it far enough, would come out in Two Marks, two miles away. Dolly ran sniffing happily after rabbits, nose down and tail waving gently as she zigzagged across the field. In the summer, it was full of glorious golden fronds of barley bowing in the wind, but now the stubble had been turned in, and the ground was bare and brown.

Rose paused for breath at the top of the hill and turned to enjoy the view. The village sat perched near the apex of the next ridge, with the church, the school and George's farmhouse close together in silhouette. One straggle of houses poured untidily down the side of the hill towards her, another clung to the ridge as it fell away towards Winchester, following the road down to Copse Lane. Even in the drab light of a November afternoon, it was a picturesque sight.

Obscurely, Rose felt that she should be worrying about Clive and where he was. Then Robert wasn't well yet by any means, and she didn't know what would happen next. But the quiet of the landscape soothed her, and she found herself strolling contentedly along the footpath, dreaming gently and happily, and absent-mindedly beating the rough dry grass with the stout piece of varnished hazel she liked to use as a walking cane.

"Dolly! Dolly! Come on. Leave those rabbits in peace." Rose looked at her watch. Soon, she must turn back if she wanted to avoid being caught by the gathering gloom. With the sky so clear, the light would last a little longer, but in any case, Liz must want to get back to her family. It was very good of her to look after Robert for a while.

She turned away from St Martin and climbed the stile by the gate into George's hay meadow, covered in untidy rough grass and a few late wildflowers. Ahead of her, she could see another walker coming towards her; a man, by the length and vigour of his stride. She looked across the field. He did not appear to have a dog with him, and in any case, Dolly was a friendly soul who never traded rude words with canine acquaintances. She would walk on a little and see who it was.

In a few paces more, she had identified him. The particular strength and grace of his movement, and the set of his head against the pale blue sky, were both now unmistakable; it was Simon. She stopped and waited for him, trying not to panic. Part of her throbbed with the pleasure of seeing him, with the memory of their last meeting and excited anticipation at the prospect of speaking to him—and perhaps touching him—again. Another part drew back, still uncertain of him and of her own feelings for him.

In her muted tweeds and green boots, she was hidden against the green and brown background of the fields, and Simon was within twenty yards of her before he became aware of her. Immediately, her doubts were laid to rest. His rather harsh expression relaxed, and his face lit up with delight.

"Rose! This is marvellous. I've been longing to see you."

He came up to her in a few strides and took her shoulders in his hands.

She smiled at him. "What are you doing up here?"

"Me? Oh, I often walk up here on a Sunday afternoon when it's fine. How's Robert?"

"He's getting better. He doesn't say anything yet, but Dr Hollins says it will come. Liz is sitting with him, so I could get out for a bit. I wish I knew what had frightened him so."

"Yes, it would be good to know. Still, perhaps when he's better, he'll be able to talk about it. Are you turning back? It'll be dark soon. I'll walk along with you." He put his arm round her shoulder and steered her back along the path the way she had come.

"I'll have to make sure Dolly knows I've turned for home. She *will* go after the rabbits, and then she doesn't notice where I am. I lost her once up here, and she didn't come home for hours. Clive was furious."

Simon looked around. "I can't see her. Did she get this far?"

"No, come to think of it, she didn't come over the stile with me. Dolly! Dolly!"

Simon moved forward again, taking Rose with him. "She must be ahead of us, in that case," he said. "Give her a shout when we get over the top of the ridge."

He stopped at the gate out of the meadow.

"Which way did you come?"

She pointed back towards the village.

"Isn't that Brian Warrendon's land? I'm surprised you dare. That man terrifies me."

Rose laughed. "I don't believe you. You're not scared of anything. It's only the last two fields and the copse that are Brian's. George's land runs within two hundred yards of the road over there. Besides, it's a public right of way. As far as I know, he's never tried to stop anyone from using it."

"All right," said Simon, grinning suddenly. "If you're game, I am."

He helped her over the stile. She did not really need any assistance, having climbed all the stiles on the route alone many times, but she did not refuse his help; and their hands remained clasped as they walked on.

Simon swung her hand happily to and fro as they turned down the hill towards St Martin. "I tried to see you on Thursday night," he told Rose casually. "I didn't expect you to be at the practice on Wednesday night, of course, and I couldn't wait indefinitely to find out how you all were. But Clive wouldn't let me in. He was pretty hostile to me, in fact." He hesitated. "Does he... does he guess something about us, d'you think?"

"No—at least I don't think so," answered Rose hurriedly. "But Simon, when did you come... I mean, what time?"

He glanced down at her, surprised at her urgency. "I'm not sure. About seven-thirty, perhaps. I was busy at school until seven, and I came straight to you from there. Why?"

"Clive disappeared on Thursday night," Rose explained. "And he hasn't come back."

Simon stopped walking and stared at her. "What!"

"He must have gone out sometime after you called. Apparently, Remy came round about ten, but I was asleep. Clive didn't answer the door, so I suppose he'd gone by then, though I can't be sure."

"Have you told the police?"

"Oh, yes, I've told the police," said Rose heavily. "They told me lots of husbands go away without telling their wives. He'll come back soon, they say. I'm to let them know in a fortnight if he hasn't returned."

Simon grimaced. "I suppose you can see it from their point of view."

"No, I can't." Rose's indignation suddenly spilled over. "Clive wouldn't just go out and not come back. It's not the kind of thing he would do at all. Something may have happened to him, and I'm worried. It won't help Clive if the police leave it a fortnight before they start searching for him."

Something very like jealousy stirred in Simon at this sign of wifely concern.

"Has he never gone away without telling you?" he asked carefully. Clive's absence could have a simple explanation, after all.

"He's gone off without me... on business, and for other reasons, yes," replied Rose. "Sometimes at short notice. But never without telling me he was going. He's lied about where he was going, and about why. I realize that now. But he's never just *gone*. It's not like him, Simon. And he wasn't himself, either... before he went, I mean. He was knocked for six by what happened to Robert. You saw that yourself, on Wednesday, didn't you? That doesn't make sense, either. Clive's usually the one who doesn't panic."

Simon moved on, but his hand gripped Rose's more firmly. "What could have happened to make him go, do you think? Did he take anything with him?"

"I haven't had a chance to look carefully, because of keeping an eye on Robert. But I don't think he's taken anything except his coat from the hall cupboard. Not even his pyjamas."

"I can't see that anything is likely to have happened to him in the village," said Simon reasonably. "Where would he go without any luggage? Did he take his wallet? Credit cards?"

"I don't know," said Rose miserably. "I haven't really looked systematically. I've been thinking about Robert. Don't cross-examine me, Simon. I can't cope with it."

He squeezed her hand. "I'm sorry. Shall I come back with you and have a look round?"

"Oh, would you? That would be such a help." Rose's earlier determination not to call on Simon for support had vanished without her even being aware of its departure. "Everyone's been so kind, but I've felt so alone."

They walked on in silence for a little, Simon struggling with himself to contain the lover's words and actions which he knew she would not respond to at this moment, Rose allowing her thoughts to wander unhappily after the possibility of an accident having befallen Clive.

"There's Dolly, up ahead of us." Simon pointed further up the path. "I think she's after a hare."

"Oh, I do hope not. They're so beautiful. I couldn't bear it if she caught one. Dolly! Dolly, come here!"

Dolly took no notice at all. At a distance, and hot on a scent, it was doubtful whether she even heard her mistress.

"Don't worry," said Simon reassuringly. "Hares and rabbits are very quick on their feet. A lurcher might keep up, but Dolly won't."

They reached the boundary of George's land and stopped to negotiate another stile. Dolly suddenly reappeared from behind them, sailed past and stopped dead, almost causing Simon to fall over her. She doubled back and bolted into the undergrowth where the copse straddled the boundary of the two farms.

"That was a strong scent," said Simon, looking after her. "I wonder what on earth it could have been, to stop her in her tracks like that."

"I can't smell anything," said Rose.

Simon laughed. "I don't suppose we would, however strong it seemed to Dolly. Dogs' noses are turbo-charged."

"I'd better go and get her. She may not follow us home if she's smelt something really interesting. I don't want her wandering about in the dark."

"I'll go," said Simon. "You're wearing a skirt. Skirts may be all very well for climbing stiles—and very neatly you do it, if I may say so—but they aren't designed for pushing through brambles."

Rose looked at his jeans and denim jacket. She had hardly noticed what he was wearing, so eagerly had she focused on his face. "I'll wait for you here," she agreed.

He paused for a moment to take her face in his hands and kiss her hungrily. This was the last private spot on this footpath. Over the next stile, they would be in full view from the village and Copse Lane. To his relief, she did not repulse him, but her lips were cool, accepting him and his longing but finding no echo of response in herself. After a moment, he let her go and turned to go after Dolly.

He pushed through the long grass and nettles, bent his head under the first line of hawthorn branches, and set out into the dense woody undergrowth. He noticed that someone else had pushed through the copse recently. There were broken small boughs and nettle fronds above the height Dolly would have touched. He hoped the dog had not crossed the boundary between the farms. Brian Warrendon struck him as the kind of man who might set illegal traps.

"Dolly!" he called, in the hope of attracting her attention.

A rustling to his left gave away her position and he turned in that direction, calling her again. She emerged from the undergrowth a few yards away, dashed up to him and then ran off again before he could grab her collar.

"Dolly! Stay!" he said authoritatively.

The dog looked round, ran a few paces towards him and then whirled about and rooted through some saplings into a small cleared area. Following her, Simon could see signs of broken earth as though someone had been digging. Dolly was following their example, scrabbling with forepaws enthusiastically and waving her feathery tail. Simon grabbed her collar and pulled her away from the hole she was making.

And then he saw the brown shoe.

The shoe was loose, laces trailing. But beneath it there was a sock-clad foot. Simon stood staring at it for a long moment before he bent down and touched it. There was no reason for his action, for the owner was clearly not able to feel anything. But it was a human reflex, to check that it was only a body, no suffering mortal being lying there in the damp earth. The foot was limp, and as cold as the soil around it. Simon straightened up.

From the pathway, he heard Rose calling. "Have you caught her, Simon?"

He backed away from the limb Dolly had unearthed and made his way quickly back to the path, dragging the unwilling dog by the collar.

Rose saw at once from his face that something was wrong. "What is it?"

Simon put his hand out to stop her instinctive movement towards the copse. "Don't – don't go in there, Rose." His voice was hoarse.

"Why not?" She stared at him. "Whatever is it, Simon? You look as though you've seen a ghost."

"You could put it that way. There's a body in there."

"A body... You mean... a corpse?"

He nodded. He was feeling rather sick.

She went white. "It couldn't... it couldn't be Clive, could it?"

"Oh, God," said Simon. "I didn't think of that."

They looked at each other in silence for a long moment.

"We oughtn't to touch anything," said Simon at last. "We ought to call the police." He checked the pocket of his jacket. "We'll have to go back to your house to phone. I didn't bring my mobile, I'm afraid."

"But supposing it *is* Clive. I can't bear not knowing. The police'll take ages to come. Didn't you see whether it was him? Let me go in there... I could tell even if..." she swallowed. "Even if we can't see his face."

"Would you know from a sock?" asked Simon abruptly. "That's all I could see... a plain sock and a shoe. Dolly had dug them up. It's a man, that's all I can tell. He's buried in among the trees. Come away, Rose." He took hold of her arm to help her. She looked close to collapse. "I'll leave Dolly here and come back for her later."

She began to weep, the tears running unchecked down her face, but she obeyed his insistent hand on her arm. She climbed the stile clumsily, this time accepting his help from need, not desire, and stumbled along the pathway blindly, leaning against him. His arm about her shoulders gave her physical support, but even Simon was not able to offer any emotional reassurance.

It was not far to the road, not far after that up the hill to the church and to Sundials on the further side of it. But to Simon, it was the longest walk he had ever taken. Rose's feet dragged, and his arm ached as he helped her along. They came out on to Copse Lane just below the estate and turned the corner by the wall where Clive's car had so nearly run into Brian Warrendon. They trudged slowly up the hill into the village, Simon hoping they would meet some other Sunday walker who could be pressed into service as messenger and sent to telephone the police. It was nearly dark, however, and other walkers had gone home to tea. Simon, aware of Rose's exhaustion, suggested they might stop at the cottages by the church, but she refused. "Please let's go home," she said wearily. "Robert needs me, and Liz will be worried."

They struggled on down the slight incline to the house. Liz had turned on the porch lamp, and it lit the path from the gate with a friendly glow. Rose's step strengthened a little as she reached the door, but she still leant against Simon as he opened the door for her.

Liz came down the stairs at a run. "Rose! What's happened? I was a bit worried, with it getting dark. Where's Dolly?" She perceived Rose's companion and said rather stiffly, "Oh, hallo, Simon."

"I left Dolly tied to a stile on the footpath, so I had both hands free to help Rose," Simon explained. "We need to phone the police," he went on succinctly.

"Are you hurt, Rose?" Liz looked baffled. "What's this about Dolly?"

Simon shook his head. "We found a corpse, buried up in the woods on the hill." He steered Rose into the sitting-room and deposited her gently in a chair. "Liz, will you get her some tea, while I phone, please?

He punched in 999 and waited. "Police, please," he told the emergency services operator firmly. Then, after a moment, "My name is Simon Hellyer. I want to report finding a body."

Liz had brought in the tea for Rose by the time the police had finished questioning Simon. When he put the receiver down, he felt weary himself and was glad to accept the cup she proffered.

"Where do the Althorpes keep their brandy, Liz, do you know? Rose ought to have something, and I wouldn't mind some myself."

Liz didn't know where the spirits were and disagreed with his intention of lacing the tea with brandy. She said so forcibly, but Simon settled the matter out of hand by putting her firmly aside, locating the brandy bottle on the sideboard and pouring a generous measure into his own and Rose's cup.

Rose herself took no part in their altercation, sitting listlessly in the chair, although when he prompted her, she drank the tea with its brandy flavouring thirstily.

"Are the police coming?" asked Liz.

He nodded.

"But what's it all about? Why is Rose in such a state? I know finding a body must be pretty horrible, but…"

"The trouble is that it may be Clive."

"Oh, Simon!" Liz digested this information for a moment. Then she said, "When you've drunk your tea, please will you go down to the rectory and tell Remy I'll have to stay here a bit longer? I can't leave Rose yet. I know Remy will understand. Tell Lorna to make something to eat for everyone, will you?"

"Can't we phone?" he said. "The police will want to talk to me again, I expect. I probably ought to stay here, too."

"No," said Liz briskly. "Otherwise Remy will want to come up here as well. And I think Rose should just sit quietly and not be asked questions by Remy… and he'll be sure to want to. Talking to the police will be quite bad enough. You can come back later to talk to the police, or I'll send them on to you at home, if you like."

Reluctantly, Simon gave way. Whatever his instinctive desire to stay with Rose and comfort her, and his qualms of conscience about leaving her to the mercy of the police, Liz's request was a reasonable one. But he recognised that it was also a means of removing him from the house, and this did nothing to improve his temper. He trudged up the road to the rectory, furious at being thus outmanoeuvred. He was close to wishing that he had not taken it into his head to go out for a walk that afternoon, and only the knowledge that if he had not been there, Rose would probably have herself followed Dolly into the wood and discovered the body prevented him regretting the whole episode.

Fourteen

Mike opened the door of the rectory and ushered Simon innocently into Jeremy's study, where he waited by the empty fireplace, his eyes running absently over the tall bookshelves, the contents of the desk sorted haphazardly into piles of paper with an empty pipe lying in the big unused ash tray beside them. There were two armchairs facing each other cosily either side of the fire, waiting for the confidences to flow.

His gaze sharpened into focus as Jeremy entered, and he saw at once that in spite of clerical etiquette, Jeremy's reaction to him was a mirror image of his own. He was accustomed to his own reasons for disliking and mistrusting the clergy and all they stood for, but he was taken aback to be met by such mistrust in return. His first reaction to it was anger. He felt the weight of Jeremy's appraisal of him and it put him on the defensive. Vicars should be kind, uncritical and accepting, he thought angrily. It was part of their job. How dare this clergyman mistrust him?

"Simon," said Jeremy quietly, as though the undercurrents of judgement, defensiveness and anger between them were non-existent, "What can I do for you?"

"Liz asked me to come," said Simon brusquely. "She said to tell you she's staying with Rose for a bit longer. She asked if Lorna would get tea for everyone."

"Is Rose upset?" asked Jeremy. "Perhaps…"

"Yes, she is upset," Simon interrupted him. "It's hardly surprising, seeing that we just found a corpse up in the wood that might turn out to be her husband."

Jeremy had learned over the years to hide shock when he felt it, but even his face expressed startled horror for a moment. Simon found himself feeling a kind of perverse pleasure in that.

"Have you informed the police?" Jeremy snapped at him.

"Yes, from Rose's house. They're on their way."

"Where is this corpse?" asked Jeremy, turning towards the door. "You'd better come with me and show me."

Simon opened his mouth to refuse and remembered that poor Dolly was still up on the hill, tethered to a stile and probably both hungry and frightened. "All right," he said rather grudgingly. "I've got to go back for Dolly, anyway. We left her up at the copse. But why do you want to see? Until they dig the body up—it's buried shallowly—there's not much to see anyway, not in the dark."

Jeremy smiled suddenly, and Simon wondered whether he had imagined the hostility. "I like mysteries," he said simply. "And whatever's happened will affect the village… it's bound to, if the police are involved, don't you think?" He went out into the hall and took his coat down from the hook on the wall. "Bodies aren't found here every day, Simon, even if it turns out to be someone we don't know. It's my job to look after the people here. So, it's my duty to see for myself."

Simon snorted as he followed him. He waited in the hall while Jeremy passed on his wife's message to Lorna. *Duty.* The same as all the rest of that hypocritical clerical clan: talking of duty, responsibility and caring, and using it as a cloak for their own busybodying. At least Jeremy had begun by being honest, saying that he liked mysteries. That was something. But it was a pity he had spoilt it by justifying his curiosity with clerical humbug.

It was quite dark outside as they picked their way down the rectory drive by the light of Jeremy's torch. Simon realised that when he had seen the police (who would no doubt have even more interminable questions for him to answer) he had still to walk home across the unlit fields, or take the long route home by the road. He looked up at the sky and tried in vain to remember whether there was likely to be a moon.

"Can you tell me a bit more about this body you found, Simon?" asked Jeremy as they emerged on to the road. "Where are we making for, to begin with?"

Simon described the location of the body. "I don't know how the police will reach it. I told them where to go, but it isn't very accessible from the road, with two stiles and the fields to cross."

"They can get in from the Church End Farm side, I think, if I've got the whereabouts of the body correctly. You said it's on George's land, didn't you? Near the boundary in the copse? There's a gateway between the two big fields. They'll bring something with four-wheel drive, I expect."

They walked down the hill in silence, busy with their own thoughts. They crossed the road to the stile which led on to Brian Warrendon's land and found a police car parked beside it. A young police officer peered at them out of the driver's window.

Simon stopped beside the car and waited until the passenger, who was speaking on the car radio, lowered his window. "Yes sir?"

"My name's Simon Hellyer. I phoned your people a few minutes ago."

The sergeant looked up at him. "We've come out in response to that call, yes. It would have been better if you had stayed at the house you telephoned from, sir," he added with a trace of severity. "We were on our way."

"I remembered we had left Mrs Althorpe's dog tied to the fence up on the hill. I need to go back for her."

The sergeant did not express either acceptance or disapprobation of this explanation but merely gazed at Simon appraisingly. In the background, Jeremy moved slightly and attracted his attention.

"Are you with Mr Hellyer, sir?" he asked, politely enough on the face of it, but with an undertone of suspicion.

"Yes. I'm Jeremy Swanson, the rector here."

The sergeant waited for further explanation, but none was forthcoming.

"Well, sir," he said to Simon. "I'm afraid I can't let you go back to the scene of the crime, so to speak, without a police escort."

"I might meddle with the body, you mean," said Simon slightly truculently.

"It's a possibility we have to take into account," the sergeant agreed equably.

He said to his colleague, "I'll stay with the car, Kev." He turned back to Simon. "Constable Stevens will go with you, Mr Hellyer. You can show him the location of the body, and he will wait for us up there. Don't touch anything," he added with emphasis. "In fact, keep away from the immediate area. The Scene of Crime Officer will want to find whatever's there to be found."

"I'll make sure he does, sir," said the constable. He emerged from the car quickly, light on his feet for his height and powerful build. "Lead the way, please, Mr Hellyer."

"Mr Swanson... is that right, sir?" asked the sergeant, turning his attention to Jeremy as the two men climbed the stile into the field. "Would you be kind enough to help me? How can we get a vehicle over these fields?"

Jeremy repeated his advice about four-wheel-drive and entry via Church End Farm, and much to his frustration was pressed into escorting the sergeant up to the farm. *So much for my efforts to see this body for myself,* he thought as they drove up the hill.

~ * ~

The farmhouse presented a dark and silent front to the yard as they drove in. The outbuildings showed only as shadows to their right, the Land Rover a darker shadow in front of them.

"Looks as though they're out, sir," said the sergeant.

Jeremy smiled. "I can see you're a townsman, Sergeant," he said. "Most farms are battened down for the night early in winter; and the living rooms in this house are all round the back, anyway."

"They should have security lights on," complained the sergeant, pushing open the driver's door. "Asking for burglars it is, with the yard as dark as this. No burglar alarm, either, I'll bet."

Jeremy sighed. "I don't suppose they have that sort of money," he said softly. "Or that much to steal."

The sergeant gave no sign of hearing him but led the way to the front door. Jeremy forbore to inform him that country people rarely use the front door of a farm house, either. He doubted the sergeant wanted to know.

There was a long pause at the door before they heard footsteps in the hall, and the sound of bolts drawn back. George seemed completely taken aback, even alarmed, at the sight of a uniformed policeman on his doorstep, but he looked relieved when he saw Jeremy.

"Can we come in, George?" asked Jeremy gently. "There's nothing to worry about. The police just need access to your land."

The sergeant glared at him. This was police business and he clearly resented the clergyman's interference in it. He trod heavily into the house but was unable to prevent Jeremy from following him.

George looked if anything more worried than before at Jeremy's explanation. "Anything we can do, Officer, of course," he murmured.

The sergeant paused, and before he could articulate his wants, Jeremy said, "They want to get over the thirty-acre field, George… to that bit of woodland just below the brow of the hill. I told them there's only the one stile at the far end… is that right?"

George looked at him. His pale skin shone with sweat. Jeremy wondered whether he and Lucinda had been quarrelling.

"The rector reckons we can get in with an off-road vehicle, sir," stated the sergeant.

"Yes, you can. Up to the copse stile, anyway. If necessary, we could take down the fence, but there's a lot of hedgerow up there." George hesitated. "May I ask what this is about, Officer?"

"A body's been found in the copse on the far side of the stile," Jeremy supplied quickly, with somewhat reprehensible amusement at the policeman's discomfort. "If you can lend us the Land Rover, George, I'll take the sergeant up there. Or perhaps you should come yourself," he went on. "You know the ground better in the dark."

"What's all this about the Land Rover?" A woman's voice came from the passage and Lucinda arrived, bristling with suspicion and hostility. "That thing isn't safe on rough ground in the dark, four-wheel drive or no. I asked you to get it serviced, George, but as usual you took no notice."

George made shushing movements at her with his hand, and Jeremy wondered whether the Land Rover was in fact unroadworthy. Lucinda never allowed caution to curb her tongue when her husband had earned her displeasure. To his regret, Jeremy had never been able to view George's wife with anything but dislike. She seemed to him a hard-faced, embittered woman with a grudge against life. Doubtless there was a reason for the grudge, and perhaps as a Christian he should give her the benefit of the doubt, but there was no denying she made it difficult.

"That won't be necessary, thank you, sir," said the sergeant, regaining the initiative. "One of our four-by-fours is on its way."

~ * ~

Simon released the ecstatic Dolly from her restraints, responded suitably to her fawning gratitude, and reattached her leash to her collar. The policeman, who had been dogging his footsteps determinedly, stood watching him. Simon expected him to reconnoitre the ground, to ask where the body was to be found, but he did not. He seemed to possess no natural curiosity at all. His instructions were to accompany Simon and make sure he stayed away from the corpse, and he needed no initiative of his own in order to obey.

Simon said half-heartedly, "I'd better take this dog home. She must be hungry. And I have to get home myself after that. I live in Two Marks... over there," he pointed across the fields. "It'll take me an hour in the dark to walk home."

"The SOCO will want to speak to you," said Constable Stevens stolidly. "You'd best wait here with me. I expect someone'll give you a lift home after."

Simon sat on the top bar of the stile, told Dolly to sit, and resigned himself to wait for police reinforcements. He had no particular commitments this evening, so the delay was no more than a nuisance. But the air was becoming cold and damp, and he had dressed lightly for a fine autumn afternoon's walk. If he had to sit there for very long, he would be frozen. This would not have troubled him unduly in other circumstances, but he resented being frozen for the sake of police delay. Besides, he wanted to get back to Rose.

Thinking of her, he allowed himself to consider what it might mean for her, and for others, if the body Dolly had unearthed was in fact that of Clive Althorpe. She would be a widow then, and the situation they faced would be quite different. How would she feel? How did he himself feel about the possibility? He had the peculiar sensation of being on an emotional roller-coaster ride, which far from slowing was racing pell mell downhill. He had no power to bring it to a halt, nor to escape from it. All he could do was to hold on tight and wait for the ride to slow down. Perhaps then, normality might return. But he had the odd feeling that whether or not Clive was dead, the tenor of their relationship had changed irrevocably.

Half an hour passed. Simon's hands and feet slowly dropped in temperature until he had hardly any sensation at all in them. He blew on his fingers to warm them, but with little effect. At length, he climbed down from the stile and accosted his companion.

"Aren't you cold?" he demanded. "This is ridiculous. I shall give your people five more minutes, and then I'm taking the dog home. They can interview me at my cottage if they want. I'll give you the address."

He felt in his pockets for some paper but found none.

"That won't be necessary," said the constable, as placidly as before. "I can hear a vehicle coming now."

The vehicle turned out, in fact, to be two. George's old Land Rover, wheezing and coughing in the cold air, led the police vehicle up the hill. In the passenger seat of the Land Rover, Simon was relieved to see Jeremy. Clerical humbug or no, a familiar face meant an ally in this alien world of official red tape. The two men left George with the Land Rover while police procedure followed its course. A stretcher, two uniformed constables, a doctor and a police photographer weighed down with lighting equipment waited while the senior plain-clothes police officer asked Simon to show him the location of the corpse. Somewhat reluctantly, Simon led the way, and without either hesitation or any request for permission Jeremy followed them. The inspector either did not notice or did not care about his presence, and without some lead from senior authority, Simon's attendant constable evidently did not feel it incumbent upon him to quibble.

It was difficult to find the place again in the dark, and Simon found the sight of a human foot sticking up out of the ground no less disturbing now than on the first occasion, even though the shock of surprise was removed. He was glad to be allowed to return to the stile under police escort and leave the police team to their work. Jeremy, he noticed without much surprise, remained behind with the corpse.

~ * ~

Jeremy was fortunately able to establish his *bona fides* with the inspector by discovering that the head of the local crime squad had long ago been a college friend. Whether or not the acquaintanceship would be remembered by the police officer in question, and whether strictly speaking the detective-sergeant should have taken his word for the friendship, remained to be seen, but for the present it had allowed Jeremy to be where he wanted to be, at the scene of the crime.

The police team was well trained and well organised. They used their powerful lamps to photograph, measure and examine the body's position from every angle before they disturbed it. They took samples of soil and subjected the ground to a minute examination in the light of torches before they walked on it. A pathologist surveyed the immediate area for clues to the time of death. Finally, they removed the soil from around the corpse. Far from looking as though it had been tumbled anyhow into the ground, the man's body had clearly been arranged carefully, hands folded across the chest, although the grave it lay in was shallow and looked hastily dug. The corpse was covered roughly with an old horse-blanket, and the officer in charge pulled this back to reveal the face.

Jeremy bent forward quickly. The man had probably lain in the ground for some days, he thought, but the body had not yet become much decomposed. The face was pale and dewy and reminded Jeremy suddenly of a pheasant he had found dead on the road earlier in the week.

"Well," he said to the Scene of Crime Officer. "At least I can tell Mrs Althorpe her husband isn't dead, or if he is, at least not here."

"Mr Althorpe went missing earlier in the week, I believe," said the policeman, guardedly. "I was told about that before I came here tonight. You say this isn't him, though. Does that mean you recognize the man, sir?"

"Certainly I do. He's the brother of the farmer who brought us up here. His name is Brian Warrendon."

~ * ~

When Simon reached the stile on his way back from the copse, he found the area around it illuminated by the powerful headlamps of the police car and, to a lesser extent, by the mud-splattered lights of the Land Rover. As he passed the passenger door of the latter, it swung towards him. Simon looked up at George.

"D'you want to hop in?" the farmer said. "It's not very warm, I'm afraid. The heater doesn't work properly. But you're welcome to the shelter. You must be perished. Leave Dolly where she is... she'll be all right."

A farmer's attitude towards dogs, Simon thought with amusement. He pulled himself up into the Land Rover and shut the door.

"What are they doing in there?" asked George after a moment. He sounded unhappy, even anxious.

Simon looked at him curiously. "It must be annoying for you," he said. "I know I wish I'd never found the damned body. Still, I suppose if it hadn't been me it might have been Rose."

"Rose Althorpe? Was Rose here?" asked George. "I wish she didn't have to be involved in this. She's got enough on her plate, poor love."

"I met her up here by chance this afternoon," said Simon, hoping fervently that George would note the words "by chance." "She was walking the dog across towards Two Marks and I walked back with her. Dolly went into the copse. When I followed her, I found this... foot..." He stopped. "We thought it might be Clive... he's missing."

George nodded. "I'd heard he'd disappeared. News travels in a place like this, doesn't it? He hasn't been right since Robert's little escapade, though. I'd put it down to that." He paused. "Did this foot look like Clive's, d'you think?"

"I didn't really think about that when I found it." He smiled wryly. "I don't know that I'd know Clive's foot from anyone else's anyway." He paused. "Finding the body... it was horrible. I wouldn't have made a soldier, never mind a policeman."

"I was a soldier for a while," said George unexpectedly. "I wasn't much good at it, either."

Simon looked at him, assessing his age. "When did you do your soldiering?"

"I signed up for a couple of years when I finished school." Was he unhappy at home, Simon speculated, because of bad relations with his brother? "I didn't enjoy it much, but I think it was probably good for me, though I never had to kill anyone. Time in the army toughens young men up. National Service was a good idea."

There was a silence. It was broken by a rustling and thumping in the copse, and a heavy-footed procession of police officers began, led by a constable with a flashlight and completed by the detective-sergeant in charge and Jeremy. In between, came two stretcher-bearers and a blanketed, muffled body.

Simon jumped down from the Land Rover. "Is it…?" He smothered the question hurriedly and waited for the procession to pass. Jeremy said to him, "It isn't Clive, Simon. Will you go back and tell Rose? She must be worried."

"But…" Simon stopped. He had been about to ask what Jeremy would be doing. But Jeremy had already opened the passenger door and taken his place in George's Land Rover. Simon turned back to the sergeant, who was waiting to speak to him.

"I'd like to go back to the village and see Mrs Althorpe, Officer. The Reverend Swanson asked me to, just now. Her husband's missing and there's the dog…"

"I know about that, sir," said the policeman. "If you'd like to come with us, we'll pick up my car and Constable Hargreaves at the farm and go down there together. I need to ask Mrs Althorpe a few questions myself."

"But if the body isn't her husband's…"

"Just so, sir. But we need to know a bit more about her husband's disappearance, in these circumstances, I think."

Simon gaped at him. Questions bubbled in his mind like a cauldron boiling. Why had Jeremy gone to talk to George? Why were the police suddenly interested in Clive, if the body wasn't his? Where on earth was Clive, anyway? And how could he, Simon, protect Rose from all this? *Damn it, I can't protect anyone. I'm all at sea myself.* Bemused, he picked up Dolly's lead and followed the policeman to the police four-by-four. He sat dumbly in the rear of it, a damp muddy Dolly leaning on his legs, while it groaned and bumped over the fields to the farm.

Liz opened the door to them at Sundials.

"I'm Detective-Sergeant Moorcroft, Hampshire police. I'd like to speak to you, Mrs Althorpe, if I may," said this individual, smoothly. "This is Constable Hargreaves." He indicated the uniformed female officer beside him reassuringly.

Liz stepped back. "Please come in," she said. "I'm not Mrs Althorpe, I'm Liz Swanson, the rector's wife." She seemed thrown slightly off balance by the arrival of the police. "Oh, you're there, Simon. I didn't see you. Is everything all right?"

"Your husband stayed up at the copse," he replied. "The body isn't Clive's, he says. I came to tell Rose, put her mind at rest. Where is she... in here?"

He released Dolly from her leash, and without waiting for Moorcroft strode forward into the sitting room and halted abruptly in the doorway. Rose sat in an armchair by the fireplace with Robert curled on her knee, his head on her shoulder. She smiled at him wearily over the sleeping boy.

"Excuse me, sir," said an authoritative voice behind him, and Moorcroft removed him gently from the doorway and moved towards Rose. "Mrs Althorpe?"

She looked up, nodding. "The corpse we found—?"

"It isn't your husband's, according to Mr Swanson. But I do need to know a bit more about your husband's disappearance."

"Amazing how much more interested the police are in Clive now than they were when she first tried to tell them he'd disappeared," remarked Simon sarcastically to Liz, who motioned him to be quiet.

Moorcroft turned. "Circumstances change, sir," he said evenly.

Simon met his eyes firmly.

"I think perhaps I might find this interview a little easier if I spoke to Mrs Althorpe on her own," said the detective-sergeant, after a moment. "Mrs Swanson, would you take the boy up to bed, please? I'm sure Mr Hellyer will assist you. Wendy, will you sit over here with Mrs Althorpe, please?"

Simon, instinctively determined to attempt Rose's protection, at least, began to protest that Robert should be left with his mother, but Moorcroft's authoritative manner brooked no opposition.

Liz patted Rose gently on the shoulder. "We'd better take him, I think, Rose. Simon, will you carry him, please? He's too heavy for me, with those stairs to negotiate."

Simon lifted Robert gently out of Rose's arms, making apologetic grimaces at her as he did so. She smiled at him rather vaguely but showed no sign of anxiety.

"The sergeant is quite right, Simon," Liz told him, as they laid Robert on his bed. "I know Robert seems asleep, but there's no knowing what he may hear, just the same."

"Rose needs some support," said Simon angrily. "The police have no business to be asking her questions just now."

"Rose will be all right," said Liz confidently. "She's stronger than you give her credit for, Simon."

Simon sighed. It was probably true. Even in distress and unhappiness, Rose's inner resources seemed to carry her through everything. He, by contrast, felt more and more useless. "Okay," he said grimly. "But what happens when her strength runs out? What then?"

Fifteen

The village grapevine spread the news of Clive's disappearance with lightning speed. Until the police became actively involved, Rose had been able to hide Clive's absence from her neighbours to a certain extent, largely owing to the discretion of Jeremy and Liz, although some, like George, had heard a rumour. But now that she had been involved in the discovery of a corpse and was being interrogated by the police, rumour and speculation were rife. Within twenty-four hours, she was overwhelmed by telephone calls, most of them supportive, a few critical, and one mildly abusive. A few people, more inquisitive or less busy than the telephone callers, visited the house. Lesley came in on Monday evening on her way home from work and advised her to face it out; hiding would only fuel the gossip. She was grateful for the visit, but dubious about the advice. Others, perhaps less helpfully, guided to her door the local press and a representative of a national tabloid. But Maddie, that normally helpful and chatty neighbour, unaccountably made no contact with her at all, even avoiding her when they almost met in the road outside.

Meanwhile Robert, sensing his mother's inner tension, relapsed somewhat into his former condition, which so terrified Rose that she refused to answer either the telephone or the door, but locked herself into the house with only her son for company.

"This will have to stop," Jeremy said to Liz when she returned from an abortive visit to Sundials late on Tuesday morning. "Apart from anything else, the police will want to see Rose again, and they certainly won't put up with her ignoring them. And if Clive becomes a murder suspect, they'll want to search the house thoroughly, and she'll have that to deal with as well."

"*Nothing* must make them suspect her of any kind of wrongdoing," said Liz vehemently.

Jeremy raised his eyebrows. "I can't think they would be likely to. Still, I see what you mean. She's had a rotten time the last few weeks, and all this will only make it worse."

"I think the two of them had better come here to the rectory, don't you? And she could bring Dolly too… the kids will enjoy looking after her. We can filter the phone calls and visitors, and make sure Robert is all right. Playing with Chris and Bethan might help him get over whatever upset him, come to think of it, and Rose can keep him out of the way when the playgroup is here… not that they would worry, but they're a noisy lot for him to cope with at present."

"That's a good idea, Liz. I'll go down and fetch her," agreed Jeremy at once. "I suppose she won't answer the phone if you ring to say I'm coming?"

"I think not," said Liz. "And the answerphone's switched off. I tried. I don't think Rose has a mobile phone, has she? If she has, I don't know the number."

"Oh, well," said Jeremy philosophically. "I expect she'll let me in if I shout loud enough. Or I can always break down the door!"

Liz frowned at him. "I wish I knew how to work out when you're joking."

"A little mental exercise is good for you," said Jeremy enigmatically. "Will you come with me, or is it too close to playgroup time?"

Liz considered. "I think I'd have time," she said. "It might need both of us to persuade her, and she'll need some help packing and so on, I expect. As long as I'm back by one o'clock, Mandy can set things up. I'll give her a ring now."

~ * ~

That evening, while Liz was helping Rose make a list of things she and Robert would need for a possibly prolonged stay at the rectory, Detective-Superintendent Phil Brent came to visit Jeremy. The ruse by which Jeremy had gained access to the scene of Brian Warrendon's unofficial burial had been reported by Moorcroft to his superiors, and Brent had decided that Jeremy's brains might be worth picking on the subject of the village and its inhabitants.

The two men sat by the log fire in Jeremy's study, and the years rolled back in the firelight and the warmth. They had hardly seen each other in the twenty years since graduation. Even the annual exchange of Christmas cards had lapsed some years before, leaving only receding memories of a college friendship.

The first few minutes of their encounter were spent catching up. While Jeremy had been a fairly wild youth, whose career pathway into the Church had surprised his friends, Phil Brent had always shown indications of the solid and responsible citizen he had since become. Spreading a little around the waistline to match his broad shoulders, his fair hair fading to grey, it was still quite easy to believe that he had once been a talented Rugby Union threequarter for the Dark Blues and a college sprint record holder.

"It's certainly good to see you again," he concluded, smiling at Jeremy. "I'd no idea our paths would cross again down here. That said, it's a real bonus for me on this case. I'm sure you must know all the people here well, and that's what we shall need now. Though I shan't be conducting the investigation personally, I'm afraid."

"I'm quite interested in trying to solve it myself," said Jeremy mildly. "It's my patch, as you might say."

"You always were keen on solving mysteries, even when we were young," Phil observed. "Keener than I was, oddly enough." He smiled. "I'm surprised you ended up in parish ministry. Doesn't it get a bit dull for you, down here in the rural backwoods?"

Jeremy thought about that one. He had not intended, in the first instance, to become a clergyman. As an undergraduate at university, dreaming of a career as an academic scientist, nothing could have been further from his mind than a life as a country clergyman. Apart from his studies, his days and nights had been full: drinking his companions under the table, taking part in light-hearted pranks, or laughing at the imaginative graffiti which decorated the dirty walls of the city before the removal of the grime of centuries restored its pale-gold stonework.

"It does sometimes," he admitted. "And I get frustrated with rural folk's attachment to tradition, and their dislike of change."

"I seem to remember you were fairly radical in the old days," Phil corroborated. "You belonged to the old Leftie tradition at Balliol, it seemed to me."

Jeremy laughed. "And you were in the Monday Club, and as True Blue as they come."

"Still am. I'm surprised we managed to agree on anything, looking back."

"There are other things than politics," said Jeremy dryly.

Phil smiled. "Agreed. The College Christian Union was our meeting ground, really, wasn't it?"

"When I was converted, I just wanted to serve God," Jeremy explained more seriously. "And being a priest seemed to be the best way of doing that. Now... I'm not so sure I'm suited to it. I still want to change things when I think I can see a better way of doing them. Plus that love of mysteries you mentioned... that's often disapproved of by my parishioners. I expect getting involved in this murder mystery will set up a few backs, though I can justify that as part of my pastoral care of the parishioners. Already people are talking behind each other's backs, and peering at each other suspiciously. Someone must have killed him, and the probability is that it's someone local... at least that's what the villagers think. Until it's solved, this mystery will be like an open sore in our community, causing division and suspicion generally."

"Mmm. Well, we'll be doing our best to get it sorted out as quickly as possible. They've set up an incident room at the Village

Hall, and forensics have been all over the place where the body was found. What use that'll be remains to be seen. He was probably killed somewhere else and just buried there, I should think. There were marks of a four-by-four in the field before we took our own vehicles up there."

"George Warrendon was hedge-cutting along the top last week," Jeremy told him helpfully. "Though he'd usually use a tractor for that, I suppose."

"Well, forensics can probably confirm the vehicle from the tyre marks, but it won't get us very far forward, if it's George's Land Rover."

"Is George suspected?"

"We haven't got a very exact idea of the time of death yet," said Phil. "But I suppose he must be in the frame somewhere, with the bad relations between him and his brother. You could throw some light on that, I expect."

"A bit, perhaps," agreed Jeremy cautiously. He could see that priestly discretion and involvement in a police murder investigation might prove to be ethically difficult bedfellows. "But I don't want anyone to be arrested just on the basis of my speculations."

"We'd need good evidence for an arrest," said Phil. "My team don't arrest people just for the sake of it, like some forces do. I'd really appreciate your help on this, Remy. You know the people and their relationships. You know what's a likely scenario and what isn't."

"Well," said Jeremy doubtfully, "I'll do my best."

"Ambrose Harding will be in charge of the case. That's Detective-Inspector Harding. He's DS Moorcroft's superior. Give him what help you can, will you?"

"*Ambrose?*"

"He hates it," Phil reassured him. "But his parents didn't give him another to choose from. Everyone uses his surname. He's going to come down and talk to you tomorrow, I think, if that's convenient."

Phil heaved himself out of his chair and reached for the coat he'd hung on the back of Jeremy's desk chair. "They're looking for a new chaplain at Balliol, did you know?"

"Are they?"

"Yes. I saw it in the *Record*. If you're fed up of parish life, you could always apply. You might like to teach undergraduates theology and take a few chapel services for a change, you never know."

"I'm settled here," said Jeremy firmly. "And the children are happy at school. Liz has her preschool commitments, too. I don't think it's time for a change. Not yet, anyway. Besides, I'm not an academic theologian any more. I haven't time to keep it up."

"Well, we're none of us getting any younger," Phil pointed out. "Don't leave it too late, if you want to change course. The opportunities get less."

Maybe it's already too late, thought Jeremy as he showed his college friend out. His current job was a good one, from a career point of view. The status of rector conferred upon him more secure job tenure and a better position in the hierarchy. The next step upwards would be rural dean, and some of his colleagues had begun to suggest that he should consider it as he approached his forty-fifth birthday.

But suddenly, meditating on his career, he disliked quite intensely what he had become. Imperceptibly, the brilliant, but wayward, student, and the curate who had given offence with his quirky sense of humour, had turned into something very close to a typical middle-aged country rector. His liking for mysteries, and his (occasional) cynicism still provoked criticism; but he had learned to cloak those failings, along with his unpopular opinions and an impatience with current theological thinking, both liberal and evangelical, and its apparent determination to destroy the broad, inclusive Church he believed in. At first, he had worn a mask for the sake of his parishioners, then to avoid being sidelined in diocesan matters. Now, it seemed to him that the mask had taken him over; that he had sold his true soul for a clerical career which he had never really wanted, and which was in danger of stalling completely. Where was the fire, the sense of vocation, that had impelled him into the ranks of the clergy in the first place? Somewhere along the way, it had burned low, and he wasn't sure how to rekindle it. Liz was happy enough to support him in his work, but she had her own priorities, and didn't see it as her job to stoke his spiritual furnace.

~ * ~

DI Harding duly called in to see Jeremy on Wednesday evening. He was a youngish man with light brown hair and hazel eyes, quietly spoken and, at first meeting, mild-mannered, but a vein of cynicism ran through him which police work had done nothing to ameliorate. He amused Jeremy by calling him Reverend, in spite of an invitation to address him more informally. He seemed prepared to enlist the rector as an ally, and, on the strength of his friendship with the superintendent, unbend to him more than he normally would with members of the public. But any alliance between them would always be on his terms. Jeremy thought he would make a good negotiator, quick to see an advantage and press for it.

"You could be very helpful to me, Reverend, if you would," said Harding, as they sat in the rectory study, a tray of coffee to hand.

Jeremy smiled reluctantly. "I can try. Inside information, you mean?"

"If you like to think of it that way. You know these people, and I don't. You can give me a general background, tell me a few things about some of the people here, that kind of thing."

Jeremy nodded. "Fire away, then."

"Clive Althorpe, the man who's missing, for a start. Tell me about him. Is his disappearance likely to be significant, d'you think?"

Jeremy thought this a barbed question, and prevaricated. "I'm not sure what sort of significance you have in mind. But you've questioned Rose about it, I suppose?"

"Yes. She'd reported him missing, but of course we hadn't taken any serious steps, because it's the kind of thing that often happens, and then the husband turns up with some more-or-less convincing explanation for his absence, and no one wants us heavy-footing about in their domestic troubles."

"But now that there's a death to investigate, it matters."

Harding nodded. "Yes. We need to find Mr Althorpe as quickly as possible. He may know something about it... or he may be in danger himself."

"Or he may be dead."

"Yes... It's a possibility. We haven't said so to Mrs Althorpe, of course."

"I think the idea may have already crossed her mind," said Jeremy dryly.

"More likely he's simply absconded, though. Let's hope only temporarily. It would also help if we knew when Brian Warrendon died. The pathologist is doing her best, but on medical evidence alone there's not enough to fix time of death exactly. Most probably before Friday evening, she thinks. Warrendon's cleaner saw him last on Wednesday morning, but that doesn't mean anything. She very often didn't see him, she says."

"Clive Althorpe disappeared sometime on Thursday evening, I think." Jeremy hesitated. He felt extremely uncomfortable discussing his parishioners like this. It felt like a betrayal, although technically he was breaking no confidences. "Clive certainly doesn't strike me as a murderer," he added, grasping the nettle, "but there's no doubt that he and Brian Warrendon were at daggers drawn."

"Were they now? I had the feeling Mrs Althorpe was holding something back on that, although she didn't tell me any lies."

"No. She wouldn't. She's a very honest person, Rose."

"Mmm. But I don't think she told me the whole truth, either." He paused. "On good terms, are they... Mr and Mrs Althorpe?"

It was asked neutrally, almost casually, but that didn't make it any easier to answer. "Well... I'm Rose Althorpe's parish priest, Inspector. There's a possible confidentiality issue there."

Harding tried a different tack. "Has Mr Althorpe ever gone off without warning like this before?"

"Not that I'm aware of. He travels... on business, a fair bit, but I think Rose always knows where, and when."

There was a small pause. "Another woman, perhaps?" suggested Harding delicately.

Jeremy shifted uncomfortably. "Inspector, I'm not sure I can answer that question. She hasn't talked to me about it, and I wouldn't pass that information on if she had. If you're asking for my private opinion, though, not based on anything but a hunch, then I'd say yes, I think there's probably another woman in it somewhere. Possibly more than one."

"Well," said the policeman, "Mrs Althorpe may have to answer some questions of this sort from a barrister in court, eventually. But if she doesn't know about her husband's affairs, she can't give us any information about them, can she?"

Jeremy twisted his mouth in a little grimace. "There'll be an inquest, presumably."

Harding nodded. "Next week. That will be adjourned, probably, so that we can complete our enquiries."

Jeremy said slowly, "His death isn't very likely to have been an accident, I suppose?"

There was a pause while the inspector considered how much to divulge. On reflection, he appeared to realise that Jeremy was more likely to be helpful to him if he gave him some information in return.

"On the face of it, that's very unlikely. If it had been, then whoever found him would have informed us, surely? But instead someone buried him. That looks much more like murder. Still, the forensic boys are working on it. It can't be suicide, anyway. He was hit pretty hard on the back of the head with a heavy sharp-edged object." He paused. "It looks a fairly straightforward homicide, except for one odd thing. His thighs are broken."

"His thighs?"

"That's the medical evidence. His thighs were broken, almost certainly before he died. The pathologist reckons he didn't die instantly. Probably his head wound bled for a bit, but he was unconscious throughout. Something hit him very hard right across the front of the thighs, just above the knee."

"That sounds rather nasty. Why the thighs, I wonder? And what could it have been, to hit hard enough to break the bones? Do your forensic people have any idea?"

"Something that's left bruising, but not much else in the way of tell-tale traces," said Harding. "A long thin cylinder of some kind. An iron bar, perhaps."

"Not a piece of wood left lying around?"

"Rotten wood wouldn't break anyone's thighs, let alone clean through like these are."

"That's true. It does sound rather deliberate," agreed Jeremy slowly.

"Yes. The blow on the head might suggest there was a quarrel, and someone hit him with the first weapon that came to hand. Could have been a large stone, possibly. But an iron bar to the legs, or something similar... well, they aren't lying around on the hillside, are they?"

"They might be lying around in a farmyard, though."

"George Warrendon killed him and then moved him up to the copse?" suggested Harding, watching him. "He had quite a lot of scratches on his face... you saw that, I expect. We think he was probably dragged along, or maybe he fell on to rough ground."

"I just meant that the farmyard up there is only just off the main road through the village," Jeremy disclaimed hurriedly. "The Warrendons don't lock everything away, and they live mainly in the kitchen and sitting room at the back of the house. Anyone could take anything from that farmyard, and no one the wiser. Your sergeant commented on it when we went round there on Sunday."

Harding frowned. "Maybe. Most murders are committed by relatives or friends, as you probably know. Tell me about George Warrendon."

Jeremy explained the reason for both brothers farming in the village, and, somewhat carefully, about the bad blood between them.

"Means and opportunity, then," concluded Harding. "Motive, even, possibly." Jeremy had the impression that the inspector was well aware of his discomfort at this line of questioning. Indeed, he was clearly enjoying the opportunity to bait him.

Jeremy resisted the temptation to react. Instead, he said evenly and objectively, "Not the character, though. George is a victim, if anything, not a perpetrator. Even if he quarrelled with Brian, he'd never pick up a stone or an iron bar and batter him with it. It's impossible."

"Victims come to the end of their tether. They're often the most likely murderers of all at that point."

"No," said Jeremy, firmly. "I really can't believe George would kill someone, even at the end of his tether. Besides, if George ever took to violence, his weapon would be a gun, not a blunt instrument. He's a very good shot. If it were one of those vandals you read about who maim animals for fun, I might believe he could take a pot shot at him. But he wouldn't kill his brother… certainly not with a blunt instrument."

"We've managed to trace Brian's son, Eamonn Warrendon," said Harding, changing tack. "What do you know about him?"

"He hasn't been seen in the village for years, as far as I know. I've never met him myself. I don't think they were on good terms, but you surely don't suspect him, do you?"

The inspector did not answer.

"You need to find someone who saw him dead earlier than Friday evening," went on Jeremy thoughtfully after a moment.

"Someone who didn't inform the police," commented Harding drily.

"Yes, I suppose so."

"That would make them an accessory to the murder, if it was a murder. Does anyone else come to mind who had a grudge against Brian Warrendon?"

"A good many people had," admitted Jeremy.

"So I gather. Tell me more about him. Why was he so unpopular?"

Jeremy gave him a thumbnail sketch of Brian Warrendon's life, unable—though he tried—to avoid making clear the opposition of both Clive and George to the murdered man's development plans.

"We can rule out the women, I take it?" he asked when he had finished.

"I think so. I haven't had the final report from the pathologist yet, but I don't think a woman would have the strength for the blow. Not unless you can come up with a twenty-stone Amazon with muscles to match."

Jeremy laughed. "No, not in this village, anyway. I think that's a dead end."

"Well," said Harding, "I like to be thorough. And we'll have to search for Clive Althorpe, too."

He paused for a moment, and then added casually, "His ballpoint pen was found in Brian Warrendon's coat pocket, by the way."

There was a moment's silence after this bombshell. Then Jeremy asked, "How can you be sure it was his?"

"Neither the brother nor the son recognised it, but Rose did. His favourite pen, apparently. Kept it in the bureau in the dining room, but it isn't there now. Quite a distinctive one, with his initials."

"Surely he wouldn't be such a fool as to leave his pen on the body."

"Well, there I have to disagree with you, Reverend. Murderers are almost always fools... one way or another. That's why we catch them."

Jeremy met his eyes. They were humorous and neutral in expression, but the hint of steel was unmistakable. Harding had unbent a little with him, indeed had been more friendly than he had expected. But he meant to solve this case, and he would certainly not hesitate to make use of Jeremy in the process.

Sixteen

On Sunday morning, Rose left the sanctuary of the rectory, rather against Remy's better judgement, and went bravely to church. Her ringing was erratic, and after two unsuccessful attempts at plain hunting, Geoff opted for Call Changes instead. In spite of her obvious distraction, Rose's presence was appreciated, not least because Ben was still wheezy and had to be relieved at the tenor after a few minutes, so that only five bells could be rung for most of the time.

At service time, Rose almost lost her courage and left, but Ben opened the door into the church for her gallantly, his blue eyes twinkling beneath his wrinkled forehead, and Lesley steered her gently through it and into the ringers' pew before she could make up her mind to resist. Simon, left chiming the treble bell, had avoided communicating with her by word or look during the whole session.

"It'll do you good to stay for church," Lesley said, as she took her place beside her.

The service itself may have been beneficial, but the inquisitive comments and glances she received after it were not. Like a frightened rabbit, Rose froze, unable to break through the crowd and escape, while the questions and innuendo flowed over and around her.

Lesley had not been quite quick enough to manoeuvre Rose out of the door before the human deluge began, but she managed to make a passage through the congregation by means of a gimlet glare and the words, "Please let us through. Mrs Althorpe doesn't want a lot of fuss made." At the door, Rose paused only to shake Jeremy's proffered hand and receive the benediction of his warmest smile before being swept away to the rectory by Liz, turning to thank Lesley briefly over her shoulder as she went.

"She ought to get right away from here," said Liz worriedly to her husband as they washed up the dishes after everyone else had gone to bed that evening.

"I doubt whether she would be willing," Jeremy observed. "She didn't even want to leave Sundials, remember, for fear Clive would come back and find her gone. We had to leave several notes in prominent places telling him where she was before she would consent. And anyway, Robert needs to go back to school and get back to normal."

"I wish Robert would talk about the night he disappeared," said Liz, laying the massive rectory teapot carefully on the draining board. "It can't be good for him to keep everything locked up inside him in this way. Supposing someone sexually assaulted him, or something? We ought to be helping the police to find out."

Jeremy dried a spoon with extreme care, and no attention at all. "Jim Hollins gave Robert a very thorough examination, you know.. He hasn't been assaulted. And in any case, the police are much more interested in Brian Warrendon's death."

"I've heard a lot of talk in the village, as well. Robert's adventure has definitely been superseded by this new nine-days' wonder. I suppose that's a good thing in some ways."

"There's always so much gossip in this place," complained Jeremy with distaste. "You know I don't listen to half of it."

"I can never avoid listening to it," said Liz. "For your information, the village is divided in its view. The majority believe that Clive Althorpe's disappearance means that he must be guilty."

Jeremy sighed. "Hence their treatment of Rose this morning. Even though, for all we know, Brian may have been alive when Clive left the village."

"The others have a number of other suspects," Liz went on.

"Let me have them," said Jeremy heavily.

"You can take your choice among George Warrendon, Eamonn Warrendon, and Simon Hellyer. I have heard a few votes for Lucinda Warrendon, Geoff Longman, and yourself, but these are outsiders in the betting."

"You ought to take this more seriously, Liz," said Jeremy.

"I'm sorry. You're right, I should. But people's ability to make rumours and spread them always exasperates me. It's so irrational most of the time, even though, occasionally, they accidentally hit the nail on the head. And in any case, I can't believe in any of these suspects as *murderers*. There must be some other explanation."

"And who is the villagers' favourite?"

"Clive Althorpe, because he's disappeared. But of the others, George and Eamonn, I think. Simon has no known connection with Brian, and it's mainly the amateur crime buffs who favour him, because he found the body, though the fact that he was out with Rose at the time *may* just influence their opinion of his possible motives. He's not well known here, either, which means not well liked, mainly because he lives in Two Marks, and of course, he hasn't been in the district all that long."

"A foreigner," commented Jeremy with some amusement.

"That's it. He only came about two years ago. Doubly a foreigner. Now who's not taking things seriously enough?"

"*Touché.* And why are George and Eamonn Warrendon favoured?"

"George, because the brothers have been enemies for years… disregarding the fact that most of the hostility was on Brian's side. Eamonn because he inherits."

"Yes," said Jeremy dryly. "Even the slowest and most dim-witted members of the police force must have thought of that one. I saw Eamonn yesterday at George and Lucinda's, when he came down to sort things out at Home Farm. Apparently, Harding went to interview him last week. Much good it will have done him, though. Eamonn spent the forty-eight hours in question sorting out a business deal in London. Apart from short breaks in a hotel room for sleep, he was in company the entire time. When—or if—we find out exactly when Brian Warrendon was killed, we'll know how good that alibi is. But at present, I would think it's likely to be unshakeable."

"Unless we're *meant* to think he was murdered during those forty-eight hours," said Liz slowly. "Could the medical evidence be faked, so that, in fact, he was murdered much closer to the time he was found? Say Saturday morning? Anyone who had a really good alibi for Wednesday to Friday might try to make it appear he was killed then, not later."

"Phew, you have been thinking hard about this, haven't you? Quite the Miss Marple. Usually, you tell me I'm the one who's too curious about mysteries."

"This is close to home," explained Liz. "It affects all of us. And it *is* serious. The village won't be at peace until the mystery is solved."

"I should think the police pathologist would spot the kind of fake you're suggesting, in any case. And your ingenious solution won't work as far as Eamonn is concerned. He went home on Friday night and developed flu. He was in bed, attended by his wife, all of Saturday and Sunday."

"Oh." Liz scrubbed hard at a dish which had contained macaroni cheese and was reluctant to relinquish the traces.

"I'm more puzzled by the burial aspect of it," went on Jeremy. "Brian wasn't tumbled into the ground just anyhow. He was carefully laid out with his hands across his chest—almost reverently."

"Could he have been *buried* by someone else…not the murderer, do you think?"

"He most certainly could have been killed somewhere else, and then brought up to the copse for burial. Whoever buried him clearly didn't want him found too quickly. And his face was quite badly scratched. The police were thinking about him being dragged along the ground."

"It would have to be someone strong."

"Or two people…or a vehicle of some kind."

"An off-road vehicle!" exclaimed Liz.

"Perhaps. And there are a fair few of those in the vicinity," commented Jeremy.

"Are you going to tell the police?"

Jeremy shook his head. "They can think of that for themselves, I'm sure. I'll answer Harding's questions if I must. But I'm not going to help get anyone arrested unless I'm very sure they're guilty."

Indeed, in spite of his abhorrence for unsolved mysteries, until more evidence turned up, he could not believe that further deduction was likely to prove fruitful; his own proper services, by contrast, were much in need. Much as he disliked village speculation, there was no doubt that village people were very much disturbed by the events of the past few days. Some were angry at the disruption of their lives; some were frightened at the thought of violence in a place which normally seemed so safe; others were merely bewildered. In the face of such troubles, some, at least, would turn to him. They might inadvertently let drop some snippet of information which would help him to solve the mystery, and to solve the mystery would be worthwhile. But it must be a side issue, a leisure pursuit, something to be kept firmly in its place. His first responsibility, he reminded himself severely, was a spiritual one, to the unhappy people of St Martin-on-the-Hill.

~ * ~

On Tuesday, Robert returned to school. He had started to speak and act relatively normally once he and his mother settled in the rectory, and was clearly beginning to recover from his ordeal. He was cosseted by Fran and watched over carefully by Chris, Bethan and Rosemary on the journey between school and the rectory. He was still refusing to describe, or even to try to remember, the events of that fateful Wednesday evening, but it had been tacitly agreed among his well-wishers that his recollections should not be forced. He would tell them when he was ready. Rose was glad that he was well enough to go back to his lessons, but she could not resist going up to the school at lunchtime to check anxiously on his progress and was persuaded with difficulty by Fran that he was more likely to settle down if she kept away.

When she reached the rectory after her lunchtime sortie, she found that Jeremy had gone to Two Marks for a funeral, and Liz was due at a Women's Institute meeting at which she had promised to speak.

"Will you be all right on your own, Rose?" Liz asked anxiously as she changed into her smart shoes. "The children will be back soon, and Jeremy will probably come straight home from the church after the funeral. I don't think he's been invited back to the house with the mourners. Or you could come with me, if you like." She thought suddenly of the scene at church on Sunday morning. "Oh, perhaps that's not such a good idea."

Rose turned a wan but perfectly composed face to her hostess. "I'll be fine, Liz. Honestly. You're being so good to me, both of you, but you have your own lives to lead as well. Robert will tell me about school, and I'll make some tea for him and the twins. We'll be quite all right."

But she knew she wasn't all right at all. It was dreadful, not knowing where Clive was, or even if he was alive. *How can I sort anything out in my life,* she said to herself, *with all this hanging over me?*

But for once, Liz heard only her vocal reassurances. She smiled at Rose gratefully and walked briskly down to the village hall.

~ * ~

Contrary to his wife's prophecy, Jeremy did not drive straight home from the funeral. He stopped at Church End Cottages on the way back, to visit Ben Cartwright. The old man had been ailing for almost a fortnight, and this was Jeremy's second visit. He found him hunched in front of a log fire, looking wizened and pale, and coughing intermittently like an old engine backfiring.

"I thought you were a bit reckless ringing the bells on Sunday," Jeremy observed, taking the chair on the other side of the fireplace and politely refusing an offer of tea from Ben's wife.

"Can't leave the others to manage them bells without me, can I?" replied Ben with a touch of belligerence.

Jeremy smiled. "I know. But we all want you to be *well*, Ben. It's too early in the winter to take any risks with that chest of yours."

"Summat I wanted to tell you, Rector," said Ben painfully, straightening his back in the chair.

"I'm listening," said Jeremy encouragingly.

"It's about this 'ere killing. Wicked, that is, though Mr Brian had it coming to 'im, I reckon. But o' course we mustn't speak ill o' the dead," he added piously.

Jeremy hid his surprise. What could old Ben possibly know about the death of Brian Warrendon? He had been ill in bed with bronchitis during the whole of last week, surely? He said nothing, however, but waited for Ben to go on.

"I hardly ever see the man… keep out of 'is way if I can. But I were up near 'is farm one day last month, near the end o' the month, I reckon it was, and I 'eard a queer thing." He paused for breath, and perhaps also for effect.

"Yes? What kind of thing?"

"Well, now, there was Mr Warrendon, him what's dead now, Mr Brian, I mean, leaning over 'is gate talking to these two official-looking folk. Dark suits, they had, and briefcases, but they was wearing rubber boots. Couldn't make 'em out at all."

"Did you hear what they were saying?" asked Jeremy.

"That were the queer thing. I 'eard one o' them officials say to Mr Brian something about antiques."

"Antiques?" repeated Jeremy blankly.

Ben nodded. "That were it. 'A line in antiques', them were his words… or summat like. What d'you make o' that?" His eyes shone with excitement, illuminating the worn face.

Jeremy frankly did not know what to make of it. He searched frantically in his mind for a suitable response.

"You're a one for mysteries, see, Rector," explained Ben. "I reckoned you'd like this one."

"I can't say I understand it at all, Ben," said Jeremy. "But I'll give it some thought and see what I can come up with."

Ben nodded, satisfied. "That'll be right, Rector. You see what you can work out."

Seventeen

Rose made a meal for the twins and Robert and poured a cup of tea for herself and for Mike, who had come in late from school while they were eating. Then she took Robert upstairs to their room while Mike set about his homework and the twins settled down with the Lego in the playroom. She was anxious about Robert even though he seemed to be adjusting into school routine again, and she felt guilty that he was in a strange house rather than his own home surroundings. It was her fault for failing to deal with all the callers properly. It had seemed a good idea to accept Jeremy's offer of the rectory as a haven, but she knew that sooner or later she must return home. She had been there a week, in her own mind at least waiting for Clive to come home. But Clive was still missing.

Whatever's best for Robert, she told herself. That must be the right thing. Robert had been under stress at home with all the local media attention. He was safer, less likely to be disturbed here. *But surely Clive will come home soon?* She would not allow herself to consider the possibility that Clive was guilty of murder, or a victim of it himself, but the thought lurked in the recesses of her mind like a monster, seen out of the corner of her eye, roaring at her in dreams when she slept.

"Rose!" shouted Mike from below. "Rose, you've got a visitor."

After a moment's hesitation, Rose told Robert to go up and play with Chris and Bethan. She wondered who this visitor could be, against whom Mike had not considered it necessary to put up defences. Surely not Clive? Wary, defensive, but willing to trust Mike's judgement nevertheless, she made her way slowly down the stairs.

Simon was standing in the hall, and she knew at once that his reticence on Sunday had been due to discretion rather than indifference. The warm light which she had become accustomed to see in his eyes had returned, and the eyes themselves smiled at her above his tight-lipped mouth, which alone betrayed something of his inner tension.

"I promised Mike the loan of a geology book of mine. I'm on my way home, so I thought I'd just see how you are," he explained easily, for Mike's benefit. "Go and do your homework, Mike," he recommended good-humouredly.

Mike disappeared into the dining room, and Rose, overcoming her instinctive reluctance to act as hostess in a house where she was only a guest, led the way into the rectory drawing room.

"Liz is at a meeting," she explained," And Jeremy isn't back from the funeral yet."

"Yes," agreed Simon unexpectedly. "I knew about the funeral. Liz's meeting is my luck. I'd hoped to see you alone."

Rose coloured.

"Has it been really dreadful?" he asked sympathetically. "I think you're wise to come here until it all blows over."

"It was awful. Everyone ringing, and calling at the door, and then the press and the local radio got involved, too. But Remy and Liz have been marvellous." She looked at him curiously. "You don't like Remy, do you?"

"It's nothing personal," he said quickly. "As clergymen go, he's not so bad. I've no time for the Church."

"But you're a bellringer—" Rose began.

Simon laughed. "I love ringing. The two don't have to conflict."

"What did the Church ever do to you?" she asked. "It's unlike you to bear a grudge. Or is it just that you can't believe?"

There was a pause. Then Simon said, "Do you remember I told you about my mother?"

"She died when you were ten," supplied Rose.

"Yes. My father was a devout Christian. He prayed and prayed for her to live. The local vicar used to come round and pray with us. I had to pray, too. My father was sure she would get better. But she didn't."

"Oh, Simon!"

"When she died, he was devastated. He never really recovered from it. He went on living, but he withdrew into himself totally… became a complete recluse. No one was allowed into the house. He never went near a church again. I suppose it's unreasonable of me. It wasn't the vicar's fault. Maybe I blame God. I'm not sure."

Rose laid her hand sympathetically on his arm. She was lifted out of her own immediate problems momentarily by this further revelation of the emotional suffering of his childhood, which it seemed had dogged him all his life. After a moment, his hand moved to cover hers. He leant over to kiss her briefly, lovingly, though there was no passion in the kiss.

Then he moved away from her, to stand by the open fireplace, his back to the room. "How is Robert?" he asked, idly poking the remains of yesterday's log fire with his foot.

She accepted the change of subject serenely. "He seems so much better," she said. "He went back to school this week, and Chris and Bethan—and Fran, too, of course—are looking after him beautifully."

"Has he said anything yet about what happened to him that night?"

Rose shook her head. "I haven't dared ask him anything, in case it upsets him again."

A tentative knock at the door at that moment announced the arrival of the boy in question, with Chris on his heels. His eyes grew larger at the sight of Simon standing in front of the fireplace.

"I'm sorry," he stammered. "I didn't know—" He fell silent.

"It's all right, Robert." Simon crouched down to bring his own face down to the boy's level. "What's the problem? Can we help?"

"We've got stuck with a game on the computer," Chris told him from the doorway. "I think there's something wrong with the computer itself, actually… it's quite old now, and it wasn't new even when we first got it."

"It isn't as good as ours," added Robert. "Could we go home and play the game on our computer, Mummy?"

Rose hesitated, floundering in a swamp of conflicting thoughts. "I don't think…" she began.

"Can I have a look, Chris?" asked Simon. "Maybe I can work out what's gone wrong."

"Do you know something about computers, Mr Hellyer? That would be great. Come on, Robert." And Chris led the way upstairs, chattering.

Rose smiled. *I wonder whether there's anything Simon doesn't know about.*

Simon, climbing the rectory stairs in the boys' wake, had his own reasons for cultivating Robert's acquaintance. Not only was Robert an important adjunct to Rose, but he was, Simon felt sure, in need of help. Although he now communicated fairly freely, the experience he had had was still locked away inside him. Simon examined the computer problem and confessed that it was beyond his expertise, but he discouraged Robert and Chris from pestering Rose into taking them to Sundials. He did not know whether it was for Robert's sake or her own that she had left the house, but he was sure that going back would not be helpful for either of them.

"Perhaps your father will be able to sort out this computer when he gets home," he suggested hopefully to Chris.

"No, Dad's hopeless with computers," Chris informed him. "It's Mum who uses it most. She does a lot of the secretarial stuff for the Church Council, you know, on the word processor. But she understands how they work, too. She studied electronics."

Simon was impressed. Liz was clearly not the kind of woman he had imagined a rector's wife to be. Was it possible that he had misjudged Jeremy, too? He smiled at Robert. "Does *your* mother understand computers?" He thought he knew the answer, and the response did not disappoint him.

"No-o." Robert was trying to be loyal. "But I'm sure she would try to, if she had the chance. I don't think she's ever had much to do with them, really. She won't touch ours in case it goes wrong. Dad would be sure to say it was her fault, even if it wasn't," he added, with devastating candour.

"So this is where we are entertaining guests today," said Jeremy's voice from the doorway.

Chris looked up. "Hallo, Dad. Mr Hellyer was trying to fix the computer… something isn't working the way it should. But he couldn't."

"I'm relieved to hear it," said Jeremy. "In this house, the women are the computer geniuses, and we mere males look on and marvel. Come and have a drink with me, Simon, and let Liz deal with the problem up here. I heard her car in the drive just now."

"I'd better not," said Simon quickly. "I called in to give Mike a book I'd promised him, and somehow one thing led to another. But I've got a case full of exercise books in the car that I should be marking."

"Another day, then," agreed Jeremy equably. "You and I have never seen very much of each other, Simon, but this business has given me the opportunity to further an acquaintance I should have pursued months ago."

Simon tried to think of a suitable excuse. "I'm too busy" would sound specious, and possibly even rude; after all, he had not been too busy to bring Mike a book and take the opportunity to see Rose.

He had the uncomfortable feeling that the rector was all too aware of his involvement with her, and probably viewed it with disapproval.

"Has anything been heard of Clive Althorpe?" he asked instead as Jeremy brought him his coat from the cloakroom.

"Nothing. Rose doesn't say much, but she must be worried."

"If he's a murderer," said Simon slowly, "perhaps it would be best—for him, for Rose too—if he never comes back."

"And leave Rose not knowing whether or not she's a widow? or married to a murderer? or simply abandoned?" retorted Jeremy indignantly. "Do you really mean that?"

Simon met Jeremy's eyes and tried not to colour under his scrutiny.

"Besides," went on Jeremy, "You can't play games with murder. If Clive, or anyone else has killed a man, with whatever provocation, he can't be allowed to escape."

"Yes, I agree," said Simon quietly. "I was just thinking how difficult all this is for Rose." He hesitated. "Can you try to get her to come and ring tomorrow evening? It would do her good to go out for a bit."

Jeremy looked at him. "I think she'll want to stay with Robert, in the circumstances, don't you?" he said mildly. "But, of course, we'll offer to babysit, if she wants to go." His tone was neutral, but Simon felt sure that Jeremy was aware of, and resistant to, his deeper reason for wanting to see Rose on his own ground, away from the rectory.

"I'd like to talk this mystery of ours over with you sometime," Jeremy went on after a moment. "If we put our heads together, you and I may be able to see things a little more clearly."

Simon began to resist the suggestion at once, but Jeremy put out his hand. "Think about it. I would really value your help. And Simon—"

"Yes?" asked Simon warily.

"I only wear a dog collar six days a week, you know. Without it, I'm only an ordinary human being, like yourself."

In spite of himself, Simon laughed. "When is your day off? Not Sunday."

"Monday. You have a standing invitation to come round any time on Monday. Forget about the Reverend Swanson, Rector of St Martin's. Let me be Remy, lover of mysteries."

Simon took the hand tentatively and shook it. "Thanks. Remy."

~ * ~

The puzzle of Brian Warrendon's murder was occupying Jeremy more than it should have, both that evening and the next morning, even when he was saying Matins. The more he thought about it, the more he was convinced that George held the key to the death of his brother. Knowing George, he could not believe that he would have been able to murder his brother in cold blood, though it was always possible that some new quarrel had arisen, and he had struck out in the heat of the moment. But in that case, George would have called the emergency services and co-operated with the police, even if it meant manslaughter charges. He would never have left Rose in doubt about her husband's safety, or let others be suspected. No, he would take his oath that George had not been responsible for Brian's death. But he knew something and wasn't prepared to divulge it to the police.

That being so, Jeremy concluded, he had better go down to Church Farm and give George the chance to tell *him*.

~ * ~

George sat silently in the shabby sitting-room of Church End Farm, angular shoulders hunched over bony knees, and looked at Jeremy dispiritedly. Every day, he knew, he was withdrawing more into himself, more fearful of the discovery that must surely come, less able to deal with farm business, less able to face Lucinda and her waspish tongue. His wife did not seem to understand his grief for his brother, for the shared memories of childhood which now seemed more vivid than ever, and for the lost opportunity to find reconciliation. But their ways of thought had been poles apart for many years. He knew how inadequate Lucinda thought him, because he had never made Church End Farm pay as Brian had done with Home Farm and had never been able to provide the luxuries she craved. Her complaints against him were nothing new, yet they jarred on him now more than they had done for a long while.

He was glad of Jeremy's presence, and especially of his sympathetic silence. George was a typically inarticulate and instinctive churchman, committed to the Established Church and all it stood for, and irrevocably conventional in his beliefs and attitudes. He respected Jeremy for his position as rector, quite apart from the qualities of the man who held the office. Nothing needed to be said, for George was aware that Jeremy understood at least some part of his suffering and was attempting to share it with him. That, in itself, was a small crumb of comfort. It would be more comfort still to confess everything to Jeremy and seek some kind of old-fashioned absolution. He felt sure he could trust Jeremy. But the secret was not his alone.

For a few minutes, he struggled with this dilemma, while Jeremy sat impassively, elbows on knees, hands clasped under his chin, waiting. At last, he made up his mind.

"Remy, I need to talk to you."

"Yes," said Jeremy calmly, in a tone that conveyed both reassurance and encouragement.

George sat up and took a deep breath; and, at that moment, the doorbell rang.

"George!" came Lucinda's voice from the kitchen. "See who that is, will you? I'm busy."

~ * ~

Detective Inspector Harding had a very frustrating week. Clive Althorpe was still missing. Meanwhile, members of his team were working through a long list of people to be interviewed. Yesterday they had eliminated from the enquiry a number of villagers who had no particular connection with Brian Warrendon, and who could account for their movements reasonably fully for the forty-eight-hour period under scrutiny. But he had decided to interview the Warrendons at Church End Farm himself.

As he was ushered in by George, he noticed the rector rising from his chair.

"I'll come and see you another day," the clergyman began to say to George, but George waved him back to his chair. *Don't leave me,* begged his demeanour.

Harding noted this silent exchange with interest. People who felt the need of support from family or friends during police interviews usually had, in his experience, something to hide. He noticed that Jeremy made no further attempt to leave. Was that devotion to pastoral duty or mere curiosity?

He took George methodically through his family background, his relationship with his brother and their recent disagreements, before turning to his movements on the relevant days. The forensic and pathology experts were narrowing the time down… they now said he had been killed sometime between Wednesday morning and Thursday morning, and buried before Thursday evening, which was a little more helpful to a police officer charged with logging the activities of a number of people in the requisite period. But the time range still made the enquiries slow and cumbersome.

There was a silence while the farmer thought about the question. "I never go far from the farm," he said, slowly. "I don't really remember one day as different from the other, you know. Lucinda may be able to tell you what we were doing on those days."

Jeremy remembered that the Wednesday in question had been the day when Robert Althorpe went missing, and he and George had been among the searchers. He opened his mouth to remind George about this, thinking that it would pinpoint the day for him, and then closed it again. Until he knew what George had been about to tell him, it was better not to be too helpful to the police.

"I'll go and talk to Mrs Warrendon, then, sir," said Harding, closing his notebook and making for the door.

"She's in the kitchen," George told him. "Across the passage."

Ahead of Harding as he turned into the corridor was a room clearly given over to office work, but to the right he heard voices, and pushing open the door, he found a small, aristocratic-looking woman with fading fair hair in a tight bun at the back of her head and an old tweed suit haranguing an elderly domestic. Her complaint died when she caught sight of Harding's uniform.

"Detective-Inspector Harding," he introduced himself. "Mrs Warrendon?"

"Yes," she said, rather haughtily. "Can I help you?"

The question was asked coldly, and it was clear that she had asked it to keep him at arm's length, without any genuine wish to be of assistance.

"I'd like to talk to you, if you have a moment," he replied quietly. His eyes met hers, and the challenging flash in them, with the same quiet determination. "About the death of your brother-in-law."

"There is nothing for me to tell you," she said impatiently. "I know nothing about this most... most regrettable occurrence."

Harding thought this an unusual way of referring to the violent death of her brother-in-law, but he made no comment. "I would be grateful if you could spare me a few minutes in private, nevertheless," he continued quietly. "There are one or two questions which I need to ask, to complete my enquiries."

"Very well." She swept out of the kitchen, bearing Harding before her, and showed him into a comfortable drawing-room with an enormous brick hearth in which an inadequate fire was burning. The furnishings were as shabby as in the small sitting-room where he had interviewed George, but the room showed signs of attention; there were flowers in a vase on a side table and the cushions on the sofa had been hand-embroidered. Clearly this was Lucinda's own personal domain.

Lucinda had left the door ajar, and Harding noticed vaguely that there was still silence between George and the Reverend in the other sitting room across the passage. "Please sit down, Inspector." The words were polite, even welcoming, but the tone in which they were uttered was as frosty as ever.

"I want to ask you about the fourteenth and fifteenth of November," began Harding, embarking on his enquiries before anything else happened to disturb them.

"What about them?"

"Can you remember whether you and your husband were here the whole of those two days?"

"I can't be expected to keep a record of everything we do," said Lucinda with irritation. "I'm often away from the farm, shopping and so forth. I visit friends."

"Perhaps you would have a note in your diary?" suggested Harding.

She seemed about to tell him that his enquiries were not worth the bother he was causing her, but thought better of it. "I was at home during those two days, I think. Except for the Wednesday evening. I was out then."

"With your husband?"

"No," said Lucinda. "I wanted him to come with me, but—"

She paused, as though considering the degree of disloyalty towards her husband she was prepared to express to this policeman.

"But—" he prompted.

"George isn't very sociable," she stated flatly after a moment. "He didn't want to come. Which made it all the more infuriating when I came home and found that he'd gone out!"

"Gone out?"

"Traipsing all over the village looking for a small boy out for an evening without his parents' knowledge. Such a fuss."

"Was this absence reported to the police, Mrs Warrendon?"

"No, they found him quite quickly. He was perfectly all right."

"What time did your husband return that evening?"

"I can't remember exactly. About ten o'clock, I think. I rang up and asked him to come home. I needed him here."

"About ten o'clock."

"Yes. I arrived home at... about nine-thirty, I think it would have been, and found a note from him. I telephoned, and he came straight home."

These times may turn out to be important, thought Harding. *And the devil of it is, they're not going to be easy to check.*

"Are you aware of your Land Rover being used at any time that evening?"

Was there a moment's hesitation before she denied it? He couldn't be sure. "I went out in the car," she said.

"Your husband didn't use it to search for the missing boy?" he pursued, instinctively feeling that something was being held back.

"No, he did not. He walked down to the village... it's only a few steps. They carried out the whole search on foot. I should have thought your men would have ascertained as much, Inspector."

Harding sighed. Attack was a useful means of defence. "Could you tell me the name of your friends, Mrs Warrendon?"

"Which friends?" she asked sharply.

"The friends you visited on that Wednesday evening, the fourteenth of November."

"What on earth for?" she demanded. "I don't want my friends involved in this."

Her refusal looked suspicious, but he was well aware that it probably stemmed from snobbery. Her friends were (or they should be) above police investigation.

"We shall involve them as little as possible, I assure you," he said. "But it is necessary for us to make our investigations thoroughly. And in this way, Mrs Warrendon," he added thoughtfully, "we can eliminate you from our enquiries."

"Eliminate me?" Her outrage fought with something very like fear. "How could I possibly be involved in this... this sordid little death?"

"I don't suspect you of any involvement," he assured her, with a certain perverse satisfaction at having thawed the iceberg. "If you would be good enough to give me the names and address of your friends, I shan't bother you with any more questions."

With an ill grace, she complied with his request. He left the house wishing he could put her on the suspect list, against all the medical evidence, for a more poisonous woman he never wished to meet.

If he was still alive, Clive Althorpe seemed to him the likeliest contender for the role of murderer, though they must pursue this matter of a boy going missing that night… that might turn out to be important. Harding's working hypothesis was that Clive had most probably quarrelled with Brian Warrendon sometime on the Thursday afternoon, killed him, buried him, and then run. He had had time to make for the airports before the body was found, too. Once out of the country, it was twice as hard to trace a man, ten times harder to get him back. But the initialled pen in the murdered man's pocket… that was an odd circumstance. It led to Clive, but at the same time it was too pat a clue to be conclusive. However, if and when, they found him alive, he would have to be pulled in for questioning, maybe even arrested.

Eighteen

While Detective Inspector Harding and his fellow policemen were busy investigating Clive Althorpe's disappearance, the object of their inquiry was staying quietly but perfectly openly in a hotel in Penzance. Rose's probable anxiety was on his conscience, together with other wrongs he had done to her on various occasions, and he was still in agony over his failure to care for Robert properly, but, perhaps mercifully, he was unaware that the forces of law were on his tail.

The weather was very mild, if sometimes blustery, in the westernmost town in Cornwall and Clive spent much of his time walking along the coastline. He walked along the front to Newlyn and watched the boats of the much-depleted fishing fleet plying their trade in and out of the harbour. He walked to Marazion and along the ancient causeway to the fortress of St Michael's Mount, where once Phoenician merchants had sent ships to buy Cornish tin. He climbed the steep and craggy hillside to the gates of the castle and followed the tourist route across the windswept battlements and through the medieval rooms. There was something at once soothing and challenging about the place.

Walking quickly back across the causeway as the tide raced to join the two stretches of water it separated, he felt unexpectedly lighthearted. It seemed such a young, boyish, and carefree thing, having to run in order to avoid getting his feet wet; the last pedestrian across before the ferry again became the only method of reaching the Mount until the next low tide.

He had never enjoyed family holidays with Rose and the children. The children were too far apart in age and diverse in character to entertain each other, and Rose always seemed ill at ease with the exotic locations he chose, and therefore at her most irritating. A week at the office had seemed preferable. By contrast, 'working' trips with Olivia were lively and had the spice of being stolen and (at least in theory) secret, but he was always on his mettle, exerting himself to match her both in and out of bed, not able truly to relax. He had never before gone away on his own, nor visited an English tourist town, at any season, and the experience unlocked thoughts and emotions that had seldom seen the light of day.

One day, he caught the bus to Sennen Cove and walked up the cliff footpath to Dr Syntax's Head at Land's End. He turned his back on the twin headland, disfigured by a theme park and other tourist paraphernalia, and gazed out across the rocky bays towards Cape Cornwall in the distance. It was a clear day with a strong on-shore wind, and as he watched, the Sennen lifeboat appeared and streaked away towards the Cape on some errand of mercy, its crew as usual perfectly willing to risk their lives in the service of seamen in trouble.

They want the adventure, he told himself with a revival of his usual cynicism. *Courting danger for its own sake, to escape from the boredom of Cornish life. They aren't heroes.* It would have been easy to believe this in London, surrounded by other people with a similar outlook on the pettiness and selfishness of humankind. It was not so easy here.

He walked back along the cliff and down into the Cove, passing the lifeboat house as he reached the bus stop. Over the railing he could see the lifeboat manoeuvering to the return slipway, ready to be winched back into its shelter. A false alarm, evidently. No bus was due, and to pass the time he climbed the steps into the lifeboat house to watch the crew put the lifeboat to bed until the next emergency.

No mere love of adventure could explain the cheerfulness and dedication with which the men were working. Suddenly, Clive envied them the camaraderie and the shared joy of such a team effort. He left the boathouse, pushing a five-pound note hurriedly into the collecting box by the viewing window, and walked briskly along the sea front until the bus hove into view. While it turned round for the return journey, he walked back to the bus stop, shivering a little in the northerly wind. He showed his return ticket to the driver and sat down, metaphorically turning his back on the sea and its associations.

Back at his hotel, he asked for the key to his room, and was surprised when the receptionist hesitated.

"My key," repeated Clive with irritation.

"Yes, sir. Er... There are some police officers to see you." The receptionist indicated the waiting area behind Clive.

Clive turned. Two uniformed policeman arose out of armchairs and moved towards him. *Damn Rose!* he thought with annoyance. *I suppose she couldn't resist reporting my absence.* But there was a certain underlying menace about the two men as they came closer, which seemed unlikely to stem entirely from Rose's anxieties.

"Mr Clive Althorpe?" the leading and more senior of the two asked him as they came within easy speaking distance.

Clive acknowledged the identification.

"I have to ask you to come with me, sir."

"I'll come home when I'm ready," said Clive furiously. "You can tell my wife that."

"I'm sorry, sir. That won't be acceptable. Your wife is worried about you, it's true. But this is a police matter as well."

Clive frowned. "What the hell are you talking about? What police matter?"

"You are wanted for questioning, sir. In connection with the death of Brian Warrendon."

Without much idea of police procedure with regard to important witnesses in a serious crime, Clive at first assumed that he was actually being arrested for murder. He blustered and shouted, which made a bad impression on his captors, and then, belatedly realising this, tried to reason with them.

"Look, this is ridiculous. I don't know anything about Brian Warrendon's death. I didn't even know he was dead until you told me. You must believe that."

"We have our orders, sir," said the more senior policeman stolidly. "At present, we are not arresting you. We are just asking you to come with us voluntarily."

"You can't expect me to walk out of here just like that. Damn it, I'm staying here on holiday."

The policeman's eyebrows expressed some doubt at this explanation. "We can wait while you pay your bill and pack, sir," he offered.

Argue as he might, it soon became obvious that the policemen would not return to their base without him. He acquiesced with as good a grace as he could muster and prepared to leave Penzance in a police car—destination, Winchester police station.

~ * ~

On Friday morning, Jeremy took a telephone call on the rectory phone from Sergeant Moorcroft, asking for Rose.

"I'm afraid Mrs Althorpe isn't available at the moment," he said, cautiously, unsure in fact as to whether Rose was in the house or not. "Can I take a message?"

There was a moment's hesitation… even perhaps a whispered consultation in the background? "Could you give Mrs Althorpe a message, please? Her husband has been found."

"Found?" repeated Jeremy, thoughts of the searching of deserted woodland and the dragging of rivers running through his mind in sinister procession.

"I mean alive and well," amended Moorcroft. "Helping with enquiries at present here in Winchester." He disconnected briskly, and Jeremy put the receiver down.

"Liz!" he called. "Where's Rose?"

"Upstairs with Robert, I think. Do you want her for something?"

"Sergeant Moorcroft just phoned. Can you ask her to come down? I don't want to talk to her with Robert there."

Liz appeared in the kitchen doorway, wiping her hands on her apron. "It isn't bad news, is it? Clive isn't—"

"He's fine," Jeremy assured her. "He's at Winchester police station. I must go down to see him in a minute. When I've talked to Rose," he added pointedly.

Liz took the apron off quickly. "I'm on my way."

~ * ~

A few minutes after he had left the house, the phone rang again. Liz answered it, her hands smothered in flour. The caller display showed a number she recognised immediately.

"Hallo, George. How are you? And Lucinda?"

"We're all right, I suppose," George replied vaguely. "I wondered about Rose. How is she bearing up?"

"Pretty well, I'd say. We've just heard that Clive has been found, so that's bucked her up. Shall I call her to the phone, George? Or she could ring back later."

"Don't trouble," he said hastily. "She's had enough to cope with already, poor girl. And how is Clive? Is he all right?"

Liz pondered for a moment how much of what she knew about Clive should be considered confidential. "The police are asking him questions at the moment," she said guardedly. That at least would be common knowledge soon enough.

"They haven't arrested him?" asked George anxiously.

"I don't know," she said, finding that she didn't. "I think it's just part of the investigation."

George sounded relieved. "Thanks, Liz," he said. "Tell Rose I'll come down and see her one day soon. She's staying with you and Remy at the moment, isn't she? When's she planning to go home?"

Liz was a little surprised at this question, but she replied readily enough. "I don't know, George. I'll tell her you phoned anyway."

~ * ~

"Clive," Jeremy said severely, "You had better tell me exactly what you've been up to."

They were sitting in a plain, impersonal room, face to face across a small table.

Clive looked back at him a little suspiciously. In this situation, Jeremy's status was not altogether clear. Was he to be regarded as police stooge, or spiritual adviser?

"I'm not in the pay of the police," Jeremy told him, reading his thoughts. "I'm ready to listen. And anything you say will be treated as confidential."

"Like the confessional," said Clive.

"If you like." *What have you got to confess, Clive?*

"There's nothing secret about where I've been and why," went on Clive after a moment, slightly belligerently. "I just don't see why I should tell them anything more."

Jeremy raised his eyebrows. "Don't you think it might smooth your path a bit? You don't want to stay here any longer than you must, do you?"

"No, of course I don't. I don't have to stay, anyway. They haven't arrested me. But I don't know what they're after—I mean, I haven't done anything wrong—or nothing illegal, anyway. But what if I happen to have been at a particular place at the wrong time?"

Jeremy nodded cautiously. "They may be able to eliminate you from the investigation altogether if you give a truthful account of where you were and when," he pointed out. "It's your choice, of course, but I can't help thinking you'd be better to do that."

There was a pause. Then Clive said stubbornly, "I'm sure my solicitor would tell me to remain silent."

"You'll be able to ask him if you want. Have you contacted him?"

"I've asked the fellow who deals with all my business in London. They'll have someone in the firm who can come down." He was trying to sound calm, but Jeremy wondered whether a commercial solicitor, used to handling business deals and tying up contracts, would be the most helpful legal representative.

"You ought to have a lawyer with you now, really," said Jeremy. "Arrest or no arrest. They're questioning you, after all, even if you're here voluntarily. *Are* you here voluntarily?"

Clive did not answer him directly. "I'm getting fed up with this," he said restively. He looked directly at Jeremy. "Is Robert all right?"

Jeremy blinked at the change of subject. "Yes. I don't think he's said much yet about the night he went missing, but he's eating and sleeping normally now."

"Good." The word was said in a tone of great relief. Jeremy waited for him to ask after Rose, but his mind seemed to have left his family and returned to his own predicament. "Listen, Remy." He cleared his throat. "You know that what happened to Robert really upset me," he began slowly. "That's why I went out that Thursday… to try to think things out."

"It was very clear that you were upset," said Jeremy at once. "But I never understood the reason."

"It's hard to explain," said Clive. He paused, and Jeremy had the impression he was considering how much to tell. "I… I don't want to talk about that. I was upset, and I felt guilty. On that Thursday night, it suddenly got too much for me. I… it wasn't just Robert. Other things… Rose and…"

Jeremy thought about what Rose had told him. "Simon Hellyer called, just before you left," he prompted. It *might* not have happened in that order, but he thought it probable.

Clive looked up quickly. "You know about that? I don't know what's between them—if anything—but it was all of a piece. I felt I'd lost control of my life completely. I went out for a walk."

Jeremy waited tautly for Clive to confess to meeting Brian Warrendon, a quarrel, manslaughter, even murder.

"Then I suddenly felt I couldn't go home. I needed some time to think. I caught the bus to Basingstoke, took a train to the West Country. I stayed the night in Exeter, first… that was as far as that particular train went. But it didn't seem far enough, somehow. Penzance was better. I've done a lot of thinking, tried to sort myself out."

There was a silence. "And have you?" asked Jeremy quietly.

"A little, perhaps. Those bloody policemen picked me up before I was ready to come back."

Jeremy thought that probably explained a great deal. "There isn't a regular bus from St Martin to Basingstoke on Thursday evenings," he pointed out. "What time did you say it was when you went?"

"I left the house about seven, I suppose. I wandered about a bit first. But there *was* a bus… on the main road. It didn't come into the village. I didn't think much about it. It said 'Basingstoke' on it, and I flagged it down and got on."

"You didn't have your wallet with you," Jeremy reminded him, remembering what Rose had said.

"No. I had enough cash in my pocket for the bus. I bought the ticket to Exeter on a credit card. I always carry one in my coat pocket, just in case."

Jeremy looked at him thoughtfully until he flushed.

"Look, what's all this third degree? You're as bad as the police."

"It's all right, Clive. I simply wanted to be sure you were telling the truth. What about the pen?"

"Pen? What pen?" asked Clive. He sounded surprised, but Jeremy was sure that the police must have asked Clive about his ballpoint pen, found in the dead man's pocket. It was something that badly needed explaining. However, perhaps if they had not, as yet, asked that question, it was unwise for him to pre-empt them.

"Do you believe me?" Clive asked, with pathetic eagerness.

There was a small, pregnant pause. Then Jeremy answered slowly, "Yes, I think I do."

~ * ~

Jeremy returned from his interview with Clive in a very thoughtful mood. He had failed to persuade Clive to co-operate properly with the police, Clive having declared that he had nothing to tell them which would be in the least material to the case. Unfortunately, Jeremy was uncertain how the police would proceed. Without anything more than very circumstantial evidence as to his guilt, they would be unable to justify proceeding with a prosecution, or even arresting him, and since he seemed willing enough to take part in their enquiries, there was no point. If they arrested him, it would be because they had discovered new evidence that tied him closely to Brian's death, evidence which would lead swiftly to prosecution.

He wasn't sure how long they would be likely to keep on questioning him without arresting him, but surely it couldn't be long? He wondered whether there was any limit to the number of questions they were legally allowed to ask *without* arresting and charging him. New legislation and police guidelines came along at bewildering speed, and he had lost track of the technicalities. But Clive was clearly in an unusually vulnerable state psychologically. Jeremy couldn't help thinking that the sooner the police found the real culprit, and let Clive go back to Rose, the better.

He had said sincerely to Clive that he believed him, but there were still areas of doubt. This Basingstoke bus business was baffling. Had Clive got a lift to Basingstoke? But if so, why not admit as much... unless he was shielding someone? He must find out whether a bus really did run on the main road to Basingstoke at that time in the evening. Perhaps there was a National Express coach that came up via Winchester. But that still left the ballpoint pen in the dead man's pocket unaccounted for. There had been a point in his account of the previous week where he had shown signs of hesitation, as though some further confidence had been hovering in the background. Whatever it was, it had not transpired. Although Jeremy felt fairly certain that Clive was not guilty of murder, it was a distinct possibility that he might be guilty of something else. The only question was, did that something else involve a crime or simply a moral lapse from which he was justified in excluding the police altogether?

He accepted a cup of tea from Liz absently, and took it to his favourite chair in the study. Without a fire, the room was rather cheerless, but in his absorption Jeremy hardly noticed. He drank the tea, reached for his pipe, and stuck his legs out in front of him towards the non-existent warmth in the hearth.

The best way of sorting out Clive Althorpe's predicament, he reflected, was to find the real murderer... if there was one. Of course, if Brian's death had been an accident, discovering the truth about it might be even more difficult. He reached for a piece of paper and began making notes.

The telephone rang at this point in his deliberations and a parishioner reminded Jeremy he had promised to take communion out to her elderly bedridden mother at Two Marks. It was a normal port of call for him once a month, but in the pell mell of events surrounding Brian Warrendon's death he had completely forgotten.

"Tell her I'll come tomorrow," he promised.

Nineteen

The following Sunday marked the beginning of Advent. Minds in St Martin on the Hill were turning towards Christmas preparations: inviting family and friends to stay, buying suitable presents for the near and dear, ordering the turkey, baking Christmas cake and mince pies. Jeremy loved the season of Advent. He enjoyed the sense of anticipation it brought him in remembering afresh not only the importance of Christmas, but the promise that one day Jesus would return and set the world to rights. For him, a world in which the Messiah had never been born would be a cold, hard, uncaring place, and he brought this conviction to his Advent and Christmas celebrations in church. The Advent wreath with its five candleholders was each year unearthed from the vestry cupboard, and five new candles bought to go in it. Lighting the candles week by week seemed to Jeremy a wonderful way of building up to Christmas itself, and the older children in the congregation always loved to help him. They gathered round while he sorted out the matches and vied with each other to be chosen as mature and sensible enough to be trusted with the naked flame.

This Advent, however, he was conscious of undercurrents in his congregation that owed little to the lighting of candles, and nothing at all to the season of goodwill. The weather had turned stormy, with one gale following another, and everyone was on edge. The fact that the mystery of Brian Warrendon's death was still unsolved had fostered speculation and suspicion. Clive Althorpe, still essentially an outsider in spite of his long-term habitation in the village, had seemed a suitable candidate for the part of villain, at first, but since the police had not yet charged him, the likelihood of him being a murderer had waned. Speculation had turned inwards again, so that gossip ran riot around the village after every new suspect thought up by the irresponsible and the vindictive. The atmosphere at the service was uncomfortable, and Jeremy shook hands with his parishioners at the end of it unhappily aware of the anger and fear in their hearts.

Rose was perhaps regarded with a little less sympathy now that her husband had reappeared, but also with less overt speculation. Many people preferred to turn their back on the wife of someone who had been arrested on suspicion of murder, and she fielded the occasional barbed question or comment with more confidence. She was glad to escape with Jeremy, however, when he walked back to the rectory to collect his car before going on to another service at Southover. Being with the Swansons gave her a feeling of security, especially as long as the press were having a field day with her family's personal affairs, but she was beginning to doubt whether she should trespass on their hospitality much longer.

"Still worrying about staying on with us?" Jeremy asked her as they walked along the road by the churchyard wall, divining her thoughts with ease as he often did. "You can stay as long as you like, you know. We've all enjoyed having you and Robert. And didn't I hear that Sundials was being subjected to forensic examination"?

She nodded. "I think they've finished for the moment, and I don't think they can have found much—because I honestly don't believe there's anything to find. I must admit I hated them poking about among our possessions. It's worse than being burgled!"

"The press will poke about, too, you know, in a different way. They shouldn't, now the case is *sub judice,* but I expect they will, and all your secrets will be laid bare."

She shivered. "That's a horrid thought. I haven't got many secrets, but I bet Clive has a few he won't want trumpeted round the Sunday papers." She looked up at him. "Staying here has been wonderful, and you and Liz have protected me so well. But I'm beginning to feel rootless, like a refugee. I need to go back home and build again. Perhaps another few days, though... until Clive comes home. They must run out of questions soon, mustn't they? I'm certain he didn't have anything to do with Brian's death."

Jeremy wondered why Clive wasn't sleeping at home. He must be staying in Winchester while the police questioned him. If they hadn't arrested him, they wouldn't keep him in a cell. He must be free to come and go. He thought back to their conversation. Clive had said he wasn't ready to come home. If he continued to say nothing to the police, they would have to give up, or go the whole hog and charge him with murder. But apart from the unexplained pen in Brian Warrendon's pocket, he didn't think they had enough evidence.

He looked down at Rose as he pushed open the rectory gate, sensing that she was summoning up the courage to ask him something. "What's the trouble?"

"Is—" She swallowed. "This murder. Is Simon suspected, too? The way Inspector Harding spoke to me about it—I mean, I know Simon found the body, but if you'd seen his face... He obviously knew nothing about it at all. And Simon was with me the whole of Wednesday evening, until Clive rang and told us about Robert disappearing—we were at a Tower Meeting, though nobody else came, and then he and I searched for Robert together. And surely, he was teaching all day on Thursday? He couldn't have done it... he wouldn't, anyway. What reason could he have? I *know* he must be innocent. But is he under suspicion?" she finished, with a gulp of fear.

Jeremy patted her shoulder. "It's all right," he reassured her. "There's no question of Simon being suspected of anything, as far as I know. Stop worrying."

They walked on in silence for a few moments.

"It seems to me," observed Jeremy dryly, "That you're a lot more concerned about the possibility of Simon being suspected than you are about Clive, who's actually under suspicion."

"Yes," she replied frankly. "That's quite true." She hesitated, then went on bravely. "I'll tell you about it, if you like. Not today," she added quickly. "You have to get over to Southover, don't you?"

Jeremy opened the front door and ushered her into the rectory. "Tomorrow," he said.

"That's your day off," protested Rose.

"Makes it easy to fit you in," he said, teasingly. "But if it'll wait, we'll say Tuesday. When I've said Matins."

"Yes," she agreed, and hoped her courage wouldn't desert her in the meantime.

In the event, Jeremy had to fit her in between appointments, much to his annoyance. He wished he had insisted on giving her unlimited time on his day off, though no doubt Liz would have objected. But to squeeze something so important in between visits that would, quite likely, turn out to be a waste of time, was very frustrating.

He came in from saying Matins in the cold church to find Rose waiting patiently for him in the drawing room, and the answer phone winking busily to alert him to messages.

He picked up the receiver to play the messages silently and confidentially, and then went to the door to ask for his wife's help.

"Liz!" he called. "Can we have coffee in my study, please? I want to talk to Rose for a few minutes before I go over to Two Marks."

Rose followed him into his study. "Remy, you shouldn't ask like that," she reproached him. His brusque demand had been all too reminiscent of Clive. "Liz is probably busy preparing lunch or something."

Jeremy raised his eyebrows. "Preparing for preschool, I expect," he said, "Don't worry," he added. "Liz accepts it's part of her role to help me this way if she can. And she'll soon tell me if I step out of line. Anyway," he added with a smile. "I did remember to say please."

Rose sat down. She felt slightly rebuffed by Jeremy's reply, as though he had told her in so many words not to interfere between husband and wife.

"Sorry," she said, attempting to explain. "I suppose it's just that it's such a horrid feeling, to be asked like that, as though one's a slave or something, with no brain, no sensitivities and no rights. But I know you don't bully Liz, and she *would* stand up to you if you did, much more than I've ever managed to stand up to Clive!"

Jeremy looked at her, half smiling. "Is the worm turning at last?" he asked, not unkindly.

"Yes," she said defiantly. "I think it is."

"Do you love Simon?" he asked her. "Is that all part of the turning?"

That was the worst of confiding in Remy, thought Rose. He never failed to put his finger on the nub of the matter immediately, before one had had time to explain one's own carefully thought out angle.

She tried to cast aside the rounded, rosy, comfortable picture she had built up of herself and Simon living in romantic and domestic harmony and answer the question truthfully and realistically. "He's such a wonderful person, Remy. I know you two don't get on that well... he's suspicious of the Church as an institution, and you don't like atheists, I expect. But he reads, and thinks, and... I think he loves me." That was the really important thing. When she was with Simon she felt loved, even though he hadn't said the words.

"You're not sure?"

"Sure about what?"

"That Simon loves you."

Her face developed a mulish look.

"Oh, I don't mean to say he's deceiving you," said Jeremy. "But has he *said* he loves you?"

Shaken, Rose tried to answer truthfully. "Not in so many words," she admitted at last, "But..."

"He finds you terribly attractive," said Remy. "I can see that. But he's never been married, or even lived with someone, has he? No long-term partner or children."

She shook her head. "I don't think so. Not as far as I know, anyway." She thought he would have told her about it, that evening they had spent together so intimately.

"Well, sometimes when a man gets to Simon's age without forming a long-lasting relationship, it's because deep down he doesn't really want to commit himself. Or he struggles with being close to someone. Some men like that are gay and aren't ready to admit it, though I don't think that's the case with Simon. Still, I don't want you to jump from one difficult relationship straight into another."

Rose thought about it. Her heart told her unreservedly that Jeremy's analysis was wrong, that Simon did love her and was committed to her; that he simply hadn't found a woman he could love properly before. But, she could see how things might look from the rector's admittedly much more objective point of view. It was hardly likely on the face of it that Simon, of all people, would fall for her rather than for a younger, more beautiful woman. But Jeremy hadn't seen Simon's tenderness towards her when Robert went missing, or his support for her during these last two difficult weeks. Surely, these were evidence of caring love, not simply passion?

"I don't think it's like that," she said, stoutly maintaining her position. "He *does* care about me."

But she could not altogether banish the memory of that fateful Wednesday evening, when passion had so nearly had its way with both of them. There was no doubt that the first impetus towards a romantic relationship between herself and Simon had been that strange, inexplicable personal attraction which had nothing to do with the mind, but instead seemed to arise somewhere in the deeper recesses of the body and resisted all attempts to rationalise and confine it within the bounds of civilised behaviour. Could that attraction be relied upon to deliver a stable emotional relationship, which was what she desperately needed?

"And Clive?" asked Jeremy.

Here, Rose felt herself to be on firmer ground. "Clive destroyed the foundations of our marriage a long time ago," she said firmly. "He treats me with contempt. *And* he's been having an affair with his secretary for years. Remy, even you can't ask me to stay with him."

"I'm not asking you to do anything, my dear Rose," he said gently. "Your life is for you to live. If you've made up your mind to leave Clive, whether to be with Simon or not, then I shan't try to persuade you out of it, though I think you must also consider Robert's needs." He smiled at her, but then added, devastatingly, "But are you sure you have made up your mind?"

"No," she said miserably. She passed her hand over her face. "I'm not sure at all. Oh, Remy, I do so want you to understand."

"I think I do understand, Rose, and I have a lot of sympathy for you, too. But I can't give you advice unless you want it. And even then, only you can decide whether to take it or not."

"I want to know more about the rights and wrongs," she said suddenly, eagerly. "So that I can make the right decision. Do you think divorce is always wrong? Surely, it's better than a lifetime of misery for everyone? Even the children?"

"I think divorce is always painful for everyone," he told her. "Have you thought of how Robert will feel? It's a tearing apart of a whole family, remember. Clive is Robert's father. Nothing can change that. The Church would say—"

"No, I don't want to hear what the Church thinks," she interrupted him. "Tell me what you think. I... I value *your* opinion."

He smiled a little ruefully. "I suspect what you mean is, you'd like me to sanction what you want to do."

"Oh, Remy," she said. "Don't say that! I truly want to know what you think. As long as it's you, as a man. Not the Church and its dogmas."

"Well," he said. "I can leave aside the fact that I'm a clergyman, if you want, and speak for myself, not the Church. But I'm still a Christian, Rose. And I take marriage seriously."

"So do I! Do you think I would have stayed with Clive this long if I hadn't?"

Even as she said it, Rose wondered suddenly whether this was, in fact, true. Was it her Christian beliefs that had made her stay? Or was it that until she met Simon she had lacked the strength to leave, had had no overwhelming reason to rock the boat? Looking back, it seemed to her that inertia might have had as much influence as anything.

"Christ spoke of adultery as though it destroys something fundamental in a relationship," Jeremy told her. "As though it breaks the whole basis for that relationship. In Jewish society, divorce was completely in the hands of the man, so he was speaking of a woman's unfaithfulness, but I think the same holds good for adultery by a husband, certainly for persistent adultery. That's a matter of choice, not a moment's aberration."

"You mean that my marriage is over as far as God is concerned?"

"Let's say I could not condemn your action if you left Clive because he had been persistently unfaithful. But that is not to say that you *have* to leave. Relationships can be rebuilt, especially where there's half a lifetime of marriage on which to build, and where there are children to be considered. There's nothing to stop you making a fresh start. Many people in a similar situation have."

Rose felt she was being put through a wringer. The thought of trying to rebuild anything of her relationship with Clive was too painful even to contemplate. It was impossible. Even if Simon had not been waiting to give her a home, she could not consider trying to revive her marriage.

"Clive wouldn't want a fresh start," she said. "He doesn't see any need to change. He'd go on just as before."

Jeremy wondered whether she was right about that. When he had visited Clive at the police station, he had become aware of some very profound transformation that was taking place in him, though he had no idea what the result would be.

There was a knock on the door and Liz brought in a tray with two cups of coffee on it. Rose jumped up to help her, trying to apologise for the extra work.

"Nonsense," said Liz. "I was making coffee for Mike and Lorna and myself, anyway. What's two extra?" She looked hard at Rose. "Are you all right? What's Remy been saying to you now?" She turned on Jeremy rather fiercely. "Don't put her through any more, Remy. She's had enough."

"I'm not doing anything of the kind," he said, reassuringly, but perhaps a little defensively. "Rose *asked* to talk to me."

"Well," answered Liz, looking from one to the other, "Don't make her miserable, that's all I ask."

She gave Rose a quick hug and went out, shutting the door behind her.

There was silence. Then Jeremy said, "I'm sorry, Rose. You did ask me what I think. But don't feel I'm sitting in judgement. I shan't condemn you, whatever you do. I know you've suffered a great deal from Clive's heartlessness."

She gave a smothered sob.

"One thing I do ask, though," he went on gently. "When you speak to Clive, don't be too hard on him… not when he first comes home. He's been through a lot, too. A man doesn't just walk out of his house and go away for a week to think about things if he isn't struggling pretty hard with the circumstances of his own life. You may even find he's actually learned something from the whole experience… stranger things have happened. But, just at first, he's going to feel very vulnerable, especially with the police questioning him. Be gentle. Don't throw all this in his face as soon as he walks through the door. Or he may go to pieces completely."

Rose sighed. "I used to feel sorry for myself, you know, Remy. I used to feel that if Clive thought a bit more about me, everything would be fine. Now I *have* found the courage to escape from being married to him, so I don't care much what he thinks, and suddenly there are so many more problems to take the place of that one!"

Jeremy smiled. He leaned over and put his hand over hers for a moment. "Come and talk to me again if you need to," he said.

Rose looked at the clock on the mantelpiece. "It's time for you to go to Two Marks, isn't it? Thanks, Remy. I've probably stolen your coffee break."

"It doesn't matter." He got up, putting his empty coffee cup on the tray. "Stay here and finish yours… you've hardly touched it."

Impulsively, Rose reached up and kissed his cheek. "You're so good to me, you and Liz," she said. "It must be difficult, being good to people for a job. How can you ever switch off and relax?"

Jeremy laughed. "I really don't think of it that way," he said. "At least most of the time I don't. It's my life, and I'm lucky enough to be paid for doing what I'd want to do anyway."

"Do you mean that?"

Jeremy thought of his reservations about so much of his existence as a clergyman, particularly here in this village. This was neither the time nor the place to air them with Rose. In any case, the pastoral aspect of his work was the one with which he felt most comfortable.

"I sincerely mean it," he said to her. "And now I must go and deal with another part of the job." He realized that, without meaning to do so, he had effectively acknowledged that the part in question was less congenial to him. Discretion and sincerity were poor bedfellows, he reflected as he opened the door for Rose.

Liz was in the hall. "I was just coming to remind you it was time," she said to her husband. "Was George in church?"

Jeremy blinked at this apparent *non-sequitur*. "I didn't see him. Did you, Rose?"

She shook her head. "I'm sure he wasn't there. Nor Lucinda... but then she doesn't often come."

"Only Christmas and Easter would be important enough festivals for her," suggested Liz.

There was enough acid in the comment to make Jeremy frown slightly. It was easy to say things in front of Rose which one would hesitate to share with other parishioners. All the same...

"I asked because I was a bit anxious about him," Liz went on. "He rang to ask how you and Robert were, Rose... on Monday. I'm sorry, I forgot to tell you. But he specifically said not to ask you to ring back, it was just an enquiry. Only, I felt he seemed a bit strained... unlike himself, somehow. And it's unlike him to miss church on Advent Sunday. Perhaps you should visit him, Remy."

"I'll make it a priority for this week," agreed her husband. "I haven't spent as much time with George as I should." *I'm sure he wanted to tell me something the other day, but just couldn't bring himself to do it before Harding came heavy-footing in. And then he just sat in silence until I had to go away.*

"I'm sure he's grieving for Brian," said Rose, thoughtfully. "Even though they were at odds for years."

"Guilt added to natural grief is a potent mixture," said Jeremy. "Thanks for reminding me about George, Liz."

He smiled at both women and set off in the car for Two Marks, yet again painfully aware of his own inadequacies. How often Liz must feel unappreciated and neglected, when he allowed his parish work to take up too much of his time, and perhaps he *had* been peremptory in his demands this morning, as Rose had suggested. How full of Church teaching his mind seemed to be, and how desperately empty of any practical solutions to the problems people were facing every day. He knew that he had highlighted the real issues for Rose, and perhaps that had been useful. If, that is, he thought bitterly, one could think it useful to strip away the pitiful shreds of outward composure with which a woman had clothed herself and replace them with raw realism and pain. Sometimes he wondered whether his belief in the benefits of such counselling was anything more than belief in an illusion.

~ * ~

DI Harding was having yet another frustrating week. Clive Althorpe had still refused to say anything, and soon they would have to decide either to charge him with the murder or give up questioning him for the moment. In his own mind, Harding was still convinced that Clive at least knew something about Brian Warrendon's death, even if he had not killed him. But he was perfectly well aware that there was little hard evidence to connect him with the murder, and some to point away from him. Yet if he abandoned Clive, he had no other suspect. Other lines of enquiry had not turned up much in the way of positive evidence as to where or how Brian Warrendon had died, nor had the pathologist come up with any plausible explanation for his injuries. The forensic experts were still painstakingly going through every shred of evidence they had. Something incriminating might still turn up.

On Thursday, after lunching on a rather tired sandwich provided by Sergeant Moorcroft from a selection that had languished in the fridge overnight, Harding decided to speak to Rose Althorpe again. It seemed unlikely that Rose was guilty of aiding and abetting her husband in a murder, but further questioning might help to clear up this aspect of the case. Clive was hiding something, that was clear. Perhaps Rose knew what it was. He knew that Clive hadn't in fact gone home during their questioning… he had been staying in a B&B in the centre of the city, apparently, which was, in itself, quite odd and possibly significant. But it also meant it was unlikely that they were colluding on a story.

Liz Swanson opened the door of the rectory to him and Wendy Hargreaves and ushered them into the sitting room where Rose was rather desultorily reading a magazine.

"I'm only doing my job, Mrs Althorpe," he said to her, slightly defensively. "This is a murder case. I'll keep my questions to you as brief as I can."

"Yes, I understand," she said. "But Inspector, I don't know anything about Brian's death, nothing at all. And Clive really can't be a murderer. You've made a mistake." There was a hint of desperation in what she said, and, in spite of his professional determination to hold on to his one suspect for as long as possible, he was not unaffected by her distress.

"If you could persuade your husband to be more straightforward with me, Mrs Althorpe," he replied, not unkindly, "We might be able to conclude our enquiries sooner and leave both of you alone. We believe that the evidence may warrant our charging him with murder, and he is doing nothing to correct that belief. If he is innocent, it would be more sensible to be open with us."

"If he knew anything, he would have told Jeremy, even if he didn't tell you," Rose told him. "Jeremy believes that he's innocent, so why shouldn't you? Besides, you don't really believe *I* have any influence, do you, Chief Inspector?" she added.

He was surprised at the bitterness in her voice. "I'm sorry you feel that," he said, and the sympathy was genuine. "Now, can you tell me what you yourself were doing on Wednesday the fourteenth and Thursday the fifteenth of November, please, Mrs Althorpe."

"Is that when you think Brian was killed… on one of those two days?"

"Just answer the question, please."

"Well, I don't remember much about the Wednesday, except for the evening. I went out to a meeting. I belong to the St Martin's bellringing band," she explained. "We had an AGM, at Simon Hellyer's house in Two Marks."

"From—?"

"Seven-thirty. It would normally have broken up, anyway, at about nine or nine-thirty, but there was a crisis at home, and Clive phoned us. It was about eight-thirty, I think, and I came straight home." She realised suddenly that she didn't know what Simon had done after Robert was found... gone home, presumably, so that he would have no alibi for the rest of Wednesday night. Fortunately, Inspector Harding didn't follow this up.

"So, your husband was at home babysitting?"

"Not to begin with. My neighbour, Maddie Archer, came in until Clive got home. I don't know when he arrived home... you'd have to ask Maddie."

Harding made a note. "This meeting... how many people were at it?"

Rose hesitated. Then she said, rather quietly, "Just Simon and me."

Something in her tone made Harding look at her sharply. She was colouring faintly. *Well, well,* he thought with some surprise. *Who would have thought it?* He looked at her with different eyes for a moment, but still could not imagine what Simon Hellyer saw in her. She was a long way from the bubbly blonde type he himself preferred. Still, there was no accounting for tastes.

"There should have been others," she explained. "Ben Cartwright and Lesley Trant from St Martin, and Ken Longman from Southover, too. But they couldn't come in the end."

"You don't have to justify anything to me," he said.

"I wasn't," she retorted, defiantly. "But Simon and I were together the whole evening. He came back with me when Clive phoned." She hesitated for a moment, wondering whether she should tell Harding about Robert's disappearance, and that she, Simon, George and the Swansons had all been out in the village looking for him. They hadn't seen anything unusual. Perhaps that would be useful information, as it concerned the Wednesday he was asking about. On the other hand, something warned her that telling Harding about Robert's escapade would turn his attention to her son, and she wanted to avoid that. The last thing Robert needed just now was to be questioned by the police.

"And on the Thursday?" If Harding had noticed the hesitation, he had obviously misinterpreted it.

"We were all at sixes and sevens on Thursday, because of Robert being unwell. He was a bit better in the evening, and then Clive decided to go away, although I didn't know that of course, until the Friday morning."

Harding made another note. It was clear that this woman thought the world of her son. Some minor ailment or other had driven all other thoughts from her mind. He felt a certain sympathy for Simon Hellyer, whom he had not personally interviewed. Moorcroft had reckoned that he fancied Rose Althorpe and wasn't having much success, and perhaps the sergeant was correct. What with an ailing son and an errant husband, Harding thought, she had too much to think about at present to take on a lover.

He left Rose and drove the half-mile down Church Lane to interview Maddie Archer.

"I don't suppose Mrs Archer will be able to tell us anything useful, either," he said to Wendy Hargreaves, gloomily. "She went home after babysitting on the Wednesday night at eight o'clock and watched television, I'll bet."

Wendy looked at him. She had been aware, intuitively, of undercurrents of hesitation and omission in Rose's statements that she would have liked to explore further. But Harding wouldn't have liked it if she'd suggested a line of questioning. He never listened to her ideas during an investigation. She was just there as female dogsbody, not expected to use her intelligence. The sooner she got away from his team the better.

Twenty

While Inspector Harding was talking to Rose and failing to ask some of the questions which would have helped his investigation along, Jeremy went looking for his wife and found her kneeling on the sitting room floor.

"What on earth were you doing at preschool this afternoon?" he asked her, bending down to retrieve a plastic railway engine from under the big sofa. "It looks as though the children had every toy out and threw them all at one another."

Liz laughed. "No, we just had a 'free' afternoon. Everyone chose their activity, instead of doing something structured. It does tend to make a lot of mess," she agreed, ruefully. "And the kitchen isn't much better... Mandy was cooking with some of them in there. But the children do enjoy it so much that I try to have a free morning every few weeks. You can have too much structured activity."

Jeremy removed some plasticine from the underside of the old pine table. "Is there a tub for this stuff?"

Liz handed him a plastic container which had once held ice cream. "Don't you worry about this lot," she said. "It won't take a minute to sort it out."

"I'll make you some tea," he offered. "Come and drink it with me in the study when you've finished."

She raised her eyebrows at this unusual request, but nodded, for it was clear that he wanted to discuss something with her.

Having piled the toys into their boxes somewhat chaotically in the interests of speed, she followed him willingly enough into the study, merely picking up her knitting from the drawing room on her way. Whatever Jeremy had to say, she might as well be usefully occupied while he said it.

She settled herself in one armchair, found her place in the pattern and began a stocking-stitch section of Mike's new sweater while she waited for Jeremy to gather his thoughts. The long silence which ensued told her that these were complex and tangled. He rarely had difficulty in coming to the point where the issue was clearcut.

"How would you feel about leaving St Martin?" Jeremy asked her at last.

Liz paused in the middle of a row and regarded him searchingly. "Do you mean, 'How would I personally feel?' or 'Do I think we should?'"

Jeremy sighed. "I'm not sure. Both, probably."

"What brought this on?" she asked briskly. "I thought we were settled now more or less until you retired. Is it this murder? Though you were preaching sermons about change even before that, I seem to remember."

"Perhaps Brian's death has something to do with it," he said slowly. "It's been rather a rainbow month, hasn't it, weather-wise and in our lives. The sun comes out for a bit and then you get another hefty shower. But it goes deeper than that. I feel—" He paused, searching for the word.

"Frustrated? Wasted? Unfulfilled? Bored?" she suggested a selection helpfully.

He laughed. "One of those, but I'm not sure which. Perhaps a mixture."

"What is it that's missing?" she asked. "Do you want larger congregations? More up-to-date worship? Quicker pace of life?"

"No-o. Certainly not the last one. I wanted the quiet and the open spaces we have here. I should miss my country walks. I'm not what they need, the people here. I'm banging my head against the proverbial brick wall half the time. No one wants to listen to what I want to share with them, even plain and simple theology. I thought if I gave them time they'd accept changes in the liturgy, new music, new ideas. But I've given them ten years, and I can't really see that they've altered their attitudes much."

"You said so in your sermon for St Martin's Day," nodded Liz. "Ruffled a few feathers, by all I hear, too. Where would you want to go, if you left here?"

"Where I'm sent, I suppose," he answered tentatively after a moment.

"By whom? God or the bishop?" asked Liz.

Jeremy laughed. "Either, or both—supposing they agree on the matter."

"Well," his wife went on, "You were sent here, and now you don't want to stay. Where you get 'sent' next might be just as bad. Before you talk of leaving here, I think you need to be clearer of your destination."

Jeremy sighed again. "I suppose what you really mean is that you're happy here and don't want to leave."

Liz smiled at him. "No, that's not quite fair. It's probably true that I'd prefer to stay here. The children are settled at school. I have friends here, I've got my evening job and I get a lot of satisfaction out of running the preschool group. But it isn't what I meant, all the same. I could get excited about another job, and a different kind of life, I expect. No, I meant exactly what I said. I know perfectly well that I shan't be happy if you're feeling unsettled and unfulfilled."

"Your feminist friends would be exceedingly shocked by that statement," Jeremy observed.

"They would. Horrified, I expect. But it's true, all the same. It's not because I'm self-sacrificing, not really. I mean, anyone who wants to stay married has to be willing to put up with a bit of self-sacrifice, don't you think? I'm only being realistic. I know you wouldn't be happy if *I* were feeling discontented, either."

Jeremy digested this.

"And while I remember," added Liz. "Simon Hellyer rang while you were out walking this morning. He asked if he could come round after school. I started to remind him today's your day off, but he said you'd specifically told him he could come any Monday."

Jeremy nodded. "The idea was to get to know the man rather than the rector, I think. I represented myself as off duty today. Although I suppose Rose may be part of the attraction. Can you stretch supper to one more, if I ask him to stay?"

Liz got up, spilling one knitting needle and a spare ball of wool on to the floor. "Really, Remy! Not so long ago he was public enemy number one, I seem to remember. Imperilling Rose's moral standards or her immortal soul, or something equally dire. Now we ask him to supper. What is happening to you?"

"I think," replied Jeremy thoughtfully, "I'm learning not to judge people so harshly." He handed her up the ball of wool, which had rolled across the carpet and halted by his foot. "Not before time, probably."

Liz forbore to comment on this piece of self-analysis, merely observing that the telephone was ringing. "Days off... when do you ever get a whole one? Do you want me to answer it in the sitting room, or will you take it in here?"

"I'll take it. If it's urgent, I can go out for a bit. As long as I'm back by five. I don't think the inspector wants to speak to me, does he?"

"He didn't say so. I can let him out. Are you going to answer that phone?"

~ * ~

Simon loaded exercise books into his briefcase with very little enthusiasm for the task they represented. He was tired after a day spent teaching teenage boys the rudiments of the English language and a superficial acquaintance with its literature. He would have preferred to go straight home rather than going to St Martin's

Rectory. He thought about phoning to rearrange the appointment, but in the end a not-quite-admitted desire to pursue his acquaintance with Jeremy, along with the possibility that Rose might be there, prevented him.

He drew up at the rectory still undecided about the wisdom of this visit, and when Mike opened the door to him, the boy's undisguised pleasure at his arrival almost caused him to turn tail and beat a retreat.

"Come in, sir," invited Mike warmly, standing back to usher him inside. "Mum said you were coming. Can I make you some tea?"

"Coffee, please, if it's going," said Simon, who hated tea. "Shouldn't you be doing your homework?"

"Almost finished," Mike told him. "Then I want to read some of that book you lent me the other day... fascinating stuff, so far."

"You'll have to come orienteering with me," said Simon, unbending a little as he followed his pupil into the study. Remy was nowhere to be seen.

"Love to," agreed Mike, with a readiness which would have surprised his father. Mike's interest in maps had, up to that point, been a completely sedentary one, with little attraction to exploring the terrain in the field.

"No sugar in the coffee, please," said Simon, recognizing that Mike was tempted to linger.

"Right. Won't be a minute." Mike half-turned towards the door, then turned back again. "Oh, I forgot to say. Dad said to tell you he'd be here shortly. He had to go and hold someone's hand."

"He what?"

"When people are really sick, or dying, or something, Dad often goes round to sit with them, even on his day off. He's quite good at comforting people," Mike informed him cheerfully. "I think it was a relative of someone who'd died suddenly, today. Down in Southover. He'll be back soon. And Mum told me to make you tea, well, coffee, if that's what you'd like. Make yourself at home."

With this vague permission, he vanished in the direction of the kitchen.

Simon wandered round the study, half-hoping Rose would appear in the hallway, or that he would at least hear her speaking to Liz or one of the children. It was like some kind of exquisite torture to be in the same house with her but unable to think of an excuse to seek her out. He found himself reading the spines of books on the shelves and remembering with a mixture of pain and pleasure the evening not so long ago when Rose had done the same in his house. Some of the titles on Jeremy's shelves were what he had expected: theology and church history, volumes of prayer, the biographies of saints and famous Christians ancient and modern, a few hymn books with music. But some were unexpected; a complete set of Dorothy Sayers' detective stories, five of Ellis Peters' *Cadfael* novels, and Edmund Crispin's *The Moving Toyshop*; and several scientific volumes on subjects as widely spread as quantum physics and the zoological implications of Darwinian evolution. Involuntarily, Simon's desire to know Jeremy quickened.

"Find anything to interest you?" asked a voice behind him, and he swung round almost guiltily. "Don't look like that, Simon. You're very welcome to examine the contents of my bookshelves. Why should I have any secrets?"

"Most people do," said Simon, smiling.

"Yourself included?"

Simon looked at him warily.

Jeremy raised a hand. "I'm sorry. It wasn't meant to become the inquisition. Sit down. Are refreshments on the way?"

"Mike promised some coffee," grinned Simon.

"You don't sound very optimistic about its arriving," said Jeremy. He went to the door. "Mike! Coffee for me as well, please. On the double, if you will."

He motioned Simon to sit down. "Glad you could make it," he said. "You look tired, Simon. Teaching's no sinecure these days."

Simon smiled. "It's not the teaching, really. The kids at Northchurch are a nice mob. Better than the comprehensive where I taught before I came here. There they threw things if you turned your back."

Jeremy was silent. It was so much an expectant silence that Simon found himself, as so many had before him, confiding more than he had intended.

"It's been a difficult few weeks," he said at last. "And I'm worried about Rose. Would she call on me if she needed me, do you think? I can't make up my mind whether it's just because she's staying here at the moment that I haven't seen her."

An idea occurred to him, and he met Jeremy's eyes challengingly. "Are you encouraging her to keep away from me?"

"I wasn't even aware that she was," answered Jeremy simply. "We have no say in who she sees while she's here... the door is open to anyone she wants to invite, and she can go where she likes. She is our guest, not a prisoner."

"But she's talked to you, hasn't she—about us—about Rose and me?"

"Yes," said Jeremy after a moment.

Simon waited for more information, but Jeremy was more practised than he at such encounters. The silence remained unbroken. "Clive has forfeited any right he had to keep her," he said fiercely. "Do you know what her life has been like?"

"Yes, a little. And I agree with you," said Jeremy calmly.

Simon's eyes opened wider. "You agree?"

"I do, and I have told Rose so."

Simon digested this in silence for a moment. "What did she say?"

Jeremy smiled. "I don't think I can tell you. You must ask her yourself. Simon, have you thought about this situation at all from your own point of view?"

"Thought about... *Of course,* I have. I'm only afraid I'm being too selfish, wanting her to come and live with me."

Jeremy raised his eyebrows, and Simon realised that Rose had told the rector less than he had supposed.

"I'm waiting for her answer," he explained quickly.

"Have you thought about it in the long term? I don't believe for a moment that you and Rose would consider a brief affair with no commitment, so I'm envisaging that you would be together for a long time. Rose is older than you are..."

"Only a few years," said Simon quickly.

"Still, those years will be significant when you're older. Rose's daughter, Sarah, is a grown woman now. Very soon, Rose will seem middle-aged, while you are still in your prime. She'll be almost seventy when you retire at sixty-five, and—"

"Stop it," interrupted Simon angrily. "I won't listen to this. Age doesn't come into it, only personality does. And Rose is—" He broke off, conscious that to say what he felt would make him sound like any foolish youth in the throes of calf-love.

"I'm sorry," said Jeremy. "I shouldn't have said so much. I just don't want you and Rose to find out the mistake too late. Forgive me."

Simon was not proof against the disarming smile with which this was said. He subsided into his chair again, but his jaw was set. He had been a fool to come near this place or listen to this man even for five minutes. No clergyman could resist cant, or moralising; and they were *always* full of unwanted good advice.

Jeremy, painfully conscious that he had mismanaged not only this conversation but also his similar discussion with Rose the previous day, wondered suddenly whether he had made a mistake in trying to appeal to self-interest in both parties. Perhaps it would have been more effective to swap his arguments and speak to Rose about the disadvantages to Simon of the age difference between them, and to Simon about Rose's difficulties. The reflection at least showed him that they were both essentially unselfish people, and in a way that was reassuring. He found he could not any longer dislike Simon as an individual, but he was still very doubtful about the good sense of his relationship with Rose. But he had not invited Simon to the rectory to talk about Rose, but about Brian Warrendon's death. He was in danger of losing an ally whose help he needed.

At this moment of uncomfortable tension, Mike tapped at the door with the toe of his shoe, pushed it open with his shoulder, and came in carrying two steaming mugs carefully in one hand and a book in the other.

Simon relieved him of the mugs and stood awkwardly looking for somewhere to put them. He longed simply to walk out of the rectory and drive home, but good manners demanded that he made a pretence at least of sampling the refreshment he had been offered.

"There's sugar in that one," said Mike, indicating his father's mug. He turned to Simon. "Sir, can I ask you a question? I'll be quick… I know you and Dad don't want me hanging around."

"On the contrary," said Simon sincerely. Mike's presence might discourage his father from delivering any more uncomfortable moral opinions.

"It's just—" Mike turned the pages. "Sir, what's an anti... antique-something."

Jeremy looked up sharply. There was something familiar about the word.

"A what?" asked Simon. He peered over Mike's shoulder. "Oh, an anticline. It's a rock formation. It's a fold shaped like an arch." He turned the page. "Look, there's a diagram here. See?"

"Doesn't it have something to do with oil?" asked Jeremy, a note of sudden urgency in his voice.

Simon turned towards him. "Well, it *can* coincide with deposits of oil. It depends on the kind of rock. You need a mixture of porous and non-porous rock. In the right kind of rock formation, any oil that was formed in the lower strata seeps upwards until it meets non-porous rock. Then it settles in a kind of lake, under an arched formation above it. You bore through the rock above it. There's oil in some of the chalk hills in Hampshire, in fact, though it's probably not economic to extract it."

"Like this chalk ridge here in St Martin's," said Jeremy.

"Well, possibly. I've never heard of anyone exploring for oil around here, though."

"No," said Jeremy, slowly. "But I think I may have."

"What?"

"Dad, what are you talking about?" Mike's eyes were glowing, for he shared his father's interest in anything mysterious or unexplained.

Simon sat down again slowly in his chair, wondering what strange and unlikely theory Jeremy was incubating. Mike, who had more trust in his father's perspicacity, folded himself and his long limbs on the carpet and gazed intently up at him.

"About a week ago, I was talking to old Ben Cartwright. I'd gone to see him because he was housebound with his rheumatism and bronchitis. He told me something which I found entirely baffling, and I think you may just have given me a notion as to its significance."

"What did he say, Dad?" asked Mike from the floor.

Jeremy repeated what Ben had said. "I couldn't for the life of me work out what antiques had to do with this murder. But an anticline... now that's entirely different."

"Because of the possibility of oil," said Simon.

"I'd think so. If someone thought Brian was going to encourage oil companies to prospect on his land..."

"Ruining the natural landscape and bringing lorries and industrial by-products..."

"The village would go mad!" exclaimed Mike. "Mass mobilisation and pickets on the oil-drilling equipment. People lying down in front of bulldozers."

"The land would become very much more valuable," said his father, ignoring him.

"But who does this implicate?" asked Simon. "Eamonn Warrendon—is that the son's name? George? Doesn't it let Clive out?"

"Eamonn has an alibi," said Jeremy. "And in any case, I would have thought he would wait until the oil riches were a reality, not just a possibility. But Clive quarrelled with Brian about oil, sometime on the Saturday of the St Martin's weekend. Rose told me. Sarah had overheard them talking about oil, apparently, but Rose thought it must be that a tanker had spilled some oil on the road down by Home Farm... it's always a bone of contention, the state of the road down there. But I think perhaps this quarrel may instead have been about Brian's plans for his land. I could ask Clive about it, though whether he'll tell me or not is another matter."

"Drilling for oil. Anyone in the village who knew about it would have wanted to stop Mr Warrendon," said Mike. "I suppose the easiest way to stop him would be to kill him, but it seems awfully drastic, doesn't it?"

"Would anyone care that much, enough to murder him?" asked Simon. "Surely there are other ways of preventing that kind of development... less final, perhaps, but a lot less risky? Planning opposition campaigns, that sort of thing."

"The village tried that when Brian sold the land for the Copse Lane estate, and it failed. But I know someone else who cared, apart from the villagers." said Jeremy slowly.

"Who?" asked Simon.

"I don't think I'd better tell you that, either of you. Not until I've talked to the person in question."

"You'll tell the police?" asked Simon, sharply.

"Yes, when I've spoken to this person."

"Be careful," Simon warned him. "For God's sake. You can't play games with murderers."

"I'll be careful," promised Jeremy.

Twenty-one

At about seven o'clock that evening, after snatching a quick meal to which Simon was not, after all, invited, Jeremy pushed open the back door of Church End farmhouse and peered into the passage. It was pitch black outside, but even after dark the Warrendons rarely locked up their house.

"George!" he called. "George, are you there?"

The tall angular figure of the farmer emerged from the farm office. It was easy to see on his face the ravages of the nightmare through which he was still living.

"Come into the kitchen," he said to Jeremy heavily. "It's a bit warmer there." He pulled out a chair by the big table, pushing aside the clutter of magazines.

Jeremy took the chair and sat down, facing the older man across the table. "I want to know about the oil, George," he said quietly.

George started, and his eyes moved wildly around the kitchen. "What oil?" he muttered.

"The oil Brian thought might be found on his land. That's what this is about, isn't it? You'd better tell me."

George groaned. "I knew it would come out," he whispered. "Lucinda said it would be all right if we kept quiet, but I knew it wouldn't. Oh God!"

"Tell me," said Jeremy again. "Maybe I can help."

George met his eyes for a long moment. "I doubt that," he said.

"Brian had an oil company prospecting on his land, didn't he?"

George nodded. "Down the slope below this house, right in my lovely view, it was. I don't know how I'd bear it, Remy, if it happened."

"But surely nothing was settled?"

"They were considering taking up an option. That means they'd put a drill down to see what was there. I only found out about it a few weeks ago... the Saturday before the fete, I think. Brian and I had words about it that morning on the phone. In fact, it was the last time I ever spoke to him."

"Go on."

"We thought Eamonn wouldn't want oil workings on the land," said George wretchedly. "Besides, they'd have to go through all the steps—planning and so on. Eamonn would have told them to go away. He's not greedy, and he's doing well enough where he is in London. Lucinda thought—I thought we might save the village that way—or put off the trouble, anyway."

"Not by murdering him, George?" Jeremy leaned forward and gazed at the farmer searchingly.

George stared at him. "You don't think I'd do that, Remy?" he asked, horrified. "We were on bad terms, I know, but he was my *brother*. No, he was dead, dead and going cold, when I found him. You saw that head wound, Remy. He couldn't have lived, even if I'd got to him earlier. And I don't know how he died, either. You do believe me, don't you?" His eyes pleaded with Jeremy for agreement, for reassurance that he had not in any way helped to cause his brother's death.

Jeremy replied slowly, "I'm inclined to, George, yes. I can't believe preventing oil from being mined in the village would be enough to make you murder your brother. But you did have something to do with it, didn't you?"

George hesitated, and Jeremy had the impression that he was struggling with some matter of conscience which he had not yet resolved. At last he seemed to make up his mind. "I found him in the field when I came back from looking for Robert, with you and Liz and the others. I took him up to the copse and buried him. I said some words over him, Remy, words out of the funeral service. Lucinda said—we thought—I thought it was the best way."

Lucinda said, repeated Jeremy to himself. That was nearer the truth. Lucinda was involved in all this somehow, and what Lucinda said was far more likely to have dictated events than what poor downtrodden hen-pecked George might think. He wondered how far he could he rely on what George had told him.

"George, you'll have to make a statement, you know. The police may charge you. It's illegal to bury someone like that, never mind not informing the police when you found a dead body. And the fact that there's a murder investigation means you'll be accused of obstructing the police in their enquiries, at the very least."

The farmer nodded. "I'll tell them anything I can, now, but I must keep Lucinda out of it, Remy. She... she couldn't cope with the disgrace."

Jeremy looked at him. "You want to make out that it was all your notion."

"Yes."

Jeremy raised his eyebrows. "Well, George," he said dryly. "You can try. But I can't see how you can protect her altogether. The police will question both of you closely. Besides, this notion that you buried him to keep the oil company out of the village—I may believe you, because I know you, but it won't cut much ice with the police, you know. They may charge you with Brian's murder instead. They haven't found enough evidence to charge Clive with it."

George nodded. "I know. But I can't help it. I've tried not to betray her," he added, bitterly. "But she'll feel it's my fault, just the same. I've been so worried about Clive. I was afraid that he would be blamed. I didn't know what to do for the best."

Jeremy left Church End Farm without feeling that he had been of much assistance to George, but with the uncomfortable certainty that the farmer had been more than a little economical with the truth, and he had not thought of George as a man to whom lies came easily. But where the lies began and ended he did not know. In what sense had he *betrayed* Lucinda, for example? He had persuaded George to let the police know what had happened straight away, but the farmer had agreed with great reluctance. He looked as though police questioning might be the final straw.

He fulfilled his promise to Simon and telephoned him when he arrived back at the rectory.

"I've spoken to the person in question," he began.

"George Warrendon," said Simon flatly. "I worked it out when I got home."

"Yes. It seems Brian must have died early that Wednesday evening." Jeremy hesitated before speaking again. He decided that he couldn't pass on all the information George had given him, promise or no promise, though he would have to tell the police the basic facts. Confidentiality somehow precluded full disclosure, even though George had not spoken to him in any way as a confessor. "But I don't think George murdered his brother, Simon. He says he merely buried him."

"Found the body lying around in the woods and buried him to delay the oil business? Does that make sense? To murder him in order to prevent oil being mined there, I could understand that. Some people are obsessive enough about the countryside even for that. But to bury him and tell no one... why not just inform the police and enjoy the fruits of someone else's misdeeds? He had an alibi, after all; he needn't have worried about being accused if he'd reported the discovery straight away."

"It doesn't make sense, I agree. I suppose," said Jeremy slowly, "I've been hoping all along that it would turn out to be some kind of accident. I can't see any of the people we've considered so far being capable of murder, but I don't think George was telling me all the truth, just the same. Could he have killed him accidentally, perhaps?"

"But surely, he'd admit to that now, wouldn't he? That would be better than being charged with murder."

"I see your point," Jeremy said. "But people really do the most extraordinary things for the most extraordinary reasons, Simon."

"Fact being stranger than fiction," said Simon.

"Sometimes, a great deal stranger."

It was good to know what Ben had been talking about, with his talk of a "line in antiques," Jeremy reflected. But in some ways, there were now more unresolved questions than before. They still didn't know why Clive had run away to Penzance, or who had taken Robert from his bedroom (if anyone had). Was George telling the truth when he said that someone had murdered Brian Warrendon and left him in a field for his brother to find (and if so, why they had). Where did Lucinda fit into all this, if anywhere? And what wasn't Clive telling the police about the Wednesday evening when Brian had probably been killed? After all, he could just have said he came home from work and didn't realise Robert wasn't there until later. Who could argue with that? What was he hiding from everyone, and why?

~ * ~

Harding put down the phone after his conversation with Jeremy next morning and whistled to himself, his eyes snapping with renewed energy. If George had buried his brother on the Wednesday night, as he'd averred to the rector, then the time of death could be narrowed down considerably. Clive Althorpe could be included in the list of suspects at least as feasibly as before, at any rate until he gave a proper account of that evening, but the more likely suspect now seemed to be George himself. Certainly, there was plenty of room for more enquiries. He set off for St Martin-on-the-Hill whistling tunelessly through his teeth, to the irritation of Wendy Hargreaves sitting beside him in the passenger seat.

His enquiries began with George himself, who repeated what he had told Jeremy, but whose answers to subsequent questions were far from satisfactory. When asked about the ballpoint pen that had been found in his brother's pocket, he hesitated for a moment and then said, "I found it by Brian. On the ground. I thought it must be his, so I put it in his pocket. I didn't want to rob him." He could not or would not recall more exactly where the pen had lain, nor could he pinpoint any specific location in the field as the spot where the body had been found. Lucinda had nothing new to add to all this, merely endorsing George's insistence that she had had nothing to do with the matter. In the course of taking her again carefully through her activities that evening, however, Harding did elicit one fact that was new to him, though well known to most of the village.

"This boy that was missing, the one that you were hunting for," he asked. "Who was that?" This boy had been out in the village at the time when the body was presumably lying in the fields somewhere. It was possible he had seen something.

"Why, Robert Althorpe, of course," said Lucinda, astounded at such ignorance.

Harding stared at her, recalling his recent interview with Rose and wondering whether he'd completely missed an important line of enquiry. "He was ill afterwards, I believe," he suggested cautiously.

"Completely traumatised," confirmed Lucinda, without the note of regret which might have been expected.

"Poor boy!" said Wendy and was frowned at for her pains by both Lucinda and Harding.

Harding got up. "Thank you for your help, Mrs Warrendon. Mr Warrendon, I am afraid that you will be in quite serious trouble over this. Not least for impeding our enquiries." If it had not been for Clive Althorpe's ambiguous position with regard to the crime, in fact, he would have been pressing for the farmer's arrest. It still might come to that. Forensic had already confirmed that the body had been in George's Land Rover.

"I realise that," murmured George. He did not look at the inspector. He did not ask whether he was under suspicion for his brother's murder.

"You will be hearing from us further about this. Please don't go away from home without letting us know beforehand. Now, if you will excuse me—"

~ * ~

Harding's interrogation of Robert had to wait until the boy returned from school, and Rose was not at all willing to allow the interview even then. Indeed, it was only when Jeremy threw his weight behind the inspector and suggested that the questions might help to unlock Robert's memory of what had happened on the evening he was missing, and that this might actually be helpful to Robert as well as to the police, that she finally agreed to it.

Harding arrived at the rectory with Wendy just after four o'clock. He shook hands with Rose and thanked her for letting him come. Then he bent down to speak to the boy. "Hallo, Robert."

Robert turned his face towards him, shyly.

Harding sat down and suggested that Rose take the chair opposite him. Robert curled up on the floor at her feet, arms round his calves, his shoulders touching her knees. He did not look at the policeman.

"Robert," said Harding as gently as he could. "I know how difficult it is for you to think about the night when everyone went looking for you, but it is very important that I know all about it. Once I know everything you can tell me, I promise I shall go away and not bother you again."

Robert said nothing. His teeth were digging into his lower lip.

"Did you see anyone that evening, when you were out on your own? Someone on foot, or in a car?"

There was a long pause. "Try to answer, darling," said Rose, stroking his shoulder.

"No," whispered Robert at last. "I didn't see anyone until Mr and Mrs Swanson came."

"Did anyone take you from your home, or did you go of your own free will?"

Robert turned scared eyes up to Harding's face. "No one took me."

"When did you leave the house?"

"I don't know exactly. I didn't have my watch on."

"Did your father know you had gone out?"

Robert whimpered.

Rose bent over him, pulling him closer to her.

"Daddy won't be cross, I promise."

Robert still said nothing.

"You must have been very quiet," Harding pursued. "What was your dad doing when you left the house?"

There was silence while Robert thought about this. "I don't know what he was doing. I mean, he wasn't there. At least, I couldn't see him anywhere."

There was a pause. "Did you say your father *wasn't there?*" Harding asked at last.

Robert looked up at him and nodded. "I was a bit worried about going out on my own," he went on more freely, "and at the last minute I thought perhaps Dad would come too, if I asked him. It was dark outside, and I was scared. I looked in the sitting room, and the lights were on, and the television. But he wasn't there."

"He must have been in another room, darling," said Rose.

Robert twisted round to look up at her. "No, really, Mummy. I couldn't find him. I looked all over."

"This is a surprise to you, Mrs Althorpe," Harding observed flatly.

"Yes. I don't know what time Clive got home, but I know Maddie would have stayed until he did. Robert, wasn't Maddie there either?"

Robert shook his head.

"I imagine your husband must have come home at some point," Harding observed, rather dryly. "Because Robert clearly thought he was there, and that means, surely, that he must have heard him come in. Is that right, Robert?"

"Yes," whispered Robert. "I wasn't asleep, you see. I was waiting for it to be time to go out. Dad came in, and I heard him and Maddie talking, and then I heard Maddie go home, so Dad must have been there."

"I don't understand it at all," said Rose, shaking her head.

Harding looked at Robert. The boy was being a little more forthcoming than he had been at the start of the interview. But there were still a lot of gaps in his narrative. He tried again. "And when you went out, Robert, what happened next?"

Robert shrank against his mother. "I don't remember," he said.

There was a moment's silence.

"Where were you going?" persisted Harding. "Why did you go out at all? It was cold, wasn't it, and wet?"

Robert turned his face away and seemed to curl up like a snail.

"If he doesn't remember, he doesn't," said Rose, just a trace showing in her voice of the fierce protectiveness she felt. "Leave him alone, now, please, Detective-Inspector."

"He must remember why he was going out, surely?"

"He was traumatised for several weeks," said Rose. "He's only just started talking about ordinary things. I don't want him to go back to being silent again. I'm sure our doctor would agree."

"I don't want to upset the boy," the policeman said. "But I have a murder enquiry to pursue, and it's become clear overnight that the Wednesday evening when Robert was out may be the evening that Brian Warrendon was murdered."

Rose shuddered. "We can't ask him to try to remember something like that, not if he isn't ready to. But I will try to ask him when we're on our own, if he saw anything."

Harding got up. He sighed. "Very well," he said. Then he looked at Robert again. "If you think of anything else you should tell me, Robert, ask your mother to telephone my office."

Robert looked up at him and said nothing. But Rose had the impression there was a great deal more to tell.

~ * ~

Jeremy had had a similar feeling when talking to Clive at Winchester Police Station on Saturday morning. It was a frustrating interview that in retrospect he felt had got him nowhere, although he had hoped that the report Rose had given him about Robert's confession to Harding would help him to break down Clive's reserve.

Clive himself, however, was glad to see Jeremy. His world seemed to have narrowed down to the four walls around him, and his life's purpose to withstanding the barrage of questions he was facing. He knew his firm must be desperately needing his presence—Olivia couldn't hold the fort forever. He knew that the problems at home would have to be faced sooner or later. He was aware, from Jeremy's concerned expression, that he must look pale and strained, but his face had set in stubborn lines. He might be sick of himself and his own sins, but he was determined not to give in to police pressure. He didn't particularly want to go home, anyway. Let them arrest him if they wanted to.

"I've told you everything I can, Remy," he insisted. "I'm not giving the police the satisfaction of breaking me down, but I haven't kept anything back from *you*. What I did that Thursday night, it happened exactly as I told you. I wasn't running away from anything except myself."

"And the Wednesday night?" asked Jeremy.

Clive looked up in surprise. "What about the Wednesday night?"

There was a pause. He had the impression that Jeremy was treading a fine line between candour and discretion.

"It seems that Brian Warrendon was probably killed on Wednesday."

Clive said nothing. The information meant little to him.

"Your movements have not been sufficiently accounted for on that evening," Jeremy went on mildly.

"They've asked me so many questions," said Clive sullenly. "I can't remember what I've told them."

"You came in at about eight o'clock, according to Maddie Archer," Jeremy told him. "You were at home later, manning the telephone while other people searched for Robert."

Clive met his gaze squarely, but his expression was defensive.

"However, when Robert left home you were not in the house."

"What! Who the hell says so? That's absolute nonsense!" A flush of annoyance spread across Clive's face. They weren't going to hear about Maddie from him. If she hadn't said anything about what they'd got up to, it wasn't for him to let her down. He wasn't adding that kind of betrayal to the rest. He felt enough of a shit as it was.

"Robert says so."

"Robert was in..." Clive stopped.

"Robert was *not* in bed at that point. He was setting out on a jaunt on his own. That is what he told the police yesterday."

Jeremy's tone was severe. Clive heard it, but it was not the rector's disapproval which felt like a weight in his chest. He groaned and put his face in his hands. "God!" he said. "What a mess!"

"But where were *you*, Clive?" Clearly this was the first Clive had heard about Robert's night-time jaunt, and Jeremy was keen to press his question home while he was still processing that new information.

"I can't tell you." Clive straightened up and met Jeremy's eyes. Beneath the shame his determination remained intact. At least Robert had gone of his own free will. No one had abducted the boy, as he'd feared, while he was at Maddie's. He didn't have to feel he'd let his son down as well the rest.

"You're shielding someone," said Jeremy with certainty.

"Maybe. But I don't know anything about this murder. You're barking up the wrong tree."

"I've told you more than once that I believe you, Clive. I don't think you killed Brian, though you hated him."

Clive winced. "It's true. He was a bloody awful bastard, and he did a lot of harm in the village and would have done more. He won't be missed. But *I* didn't kill him. And I don't know who did."

"And you won't tell me where you were that evening? In confidence, Clive."

Clive shook his head stubbornly.

"How do you explain the ballpoint pen the police found in Brian's pocket?" asked Jeremy abruptly. His voice had hardened.

Clive looked up. "I don't know anything about a pen." The police had asked about it too, but he'd ignored the question, which had made no sense to him.

"Rose recognised it as yours."

Damn Rose, thought Clive irritably.

"The last time I saw that pen, it was in the bureau at home, where I keep it." He felt squeezed by all these questions, like a rat in a trap. But he'd answered them honestly… all except the one he wasn't willing to answer at all. It was odd how strongly he felt about protecting Maddie. In the past, he wasn't sure he would have cared. He didn't have any special feeling for her; he couldn't see himself starting any kind of long-term affair with her, especially not with her living in the house next door. But at the same time, he couldn't bring himself to let on, not to the police, not even to Remy, that he'd been with her, unless she was prepared to publish the fact herself. And he was ashamed, too, that he had been out on such a shoddy, casual fling when he should have been in charge of Robert. He still felt that it was at least partly his fault the boy had ended up traumatised that evening.

Jeremy looked at him. "I can't help you, Clive, if you won't tell me… it isn't the same as telling the police, you know that. I can keep secret anything you want to tell me. But I have to know, if I'm to work out who did murder Brian. It's the only way you'll be clear of this."

Clive shook his head. "I've told you everything I can, Remy," he said, and his jaw set hard. It was clear there would be no moving him, even if it put him in the dock.

Twenty-two

Simon sat peacefully in front of the fire, with a mug of coffee on the floor beside him and a pile of corrected exercise books on the table. It was five o'clock on a Monday, and he had the whole evening before him. Relaxed, his mind wandered, as it often did these days, to Rose and Robert and their current sojourn at the rectory. He wondered when they would return home. Rose at the rectory, protected by Jeremy and Liz—who, for all their outward friendliness to him, resembled a garrison guarding a besieged castle—was unapproachable; a fairy princess immured amid thorns. Even at bellringing practice the previous evening, she had been awkward and distant, as though afraid to attract further notice by responding to his concern. Rose at Sundials would be a different being altogether... wouldn't she?

It was selfish of him, he told himself, to chafe against the bounds that the Swansons had set about her. She had found a haven there from trouble, as well as from the press and her less sympathetic neighbours. He could not grudge it to her. But at the same time, he longed to be the one who was guarding and protecting, and he fretted at his separation from her.

He could not help believing, too, that given free access to Robert, he could have helped him to recover from trauma more quickly. Locked up inside Robert's damaged mind, he felt sure, were clues to the St Martin's mystery. He had, after all, been out on the night when Brian Warrendon had probably been murdered. It seemed very unlikely that Darren knew anything more than he had told Simon, for Darren had shown no sign of having seen anything untoward. Perhaps Jeremy's younger son Chris might be able to help. He would understand his friend, notice small things he let slip.

This thought turned abruptly and came back metamorphosed into a completely different idea.

"Chris," said Simon to himself thoughtfully. "Now, I wonder whether Chris too—"

He picked up the telephone and rang the rectory.

"Liz? Is Remy there?"

"He's out visiting, I'm afraid, Simon," came the reply. "Even though it's his day off. I'm sorry. He isn't very good at saying 'no'."

"Oh." On the whole, Simon thought better of Remy for this, but he could see that it might make rectory family life difficult. "Well, are Robert and Chris around?" He looked at his watch. It was too early for them to be in bed.

"Y-yes, they're upstairs with Bethan. But Simon—"

"Could I come over and talk to them for a little? It is important."

"Well, I suppose so—" Liz was clearly taken aback at this suggestion.

"Good. I'll be over shortly."

~ * ~

By the time Simon arrived at the rectory, it seemed as though the entire juvenile household had assembled in the drawing room. Mike had folded himself up on the floor in front of the fire, Lorna was curled up in a corner of the sofa, and the three younger children stood a little diffidently in the middle of the room, gazing at Simon. Liz, having ushered him in, disappeared in the direction of the kitchen, but Rose sat silently in the corner and watched them relax and become receptive as Simon spoke to them.

"Hi," he said cheerfully. "Nice of you all to be here." He sat on the floor, indicating that they should do so, too.

"I'm looking for a badger," he said. "Do any of you know where we could find one?"

"There's a sett down Copse Lane in the wood there," volunteered Chris. "Dad and I saw it once last year. But when—"

He stopped.

Simon did not appear to notice that the boy hadn't finished the sentence. "I wondered whether you'd all like to come and help me search," he continued smoothly. He seemed to include Mike and Lorna in the invitation, but he was looking at Chris and Robert.

Chris and Bethan immediately expressed great enthusiasm for the project. Lorna said nothing, but Mike offered to come if Simon thought he would be useful. Robert merely looked worried.

"I'm free tomorrow evening," went on Simon. "Check with your parents, then Mike can give me a ring to confirm." He looked at Rose. "May Robert come?"

"If he wants to," replied Rose steadily. She couldn't quite understand what Simon was doing, but she was prepared to follow his lead.

Robert crept up to her and took her hand. She felt him trembling. Simon was watching them implacably. Whatever Simon was after, Robert's fear would not cause her to draw back. Maternal protectiveness overwhelmed her for a moment.

"Simon," she begged fiercely, "Don't press it." She thought of the effect of Detective-Inspector Harding's interview with Robert the previous day and felt he had had enough.

"I think we have to know," he said quietly but inexorably, "what really happened that night."

"Not with everyone here. Let the others go." She put her arms round Robert.

"I'd like to speak to Robert," Simon told the other children. "And Chris."

Mike got up immediately and took Bethan by the hand. "Come on, half-pint," he said to her. "I'll run the railway for you."

Bethan skipped out with him, eager for the treat.

Lorna hesitated, sensing some menace in the tableau before her, but not able to analyse it. "Do you need me, Rose?" she asked at last.

Rose smiled at her. "I think it will be best not to have too many people," she said. "I'll call you if we need anything." As the girl left the room, Rose called after her softly, "Thank you, Lorna."

Simon guided Rose and Robert to the sofa and pulled up a chair close to them. Chris sat down willingly at his feet, eyes fixed intelligently on the teacher's face.

"I'm going to tell you a story," said Simon quietly. "I don't know all of it, so you'll have to fill in the gaps for me."

"We do that at school sometimes, with Miss Baker," said Chris.

"That's right. But this is a true story." He paused for a moment, watching Robert's white face. He hated to put the boy through a new ordeal when he was just beginning to recover from his trauma, but he could see no other way. Not only was it important to cauterize the psychological wound, to get Robert to face up to his experience and remember it properly, but he had now realised that to know what had happened might be vital for other reasons. And if he didn't do the job, the police would, eventually.

"Once upon a time," suggested Chris, grinning.

The grin lightened the atmosphere for a moment. Simon smiled his appreciation at the boy but told him to pipe down. Then he went on, "My story is about some boys who went out one evening for a lark. I think there were three of them, but there may have been more. They went to visit the badger's sett."

Chris stopped grinning. Robert's face, if anything, grew whiter.

"They left their homes secretly and met at an agreed rendezvous. I'm not sure where that was… on the village green, perhaps?" He looked at Chris.

After a moment the boy nodded. "At the Copse Lane end."

There was something to be said for a rectory upbringing, Simon reflected. Chris was likely to tell him the truth.

"They went down Copse Lane and up the footpath into the wood. They waited there for quite a while, but they didn't see the badger. One of them, the youngest, had come out in his pyjamas. He was cold and wet, and he started to complain."

Simon raised an eyebrow at Chris, and again the boy nodded. Robert had turned his face into Rose's shoulder. Rose herself was listening in fascinated horror.

"In the end, the boys decided to come home. One of them left the others at the entrance into the Copse Lane estate, because he lived there. The others started to walk back towards the village. But for some reason, they separated."

He looked at Chris.

"Y-yes," stammered Chris. "That's right. Darren went straight home. Rob and I got as far as the green. Then Rob said he'd lost his wristwatch. It must have fallen off in the road. We… we had an argument about it."

He looked at Robert for help, but Robert was still buried in his mother's shoulder.

"Did you go back?" asked Simon quietly.

"Rob did," answered Chris in a very small voice.

"Didn't you go with him?" asked Rose hotly.

Simon waved at her to be quiet. "Why didn't you go, Chris?" he asked gently.

"A Land Rover or something passed us, going really fast. It nearly knocked us down. The driver must have seen our torches at the last moment. I was walking in front of Rob, and the Land Rover sent mud all over me. I was drenched. I said we'd go back for his watch in the morning. We wouldn't be able to see anything in the dark, anyway. We were nearly here then, and I didn't want to walk back up Church Lane with Rob, all wet like that. I'd have frozen. I thought he would follow me when I went. His house isn't very far the other side of the green…" His voice trailed off.

"But you went back to look for your watch, didn't you, Robert?" said Simon, projecting his voice a little more to penetrate the psychological cotton wool with which Robert had surrounded himself.

There was no answer.

"Robert," said Rose gently. "I think you should tell us. Maybe we need to know, too. You'll feel better if you share it with us."

There was silence.

"I think the youngest boy went back to look for his watch," Simon said, reverting to his story-telling voice. "He walked back along the lane. And something horrible happened. Something so horrible that he was frightened almost to death. He ran away, but he didn't go home. His mother was out, and he didn't know where his father was. Besides, he was afraid his father would be angry. He went to the church."

There was silence.

"He went to the church," repeated Simon. "He thought he would be safe there. But it was night, and the church was locked."

A small sob escaped Robert.

"After a long time, people came and found him in the churchyard and took him home. Then he was safe. He's quite safe now. No one can hurt him. Nothing he saw can hurt him, unless he goes on keeping it inside. Tell us, Robert. What happened?" He paused. "What did you see?"

There was silence for a while. Then Robert turned his head to look at Simon. Their eyes met and held for a long moment. "I saw a man," he said. His voice was so quiet they could hardly hear it.

Rose held him tightly. "What was the man doing?" she asked him. "What did he do to you?"

Robert shook his head.

Suddenly, Simon was quite sure what it was that Robert had seen. "The man wasn't doing anything, Robert, was he?" he said. "He was just lying in the road."

"Yes," said the thread of a voice.

Chris reached out for Robert's hand. "Oh, Rob," he said. "I'm so sorry I left you."

"Did you recognise the man?" asked Simon.

Robert nodded.

"Was it Brian Warrendon? The farmer from Home Farm?"

The boy nodded again. "He was bleeding," he said, shuddering. Suddenly the words all came tumbling out in a rush. "His head was bleeding, and his nose, and his ears, and he was all crumpled up. He was… he was moaning. I couldn't understand what he was saying. I ran away. I ran and ran. I should have come home. I could have told Daddy when he came home, and the doctor could have come and helped the man. It was all my fault. What… what happened to the man?" His eyes turned appealingly to his mother.

Rose realised suddenly that although everyone else in the village knew that Brian Warrendon had been killed, Robert possibly did not.

"He died, Robert," she told him sadly. "But I don't think he would have lived, even if you had gone straight home. I don't think it would have made any difference at all." *I hope that's true*, she thought. She couldn't remember why she and Simon or the Swansons hadn't walked down to the corner, when they were looking for Robert. But clearly nobody had.

Robert gave a deep sigh and turned his face from sight again. The tension left his body and he sagged against Rose. She looked bleakly at Simon, who smiled a little wryly.

From the doorway, Jeremy said, "That was very well done, Robert. You've been a brave boy. Your mother is proud of you, and so am I." His eyes fell upon his younger son, and the message in them was not so congratulatory.

Simon looked round. "I'm sorry," he said. "I didn't hear you come in."

"Well," said Jeremy dryly. "You seem to have turned my drawing room into some kind of counselling chamber… or was it the witness box? And well done, if I may say so; you've succeeded where the rest of us had failed."

Simon looked at Rose. "Do you want to take Robert upstairs? Give him a hot drink, and I think he may sleep."

She was conscious of the authority he still carried from the meeting he had organised and led so deftly. Blindly, half-carrying Robert, she went out of the room.

"I'll talk to you in a few minutes, Chris," said Jeremy. "Don't say anything about this to Bethan, please. You can tell her later, when I've spoken to you again. But for the moment, keep quiet."

Chris nodded and disappeared upstairs. It was clear he was glad to have escaped a lecture from his father, albeit temporarily.

Simon met Jeremy's eyes.

"We'll have to report this to the police, of course," said Jeremy. He took a breath. "I had no idea of all that went on that evening. You must know things about it that you never told me."

"I'd talked to Darren Turner at the time, when we were looking for Robert, but it didn't seem to lead us anywhere. I didn't realize until this evening that Chris must have been out with them, too. It was only while I was talking to them that I thought of what Robert might have seen. It was obvious once I thought of it. But perhaps I should have waited for you to come in."

"It was probably easier done this way," said Jeremy, fairly. "Would you have told me, if I hadn't arrived when I did?"

Simon smiled. "There's no choice now," he answered obliquely. "The police will have to know. We couldn't have kept it to ourselves."

"Just so," agreed Jeremy. "This alters the case completely, don't you agree?"

"I think I can see how he must have been killed," said Simon slowly. "But as to the details, and who moved him—"

"I'll go and telephone," said Jeremy. "Don't rush off, will you, Simon? We'll have a drink and see whether we can tie up all the loose ends."

"Will you be able to get hold of the detective-inspector? Won't he be off duty?"

"Oh, they'll be able to contact Harding, I'm sure, if they want to."

~ * ~

"If Brian was killed shortly before you and Liz found Robert," said Simon to Jeremy thoughtfully, half an hour later, holding up a tumbler of scotch to the light, "Clive had nothing to do with it. He was at home manning the phone."

"I hope you're right. Clive is certainly hiding something about that evening, and he could still be involved, even if his protestations about murder are all true."

"And George? The boys said a Land Rover passed them, remember."

"George went home at about ten o'clock, according to Lucinda, and that fits with what Rose remembers. She phoned and asked him to go home. He could have gone back to collect and bury the body then, I suppose. But why not pick it up straight away, if he'd killed him? This business looks more like hit and run."

"But hold on, Remy," said Simon quickly. "George didn't bring the Land Rover down on the search for Robert. We were all on foot."

"That's true," said Jeremy, brightening. He didn't want to think of George being involved in his brother's death, even accidentally.

"And that gives us more information about Clive, doesn't it? Clive was at Sundials just before George went home, before you and Liz found Robert. Fran was there, too, for a bit, wasn't she? They can't all four of them be in cahoots."

Jeremy looked doubtful. "I see what you mean. But anyone could have gone out and knocked him down in ten minutes or so. As you say, it looks as though it must have been a hit-and-run incident, not murder at all. Though that doesn't explain why George buried him like that." He felt sure that Inspector Harding and his team would shortly be carrying out a thorough forensic check of the sharp bend below Copse Lane. But it was a matter of personal satisfaction to him to work the mystery out logically before the police solved it by painstaking collection of the facts.

"I can't for the life of me work out why the person responsible didn't report the death, though," said Simon.

"Scared, perhaps? Panic."

"Perhaps. Robert's adventure, by the way, may explain this odd business about the ballpoint pen."

Simon raised his eyebrows. "What ballpoint pen?"

"Haven't you heard about that?" said Jeremy. He explained. "I think Robert must have borrowed his father's pen on the way out. Maybe put it in his coat pocket."

"To make notes on badger-watching, perhaps," supplied Simon helpfully.

"Possibly so. He wouldn't notice he'd dropped it by the body, in the circumstances. Anyway, I'm sure the police will ask Robert about the pen, and it may help to destroy the circumstantial evidence against his father."

"Poor kid," said Simon. "He's had enough. They ought to leave him alone."

"As you did?" asked Jeremy.

Simon winced. "I guess you're right."

There was silence for a minute or two, a silence not exactly hostile, but certainly not companionable.

"We know Brian Warrendon was knocked down before ten-thirty," Jeremy went on doggedly. "Because Robert saw him more or less alive, and Robert was found in the churchyard around ten-thirty."

Simon made an effort. "I think Darren must have got home just before ten, but I didn't specially check the time. I was too concerned to try to get Darren to tell me the truth about where they'd been, so we could find Robert. That would mean the boys must have been at the bottom of the Copse Lane Estate about nine-fifty, say."

"Allow ten minutes for Robert and Chris to walk up to the Green, and for Robert to walk back—"

"That's right. We know Brian Warrendon must have been dying then, but how long had he lain there?"

"It's not unusual for the roads to be very quiet at night," said Jeremy sombrely. "He could have lain there for ages, except that Lucinda says she drove past in her car about nine-thirty. She would have seen him lying there. So, it must have been after that. The boys were splashed with mud by a vehicle, weren't they, now I come to think of it… that was why Chris wanted to come home. Unless..." He stopped, as another possibility struck him.

"George is definitely out of it," went on Simon, after waiting for a moment to allow Jeremy to complete his sentence. "He was with Fran from about eight-thirty onwards, then went straight home. And as I said, he was on foot, not in the Land Rover. He may have *buried* the man illegally, but he can't have killed him."

There was silence. "And the body could have been retrieved and buried at any time during the night," said Jeremy. "Possibly in George's Land Rover, though George *said* he found the body in the woods, not on the road. Which brings us to why," he added.

"Why he was killed? But surely, if it was an accident…"

"No, I meant why he was buried. Was it an attempt to cover up the time of death, or to slow down the discovery of the body? I must tackle George again… I'm convinced he told me a pack of lies last time I spoke to him. But the motivation baffles me. This business of the oil can't really have been that important as a motive for burying him, though I suppose it might have been for murdering him. But nobody did murder him, did they?"

"It looks that way," replied Simon, "But as for motives… I simply have no idea. It makes no sense to me at all."

Twenty-three

At breakfast the next morning, Rose declared her intention of going home, and, in spite of a number of objections from her host and hostess, she remained adamant.

"It's time for Robert to sleep in his own bed in his own room," she said stoutly.

Jeremy did not quite have the heart to break the news to her that the police would quite likely want another interview with Robert.

"And Clive will be coming home soon," she added with confidence. "He'll expect me to be there when he comes."

Liz looked at her sceptically but said nothing.

"Will you give me a lift home, Remy, please?" persisted Rose.

Jeremy capitulated. "Yes, of course, I will. You must do what you think best."

When he had taken Rose home, together with two suitcases, Robert's teddy bear and Dolly, Jeremy went into his study and sat at his desk. He must find time during the morning to visit George and Lucinda; there was pressing parish business, and he had not yet said Matins. On the other hand, his day off yesterday had consisted of a number of urgent parish demands, and he felt badly in need of some quiet respite from the demands of life. He sat for a few minutes quietly, letting his inner thoughts settle, seeking awareness of a deeper reality, a presence which the clamour of a busy life could so easily drown.

Then the telephone rang.

"Hallo," he said into the receiver, with difficulty surfacing into the everyday world. "St Martin's Rectory."

"Rector, it's Maddie Archer."

Just for a moment, Jeremy had to work hard to place the name.

"I live next door to the Althorpes... you know."

"Yes, of course," he said relieved. "What can I do for you, Mrs Archer?"

"It's... I don't really know how to say this. I ought to go to the police, but—"

"Would you like me to come round to you?" he asked, courteously. "It's no trouble."

"No... I... not here. I'll come to the rectory... may I?"

She sounded quite distraught and automatically Jeremy answered reassuringly. "Yes, of course. Come round at once, if you like."

"Oh, thank you. I took today off work to talk to the police, and I put my coat on to catch the bus into Winchester. But I... I just couldn't face it. Rose isn't at the rectory at the moment, is she?"

Jeremy did not know quite what to make of this. "Should she be?" he asked, bemusedly.

"N... no. But she was staying with you for a bit; I thought she might be still there. I... I don't want to see her at the moment. I thought I heard her next door this morning, but I wasn't sure."

Curious, thought Jeremy. Rose had always seemed to be on excellent terms with her neighbour. He would have expected Maddie to go round and welcome her neighbour home, in the circumstances.

"Rose went home this morning," he confirmed. "You can talk to me quite privately."

Within ten minutes, she was sitting on the edge of a chair in Jeremy's study, twisting her hands together in a classic gesture of distress and seemingly unable to meet his eyes.

"My dear Mrs Archer... Maddie," Jeremy said gently. "Please tell me what is upsetting you so."

"It's about Clive," she began incoherently, "I know I'm not the first, but I feel so bad about it. I've been trying to bring myself to tell the police, but I kept thinking... well, they can't really have anything on him, can they? But they're still holding him, aren't they? I'm sure he's kept quiet about... about what happened, for my sake. I feel I'm responsible for his being questioned all this time, when perhaps I could have got him out."

Jeremy listened in some amazement to these maunderings. Their overall implication, however, was plain. "You were with him on the Wednesday evening when Brian Warrendon was killed," he said flatly. "You *know* Clive couldn't have been involved."

She looked at him, tear-stained face and wild eyes showing the conflict that had kept her from earlier confession. "Yes," she whispered. "I mean... I didn't know which day the police thought Brian... But—" She took a deep breath. "The night Robert went missing, Clive came home from work, and I was babysitting—" Her voice dropped still further. "I went home, and he... he came too."

"Leaving Robert in the house alone."

She looked away. He could hardly hear her voice as she said simply, "Yes."

"And something happened between you." Jeremy's voice was quiet but stern, inexorable.

"He... we... we went to bed together." Maddie took a deep, sobbing breath. "I haven't been able to face Rose since."

For one dreadful moment, Jeremy was torn between a flame of righteous anger at the wicked, irresponsible self-indulgence shown by Clive and Maddie, without any thought for the proper care of an innocent child or the rights of a wife, and a deplorable desire to laugh. For at the precise moment of that irresponsibility for which he wanted to condemn Clive and Maddie, Rose, the wronged wife, had been playing with a fire of her own in the cottage at Two Marks with Simon; and that innocent child, Robert, had been about to gallivant around the countryside in an illicit fashion with companions who included Jeremy's own son.

Then he regained control of himself and managed to find some pity in his heart for poor Maddie. "You did right to tell me," he said soothingly. "I'm afraid we must pass the information on to the police, but it certainly gives Clive an alibi. I'm sure they will let him go."

She sniffed miserably.

"It was wrong," Jeremy went on. "Of all people, as your pastor I have to say that. But I think you're right in believing that this is not the first time Clive has been unfaithful to his wife. And Rose knows that."

"Now she'll have to know about me," wailed Maddie. "And she thinks I'm her friend!"

Jeremy's mouth twisted. "Let's go to the police station now," he said. "I'll take you in the car. It's best to get it over quickly, don't you agree?"

Maddie got up, sniffing, and let Jeremy help her on with her coat. Still stifling an unclerical urge to laugh, Jeremy drove her to Winchester. It was perfectly clear to him now why Clive had been so unwilling to tell the whole truth, and why he had seemed so ashamed; and all the time the man had had a perfectly good alibi, which he had refused to use, simply because of the ruin it would make of a woman's reputation! Who would have thought Clive was capable of such chivalry?

On their arrival, Harding insisted on interviewing Maddie himself, and after the interview she became more distressed than ever, depending on Jeremy for comfort, reluctant to let him leave even when he had conducted her to her own front door. So it was mid-afternoon before he was able to detach himself from a still mournful Maddie and concentrate on pumping George Warrendon for some true answers to replace the tissue of lies he had told last time.

He drove his car back to the rectory and walked the few yards across to Church End Farm. As he made his way through the yard to the side door, passing George's battered old Land Rover with its stained and bent bull bars, the last piece of the jigsaw fell suddenly into place. He knew who was responsible for Brian's death, and why it had been so desperately important for George to bury his brother before anyone found him.

At the farm door, he met Lucinda. She looked pale and her eyes were red-rimmed and slightly bloodshot. Her grey hair was unkempt and staring and any attention to personal grooming seemed to have deserted her altogether.

"Lucinda, how are you?" he said, as sincerely as he could. "I was just calling to see you and George. This whole business must have been very trying for you."

She looked at him vaguely for a moment, then her focus seemed to sharpen. "Trying? I should think it has! The police around the place the whole time, prying and asking questions, traipsing about in their muddy boots. No peace at all. And no nearer finding out how Brian was killed, either. I don't believe for a moment Clive Althorpe was involved… such a charming man. I can't think why they don't just leave well alone and go away." Lucinda snorted, and her eyes snapped with annoyance.

Jeremy opened his mouth to answer her, but she went on, shrilly. "Silly fuss. Brian wasn't murdered. No one in the village would do such a thing. And you're just as bad as the police. I hear you've been asking everyone questions as though you were a policeman yourself."

Jeremy raised his eyebrows in surprise at this gratuitous attack. "Come inside, Lucinda," he said, taking her arm. "I very much want to talk to you both."

She shook him off. "I can't spare long," she said. "I'm very busy this afternoon."

"All right," said Jeremy soothingly. "It won't take many minutes. Where is George?"

"Really, Rector, how should I know? He might be anywhere on the farm."

This gambit failed, since as they walked through the hall he could hear the click-click of a computer keyboard from the little farm office. With a little effort, Jeremy managed to persuade the couple to sit down with him in Lucinda's sitting room.

"George, Lucinda... since I last spoke with you, I have found out a lot more about what happened the Wednesday evening Robert was missing. I am sorry to have to say this, but I think both of you have been telling me lies."

Their reactions were quite different, as might have been expected. Lucinda bristled, and said the rector had no right to ask her any questions at all. George lowered his head into his hands in mute admission.

"Yesterday afternoon," went on Jeremy, "Simon Hellyer managed to persuade Robert to tell us what he saw that night which so frightened him."

George's head came up. "Remy! I never thought... Not—"

"Yes. Robert saw Brian dying in the road near the Copse Lane bend."

"Oh God," groaned George wretchedly. "That poor boy."

"I don't think it will take the police long to work out what must have happened, now they know where and when he was killed. Their forensic boys will be all over your Land Rover again tomorrow, I'll bet."

Lucinda got up. "I've already told you, Rector, I know nothing at all about Brian's death. This whole business is driving me to distraction. If you'll excuse me, I have better things to do than listen to you drivelling on about the death of a man I never liked and do not grieve for. The village is better off without him." And with this blunt speech, she left the room.

Jeremy half-rose to follow her, feeling vaguely that he should detain her pending police involvement. But his pastoral instincts told him that George needed him more than Lucinda did. She was unlikely to go far, after all.

"You'd better tell me, George."

George shook his head.

"I'll tell *you* what I think happened, then, shall I?" He was suddenly reminded of Simon's technique in telling the boys a story the previous afternoon. "You can set me right if I get anything wrong."

There was no movement from the other man.

"The oil business was a smoke-screen, wasn't it, George? Of course, it horrified you. You didn't want the valley spoilt by oil drills and prospectors, let alone an oil strike. That could have been a real motive for murder, but it wasn't a motive for hiding Brian's body when he was killed accidentally. You had to have another reason for that." He paused for a moment. "Lucinda took the Land Rover that evening, didn't she? What was wrong with the car, I wonder—wouldn't it start?"

"Had a flat," mumbled George into his hands.

"She came back about nine-thirty, as she said, driving fast up the hill round that dark corner, and she hit Brian as he walked down the road. I expect he was carrying no torch, as usual. You've got bull bars on the front of the Landie, haven't you, George? The impact broke his legs clean across and threw him back into the wall there where it hangs outwards. He hit his head on one of the flints that stick out of the wall at that height and was fatally injured."

George was silent. After a moment, Remy went on. He was working more of the details out as he spoke, building up the story as it surely must have happened, whether George and Lucinda were prepared to admit it or not.

"Lucinda panicked, I think. She drove home, found you out looking for Robert—I expect you left her a note, didn't you?—and rang Clive to ask you to come home. She demanded you hide the body. She couldn't face being involved in a criminal trial, and she couldn't do the job herself because Brian was too heavy for her to lift. Why didn't you report Brian's death immediately, George? Lucinda might not have been blamed. It was only an accident, though she shouldn't have driven on, of course,"

George stirred. "She'd had a few drinks at her friends' house."

"Oh, I see. Of course. She was over the limit."

"She said she wasn't drunk; she was perfectly capable of driving. I *told* her it was better to own up. I knew we'd never get away with it. But... You know what she's like, Remy."

Jeremy sighed. "Yes. I do." He leaned over and patted the farmer on the shoulder. "You can't shield her any longer, George. She can deny everything if she wants, but the facts are plain to see. I've already reported back to the police. They know Robert was there, and the probable time of death."

A faint feeling of dread touched him, like a cold breath of wind on a sultry autumn day. It was less than a premonition, no more than a half-formed thought, but he could not push it away. Once or twice before he had experienced such a feeling, and it had proved wise to take notice of it. So he sat listening to it, searching desperately for something specific to explain what it meant. He must have some reason for that faint unease, that vague sense of impending disaster; and if he could not identify it, someone else might be in danger.

"I'll tell the police what I know," said George heavily. "But Lucinda won't admit it; I know she won't."

"I think the police must be on the verge of putting the pieces together themselves, in fact, if they haven't already. We'll ring them from here and let them know. When Robert tells the police exactly what he saw—"

His voice trailed off. Where *was* Lucinda, he wondered suddenly. Perhaps he did need to detain her after all.

~ * ~

Simon took advantage of two consecutive free periods that afternoon and left school early, having cleared his absence with the head. He had a parents' evening to come back for later and was heavily involved in the school Christmas play the following Monday and Tuesday. He badly needed some time off. In spite of all his efforts, he had not found it possible to accept the stalling of his relationship with Rose. His hitherto complex emotions had been pared down to a simple, unrelieved longing to see her alone, even for a short while. He telephoned the rectory in an attempt to take her out for a drive and found that she had returned home to Sundials that morning.

He looked at his watch. It was two-fifteen. For one precious hour, before Robert finished school, he might be granted the felicity of being alone with her without interruption. He would neither demand anything of her nor press anything on her. He would be in her presence, and that was enough. He drove straight to Sundials with a lifting heart.

Fortune, however, refused him even this small boon. When he reached the house, he discovered that at lunchtime Fran Baker had telephoned from the school to tell Rose that Robert had suffered a relapse of his nervous withdrawal, and she thought he should go home. He found Robert curled up on the sofa, tucked under a rug and being regaled with excerpts from *The Hobbit*, while a distracted Rose seemed hardly to notice his own arrival.

He sat in an armchair quietly and drew in what comfort he could from the sound of her voice. Of medium pitch, its tone was clear and sweet and moved among Tolkien's paragraphs like a dancer. He tried to remember whether he had ever heard her sing. A kind of peace fell upon him as he listened to her. A melancholy, unsatisfied peace it was, its edges disturbed by banked-down desire and emotional hunger, but the closest to the reality he could come.

Her voice stopped. As he listened, it had grown rough and croaking. She coughed a little and then picked up the book again.

"Rose, would you like a drink?" Simon jumped to his feet. "Some water or fruit juice. Are the glasses in the kitchen?"

She shook her head. "I'll have to stop. My voice always goes like this if I read for too long. Simon—" she hesitated.

"Yes?" His eyes were eager.

"Will you read to Robert for me? Or recite some poetry—"

Simon looked down at Robert for his reaction. Poetry was not, in his experience, the favourite literature of boys of this age.

"'Now We Are Six,'" said Robert instantly.

"Oh, yes!" Rose's eyes shone. She looked up at their guest. "Do you know the A.A. Milne poems, Simon?"

He smiled. "I was brought up on them. My father used to read them to me." *Before my mother died. There wasn't any poetry reading after that.*

He sat down again, on a chair nearer the sofa this time. "How about 'Bad Sir Brian Botany'? I know that one off by heart."

"Yes, please!" Robert's pale, strained face became animated for a moment. "That's one of my favourites."

Simon leaned forward, fixing the boy's eyes with his own, and made a dramatic gesture. "'Sir Brian had a battle axe with great big knobs on—'"

Rose smiled at both of them lovingly and went out to the kitchen to make some coffee. Her thoughts were far removed from the coffee, and she made it inefficiently, so that it was weak and pale, and some of the grounds escaped from the lower part of the cafetiere jug and swam around in the liquid above the filter where they had no business to be. She poured milk from the bottle, partly into a jug and partly on to the table and wiped it up absent-mindedly with a sponge from the sink. Just as she was drying the work surface with a teacloth, Simon walked in.

She looked up quickly and flicked the end of the teacloth into the milk jug. "Is Robert all right?"

Simon came over to her and took the teacloth out of her hands. "He's fine. He's gone to sleep, I think. Do you want us to go and sit with him?"

"No. If he's asleep, he'll be better if we leave him undisturbed. Do you mind having coffee in here?"

Simon looked around. He had never been in this room, and he was immediately conscious of the difference in atmosphere. The sitting room, though clean and tidy and expensively furnished, lacked the human presence of this shabby, rather chaotic kitchen. A rush of pure affection for Rose welled up in him and he put his arms round her and gave her a hug. "Of course, I don't mind," he said. "Let's have it here at the table."

She set the mugs down, and they sat down facing each other. Rose took a sip from her mug and sighed deeply. "This is nice," she said simply. "The coffee isn't much good, though. I didn't measure it out properly."

Simon smiled. "It doesn't matter, my love." It was enough just to be here with her, sitting face to face with the coffee mugs between them. He would not have believed that his hunger for her could be even partially slaked by such a mundane activity as drinking coffee at a kitchen table. He felt as though he could have remained there looking at her across the table indefinitely without any diminution of happiness.

"It's just so good to see you," he said, trying to express an iota of what he felt. "How are you coping?"

"I'm glad to be home," she said. "But I'm still worried about Robert."

"Give him time," said Simon. "Yesterday was hard on him... I'm sorry about that, Rose. But we needed to know."

"Yes," she said. "I understand that. I think he's fretting about his father, too. But maybe now Clive will come home."

Simon looked at her and thought he had never loved her more than at this most unromantic of moments, when all her attention was devoted to her family. He tried to think how to say what he felt without putting pressure on her.

Fate, however, was still in an uncooperative mood. As he opened his mouth to speak, the doorbell rang.

Twenty-four

"Bother," said Rose. "I'll go and get rid of whoever it is and come back."

She looked in at Robert for a moment on her way to the front door and saw with relief that his eyes were still closed peacefully. The sound of the doorbell had not disturbed him. She opened the door. Lucinda was standing on the step.

Rose gaped at the sight, and her surprise was mingled with dismay. Lucinda had never visited Sundials during the time Rose had lived there. She was also reputed to be extremely difficult to eject from a house, once she had gained an entry. In short, she was the very last person Rose wanted to see at this moment.

In the split second it had taken Rose to form this train of thought, Lucinda was already moving over the threshold into the hall. To stand in her way would have been about as effective as trying to stop a tank.

"Lucinda," Rose said instead, trying to inject some hostessly pleasure into her voice. "This is a surprise."

She carried out a rapid mental review of the rooms available for Lucinda's reception. It seemed to her vital that Robert should rest, and to move him into bed at this juncture might easily result in his waking. The kitchen was out of bounds... no one must know Simon was there. The dining room was rather cold, unless you turned the radiator on full, but—

Her mental review, however, had taken too long. Lucinda was already in full sail towards the sitting room door. In vain, Rose darted in front of her, murmuring about Robert and quiet.

"Dear little Robert," said Lucinda with uncharacteristic sweetness. "I shan't disturb him. I just came to see how you were, after all your troubles. How is your husband? Isn't he home, yet?"

She sat down on a chair in the window, and turned her face, wreathed in insincere smiles, towards Rose.

Rose stood in the doorway, outmanoeuvred and forced to change course. "I'll make some tea, Lucinda," she said desperately, glancing at Robert to see whether he was stirring. "Please be quiet and don't wake Robert. I won't be long."

She scuttled away. Simon would have to leave. How frustrating it was, when they had had so little time together, that this particular afternoon should be spoilt. His presence was such a comfort to her.

Lucinda, left unsupervised in the sitting room, turned unfriendly eyes upon the sleeping Robert. She had come to find out exactly what Robert had seen on the night of Brian's death and stop him from divulging any more of it, particularly to the police. She had expected him to come in from school soon after her arrival this afternoon. Instead he was already here, sleeping.

Unreasonably, perhaps—but Lucinda never considered whether her attitudes might seem unreasonable to other people—she blamed Robert for all the misfortunes of the past weeks. George's lack of efficiency as a grave-digger, coupled with the inquisitiveness of Dolly's canine nose, had resulted in Brian's body being found. But without Robert's nocturnal activities on the night the man had died, no one would have discovered where or when he had been killed, and no one would have begun to question her account of her movements on that particular evening. To make matters worse, Robert had talked about what he had seen. In spite of his trauma and nervous reaction, which should have kept him silent, he had talked – and to Remy and that schoolteacher Simon, who would make sure the information was passed on to the authorities. How much more trouble would he cause, if he talked again?

Bitter resentment of the boy began to take hold of her as she sat watching him. It seemed to her that he was part of the malignant fate which had ensured that she had never enjoyed the good fortune she deserved. Bad luck and other people's inadequacies had plagued her all her life. She dwelt for a moment upon the particular inadequacy of George, who was spineless and unsuccessful, as well as socially her inferior. She should have abandoned him long ago and made some effort to rediscover her place in good society. She had a right to live her life and find some happiness, hadn't she? And now this insignificant small boy might rob her of even that possibility. She was in danger of going to prison, and he could confirm the evidence that would put her there. She had no illusions about that.

Her eye fell upon the pillow which Rose had used to prop Robert up against the arm of the sofa, but which had now fallen to the ground beside him. She got up from her chair, went across to the sofa, and stood looking down at the boy. His face was upturned, mouth slightly open. She bent down and picked up the pillow. It felt soft and heavy and its own gentle gravity seemed to pull it downwards. Smiling, she began to lower it towards Robert's face.

A few minutes later, she went to the door and called. "Rose! Something's wrong with Robert. I think... I think he's stopped breathing." Her voice sounded concerned but gave no indication of the pounding of her heart. She held a hand out in front of her. It was perfectly steady.

Rose appeared like a gale of wind, swept Lucinda aside in what seemed to the older woman a most disrespectful manner, and swooped on her son. The pillow lay on the floor beside the sofa as before. The boy's face was quiet, and his hair unruffled. There had been no struggle. Rose gave a wail of despair. "Oh no!"

She ran to the door and across the hall, all discretion quite forgotten, in the face of this overwhelming maternal disaster. "Simon! Simon, help!"

Lucinda stood rooted to the spot. This scene should have been played out between Rose and herself. She would have held Rose and comforted her, telephoned the doctor with deceptive slowness, done everything to give the impression of a concerned and capable friend. No suspicion could have attached to her, but Robert would still not breathe again. Suddenly her planned scenario was being swept aside by unforeseen circumstances, and for a moment she was at a loss.

Simon had been at the kitchen door, on the point of departure, his coat in his hand. The sharp urgency of Rose's cry brought him in a few strides to the hall. "What is it?" he asked quickly. "What's wrong?" He put his arms around her.

"Robert. It's Robert. Simon... he's... I think he's dead." She broke from him, dragging him by the hand into the sitting room, and fell on her knees beside the sofa sobbing.

Simon put his hand down and felt for a pulse.

"Was he all right when you came in with Lucinda?" he asked.

"Yes. It was just a few minutes—"

"Ring for an ambulance, Rose. Quickly."

Simon picked Robert up and laid him down on his back on the floor. He knelt beside him and without hesitation lowered his open mouth over the boy's face. Stunned, but with a new, slight hope, Rose watched him massaging Robert's chest rhythmically but gently, then breathing into Robert's lungs, making them exhale again, taking in new oxygen for another breath; over and over until it seemed that the process had gone on for hours. She looked at her watch. Lucinda had been in the house a little over five minutes.

Suddenly there was a convulsive movement on the floor, and Robert's lungs were heaving, drawing in breath without help. Simon sat back on his heels, his hand on the boy's wrist, panting a little and considering what he should do next. He thought the danger was over, but he would be happier if a doctor saw Robert. Quite apart from the physical effects of suffocation, this constituted one more trauma in a line of them. He could take Rose and Robert to the hospital in his car.

He picked up the pillow from the floor and moved to put it back on the sofa. Then he looked up, and his eyes met Lucinda's. He said nothing, but it seemed inadvisable to leave Lucinda to her own devices while he ferried Robert to hospital. He heard Rose briefly giving the required details to the woman on the switchboard. She added, the fear evident in her voice, "Please hurry."

Lucinda waited until Simon looked away again, to check Robert's pulse and breathing, and then she began to walk quietly towards the door.

Rose noticed nothing. Her eyes were fixed on her son's face. "Will he be all right, Simon? For a moment I thought he was dead."

Simon straightened up. "The hospital will check him over," he said. "It's... possible... there could be brain damage. But I don't think he stopped breathing for long enough to make that likely. We caught him in time." He said nothing to Rose of his other suspicions, but he noticed that Lucinda had disappeared.

"Oh, Simon, thank you. How wonderful you are!" cried Rose. She cast herself on his chest with enthusiasm, throwing her arms round him. Her embrace was born purely of gratitude, but he welcomed it just the same and bent to kiss her. Even in these circumstances he savoured her sweetness like a man finding dew in the desert.

"Well," said a voice behind Rose. "This is a fine welcome, Rose. I'm glad you haven't been lonely while I've been away."

Simon looked up, still holding Rose against him. Clive stood in the doorway. The two men gazed at each other over the top of her head. Clive's eyes were like steel, full of an icy anger perfectly under control. Simon's blazed. He let Rose go and stepped back.

"Clive!" she said. "You've come home. I am so glad." She seemed quite unembarrassed, and her sincerity was obvious, but Clive was clearly not in the mood to welcome it.

"I bet you are," he said with savage sarcasm. "Did you have to turn my house into a love nest for yourself and your toy boy? Or doesn't he have a place of his own?"

Rose quailed. "It isn't like that," she began.

"No. It never is, is it? There's always some wonderful excuse for misbehaviour."

"Well, you should know!" Rose retorted with a sudden flash of spirit.

There was a tense silence. Simon checked Robert's pulse and moved around Rose towards the door, but Clive barred his way. "I've got a few things to say before you go," he said. He began a furious tirade, not against the man in front of him, but against Rose.

In the moment of discovering his wife in Simon's arms, his contrition and self-loathing had vanished. It seemed to him that all his humiliation, all his confusion and shame, all his guilt, were the result of her inadequacies. If she had been different—firmer, more of an equal partner in their marriage—he would not have become the man he saw himself to be, successful and sophisticated on the outside, but rotten, selfish and corrupt within. Why should she find happiness when he had forfeited his? Her unexpected unwillingness to wilt under his sarcasm caught him on the raw. He railed at her, shutting his heart to her growing misery as she stood in front of him, her eyes blinded by tears, while all the time he knew her retort was justified, and his anger should have been turned upon himself.

Goaded beyond endurance at the ferocity of Clive's attack on his wife, Simon stepped between them. "Be quiet, damn you!" he said. "How dare you say such things to her?"

Clive ignored him totally. All his vengeful attention was focused on his wife, and his words flayed her like emotional whips.

Simon shouted at him again to be quiet, but Clive took no notice. Rose had begun to sob, and the sound of her weeping was suddenly more than Simon could bear. He strode up to Clive and with one swift blow to the chin, carrying all his weight behind it, laid him flat on his back on the hall floor.

The excess of chivalry which had prompted this action left Simon abruptly. Suddenly the little scene seemed sordid and ugly. He turned towards Rose and would have taken her into his arms to comfort her. But Rose, sobbing, had knelt down beside Robert, cradling him against her. She did not look at Simon.

The repentant knight-errant bent down and studied his fallen adversary closely. Clive was beginning to stir, murmuring slightly incoherently. Simon looked back at Rose. She was about to replace the pillow behind Robert's head.

"Rose," he said to her quickly. "Don't touch that pillow. It may be evidence."

She half-turned towards him. "Evidence of what?"

"I can't tell you now. Just keep it until I can send the police down."

He went out into the hall and picked up his coat from the floor where he had dropped it in his haste to come to Robert's aid. Lucinda was standing outside the front door, apparently listening to the altercation.

"You've got some explaining to do," Simon said to her roughly. "Where do you think you're going?"

"I thought my presence here might be unwelcome," said Lucinda acidly. She had clearly recovered her composure, and her eyes met his with a kind of manic fury. "Your explanations don't seem to have met with much success."

"I didn't make any," replied Simon briefly. "But you're going to make plenty." He put his hand on her arm. "Come on. I'll take you to the police station."

She shook him off. "Don't touch me," she told him shrilly. "I have nothing to say to those unspeakable policemen."

Off balance as a result of his encounter with Clive, Simon could not think how to make her do what he wanted. He moved between her and the gate. "I'm not leaving here without you. *And I'll give evidence against you, too.*"

She shot him a look of such venomous hatred that he stepped back involuntarily. In that moment's recoil, he was no longer in her path. She opened the gate, sped through the opening, and slammed it shut behind her. She almost sprinted along the lane. Behind her she heard Simon's voice shouting at her, but she neither knew nor cared what he was saying. All her attention was on planning her next move. Her paramount need at this point was to return home. If the police came for her, they would find her gone. A car would be useful, and there, ready to her hand, was a lively-looking sports model, relatively new and evidently capable of speed.

Simon had wrestled briefly with the gate and was running down the lane at speed when he saw her move in the direction of his car.

"Hi!" he shouted, as much in warning as in anger. The car door was unlocked but the ignition key was in his pocket. She wouldn't be able to start the engine, and if she tried to roll the car down the hill, she would crash it at the first corner, since the steering wheel had an automatic lock. Worse still, he could hear the rumble of a powerful engine pulling a heavy vehicle up the hill towards them.

He watched with horror as Lucinda opened the door and climbed into the driver's seat. Presumably with some notion of bump-starting the car on the long slope, she let off the handbrake and the car began slowly to roll forward.

Simon threw himself across the bonnet, his body covering the driver's side of the windscreen, which forced her to brake momentarily. The vehicle he had heard coming towards them hove into view. It was the ambulance. Presumably manned by at least two able-bodied people, it represented some hope of assistance. He jumped off the bonnet and dived for the driver's door. Lucinda resisted him, pulling on the door handle from the inside. She released the brake again and the car began to move. Simon managed to wrench open the door and put his foot on the sill, reaching across for the handbrake. She elbowed him viciously in the ribs and his foot slipped. He fell back into the road as the car gathered speed.

The ambulance pulled up immediately in its path, and a paramedic jumped out. Numbly, Simon watched as Lucinda tried to swerve around it. The steering wheel locked, and she braked hopelessly late, trying to avoid a head-on collision. With one vehicle stationary and the other still travelling quite slowly, the impact was much less than it might have been, but it was far from negligible. The bonnet of Simon's car crumpled, the bumper folding upwards at a crazy angle, as it met the immovable resistance of the larger vehicle, and Lucinda was flung forward into the windscreen. She emerged, shaken and bruised, blood dripping from a cut in her forehead, straight into the arms of the paramedic.

Simon picked himself up from the road a little gingerly and went to meet them. He gazed ruefully at his car, its radiator bent against the stout bumper of the ambulance, before turning to face the young ambulance driver.

"What's going on?" demanded that individual, with pardonable indignation.

"It's a long story," said Simon wearily. "Is she okay?"

The ambulance driver lowered Lucinda on to the verge gently. "A bit stunned," she said. "I'll have a proper look at her presently. You all right, yourself? I'm looking for Mrs Althorpe, and her son Robert."

"I'm fine," said Simon, rubbing his back. "Mrs Althorpe's with Robert in that house back there." He pointed to Sundials. "He stopped breathing, but I resuscitated him, and I think he's okay. You'd better check on him, though."

"Right," said the paramedic briefly. She waved to her colleague. "Can we have a blanket here, Les, please?"

"I'll look after Mrs Warrendon for you," Simon offered. "Go and see to the boy. Oh, and there's a man who was knocked out, too. I punched him. You'd better take a look at him as well."

"Sounds like a battlefield you've got around here," commented the ambulance driver cheerfully. "Don't move her, will you? Les'll see to her in a minute." She hurried away in the direction of the house.

Simon stood looking down at Lucinda, his stance one of guard duty rather than succour. He was still standing there while the second paramedic examined her, when George and Jeremy drove up in the Land Rover. They manoeuvred carefully round the dented car and the ambulance and pulled up the other side of Sundials.

George ran, staggering slightly like one enebriated, in the direction of his supine wife, whom the paramedics had covered with an ambulance blanket. Jeremy, following more slowly, put a hand on Simon's arm. "What's been going on?" he asked. "Is Robert all right?"

Simon looked round at him. How had Jeremy known Robert might be in danger? "He's fine," he said. "No thanks to this monster of a woman, though. I don't know what she has to do with Brian Warrendon's death, Remy, but I'm almost sure she tried to murder Robert this afternoon."

George, kneeling beside his wife, gave a moan.

"If I hadn't been there to resuscitate him," went on Simon inexorably, "Robert possibly wouldn't have lived. She suffocated him with a pillow, at least I think that's what she did. I told Rose not to touch the pillow, so the police can have a look at it."

Jeremy rested his hand on Simon's shoulder for a moment. "You've done well," he said quietly. The gesture had an oddly warming effect. "Is Rose all right?"

Simon grimaced. "She was distraught when she thought Robert had died. And I don't suppose I made things much better by knocking Clive down, though the bastard deserved it."

Jeremy raised his eyebrows. "You seem to have been having an exciting time down here," he said dryly. "Clive's home, is he? Should we take Lucinda inside with us, or is she going to the hospital?"

"The paramedic said to not to shift her," said Simon. "She slammed my car into the ambulance, so she's probably a bit shaken. It's routine not to move head or spinal injuries, even minor ones, just in case."

"I'll stay with her," said George.

Simon and Jeremy looked at each other.

"Have you telephoned the police, Simon?"

"I haven't had much chance. Rose may have thought of it, but to be honest, I doubt it."

"Would you do that for me? I'd better stay with George and Lucinda, I think." He did not need to give any reason. He was sure Simon would understand the mixture of pastoral responsibility and sleuthly interest involved.

Simon felt in his pocket and found that his phone wasn't there. He must have left it in his coat. He turned and ran back towards Sundials. In the hall, he found Clive sitting up against a wall, attended to by Dolly's tongue. Simon's coat was lying on the floor nearby.

Clive's eyes followed Simon as he went into the sitting room and telephoned the Winchester police, but he seemed too dazed to say anything. Simon asked to speak to Harding and was fortunate enough to find him available. After the briefest of resumés, the detective inspector cut him short, saying "I'm on my way."

Simon knelt beside Rose where she still sat, arms wrapped around Robert. The ambulance driver was already gently trying to attract her attention. "Come on, Rose. They need to take him to hospital."

She looked up vaguely and began to scramble to her feet. The paramedic gave Robert a brief examination and then carried him out of the house. Rose followed, accepting meekly the coat Simon handed her from the cupboard, and her handbag from the hall table. Simon looked at Clive. The second paramedic was kneeling beside him, talking to him in a low voice whilst fending off Dolly with one hand.

Simon stopped. "Dolly!" he said peremptorily.

She came over to him, wagging her feathery stump of a tail gently.

"Go to bed, Dolly," he said. She looked at him for a moment and then slowly slunk away into the kitchen. He heard the slither and thump of her basket as she climbed into it.

"Thanks, mate," said the ambulanceman.

As Simon went outside, he heard sounds of argument from the roadside. George was attempting to hold on to Lucinda as she struggled to her feet, ignoring the paramedic's instruction to the contrary. Rose was nowhere to be seen and must already have been helped into the ambulance with Robert.

"Get away from me!" Lucinda shouted. She struck at her husband and pushed him away.

He stepped back, the hurt and bewilderment plain in his face.

"It's all your fault," she stormed. "If you'd buried him deeper, no one would ever have known! We could have gone on living our lives in peace. Now, I never want to see you again."

She spat in his face and turned away, to be gripped by the guiding hand of the ambulanceman. Her waving arms were pinioned as she tried to swipe at his face. Jeremy moved to go with her, but her expression stopped him in his tracks. Instead, he turned back to attend to George, who stood with his head down, utterly crushed.

"I've sent for another crew to bring Mr Althorpe in," the ambulance driver told Jeremy. "I think we've got enough to cope with as it is."

Simon hurried forward, reaching Lucinda just as the ambulance crew were about to help her into the back of the ambulance. "Wait," he said vehemently. "You can't take a boy to hospital in the same ambulance as the woman who tried to murder him! Make her wait and let the boy's father go with them instead."

The ambulance crew looked at him rather helplessly. "I don't know anything about any attempted murder," began the driver.

"The police will be here in a moment," said Jeremy, looking up from his preoccupation with George. "They'll endorse what I say, I'm sure."

The ambulanceman made a move to go on loading Lucinda into the vehicle, and it seemed possible for a moment that Simon might crown his afternoon's activities by physically intervening in this situation as well, for the same chivalrous reasons and, in all probability, with the same humbling aftermath. On this occasion, however, he was given no opportunity to influence the course of events. The ambulanceman, who was operating a kind of strong-arm human straitjacket on Lucinda, looked up and saw the tall figure who had materialised behind Simon.

"I've sent for another ambulance to bring you in, sir. We're a trifle crowded in here, I'm afraid."

"I don't need any attention," said Clive calmly, stepping up into the back of the ambulance. "And I want to make sure my son has come to no harm. I know you want to fuss over me because I was knocked out for a moment, but I feel perfectly all right now, barring a slight headache. Believe me," he added, moving past Lucinda with the type of circumspection one might use towards a snake. "After what I've been through in the last few weeks, a blow to the chin comes almost as light relief."

He found a place to sit near Robert and lowered himself carefully into it. He reached for Robert's hand and held it gently. The hand grasped his tightly. Rose glanced up at Clive once, quickly, and looked away again, but Simon could see no fear or hostility in the glance. At Simon himself, she did not look at all.

Jeremy touched him comfortingly on the arm. "I think we'll leave them together for the moment, Simon," he said, watching the strained yet still oddly cohesive family unit reforming under these stressful conditions. He turned to the bemused paramedic. "I think Mr Althorpe will be a help to you with his family," he told him.

"Though it's probably best if he's checked over at A&E when the doctors have time. We can look after Mrs Warrendon until the second ambulance arrives. Are you ready now?"

The ambulanceman, somewhat overawed by the clergyman's cool assumption of authority, nodded, let go of Lucinda and handed her over to Jeremy before calling to the driver to set off. Jeremy helpfully shut the doors and left them to their task. He motioned to Simon to grasp Lucinda by the other arm. As they turned, a police car drew up smoothly outside the gate.

Twenty-five

Detective Inspector Harding had taken the phone call from Simon while perusing the latest forensic report from the team on the Warrendon case. It certainly looked like a hit and run incident, serious enough to warrant manslaughter charges, possibly, but no longer a murder case. In view of the downgrade, he would probably hand it over to Moorcroft to finish off. Hit and run cases were rarely solved unless there were witnesses. The boys' evidence, as he understood it—and Moorcroft would probably have to interview Chris Swanson and Robert Althorpe again—was that a 4x4 had passed them on the road just before they split up. In all likelihood, this was the vehicle that had done the damage. George's Land Rover might bear some more checking by forensic. He wasn't quite satisfied with the thoroughness of the job they'd done last time.

Simon's call delayed the transfer of the case, however. It sounded as though there had been developments, although Simon hadn't given him any details, and he had better see for himself what they were. In his experience, once Joe Public got involved in a serious criminal case, he was liable to do more harm than good. He had best get down there quickly before the reverend and this teacher sidekick of his got themselves into trouble. On-the-spot action by eye witnesses was one thing, but it was quite another when the action in question arose from deductions made by amateurs such as the reverend, however well-meaning they might be.

He arrived to find his two amateur detectives holding Lucinda Warrendon by the arms. Alarmed, he advanced swiftly towards them. "What on earth's been going on here?" he demanded.

"We have made what you might call a citizen's arrest," Jeremy explained. "Of Lucinda Warrendon, for the attempted murder of Robert Althorpe."

Harding blinked. What was this? Attempted murder of the child? What were they thinking of?

"She was probably also," went on Jeremy, "responsible for the accident which killed Brian Warrendon. She has been slightly injured in this latest accident, caused by her attempt to steal a car." He indicated the wreck of Simon's car beside them. "Another ambulance is on its way, I understand, to take her to hospital for a check-up. I imagine you may want to send an officer with her."

Harding had listened open-mouthed to this rather formal recital, but it certainly covered the facts. "Wendy!" he called.

PC Hargreaves emerged from the car, mobile in hand.

"We're going to need you. Now," he said to Jeremy and Simon. "I shall leave Mrs Warrendon with PC Hargreaves to wait for the ambulance, and you two are going to explain to me what has been going on since I saw you last."

"May I suggest you use handcuffs, Inspector?" said Jeremy mildly. "Mrs Warrendon has already caused a great deal of trouble to the irregulars."

Harding looked at him, slightly irritated at this trespass on his authority. On the other hand, it had been very diplomatically put.

"I agree with Remy," said Simon, who had been silent up to now. "She is a very dangerous woman."

As if to confirm his opinion, Lucinda twisted violently in their hold and threw herself backwards in an attempt to wrench herself free. Within two steps, however, Harding and Wendy Hargreaves had taken a strong grip of her, and Harding snapped the handcuffs on.

The second ambulance drew up at that moment, and with a minimum of fuss, PC Hargreaves explained the situation to the ambulance crew, and helped them propel her charge, struggling, into the back of the ambulance, before climbing in after her.

"There certainly doesn't seem to be much wrong with her," said Harding. "But I suppose they'll want to give her the once-over. I'll be along to join you shortly," he added to his subordinate as the ambulance doors closed.

The door of the house still stood open, and Harding ushered them all inside. The hallway looked disordered, which was not, he remembered, its normal state. A man's coat lay on the floor, and there was a ruffled pillow in the doorway.

Simon pointed to the pillow. "That may be evidence, Inspector," he said.

"Of what?" asked Harding, bemused.

"The attempted murder Remy mentioned. Lucinda tried to suffocate Robert, I think."

Harding shut the front door firmly. "Leave it where it is for the moment," he said. "I'll bag it up properly before I go. For the moment, I want the facts, and in order, please."

"You seem to know your way about in this house," he heard Jeremy say to Simon. "See if you can find the coffee, will you? I think we all need some."

~ * ~

A few minutes later, mugs in hand, they were ensconced around the kitchen table where Simon and Rose had sat together earlier that afternoon. Harding had wanted to exclude, for the moment, the formality and bureaucracy which would all too soon overtake this investigation again and reduce it to the procedures of arrest and criminal prosecution. The incident room was only a few hundred yards away, but Sundials had stood open and inviting, and he was human enough to prefer it to some more official, and less comfortable, venue.

"Now, Reverend," he said.

"It was partly my fault, I suppose," said Jeremy slowly. "I precipitated Lucinda's actions this afternoon. I made it clear to Lucinda and George that I knew it must have been Lucinda who was driving the Land Rover that killed Brian, and while I was talking to George about it, she slipped out and came down here. She must have thought there was no evidence without Robert and tried to get rid of him. She can't have thought it through, though. I imagine you would have made the connection anyway. After all, it must logically have been George's Land Rover, and you could have checked that anyway, I expect. Besides, George would have picked up his brother straight away, if he'd hit him. He didn't have any reason to leave him in the road and go back for him later, and it would have been quite out of character."

George sat silently throughout this recital, giving no indication that he had heard any of it.

"But Lucinda might have panicked," went on Jeremy, wondering how much he should tell Harding. "I think she was probably over the limit and didn't want the Force breathalising her."

"Ah," said Harding, making a note. "And what have you to say about that, Mr Warrendon?"

"I'm not saying anything," said George heavily. "You'll have to ask Lucinda. I told you I buried Brian, and I'm not telling you anything about Lucinda. I tried to keep her out of it," he added, sadly.

Jeremy sighed. Lucinda would probably get herself into worse trouble through resisting their questions, and it would do George's position no good. Still, at least the farmer was no longer to be considered an accessory to murder. Perverting the course of justice was quite bad enough.

"You'd better tell the inspector what happened down here, Simon," he said at last.

Simon tried to make his account as clear as Jeremy's had been, but the events had happened too quickly, and he had been under emotional strain. The salient facts were simple, however. Lucinda had been in the room with Robert alone for five minutes or so, had called Rose, and had obviously expected to be able to delay the summoning of medical assistance until it would be far too late to revive Robert.

"But I knew some child resuscitation techniques," explained Simon simply. "So, I got him going again. With luck, he won't suffer any permanent damage."

Harding looked at him with respect. Resuscitating a child was a delicate affair, balancing controlled strength, rhythm and a gentle touch.

"And then I ran after Lucinda," Simon went on, "Leaving Rose to get the ambulance." He deliberately said nothing about the altercation with Clive. If Clive wanted to press assault charges later, he would have to own up. But for now, he didn't want to go over it again. "She got in my car and tried to drive it away, but I had the ignition key in my pocket, although I hadn't locked it up. The steering lock stopped her turning the wheel, and she smashed it into the front of the first ambulance. That put paid to her escape attempt." He shrugged. "That's about it, really."

There was silence for a while after he had finished. Then Harding got to his feet. "Well, thanks for that. We'll need a statement from both of you, of course. But just now, I think I'd better go and interview the lady." He went off to his car, taking the pillow with him in a polythene bag.

Simon picked up the coffee mugs and washed them up in the sink. When he had finished, he found his jacket and said to Jeremy, "I'd better be off, too. I've got a parents' evening tonight… and I don't suppose the Althorpes would thank me for being here when they get back, anyway."

Jeremy looked up, as though he had heard the ache in Simon's voice. "You haven't told me anything about what happened this afternoon," he said. "Apart from what you did for Robert, for which both Rose and Clive will be very grateful."

Simon shrugged his shoulders irritably. "Rose, maybe. I don't suppose Clive appreciated being knocked down, though. As for the rest, there's nothing much you don't know already," he added. "I... I don't really want to go over it again. D'you mind?"

Jeremy shook his head. "All right," he said.

George did not look up as Simon said goodbye to him. His thoughts were clearly far away from the sunny Sundials kitchen.

Simon caught Jeremy's eye across the table and shrugged slightly. "I'll be seeing you, Remy." There was a faint interrogation in the words. He was conscious that the afternoon's events had brought a chapter of their lives to a close, and it was hard to be sure which of the relationships that had developed in the past few weeks would survive into another chapter.

Jeremy smiled at him. "Soon," he said, and the word sounded like a promise. "Liz and I really do want you to come and have dinner with us."

Simon smiled. "Fine," he said. He looked at George again, and sadness crept into the smile. "I'll leave you to it, then." He slung the jacket over his shoulder and walked through the hall to the front door. He looked his car over sadly for a while where it stood, bonnet crumpled from its encounter with the ambulance. He had been rather fond of that car, but it looked like a write-off now. He took out his phone and rang the local garage to explain the situation. They would probably let him hire one of their demo cars, or even give him a courtesy one. No doubt Jeremy or Harding would have given him a lift, if he'd asked them, but he preferred to be alone. He could walk home easily enough across the fields and get one of the other teachers to give him a lift in to school for the parents' evening.

~ * ~

The Althorpes sat silently in a hospital cubicle, waiting for the consultant to return and confirm that Robert could go home. The boy lay between them, asleep and peaceful on his trolley.

Clive reached across him and touched Rose's arm. "I'm sorry," he said awkwardly.

Rose looked up and her eyes met his. There was neither anger in them nor warmth.

"Simon saved Robert's life," she said neutrally. "I think he deserved some thanks, not a tirade, particularly not one directed at me… he wasn't going to take kindly to that, you know."

Clive swallowed a protest at the particular method of thanking Simon that she had chosen.

"Besides," she went on firmly. "You're judging me by your own standards. I've done nothing to be ashamed of. Nothing has happened between Simon and me while you've been away." She paused, and then added, deliberately, "Not yet."

Robert stirred, murmuring in his drug-induced sleep, and Clive laid his hand on the boy's as it moved on the blanket. Robert's fingers closed upon his father's tightly again, as if on a lifeline. Clive put his head down against the side of the bunk, and Rose remembered Jeremy's warning to her of his state of mind. And he had been knocked out, too, albeit briefly. The A&E people had said something about mild concussion.

"We'll talk about it later," she said more gently. "When we get home."

~ * ~

But when they reached Sundials, two hours later, after Robert had been pronounced fit and well, Clive was too exhausted to do more than sit in a chair with a drink, and Rose found herself ministering to his needs as well as Robert's, making him a meal and cajoling him into eating it, as solicitously and selflessly as ever. She despised herself for it, but she could not break the habit of a lifetime. Was nothing ever to be resolved? Were the decisions about her life to be made by default as so often before? No, she told herself firmly. *It will be different this time.*

At ten o'clock she persuaded Clive to go to bed, while she cleared up the debris of the meal. When she reached the bedroom, she found him sitting up, waiting for her.

"Rose, when I said this afternoon that I'm sorry, I didn't mean only for what I said to you earlier. It goes deeper than that." He stopped, then went on, clearly with an effort, "I've treated you abominably for years. Worse than you know."

"With Olivia?"

"With her... and others." He hesitated. He didn't think she knew about Maddie, and only Maddie should tell her.

"I think I've known for years, if I had really thought about it," said Rose. "I didn't think, because I didn't want to know. It was easier to pretend."

"It always is," he replied unexpectedly. "You should have brought it out in the open a long time ago, Rose."

She looked at him. "I know. I've been a coward all our married life, and I suppose that's made it easy for you to be a bully."

He winced. "I've never raised a hand to you!"

"No," she agreed. "That's not your style, Clive. Words are your style. You've raised your voice often enough."

She had the feeling that her temerity surprised him. Had he expected her to forgive him out of hand and tell him it didn't matter?

"I'm sorry," he said again, helplessly.

She undressed quickly, pulling on one of the warm shapeless nightdresses she always wore in the winter. Clive watched her silently, at least outwardly unmoved. She had a momentary vision, quickly extinguished, of Simon's face as he had led her to the bed-alcove in his sitting room; full of passion and excitement, alive with an expressive fire. Suddenly, she felt that she could not share a bed with Clive tonight. She picked up her dressing gown and opened the bedroom door.

"Rose, please—"

She turned towards him, moved in spite of herself by the raw misery in his voice, the strain in his normally cool, composed face. "What is it you want?" she asked. "I accept your apology. Is that what you want... my forgiveness?"

"Yes," he said. "That... and another chance."

"Another chance?" she repeated stupidly. "At what?"

"Loving you."

She was aware that these were new sentiments; contrition instead of criticism, requests rather than demands. There was even a hint of humility. But the response he asked for was more than she could give.

"You haven't loved me for years," she said. "And I should have stopped trying to, long before I did. Loving you nearly destroyed me. And fearing you hasn't been much better. What do you suggest?" she added, bitterly. "Begin again where we left off?"

"Make a new start," he said urgently, reaching for her hand and imprisoning it. "I promise it will be different this time. No more affairs, no more despising you, criticizing you. I know how much I've hurt you in the past. But I've come to realize just recently how stupid I've been. When we were young, I thought we could mean a lot to each other, but I let it slide. There could still be something left in our marriage, for both of us, if we try." He reached for her other hand, began to pull her gently towards him.

It was an effort to resist his new sincerity. Against her will, she found herself allowing him to succeed. Then she looked down at him and remembered the lies, the deception and the heartless domination of so many years. At the beginning, he had seemed just as charming as he was trying to be now. Later, he had not thought the charm so necessary. Her attractiveness to Simon, and the possibility that she might leave him, had made him see her with different eyes, but that was all. With an effort, she began to move away from him.

"Rose," he said desperately. "For Robert's sake—"

She halted. *For Robert's sake.* Whatever her own reservations about Clive's sincerity, whatever her doubts about any future happiness with him, it was not herself alone that she must consider. Robert had been afraid of his father, but what if Clive did change? Could she rob her son of his father?

She pulled her hands free, left the bedroom and went across the landing to where Robert was sleeping, the sedatives which the hospital had administered still ensuring his rest. As on so many previous occasions, she gazed down at the person she loved most in the world, but never before had she experienced so many conflicting emotions while she did it. He was safe, and she felt relief because of that. But the traumas of the past few weeks would leave their mark. He might relapse further into silent withdrawal or need special therapy to help him recover. It might be months before he would be able to return to the normal concerns of childhood. She had been warned of possible nightmares, loss of concentration at school, fear of friends or ordinary play situations... the list was alarmingly long.

She sat beside him in the chair by his bed. Clive's own harsh experiences, and the apparent breaking of his spirit, might make him, too, in need of her care. There was no guarantee he would be able to help her to look after Robert. But in any case, it was clear that to remove Robert from his home and break his relationship with his father would probably make matters worse for both of them. She wondered miserably whether she was entitled to injure another human being in that way, for the sake of her own happiness. She closed her eyes and prayed, wordlessly, desperately, for release from Clive, from the demands of her marriage that seemed to ask so much of her and give so little back.

Suddenly she longed for Simon. His warm, vital presence, and his certainty that their own personal happiness was important, would make her indecision seem stupid and unnecessary. Since the night of the dance, he seemed to have had no doubts about their relationship; he knew what he wanted. The doubts were all hers, and even now she could not rid herself of them.

It was at that moment, ironically, that she knew she would not be able to do what Simon wanted her to do, what she herself longed to do. The burden of her husband and her son, their needs and longings, their weaknesses and failings, would always weigh too heavily on her. She was not strong enough to fight for her own happiness and hope to win. *If I fail Robert now, there will be no happiness for me anywhere. Whatever Simon and I might have had will be blighted from the start.*

She sat beside Robert for a long time, the tears trickling slowly, unchecked, unnoticed, down her face, her heart wrung by grief and self-contempt, as the hours of darkness crept on, and, at last, the dawn came.

Twenty-six

"Well, at least we no longer have to fear the presence of a murderer in our midst," said Liz cheerfully over breakfast the next morning. "Lucinda will be charged with manslaughter, I suppose. Or will it be attempted murder? Or both?"

"There never was any murder," Jeremy reminded her. "Brian's death was an accident."

"I know. But Lucinda nearly killed Robert. That wasn't an accident."

"I suppose you're right," agreed Jeremy sadly.

"George tried to protect her," Liz went on. "He always has. Such a mistake. It means she's never recognised that actions have consequences."

"People don't use logic when they're afraid," Jeremy reminded her. "Lucinda simply began to believe that Robert was spoiling everything for her, getting in her way. So he must go. I believe it's not uncommon for psychopathic murderers to begin that way, with a kind of over-weaning conceit. *What's best for me is the only thing that matters,* is the way the argument runs. If she hadn't killed Brian accidentally and tried to wriggle out of the consequences, perhaps she wouldn't have started to think like that. Fortunately, Simon was there to resuscitate Robert. Otherwise—"

"You knew Robert was in danger, didn't you?"

"Not really. I didn't *know*. But I felt uneasy, so George and I went down to Sundials just to make sure."

Liz said nothing for a moment. Her husband often had these moments of uncanny knowledge… she didn't know whether to call them telepathy, extra-sensory perception or something more spiritual. She accepted that they were real without trying to understand them.

"Is Lucinda mad, Remy?" she asked instead. "She must be, to do something like that."

"I don't know. I can't help remembering the way she looked when I saw her at the farm on Friday afternoon. Very wild-eyed, on the edge of breaking down, I thought at the time. She nearly fractured the paramedic's arm when he tried to get her in the ambulance. I suppose the psychiatrists will assess her. Fear," he added, grimly, "is a terrible emotion. If only she could have faced up to it."

"She'll have to face up to it, now," said Liz, briskly. "The criminal justice system will see to that. Will you go to see her?"

Jeremy sighed. "I suppose so. She's still one of my parishioners, after all. The prospect doesn't thrill me, I admit. She won't want my help or counsel. I may be able to do something for George, though, perhaps," he went on more cheerfully. "He'll face charges too, I imagine."

"And what about you?" she asked.

"Me?"

"Have you decided what you're going to do?"

"About what?"

"About staying here, of course!" A hint of exasperation crept into her voice. "You asked me how I'd feel about moving."

"Oh. That. I'd forgotten, with everything that's happened."

"If you leave now, you'll be welshing on your own parish responsibilities, I suppose," she said, tentatively.

He smiled. "Perhaps. I don't know. I haven't had much time to think about it lately."

She got up and began to clear the breakfast dishes. "Well, leave it for now," she said, carefully keeping the disappointment out of her voice. "We'll be here next term anyway. I need to start planning for next year's preschool activities soon. If I survive the nativity play this week, that is."

"Christmas," said Jeremy, brightening. "That's something to look forward to. Advent always is my favourite season of the year."

~ * ~

At supper, Rose watched Robert, awake and physically recovered, though subdued and silent again, while he ate very little and even pushed away his mashed banana. She hugged him reassuringly and helped him to run his bath and find his pyjamas. His appetite would return in time. But she hoped very much that no more disturbances would set back his recovery. He needed time and peace.

By contrast, when she put their own dinner on the table, Clive ate everything that was put in front of him and insisted on clearing the dishes for her afterwards. "I can hear the bells," he said. "Go to ringing practice, Rose. It'll do you good."

Rose pushed back her hair. "Is it Wednesday? I've lost track." She opened the back door and listened for a moment. "You're right. They're short of people, too, by the sound of it. I can only hear five. I hope Ben isn't ill again. He looked better on Sunday."

How long ago last Sunday seemed, she thought, as she put her coat on. The last thing she wanted to do this evening was to ring. Even an evening spent with Clive, this new and disarmingly eager-to-please Clive, would have been preferable. But she must see Simon, and Simon (hoping to see her?) would surely be at the tower tonight. She wondered whether Clive had realised this, whether he was deliberately engineering an encounter between her and Simon, and if so, what he expected of it.

She walked down the lane leaning into a cold blustery wind, hugging her coat round her for warmth, her torch lighting the wet ground inadequately as she picked her way. The church rose tall and imposing on her left, an outline against the faint town-glow on the horizon beyond it. Its bulk was vaguely comforting.

Inside, the tower was warm with heat from the electric fire, and the rhythmic swinging of the ropes and their coloured sallies was familiar, almost cosy. She leaned against the tower wall and watched the movements of the ringers, remembering the evening, only six weeks before, when she had come here smarting from Clive's steamroller tactics over Robert's schooling. It seemed a lifetime away, and herself a different person, yet outwardly the scene was an exact replica.

She tried not to look at Simon. To meet his eyes risked giving away everything, and that could not be done here, in front of everyone. Yet she knew she had come in order to speak to him, that nothing else mattered at all.

The practice continued for over an hour. A car full of visiting bellringers turned up, even later than Rose, and allowed the more proficient of the St Martin's ringers, including Simon, to ring Stedman and Kent Treble Bob. When they rang Plain Bob and Grandsire, she took her turn on the treble and rang badly, her thoughts elsewhere, and the others were kind to her about it and pretended not to mind that she ruined every method in which she took part. Once Simon rang beside her, correcting her mistakes as he had done during the quarter-peal, seeming to turn a knife in her heart by his closeness and the sound of his voice.

At last the practice was over. She knew Simon would hold back until they had left the tower with the others; that he would walk beside her casually, and, as casually, offer to take her home, and that he would somehow contrive to do it so that the other ringers melted away into the darkness, to their cottages or with Geoff and Ken to the local pub, and left them walking in the dark, alone.

And so it was. They said goodbye to the others and went out into the little car park by the church. When the last of the local cars had gone, and Geoff and his son had invited the visiting ringers for a drink at the Bell, Simon took her torch from her and put an arm round her shoulders. "Shall we take the car? Mine's at the garage, but they gave me one to drive for the moment."

She shook her head. "It's not raining. I'd rather walk."

He turned her towards home and began to walk up the lane.

"Simon, wait. I… I want to talk to you."

He stopped at once and went back into the churchyard. Geoff had locked up the church, but there was shelter from the wind behind the tower where an enormous flying buttress anchored the ancient north wall. Simon found the tomb of a long-dead noble family, marked by a great flat stone, and swept the leaves from it to make a seat for her. The faint glow from the security lights on the village school lit her face dimly. He propped himself against the buttress a few feet away.

"What is it?" he asked her. "Something's happened, hasn't it? Is Robert okay?"

She nodded. "Yes, it's not Robert."

This was the interview she had sought, but now she could find no words to tell him what she wanted him to know. It was impossible to explain the tangle of reason, unreason and conviction which had brought about her decision.

"Darling," he said at last, very low. "Please tell me."

At this she began to cry, quietly and painfully, but when he would have come and taken her in his arms, she held him off.

"Simon, it isn't any good," she said sadly. "There just isn't any way for me to leave Clive and… try to find happiness with you. It simply won't work."

He was silent. He felt that deep down he had known for a long time that their relationship would end this way. That sense of inevitability left him bereft of words to answer her.

"I've found something with you that no one else has ever given me," she went on after a moment. "I'll never forget that… I'll always be grateful. And for Robert's life."

"Grateful!" he said bitterly. He felt as though an enormous gulf had opened between them. "Rose, I don't want your gratitude. You know what I want… what I have always wanted."

"It's partly because of Robert," she gabbled on, ignoring his words, trying to find some explanation that he would accept, that would leave him feeling less rejected, less bitter. "I couldn't uproot him now; he's been through too much."

"You know I don't ask you to do that." *A few stolen moments are all we've ever had,* he thought. *But I could live on stolen moments, if I can't have more.*

"And it's Clive, too. He's had a rough time. When you've lived with someone for years, leaving them is like leaving half your life behind. And I'm too old for you, I see that now."

"Rose, you don't really think any of these are *reasons,* do you? In forty years, we'll all be old… what does it matter?" The words rose up and choked him.

"No," she cried desperately. "I'm no good at reasons, I know I'm not. I can't tell you why I have to do this, but I know I do. It can't be. I can't go on with it. I want to, but I can't. Oh, Simon, I'm so sorry!"

Simon put his hands on her shoulders and pulled her towards him. He longed to over-persuade her, to take her in his arms and kiss her into submission, to sweep all her crazy notions away and crush her resistance with the sheer force of his passion. But as he looked into her eyes, he saw that, vulnerable though she was in many ways, weak though her arguments might seem to him, in this, her will was stronger than his own. She had made up her mind, and nothing he said or did would deflect her from her decision. His resistance would only cause a quarrel and make their parting bitter and irrevocable.

His hands dropped to his sides. "Oh, Rose," he said, his voice breaking. "I could have loved you so much… so much."

She gave a sob, then stood silent, her eyes fixed on him. They stood there, a few feet apart, for a long time, as though an invisible cord kept them from moving away. At length, he turned towards the path. "I'll take you home," he said huskily.

They walked, still not touching, along the lane to the white gate. He opened it for her and let her go past him to the front door. Then he turned and began to walk back to where his car was parked by the church. He strode steadily away from her and didn't look back.

Rose watched him until she could no longer make out the bobbing light of the torch beam. Then she went inside the house and closed the door.

Robert came out of the sitting room in his pyjamas and put his arms round her, his head leaning against her stomach.

"Daddy wanted me to go to bed. But I couldn't go to sleep until you came home, Mummy."

She bent over him and kissed the top of his head.

"Well, I'm home now," she said.

~ * ~

Simon drove home in a hell of grief that turned rapidly to fury. He couldn't see how he could ever become reconciled to a situation where Rose would revert to being just an acquaintance, a fellow bellringer, the wife of a man he despised and distrusted, instead of becoming his lover as he had hoped. She had come very close to leaving Clive for him, he knew that beyond doubt. But not close enough.

It seemed to him that the relationship had always been fragile. A wrong choice, the wrong circumstances, and it had been all too probable that it might vanish like summer mist. And Robert's traumatic experience had proved the catalyst. Because of Robert's need, Rose would not leave Clive and take the boy from his father, however inadequate that father had been. And Clive had even shown penitence, damn him! Simon banged his fist on the steering wheel with frustration. He was not in the least convinced that Clive's penitence was real. After all, in the past Clive had never acknowledged that Rose had any right to anything... not faithfulness or kindness or consideration. Why should he suddenly change his tune now?

He pulled up outside his house and sat in the car fuming. Even without Clive's penitence, he wondered whether Rose would have left him. She wouldn't have embarked on a new relationship while her son was still suffering emotional trauma. It had been naive of him to think that she would, he could see that. But perhaps later, if Clive were to let her go, she might… But it was no use thinking of that. Clive was still there, in possession. It was over. Over before it had properly begun. He had to put it behind him and move on.

Move on. The words echoed around his mind as he locked up the car and went inside. The room was cold, the fire unlit, his supper dishes still stacked on the draining board in the kitchen area. Dregs of coffee stained a mug on the table beside his chair. Instead of mellow, warm and inviting, it was suddenly a lonely wasteland.

He enjoyed the job at Northchurch College. It suited him. He liked the boys, and they liked him. He had been happy there, and in this cottage. But everything had changed. Did he want—could he bear—to stay here with Rose just a few miles away, and watch her struggling on with a rotten husband and a traumatised child, by her own choice living without him and the support he could have offered her?

He sat by the empty fireplace with his face in his hands, and remembered that magical but ill-wished evening, a scant month ago, when the two of them had sat there together. The depth of his need of her horrified him. He had never felt anything remotely like this for anyone. She was everything he had always longed for in a woman, and more. She fulfilled something in him that had been an aching void. And now she was lost to him… worse than lost. She herself had chosen… *chosen* to turn her back on what they could have had together, to reject him for reasons he couldn't understand. How could she? *How could she!*

He took a breath. He mustn't blame her. He didn't want to blame her. She had done what she thought was right. How many women would have had the courage and the certainty to do that? She had rejected him not because of Clive but because of Robert.

And Robert needed her, too. He thought about Robert for a while and felt calmer. Rose's anxiety for her missing son, her insistence on dropping everything to look after him when he returned traumatised, had evoked that deep maternity in her which Simon both loved and feared—loved because it healed some deep sense of deprivation caused by the loss of his mother; feared because it threatened the romantic love he wanted from Rose for himself. But it occurred to him that a Rose who let her son's needs come second to her own wouldn't be the Rose he loved. It was important to him that her essential goodness and selflessness remained unsullied. Idealism in some circumstances irritated him, but in Rose it wasn't high-minded rubbish but pure untarnished gold.

He washed up the dirty dishes, made himself more coffee, and turned on the electric heater; he couldn't be bothered to light the wood burner. He sat and started to mark the exercise books still stacked in a pile beside his chair. They were about the normal standard for Year 7… smudged and untidy and full of spelling mistakes, but a few of them showed some dim understanding of the novel they were studying. Only a few, but then it was always the few that made teaching worthwhile. You could put up with the mass of mediocrity, even with the troublemakers, for those few; their interest and achievement were the reward you needed. Slightly soothed, though still sore at heart, he put away his pen and got ready for bed, though he doubted that sleep would come.

~ * ~

After she had checked that Robert was sleeping peacefully, Rose sat quietly in the kitchen, rocking herself gently to and fro in the chair by the Aga. Clive had made coffee for both of them, but then had mercifully gone away to his study, perhaps sensing that some crisis had passed, and she needed solitude to assimilate it. At first, she felt rather numb, not quite able to believe that her St Martin's Summer was over—the promise and excitement and sheer warmth of her love for Simon that, in the end, had led nowhere but this bleak sacrifice of hope. They had begun a journey towards each other, only to find an insurmountable barrier across their way, a permanent Road Closed sign that had forced them to travel in different directions, forever bypassing the route they would have chosen.

The tears sprang to her eyes as she remembered Simon's face when she told him it was over. Incredulity and pain had struggled there, and then all emotion had been wiped from his expression as he let go of her. They had walked home in a dreadful silence, while she tried to work out what he was feeling. He had shut her out, just as he did everyone else. *I've lost something so precious,* she thought, as the tears ran unchecked down her cheeks, *and perhaps so has he. But what else could I do?*

She sat silently weeping for a long time. At last, Clive came into the kitchen.

"Come to bed, Rose," he suggested.

She shook her head. She had not shared a bed with him since the night of the St Martin's ball, when he had left her to go with Olivia, and Simon had taken on the role of escort. Perhaps one day she would have to do so again, if any real relationship were to be revived between them, but not tonight.

"You should try to get some sleep, anyway," he encouraged her, to show that he wasn't pressing her to share a bed with him. "Have a lie-in, in the morning. I don't have to go into work early tomorrow, so I can take Robert to school, if you like."

"I'm not much good at lie-ins," she said drearily.

Clive pulled out a chair and sat down. "You've said goodbye to him, haven't you?" he asked... more gently than she had expected. But Clive didn't seem to be acting the way she expected, in a number of respects.

"To Simon?" she said, not pretending to misunderstand him. "Yes, I have." She looked up at him. "If I'm to stay with Robert— and you— it couldn't have worked out for him and me. And you... will you say goodbye to Olivia?" It was a challenge, to see whether he was serious about trying to make a fresh start in their marriage. Only for Robert's sake was she countenancing even the attempt. Clive must make sacrifices, too.

"Yes," he replied steadily, meeting her eye. "To Olivia, and to anyone else who comes along. There'll be no one but you from now on, Rose."

She swallowed. Had there still been a tiny hope in her heart that he might fail, that he might want to end the marriage after all? Deliberately, she extinguished it. She doubted whether Simon would give her a second chance, anyway. His bitter hurt and chagrin would see to that. And Robert needed both his parents to support him, together, united in whatever affection and commitment they could find. Only so would he recover, and the terror of Brian Warrendon's death fade and leave no mark. Robert must be their priority, their focus, now and for a long time to come. But he was worth the effort. Even if Clive were to fail her, she could never regret putting Robert first, even above her own happiness. He was her son, and her love for him was the greatest thing in her life.

Coming soon…

You Owe Me Five Farthings – When husband Clive leaves her, can Rose rekindle the romance she found with Simon in *St Martin's Summer*?

Meet Jane Anstey

Jane Anstey began writing before she left junior school, and had her first story published in the school magazine when she was eleven. She took a degree in Modern History from Oxford University then taught in high school for four years before her first child was born in 1982. After that she took up copy-editing, indexing and educational writing. She now lives in Cornwall, UK, overlooking the moors, with her husband and younger daughter, aged 16, along with a dog, a cat, and five guinea pigs.

Other Works From The Pen Of
Jane Anstey

Beauty for Ashes - When Hollywood actor Luke Carson falls for English college student Samantha, he finds himself on an emotional roller-coaster ride to disaster.

VISIT OUR WEBSITE FOR THE FULL INVENTORY OF QUALITY BOOKS:

www.wingsepress.com

Quality trade paperbacks and downloads in multiple formats, in genres ranging from light romantic comedy to general fiction and horror. Wings has something for every reader's taste. Visit the website, then bookmark it. We add new titles each month!

34039405R00169

Printed in Great Britain
by Amazon